HOMECOMINGS

Novels by C. P. Snow

*

STRANGERS AND BROTHERS
THE LIGHT AND THE DARK
TIME OF HOPE
THE MASTERS
THE NEW MEN

These novels, and also HOMECOMINGS, *form part of the sequence of novels entitled* STRANGERS AND BROTHERS

HOMECOMINGS

BY

C. P. SNOW

LONDON

MACMILLAN & CO LTD

1957

First Edition 1956
Reprinted 1957

MACMILLAN AND COMPANY LIMITED
London Bombay Calcutta Madras Melbourne

THE MACMILLAN COMPANY OF CANADA LIMITED
Toronto
ST MARTIN'S PRESS INC
New York

To
WILLIAM COOPER

PRINTED IN GREAT BRITAIN

CONTENTS

PART I

HOMECOMING

PART II

THE SELF-DEFEATED

CONTENTS

Part III

CONDITION OF A SPECTATOR

CONTENTS

PART IV

THE UNDETACHED

PART V

ANOTHER HOMECOMING

PART I

HOMECOMING

CHAPTER I

LIGHTED WINDOW SEEN FROM THE STREET

IT WAS a February afternoon of smoky sunshine, as I walked home along the embankment to my wife. The river ran white in the sun, the plume from a tug's funnel came out blue as cigarette-smoke; on the far bank the reflections from windows shone through haze, and down towards Chelsea where I was walking, the smoke was so thick that the skyline, the high chimneys, had smudged themselves into it.

The day was a Tuesday, the year 1938; I had not been home since the Thursday before, which was my usual routine, as I had to spend half my week in Cambridge. I felt an edge of anxiety, a tightness of the nerves, as I always did going home after an absence, even an absence as short as this. Ever since I could remember, seeking deep into my childhood, I had felt this dread on the way home, this dread of what might be waiting for me.

It was nothing serious, it was just one of the reasonless anxieties one had to live with, it was no worse than that. Even now, when sometimes it turned out not so reasonless, I had got used to it. On those Tuesday evenings, walking home from Millbank to Chelsea along the river, I was anxious as I always had been, returning home, but I had put out of mind the special reason why.

Yet that day, as soon as I reached Cheyne Walk, my eyes were straining before I was in sight of our house. When I did see it, the picture might to a stranger have looked serene and enviable. The drawing-room lights were already on, first of the houses along that reach; the curtains had

3

not been drawn, and from the road, up the strip of garden, one could see the walls, high with white-painted panels. If I had been a stranger, looking up the garden from Cheyne Walk, that glimpse of a lighted room would have had for me the charm of domestic mystery and peace.

As I walked up the path, I did not know how she would be. The hall was brilliantly lit, pernicketily tidy, the hall of a childless couple. No voice greeted me. I went quickly inside the drawing-room. Here also the lights attacked me, as in the dazzle I saw my wife. Saw her quiet, composed, pre-occupied. For she was sitting at a small table, away from the fireplace, looking down at a chess-board. On the board were only a few pieces, each of them much bigger than an ordinary chess-man, part of an Indian set which, out of some whim, Sheila had bought herself the year before. So far as I could see, she was not playing a game, but working out a problem. She looked up.

"Hallo, you're in, are you?" she said. "You'd better help me with this."

I was flooded with relief, relief so complete as to be happiness, just as I always was when I found her free from strain. Whatever I had expected, it was not this. I drew up a chair opposite her, and, as she bent her head and glanced at the board, I looked through the tall pieces at her forehead, the lines of which were tightened, not as so often with her own inner care, but with simple calculation.

"I don't see it," she said, and smiled at me with great light-filled grey eyes.

At this time she was thirty-three, the same age within months as I was myself. But she looked much older than her age. When I first fell in love with her, as long ago as fourteen years before, men had thought her beautiful. Since then her face had changed, though I, who had watched it as no one else had, would have been the last to recognise how much.

The lines, which when she was a girl had been visible on her forehead and under her eyes, were now deep; her fine, strong nose had sharpened; her expression had become both harder and more still, drawn and fixed with unhappiness. Only her eyes were untouched, and they, so large that they might have been mournful as a lemur's, had not shared in the sadness of her face. Even at her worst, they could still look lively, penetrating, not-taken-in; just as her body, beneath the lined, overwrought face, was strong, almost heavy, the body of a woman powerful, healthy and still young.

Seeing her through the chess pieces, I noticed none of these changes, for I was only concerned with her state from day-to-day. I knew the slightest change in her expression, but I could not see what would be obvious to others. Trying to keep her steady, over the hours, the days, the years, I had lost my judgement about whether she was getting better or worse. All I knew was that tonight she was gay, anxiety-free, and that for this night, which was as far as I could see ahead, there was nothing to worry about.

I had loved her all through my young manhood, and, although my love had changed because of what had happened to us, I loved her still. When I first met her, I thought that the luck was on her side; she was beautiful, she was intelligent, she was comfortably off, above all she did not love me when I passionately loved her. That meant that she had power over me, and I none over her; it meant that she could tantalize me for years, she could show me the cruelty of one who feels nothing. It meant also, but I did not realise it then, that she was the more to be pitied. For it turned out that it was not only me she could not love, but anyone. She craved to; she tried to find someone to love; she tried to find psychiatrists and doctors who would tell her why she could not. Then, all else failing, she fell back on me, who still loved her, and let me marry her.

It could not have gone well. It might have gone a little better, I sometimes thought, if we had had children, which each of us longed for. But we were left with nothing but ourselves.

"I must get it out," she said, staring long-sightedly at the board. With two fingers she touched a piece shaped like a howdahed elephant, which in a European set would have been a castle. Out of anxious habit, my glance fixed, not on the strong broad-tipped fingers, but on the nails. Once again that night I was relieved. Though they were not painted, they were clean and trimmed. There had been times when her sense of deprivation froze her into stupor, when she no longer took care of herself. That frightened me, but it had not happened for some years. Usually she dressed well enough, and as she walked by the embankment pubs or along the King's Road, people saw a woman with her head high, a muscular stride, a face handsome and boldly made up.

"You'd better start again systematically," I said.

"Teach me," said Sheila.

It was like her to be willing to take a lesson in the theory of chess problems. It was like her also not to have asked a single question about what I had been doing, although she had not seen me for four days. Cambridge, my London job, they did not exist for her. From before our marriage, from the time when she no longer hoped that all would come well for her, she had become more shut up within herself. In fact, trying to look after her, I had broken my career.

When I married, I thought I knew what it would be like. I should have to watch over her dreads; I had seen something of the schizoid chill; I could imagine how tasks trivial to the rest of us were ordeals to her, how any arrangement in the future, even the prospect of going to a dinner party, could crack her nerves. But I had been borne along

6

by passionate love for her, physical passion pent up for years, and perhaps more than that. So I went into it, and, like others before me, soon knew that no imaginative forecast of what a life will be is anything like that life lived from day to day.

I did my best for her. It scarcely helped her at all. But it left me without much energy free. When we married, I had just got a foot in at the Bar, I was being thought of as a rising junior. Unless I parted from Sheila, I could not keep up that struggle. And so I found less strenuous jobs, a consulting one with Paul Lufkin's firm and a law fellowship at Cambridge, the latter taking me away from the Chelsea house three or four nights a week. When she was at her most indrawn, sitting by her gramophone for hours on end, I was glad, although it was a cowardly relief, to get away.

That February evening, as we sat opposite each other at the chess table in the bright room, I thought of none of these things. It was quite enough that she seemed content. It gave me—what sometimes can exist in the unhappiest of marriages, although an outsider does not realise its power—a kind of moral calm. Habit was so strong that it could wipe away ambitions put aside, crises of choice, a near-parting, all that had gone on in my secret life with her: habit was sitting near her, watching her nails, watching for the tic, the pseudo-smile, that came when strain was mastering her.

"I saw R.S.R. today," she said out of the blue.

"Did you?"

"I've got an idea he was looking for me."

"I shouldn't be surprised," I said.

"We had a drink. He was in good form."

Once that would have been a way to provoke my jealousy. Not now. I welcomed anything that would give her interest or hope. She still had bursts of activity

7

in which she lost herself—once or twice, for those were the thirties, in politics; but usually in trying to help some lame dog whom she had met by chance. A little backstreet café where she went by herself—I found that she had lent the proprietor money to keep on the lease. A derelict curate, terrified that he was going to be prosecuted—she was on call for him at any time he wanted. Utterly uninterested in my goings on, her family's, her old friends', she could still become absorbed in those of someone new. With them she was selfless, they gave her a flash of hope, she became like the young woman I had first known.

"He began to talk very airily about getting himself financed again," said Sheila.

"He's not losing any time, is he?"

"I wonder if I could do anything for him," she said.

"Plenty of people have tried, you know," I said.

It was true. I had only met R. S. Robinson once; he was a man of sixty, who before 1914 had made a reputation as the editor of an avant-garde monthly. Since then, he had been a hanger-on of letters, ghosting for agents, bringing out uncommercial magazines, losing money, making enemies, always ready with a new project. It was not long since he had manœuvred an introduction to Sheila; the manœuvres had been elaborate, he might as well have shouted out loud that he had heard she was well-off.

"Yes, plenty have tried," she said. "So much the worse for them."

She gave me a realistic jeering smile. She always met her down-and-outs with her eyes open. She added: "But that isn't much comfort for him, is it?"

"But if other people have got involved," I said, some second-hand rumour running through my mind, "it isn't encouraging for you."

"You've heard things against him?"

"Of course."

"I expect," said Sheila, "*he's* heard things agai

She gave a curious mocking laugh, almost braze
ing, a sign that her hopes were high. It was a long ti
I had seen them so.

"Perhaps even against you," she said.

I smiled back, I could not depress her, at momen
this her spirits could still make mine spring from the
But I said:

"I tell you, he's run through plenty of well-wis
There must be something the matter."

"Of course there's something the matter. If not,"
said, "he wouldn't have any use for me." Again
smiled: "Look, it's those with something the matter w
need someone. I should have thought even you might ha
grasped that by now."

She stood up, went over to the fireplace, grasped t
mantelpiece and arched her back.

"We're all right for money, aren't we?" she asked
Just for once, she, who usually spoke so nakedly, was being
disingenuous. She knew our financial state as well as I
did. She would not have been her father's daughter otherwise. Actually, prepared to throw money away as she was,
she had a shrewd business head. She knew exactly just
how much money need not trouble us. With my earnings
and her income, we drew in more than two thousand a
year, and lived well within it, even though we kept up this
comfortable home and had a housekeeper to look after us.

I nodded yes, we were all right.

"That's one thing settled then."

"As long," I said, "as you're not going to be too disappointed——"

"I don't expect too much."

"You mustn't expect anything," I said.

"But he is a gifted man, isn't he?" cried Sheila, her
face softer and less worn.

"I think he is," I said.

"I might be able to get him going again," she said. She went on, wistfully and yet with something like bravado:

"That would be *something*. If I haven't done anything else, that would be something, wouldn't it?"

TWO KINDS OF BUSINESS METHOD

O N THE track of someone she might serve, Sheila worked as fast as a confidence trickster. It must have been that same week, probably the very next day, that R. S. Robinson came to dine. Certainly I arrived straight from Lufkin's office; for long afterwards the juxtaposition struck me as ironic.

I had spent all day in Lufkin's suite. To begin, he had asked me to be available in the early morning and had then kept me waiting, which was not unusual, for a couple of hours. Outside his office, in an ante-room so thickly carpeted that men walked through it with no noise at all, I passed the time with the member of Lufkin's entourage whom I knew best, a man of my own age called Gilbert Cooke. He was a kind of personal assistant to Lufkin, in theory giving advice on export problems, just as in theory I gave advice on legal ones; but in practice Lufkin used us both as utility men. The company was one of the smaller oil-businesses, but the smallness was relative, and in 1938, the fourth year of Lufkin's chairmanship, he had already a turnover of thirty million pounds. He had also his own legal staff, and when he offered me a consultant's job he did not want another lawyer; but it suited him to pick up young men like me and Cooke, keep them on call, and then listen to them.

In the ante-room, Gilbert Cooke pointed to the office door.

"He's running behind time," he said, as though Lufkin were a train. Cooke was fleshy, powerfully muscled, with a high-coloured Corinthian face and hot brown eyes; he gave at once an impression of intimacy, kindness and considerable weight of nature. In fact, he spoke as though we were more intimate than we actually were.

"How is Sheila just now?" he asked me while he waited, as though he knew the whole history.

I said she was well, but he was not put off.

"Are you absolutely sure she's been to the right doctor?" he said.

I said she had not been near one for some time.

"Who did she go to?"

He was intrusive, pressing, but kind: it was hard to remember that he had only been inside our house twice. He had taken me often enough to his clubs, we had talked politics and games and Lufkin's business, but I had not given him a confidence.

At last we were shown into Lufkin's office: in that suite, as one moved from room to room, the air wafted against the skin like warm breath.

Lufkin sat up straight in a hard chair. He scarcely greeted us: he was inconsiderate, but also informal and without pomp. He was off-hand in personal relations because he was so bad at them, and yet, perversely, they gave him pleasure.

"You know the point?" he said.

Yes, we had both been briefed.

"What do I do?"

It sounded as though we should have finished in ten minutes. In actuality, it took all day, and nothing we said mattered much. Lufkin sat there, indifferent to time, straight, bony, skull-faced. He was only ten years older than Cooke or me; his skin was dark, and his business enemies put it about that he looked Jewish and that his name was Jewish, while as a matter of fact his father was a noncomformist parson in East Anglia.

The point before us was simple enough. He had been asked whether he wanted to buy another distributing business; should he? From the beginning of the talk, throughout the long, smoky, central-heated, unromantic hours, two things stood out. First, this was a point on which neither Cooke's judgement nor mine was worth much—certainly no more than that of any moderately intelligent man round the office. Second, I was sure that, whatever we or anyone else argued, Lufkin had already made up his mind to buy.

Yet all day Cooke behaved like a professional no-man. He became argumentative and rude, oddly so for a middle-rank employee in the presence of a tycoon. The tone of the discussion was harsh and on the whole impersonal; the arguments were prosaic. Cooke was loquacious, much more than Lufkin or me: he went on pestering, not flattering: as I listened, I knew that he was closer to Lufkin than most people in the firm, and wondered why.

Most of the men Lufkin bought had a bit of professional success behind them; but Cooke had nothing to show but social connections, except for his own curious kind of personal force.

Once, in the middle of the afternoon, after we had lunched on sandwiches and coffee, Cooke switched from his factual line. Suddenly, staring at Lufkin with his full eyes, he said:

"I'm afraid you're liable to overstretch yourself."

"Maybe." Lufkin seemed willing to consider the idea.

"I mean, with any empire *like yours*"—their eyes met, and Lufkin smiled bleakly—"there comes a time when you've got to draw in your horns, or else——"

"What do you say to that, Eliot?"

I said that the firm was short of men, and that the able men were spread thin. He ought to acquire a dozen future managers before he bought much more.

"I agree that," he said. For half-an-hour he got down to detail, and then asked:

"That make you feel any better, Cooke?"

"No, it seems easy to you, but it's not easy."

"What seems easy?"

"Biting off more than *anyone* can chew."

Underneath his remote, off-hand manner, Lufkin was obscurely gratified. But he had a knack of pushing away his own gratification, and we returned to figures again.

The sky outside the office windows darkened, the air seemed more than ever hot. Nothing was settled. There had scarcely been a flight of fancy all day. No one would have guessed, though it was the truth, that Lufkin was a man of remarkable imagination; nor that this marathon talk was his technique of coming to the point of action; nor that Gilbert Cooke was swelling with pride, ardent but humble, at being in on anything so big.

When at last we parted, it was nearly seven and still nothing was settled. The whole range of facts about the new business had been re-sorted, except the purchase price, which Lufkin had only mentioned once, and then obliquely. "There's always money for a good business," he had added indifferently, and passed on. And yet that purchase price gave a tang to the repetitive, headachey hours, the only tang I was left with on the way to Chelsea in the cold taxi, for it could not have been less than a million pounds.

When I reached home, I met a different kind of business method. R. S. Robinson was already there in the drawing-room; he was standing plumply by the fire, soft silver-shining hair venerable above smooth baby skin. He looked comfortable, he looked sedate; behind his spectacles, his eyes glinted from Sheila to me, sharp with merriness and suspicion. He made no secret that he wanted Sheila's backing for a sum as great as he could persuade out of her, as great as a thousand pounds.

"I've not come here just for the sake of your intelligent conversation," he told her. His voice was fluent, modulated, flattering, high-spirited.

"I mustn't come on false pretences, must I?" he said. "I warn you, I'm a dangerous man to let into your house."

A thousand was the maximum which he let himself imagine; he did not hope to get away with so much, although he was not too delicate to mention it. He set himself to persuade her, and incidentally me as a possible influence, with all the art of which he was so proud.

Strange, I was thinking as we tasted our drinks, that fifteen, sixteen years before, he had been part of our youth. For he had done, on his own account, a little coterie publishing in the days of the *English Review*, the Imagists, the rebels of the first war. It had been R. S. Robinson who had published a translation of Leopardi's poems under the inept title of *Lonely Beneath the Moon*. Both Sheila and I had read it just before we met, when we were at the age for romantic pessimism, and to us it had been magical.

Since then everything he had touched had failed. He was trying to raise money from Sheila for another publishing firm, but himself was not able to put down five pounds. And yet we could not forget the past, and he did not want to, so that, as he stood between us on our own hearthrug, it was not Sheila, it was not I, it was he who dispensed the patronage.

"I was telling Mrs. Eliot that she must write a book," he told me soon after I joined them.

Sheila shook her head.

"*I'm sure you could*," he said to her. He turned on me: "I've just noticed that you, sir, you have artists' hands." He had lost no time getting out his trowel; but Sheila who shrank with self-consciousness at any praise, could take it from him. Unlike our Chelsea acquaintances of our own generation, he had not begun by using our christian names, but instead went on calling me "sir" and Sheila "Mrs. Eliot", even when he was speaking with insidious intimacy face-to-face.

Standing between us, he dispensed the patronage; he had dignity and presence, although he was inches shorter than Sheila, who was tall for a woman, and did not come up to my shoulder. Round shouldered and plump, he touched a crest of his silver hair.

He had come to the house in a dinner-jacket, which had once been smart and was now musty, while neither Sheila nor I had dressed; and it was Robinson who set to work to remove embarrassment.

"Always do it," he advised us, as we went into the dining-room. I asked him what.

"Always put people at a disadvantage. When they tell you not to dress, take no notice of them. It gives you the moral initiative."

"You see," he whispered to Sheila, sitting at her right hand, "I've got the moral initiative tonight."

In the dining-room he congratulated Sheila on the fact that, since the food came up by the serving hatch, we were alone.

"So I needn't pretend, need I?" he said, and, tucking into his dinner, told stories of other meals back in the legendary past, at which he had tried to raise money to publish books—books, he did not let us forget, that we had all heard of since.

"I expect you've been told that I was better off then?" He looked up from his plate to Sheila, with a merry, malicious chuckle.

"Don't you believe it. People always get everything wrong." Stories of multiple manœuvres, getting promises from A on the strength of B and C, from B on the strength of A and C. . . . "The point is, one's got to refuse to play the game according to the rules," he advised Sheila. Stories of personal negotiations of such subtlety and invention as to make my business colleagues of the afternoon seem like different animals.

All the time, listening to him, I had spent most of my attention, as throughout our marriage, watching how Sheila was. She had turned towards him, the firm line of her nose and lip clear against the wall; her face had lost the strained and over-vivid fixity, there was no sign of the tic. Perhaps she did not show the quiet familiar ease that sometimes visited her in the company of her protégés; but she had never had a protégé as invincible as this. It took me all my time to remember that, on his own admission, Robinson was destitute, keeping an invalid wife and himself on £150 a year. More than anything, Sheila looked—and it was rare for her—plain mystified.

Just for an instant, out of dead habit, I wondered if he had any attraction for her. Maybe, those who are locked in their own coldness, as she was, mind less than the rest of us about the object of attraction, about whether it is unsuitable or grotesque in others' eyes. Doing a good turn for this man of sixty, whom others thought fantastic, Sheila might have known a blessed tinge of sexual warmth. At any rate, her colour was high, and for an hour I could feel responsibility lifted from me; she had managed to forget herself.

Robinson, as natural about eating as about his manœuvres, asked her for a second helping of meat, and went on with his recent attempts at money raising. Some prosperous author, who had known him in his famous days, had given him an introduction to an insurance company. Robinson digressed, his elephant eyes glinting, to tell us a scandalous anecdote about the prosperous author, a young actor, and an ageing woman; as he told it, Robinson was studying Sheila, probing into her life with me.

Pressing the story on her, but drawing no response, he

got going about the insurance company. They had made him go into the City, they had given him coffee and whole-meal biscuits, and then they had talked of the millions they invested in industrial concerns.

"They talked to me of *millions*," he cried.

"They didn't mean anything," I said.

"They should be more sensitive," said Robinson. "They talked to me of millions when all I wanted was nine hundred pounds."

I was almost sure he had dropped the figure from a thousand for the sake of the sound, just as, in the shops where my mother used to buy our clothes, they did not speak of five shillings, but always of four and eleven three.

"What's more," said Robinson, "they didn't intend to give me that. They went on talking about millions here and millions there, and when I got down to brass tacks they looked vague."

"Did they offer anything?" said Sheila.

"Always know when to cut your losses," Robinson said in his firm, advising tone. It occurred to me that, in a couple of hours, he had produced more generalisations on how to run a business than I had heard from Paul Lufkin in four years.

"I just told them, 'You're treating me very badly. Don't talk of millions to people who need the money,' and I left them high and dry."

He sighed. "Nine hundred pounds."

At the thought of humiliation turned upside down, Sheila had laughed out loud, for the first time for months. But now she began asking questions. Nine hundred pounds: that would go nowhere. True, he had kept his old imprint all those years, he could publish a book or two and get someone else to distribute it—but what good was that? Surely if he did that, and it went off half-cock, he had dissipated his credit, and had finished himself for good?

Robinson was not used to being taken by surprise. He flushed: the flush rose up his cheeks, up to the forehead under the white hair. Like many ingenious men, he constantly underrated everyone round him. He had made his judgement of this beautiful hag-ridden woman; he thought she would be the softest of touches. He had marked her down as a neurotic. He was astonished she should show acumen. He was upset that she should see through him.

For, of course, he contrived to be at the same time embarrassingly open and dangerously secretive. Was he even truthful about his own penury? He had been trying on Sheila an alternative version of his technique of multiple approach. This time he was working on several people simultaneously, telling none of them about the others.

"Always keep things simple," he said, trying to wave his panache.

"Not so simple that they don't make sense," said Sheila, smiling but not yielding.

Soon she got some reason out of him. If he could collect it, he wanted several thousand; at that period, such a sum would let him publish, modestly but professionally, for a couple of years. That failing, however, he still wanted his nine hundred. Even if he could only bring out three books under the old imprint, the name of R. S. Robinson would go round again.

"You never know what might happen," he said, and blew out wonderful prospects like so many balloons. With three books they would remember him again, he said, and he gave up balloon blowing and spoke of the books he would bring out. He stopped flattering Sheila or using the other dodges which he believed infallible, and all of a sudden one saw that his taste had stayed incorrupt. It was a hard, austere, anti-romantic taste, similar to Sheila's own.

"I could do for them," he said, "what I did before."

"You want some money," said Sheila.

"I only want enough to put someone on the map," he cried.

She asked: "Is money all you need?"

"No. I want someone like you to keep people from getting the wrong impression. You see, they sometimes think I'm a bit of an ass."

He was not putting on one of his acts. He had said it angrily, hotly, out of resentment, not trying to get round her. But soon he was master of himself again, enough to calculate that he might extract an answer that night. He must have calculated also that she was on his side and would not shift—for he made an excuse to go to the lavatory, so as to leave the two of us alone.

As soon as I returned without him to the dining-table, where we were still sitting, Sheila said the one word:

"Well?"

We had been drinking brandy, and with a stiff mass-production gesture, she kept pushing the decanter with the side of her little finger.

"Well?" she said again.

I believed, then and afterwards, that if I had intervened I could have stopped her. She still trusted me, and no one else. However much she was set on helping him, she would have listened if I had warned her again. But I had already decided not to. She had found an interest, it would do more good than harm, I thought.

"If you want to risk it," I said, "I don't see why you shouldn't."

"Do you think any better of him?"

I was thinking, he had raised the temperature of living for her. Then I realised that he had done the same for me. If she was taken in, so was I."

I grinned and said:

"I must say I've rather enjoyed myself."

She nodded, and then said after a pause:

"He wouldn't be grateful, would he?"

"Not particularly."

"Don't soften it." Her great eyes swung round on me like searchlights. "No one's grateful for being looked after. He'd be less grateful than most."

It was the kind of bitter truth that she never spared herself or others, the only kind of truth that she thought worth facing. Who else, I wondered, would have faced it at that moment, just as she was committing herself? Other people could do what she was doing, but not many with that foresight of what lay ahead.

We sat silent, her eyes still levelled at mine, but gradually becoming unfocused, as though looking past me, looking a great distance away.

"If I don't do it," she said, "someone else will. Oh well, I suppose it's more important to me than it is to him."

Soon afterwards Robinson came back. As he opened the door, we were quiet, and he thought it was because of him. His manner was jaunty, but even his optimistic nerve was strained, and as he sat down he played, too insidiously, too uneasily, his opening trick.

"Mrs. Eliot, I've been thinking, you really ought to write a book yourself."

"Never mind about that," she said in a cold, brittle tone.

"I mean it very much."

"Never mind."

The words were final, and Robinson looked down at the table.

She remarked, as though it were obvious:

"I may as well tell you straight away, I will do what I can to help."

For the second time that night, Robinson flushed to the temples. In a mutter absent-minded, bewildered, he thanked her without raising his eyes, and then took out a handkerchief and wiped it hard across his forehead.

"Perhaps you wouldn't mind, sir, if I have another little drink?" he said to me, forcing his jollity. "After all, we've got something to celebrate." He was becoming himself again. "After all, this is an historic occasion."

CHAPTER III

THE POINT OF A CIRCUITOUS APPROACH

AFTER that February evening, Sheila told me little of her dealings with Robinson, but I knew they preoccupied her. When, in the early summer, she heard that her parents wished to spend a night in our house, she spoke as though it were an intolerable interruption.

"I can't waste the time," she said to me, her mouth working.

I said that we could hardly put them off again; this time Mr. Knight was visiting a specialist.

"Why can't I put them off? No one will enjoy it."

"It will give more pain not to have them."

"They've given enough pain in their time. Anyway," she said, "just for once I've got something better to do."

She wrote back, refusing to have them. Her concentration on Robinson's scheme seemed to have become obsessive, so that it was excruciating for her to be distracted even by a letter. But Mrs. Knight was not a sensitive woman. She replied by return, morally indignant because Sheila had made an excuse not to go home to the vicarage last Christmas, so that we had not seen them for eighteen months; Sheila's father, for all Mrs. Knight's care and his own gallantry, would not always be there for his daughter to see; she was showing no sense of duty.

Even on Sheila, who dreaded their company and who blamed her torments of self-consciousness upon them, the family authority still held its hold. No one else could have overruled her, but her mother did.

23

So, on a morning in May, a taxi stopped at the garden gate, and, as I watched from an upstairs window, Mr. and Mrs. Knight were making their way very slowly up the path. Very slowly, because Mr. Knight was taking tiny steps and pausing between them, leaning all the time upon his wife. She was a big woman, as strong as Sheila, but Mr. Knight tottered above her, his hand on her heavy shoulder, his stomach swelling out from the middle chest, not far below the dog collar; he was teetering along like a massive walking casualty, helped out of battle by an orderly.

I went out on to the path to greet them, whilst Sheila stayed at the door.

"Good morning, Lewis," said Mr. Knight very faintly.

"No talking till we get him in," Mrs. Knight announced.

"I'm sorry to lay my bones among you," whispered Mr. Knight.

"Don't strain yourself talking, dear," said Mrs. Knight.

At last the progress ended in an armchair in the drawing-room, where Mr. Knight closed his eyes. It was a warm morning, and through a half-open window blew a zephyr breath.

"Is that too much for you, dear?" said Mrs. Knight, looking accusingly at me.

"Perhaps a little," came a whisper from the armchair. "Perhaps a little."

At once Mrs. Knight rammed the window up. She acted as though she had one thought alone, which was to keep her husband alive.

"How are you?" I asked, standing by the chair.

"As you see," came the answer, almost inaudible.

"What do the doctors say?"

"They know very little, Lewis, they know very little."

"So long as we can keep him free from strain," said Mrs. Knight implacably.

"I sleep night and day," breathed Mr. Knight. "*Night and day.*"

Once more he composed his clever, drooping, petulant face. Then he whispered, "Sheila! Sheila, I haven't seen my daughter!" As she came near, he turned his head, as though by a herculean effort, through a few degrees, in order to present her his cheek to be kissed. Sheila stood over him, strained, white-faced. For an instant it looked to me as though she could not force herself. Then she bent down, gave him a token kiss, and retreated out of our circle into the window seat.

To her mother, it seemed unnatural; but in fact Sheila believed he was making a fool of himself, and hated it. Valetudinarian: self-dramatising: he had been so since her childhood, though not on such a grandiose scale as now, and she did not credit that there was anything wrong with him. In her heart she wanted to respect him, she thought he had wasted his ability because he was so proud and vain. All he had done was marry money: for it was not the pug-faced, coarse-fibred Mrs. Knight who had climbed through marriage, but her husband, the self-indulgent and hyper-acute. Sheila could not throw off the last shreds of her respect for him, and at the sight of his performances her insight, her realism, even her humour failed her.

When we were sitting round the dining-room table, she could not make much pretence of conversation. I was on edge because of her, and Mr. Knight, with eyes astute and sly, was surreptitiously inspecting us both. He had time to do so, for Mrs. Knight would not let him eat more than a slice of cold ham. It was an effort for him to obey, for he was greedy about his food. But there was something genuine in his hypochondria: he would give up even food, if it lessened his fear of death. Disconsolately, he ate his scrap of ham, his eyes under their heavy lids lurking towards his daughter or me, whenever he thought he was unobserved.

Of the four of us, the only person who came carefree from the meal was Mrs. Knight. We rested in the drawing-room, looking down the garden towards the river, and Mrs. Knight was satisfied. She was displeased with her daughter's mood, not upset by it, and she was used to being displeased and could ignore it. For the rest she was happy because her husband had revived. She had put away a good meal; she was satisfied at least with her daughter's kitchen and the bright smart house. In fact, she was jollying me by being prepared to concede that Sheila might have made a worse marriage.

"I always knew you'd have a success," said Mrs. Knight. Her memory could not have been more fallacious. When as a poor young man I was first taken by Sheila to the vicarage, Mrs. Knight had thought me undesirable in the highest degree, but in our comfortable dining-room she was certain that she was speaking the truth.

Complacently, Mrs. Knight called over the names of other men Sheila might have married, none of whom, in her mother's view, had gone as far as I had. For an instant I looked at Sheila, who recognised my glance but did not smile. Then came Mr. Knight's modulated voice:

"Is he, is our friend Lewis, content with how far he's gone?"

"I should think so," said Mrs. Knight sturdily.

"Is he? I never have been, but of course I've done nothing that the world can see. I know our friend Lewis has been out there in the arena, but I should like to be certain that he is content?"

What was he getting at? No one had a sharper appraisal of worldly success than Mr. Knight.

"Of course I'm not," I said.

"I rather fancied you might feel that." Circuitous, not looking at me, he went on: "Correct me if I'm wrong, I am a child in these matters, but I vaguely imagined that between the two activities you've chosen, you don't expect the highest position in either? I suppose there couldn't be anything in that impression?"

"It is absolutely true," I said.

"Of course," Mr. Knight reflected, "if one were of that unfortunate temperament, which some of us are spared, that doesn't feel on terms with life unless it collects the highest prizes, your present course would mean a certain deprivation."

"Yes, it would," I said.

He was talking at me, painfully near the bone. He knew it: so did Sheila, so did I. But not so Mrs. Knight.

"Most men would be glad to change with Lewis, I know that," she said. She called out to Sheila, who was sitting on a pouf in the shadow:

"Isn't that true, Sheila?"

"You've just said it."

"It's your fault if it's not true, you know."

Mrs. Knight gave a loud laugh. But she could see Sheila's face, pale with the mechanical smile, fixed in the shadow; and Mrs. Knight was irritated that she should not look more hearty. Healthy and happy herself, Mrs. Knight could see no reason why everyone round her should not be the same.

"It's time you two counted your blessings," she said.

Mr. Knight, uneasy, was rousing himself, but she continued:

"I'm speaking to you, Sheila. You're luckier than most women, and I hope you realise it."

Sheila did not move.

"You've got a husband who's well thought of," said Mrs. Knight, undeterred, "you've got a fine house because your parents were able to make a contribution, you've got enough money for anything in reason. What I can't understand is——"

27

Mr. Knight tried to divert her, but for once she was not attending to him.

"What I can't understand is," said Mrs. Knight, "why you don't set to work and have a child."

As I listened, the words first of all meant nothing, just badinage, uncomprehending, said in good nature. Then they went in. They were hard enough for me to take; but my wound was nothing to Sheila's wound. I gazed at her, appalled, searching for an excuse to take her out and be with her alone.

Her father was gazing at her too, glossing it over, beginning some preamble.

To our astonishment Sheila began to laugh. Not hysterically, but matily, almost coarsely. That classical piece of tactlessness had, for the moment, pleased her. Just for an instant, she could feel ordinary among the ordinary. To be thought a woman who, because she wished to be free to travel or because she did not like to count the pounds, had refused to have a child—that made her feel at one with her mother, as hearty, as matter-of-fact.

Meanwhile Mrs. Knight had noticed nothing out of the common, and went on about the dangers of leaving it too late. Sheila's laugh had dried; and yet she seemed ready to talk back to her mother, and to agree to go out with her for an afternoon's shopping.

As they walked down the path in the sunshine, Sheila's stride flowing beneath a light green dress, our eyes followed them, and then, in the warm room, all windows still closed to guard Mr. Knight's health, he turned his glance slowly upon me.

"There they go," he said. His eyes were self-indulgent, shrewd and sad: when I offered him a cigarette, he closed them in reproof.

"I dare not. I dare not."

As though in slow motion, his lids raised themselves, and,

not looking at me, he scrutinised the garden outside the window. His interest seemed irrelevant, so did his first remark, and yet I was waiting, as in so many of his circumlocutions, for the thrust to come. He began:

"I suppose that, if this international situation develops as between ourselves as I believe it must, we shall all have too much on our minds. . . . Even those of us who are compelled to be spectators. It is a curious fate, my dear Lewis, for one to sit by in one's retreat and watch happen a good deal that one has, without any special prescience, miserably foretold."

He continued, weaving his thoughts in and out, staying off the point but nevertheless leaving me in apprehension of the point to come. In his fashion, he was speaking with a kind of intimacy, an intimacy expressed in code. As he described his labyrinthine patterns he inserted some good sense about the world politics of that year, and what we had to look forward to; he always had a streak of cool detachment, startling in a selfish, timid man. With no emphasis he said:

"I suppose that, if things come to the worst, and it's a morbid consolation for a backwoodsman like myself to find that someone like you, right in the middle of things, agree that it is only the worst they can come to—I suppose that to some it may take their minds, though it seems a frivolous way of putting delicate matters, it may take their minds off their own distress."

This was the beginning.

"It may," I said.

"Will that be so with her?" he asked, still with no emphasis.

"I do not know."

"Nor do I." He started off circuitously again. "Which ever of us can claim to know a single thought of another human being? Which ever of us can claim that? Even a man like you, Lewis, who has, if I may say so, more than his share of the gift of understanding. And perhaps one might assume that one was not, in comparison with those one meets, utterly deficient oneself. And yet one would not dare to think, and I believe you wouldn't, that one could share another's unhappiness, even if one happened to see it under one's eyes."

His glance, sly and sad, was on me, and once more he shied off.

"Perhaps one feels it most," he said, "when one has the responsibility for a child. One has the illusion that one could know"—just for a moment the modulated voice hesitated—"him or her as one does oneself. Flesh of one's flesh, bone of one's bone. Then one is faced by another human being, and what is wrong one can never know, and it is more grievous because sometimes there is the resemblance to one's own nerves. If ever you are granted a child, Lewis, and you have any cause for anxiety, and you should have to watch a suffering for which you feel responsible, then I think you will grant the accuracy of what I have tried, of course, inadequately, to explain."

"I think I can imagine it."

As he heard my sarcasm, his eyelids dropped. Quietly he said:

"Tell me, what is her life like?"

"It hasn't changed much," I said.

He considered. "How does she spend her time in this house?"

I said that she had recently found another occupation, she was trying to help a man who had fallen on bad days.

"She was always good with the unfortunate."

His mouth had taken on a pursed, almost petulant smile: was he being detached enough to reflect how different she was from himself, with his passionate interest in success, his zest in finding out, each time he met one, exactly what

30

price, on the stock exchange of reputations, one's own reputation fetched that day?

He began on another circuit, how it might be a danger to become sentimental about failure: but he cut off short, and, his gaze on the middle distance, said:

"Of course it is not my responsibility any longer, for that has passed to you, which is better for us all, since I haven't the strength to bear responsibility any longer, and in fact the strain of talking to you confidentially like this means that I am likely to pay the price in my regrettable health. Of course it is your responsibility now, and I know you take it more willingly than most men would. And of course I know my daughter has never been at her best in the presence of my wife. It has been a grief to me, but for the present we must discount that. But even if today has given me a wrong impression, I must not leave undone those things I ought to have done. Because you see, allowing for everything, including the possibility that I may be totally mistaken, that is something which I should feel culpable if I did not say."

"What is it?" I cried out.

"You told me a few minutes ago that you thought she was much as usual."

"Don't you?"

He said:

"I'm afraid, I can only hope I'm wrong and I may well be, but I'm afraid that she has gone a little further from the rest of us than she ever was before."

He shut his eyes, and as I started speaking shook his head.

"I can only leave her with you. That's all I can say," he whispered. "This room is just a little stuffy, my dear Lewis. Do you think it would be safe to open a window, just the smallest chink?"

CHAPTER IV

HANDCLASP ON A HOT NIGHT

ONE evening, soon after the Knights' visit, I broke my walk home from Millbank at an embankment pub, and there, sitting between the pin-tables and the looking-glass on the back wall, was a group of my acquaintances. As I went up to them, it seemed that their talk damped down; it seemed also that I caught a glance, acute, uneasy, from the one I knew best, a young woman called Betty Vane. Within moments, though, we were all, not arguing, but joining a chorus of politics, the simple, passionate politics of that year, and it was some time before Betty and I left the pub together.

She was a smallish, sharp-featured woman of thirty, with a prow of a nose and fine open eyes. She was not pretty, but she was so warm and active that her face often took on a glow of charm. She did not expect to be admired by men; her marriage had failed, she was so unsure of herself that it prevented her finding anyone to love her.

I had met her first in circumstances very different, at the country house of the Boscastles, to whom she was related. But that whole family-group was savagely split by the political divide, and she was not on speaking terms with half her relations. She had become friendly with me because we were on the same side; she had gone out to find like-minded persons such as the group in the pub. Sometimes it seemed strange to me to meet her in a society which, to Lord Boscastle, would have seemed as incomprehensible as that of the Trobriand Islanders.

Upon the two of us, as we walked by the river, each with private worries, the public ones weighed down too; and yet, I was thinking, in other times Betty would have been as little political as Mrs. Knight. She had dropped into her long, jostling stride that was almost mannish; yet there was no woman less mannish than she. It was her immediate self-protective manner, drawn out of the fear that I or any man might think her ready to make advances. It was only as the evening went on that her gait and her speech became relaxed, and she was warmed by the feeling that she had behaved serenely.

We had fallen into silence when I asked: "Were you talking about me when I came in just now?"

She had dropped out of step with me: she gave a skip to right herself. "Not exactly," she said. She looked down. I saw her lips tighten.

"What about, then?" As she did not at once reply I repeated: "What about?"

It was an effort for her to look up at me, but when she did so her glance was honest, troubled, steady.

"You must know."

"Sheila?"

She nodded. I knew she did not like Sheila: but I asked what was being said.

"Nothing. Only nonsense. You know what people are."

I was silent.

She burst out, in a curiously strident, social voice, as if rallying a stranger at a party: "I don't in the least want to tell you!"

"That makes it harder for me."

Betty stopped walking, put her hand on the embankment wall, and faced me. "If I do tell you I shan't be able to wrap it up." She knew I should be angry, she knew I had a right to hear. She was unwilling to spoil the evening for

33

herself and could not keep out of her voice resentment that I should make her do it.

I told her to go on.

"Well, then"—she reverted to her social tone—"as a matter of *fact*, they say she's as good as left you."

I had not expected that, and I laughed and said, "Nonsense."

"Is it nonsense?"

"Whom is she supposed to be leaving me for?"

She replied, still in the same social, defensive voice: "They say she prefers women."

There was not a word of truth in it, and I told Betty so.

She was puzzled, cross because I was speaking so harshly, though it was only what she had foreseen.

I cross-questioned her. "Where did this start?"

"Everyone says so."

"Who does? Where do they get it from?"

"I'm not making it up," she said. It was a plea for herself, but I did not think of her then.

I made her search her memory for the first rumour.

The effort of searching calmed her: in a moment her face lightened a little. "I'm sure it came," she said, "from someone who knew her. Isn't she working with someone? Hasn't she something to do with that man who looks like a frog? The second-hand bookseller?"

Robinson had had a shop once, but had given it up years before: I could scarcely believe what I seemed to be hearing, but I exclaimed:

"Robinson? Do you mean him?"

"Robinson? He's got beautiful white hair, parted in the middle? He knows her, doesn't he?"

"Yes," I said.

"Well, he started the word round that she's mad about women."

I parted from Betty at the corner of Tite Street without

taking her to her flat, blaming her because she had brought bad news. The falser the gossip, it sometimes seemed, the more it seared. On my way home, I continued angry with Betty: I should have liked to have believed that she had garbled it, she who was both truthful and loyal.

But Robinson? It made no sense: he could not have done it, for reasons of self-interest alone. No one had more to risk from upsetting her.

I wondered whether I should tell Sheila the rumour, and decided not to. Maybe in itself it would not disturb her much; I was not sure: we had both lived in a society which set out to tolerate all the kinds of sex. And yet gossip, this gossip that pawed, had something degrading about it, especially for one like Sheila. The story that it originated in Robinson, credible or incredible, had been shameful for me to hear, let alone Sheila; if I could, I wanted to spare her that.

Instead of telling her the gossip that night, I listened to her invoking my help for Robinson. He planned to start with three books in the following spring. "That may be all he ever does," said Sheila, with her business feet on the ground, "but if they are all right——" She meant, though she did not finish, for the phrase was too high-falutin for her, that she would have achieved a purpose: she thought she would have saved his self-respect.

The trouble was, of the foreign books he had counted on, he had only acquired the rights of one. The balloons he had blown up at our dinner table had most of them exploded, she admitted that; he had believed in his own fancies, he always did, he had only to wish for a property hard enough to feel that he possessed it. Yet, in another sense, he kept his judgement. Nothing would make him substitute bad, or even mediocre, books for those he had fancied were in the bag: either something good, or nothing.

35

Could I help him find an author? There must be one or two pioneer works going begging, and she knew that I had friends among writers. In fact, although she neither had, nor pretended to have, even a remote acquaintance with my official life, she assumed that it was to writing I should devote myself in the end. Mysteriously, the thought gave her some pleasure.

Could I help Robinson?

I wrote several letters on his behalf, because Sheila had asked me; one reply was encouraging enough for her to act on. Then, a fortnight later, I had other news of him.

I was working in the Lufkin suite, when a telephone call came through. Betty Vane was speaking in a sharp, agitated, seemingly angry voice: could she see me soon? That same afternoon she sat in an armchair by my desk, telling me that she was unlucky. More gossip had reached her, and in decency she could not keep it from me. She did not say it, but she knew my temperament, she had watched me last time: I should not be pleased with her for bringing such news. Still, there seemed to her no choice.

By now the rumours were proliferating. Sheila was not only eccentric but unbalanced, the gossip was going round. She had spent periods in the hands of mental specialists; she had been in homes. This explained the anomalies in our married life, why we had given up entertaining, why she was not seen outside the house for weeks at a time, why we had not dared to have a family.

Some of the rumours referred to me, such as that I had married her, knowing her condition, only because her parents had bribed me with a settlement. Mainly they aimed at her, and the most cruel was that, if we had been poor and without influence, she would have been certified.

Nearly all this gossip was elaborate, circumstantial, spun out with rococo inventiveness, at one or two points just off-true; much of it an outsider could believe without bearing her any ill will, once he had observed that she was strange. One or two of the accretions, notably the more clinical, seemed to have been added as the rumours spread from the point of origin. But the original rumours, wonderfully and zestfully constructed, with a curious fluid imagination infusing them, were unlike any I had heard.

This time I could not pretend doubt to myself, not for a minute; there was only one man who could have begun to talk in such a style. I knew it, and Betty knew I knew it.

She said that she had denied the stories where she could. "But who believes you when you deny a good story?" she asked, realistic, obscurely aggrieved.

Walking along the river that evening, the summer air touching the nostrils with pollen, with the rotting, sweet water smell, I found my steps heavy. That morning, I had left Sheila composed, but now I had to warn her; I could see no way out. It had become too dangerous to leave her ignorant. I did not know how to handle the news, or her.

I went upstairs to our bedroom, where she was lying on her bed, reading. Although it was rarely that I had her— (as our marriage went on, it was false to speak of making love, for about it there was, though she did not often refuse me, the one-sidedness of rape)—nevertheless she was easier if I slept in the same room. That evening, sitting on my own bed, I watched her holding her book under the reading lamp, although the sunlight was beginning to edge into the room. The windows were wide open, and through them came the smell of lime and petrol; it was a hot still night.

It was the heat, I took it for granted, that had sent Sheila to lie down. She was wearing a dressing-gown, smoking a cigarette, with a film of sweat on her forehead. She looked middle-aged and plain. Suddenly, I felt close to her, close with the years of knowledge and the nights I had seen her so, and my heart and body yearned for her.

"Hot," she said.

I lay back, longing not to break the peace of the moment.

In the room, the only sound was Sheila's turning a page: outside, the skirl of the embankment traffic. On her bed, which was the further from the window, Sheila's back was half turned to me, so as to catch the lamplight on the book.

In time—perhaps I put off speaking, for half-an-hour—I called her name.

"Hallo," she said, without stirring.

"We ought to talk a bit."

"What about?" She still spoke lazily, she had caught nothing ominous yet.

"Robinson."

All of a sudden she turned on her back, with her eyes staring at the ceiling.

"What about him?"

I had been thinking out the words to use, and I answered:

"If I were you, I should be careful how much you confide in him."

There was a long silence. Sheila's face did not move, she gave no sign that she had heard.

At last she said, in a high cold voice:

"You're telling me nothing that I don't know."

"Do you know what he's actually said?"

"What does it matter?" she cried.

"He's been spreading slander——"

"I don't want to hear." Her voice rose, but she remained still.

After a pause, she said, into the silent room:

"I told you that he wouldn't be grateful."

"Yes."

"I was right."

38

Her laugh was splintered. I thought how those like her, who insisted on baring the harsher facts of the human condition, are those whom whose facts ravish most.

She sat up, her back against the bed-head, her eyes full on me.

"Why should he be grateful?"

"He's tried to do you harm."

"Why should he be grateful?" Her glacial anger was rising: it was long since I had seen it. "Why should he or anyone else be grateful just because someone interferes with his life? Interferes, I tell you, for reasons of their own. I wasn't trying to do anything for R.S.R.'s sake, I just wanted to keep myself from the edge, and well you know it. Why shouldn't he say anything he wants? I don't deserve anything else."

"You do," I said.

Her eyes had not left me; her face had gone harsh and cruel.

"Listen," she said. "You've given years of your life to taking care of me, haven't you?"

"I shouldn't call it that."

"What else would you call it? You've been taking care of someone who's useless by herself. Much good has it done you." In a cold, sadic tone, she added: "Or me either."

"I know that well enough."

"Well, you've sacrificed things you value, haven't you? You used to mind about your career. And you've sacrificed things most men want. You'd have liked children and a satisfactory bed. You've done that for me? —Why?"

"You know the reason."

"I never have known, but it must be a reason of your own." Her face looked ravaged, vivid, exhausted, as she cried out:

"And do you think I'm grateful?"

After that fierce and contemptuous cry, she sat quite still. I saw her eyes, which did not fall before mine, slowly redden, and tears dropped on to her cheeks. It was not often that she cried, but always in states like this. It frightened me that night even though I had watched it before—that she did not raise a hand but sat unmoving, the tears running down her cheeks as down a window pane, wetting the neck of her dressing-gown.

At the end of such an outburst, as I knew by heart, there was nothing for me to do. Neither tenderness nor roughness helped her; it was no use speaking until the stillness broke, and she was reaching for a handkerchief and a cigarette.

We were due at a Soho restaurant at half-past eight, to meet my brother. When I reminded her, she shook her head.

"It's no use. You'll have to go by yourself."

I said that I could put him off without any harm done.

"You go," she said. "You're better out of this."

I was uneasy about leaving her alone in that state, and she knew it.

"I shall be all right," she said.

"You're sure?"

"I shall be all right."

So with the familiar sense of escape, guilty escape, I left her: three hours later, with the familiar anxiety, I returned.

She was sitting in almost the same position as when I went away. For an instant I thought she had stayed immobile, but then, with relief, I noticed that she had fetched in her gramophone; there was a pile of records on the floor.

"Had a good time?" she asked.

She inquired about my brother, as though in a clumsy, inarticulate attempt to make amends. In the same constrained but friendly fashion, she asked:

"What am I to do about R.S.R.?"

She had been saving up the question.

"Are you ready to drop him?"

"I leave it to you."

Then I knew she was not ready. It was still important for her, keeping him afloat; and I must not make it more difficult than need be.

"Well," I said, "you knew what he was like all along, and perhaps it doesn't alter the position, when he's behaving like himself——"

She smiled, lighter-hearted because I had understood.

Then I told her that one of us must let Robinson know, as explicitly as we could speak, that we had heard of his slanders and did not propose to stand them. I should be glad, and more than glad, to talk to him; but it would probably do more good if she took it on herself. "That goes without saying," she said.

She got up from her bed, and walked round to the stool in front of her looking-glass. From there she held out a hand and took mine, not as a caress, but as though she was clinching a bargain. She said in an uninflected tone:

"I hate this life. If it weren't for you, I don't think I should stay in it."

It was unlike her to go in for rhetoric, but I was so relieved that she was stable again, so touched by the strained and surreptitious apology, that I scarcely listened to her, and instead just put my other hand over hers.

CHAPTER V

INADMISSIBLE HOPE

WHEN Sheila taxed Robinson with spreading slander
he was not embarrassed; he just said blandly that his
enemies were making mischief. When I accompanied her
to his office a few days later, he received us with his twink-
ling old-fashioned politeness, quite unabashed, as though her
accusations were a breach of taste which he was ready to
forget.

He had taken two garret rooms in Maiden Lane.
"Always have the kind of address that people expect from
you," he said, showing me writing paper headed R. S.
Robinson, Ltd., 16 Maiden Lane, London, W.C.2. "It
sounds like a big firm, doesn't it? How is anyone to know
anything different?" he said, with his gusto in his own
subtlety, his happy faith that all men were easy to bam-
boozle.

He was dead sober, but his spirits were so roaringly
high that he seemed drunk. As he spoke of his dodges, he
hiccupped with laughter—pretending to be a non-existent
partner, speaking over the telephone as the firm's chief
reader, getting his secretary to introduce him by a variety
of aliases. He called to her: she was typing away in the little
room beyond his, the only other room he rented, just as
she was the only other member of his staff. She was a soft-
faced girl of twenty, straight from a smart secretarial
college—as I later discovered, the daughter of a headmaster, blooming with sophistication at being in her first
London job, and confident that Robinson's was a normal
way for literary business to be done.

"We impressed him, didn't we, Miss Smith?" he said, speaking of a recent visitor, and asking Miss Smith's opinion with much deference.

"I think we did," she said.

"You're sure we did, aren't you? It's very important, and I thought you were sure."

"Well, we can't tell till we get his letter," she said, with a redeeming touch of realism.

"Don't you think he must have been impressed?" Robinson beamed and gleamed. "We were part of the editorial department, you see," he explained to Sheila and me, "just part of it, in temporary quarters, naturally——"

He broke off, and with a sparkle in his eye, an edge to his voice, said:

"I've got an idea that Sheila doesn't altogether approve of these bits of improvisation."

"It's waste of time," she said. "It gets you nowhere."

"You know nothing at all about it," he said, in a bantering tone, but rude under the banter.

"I know enough for that." Sheila spoke uncomfortably and seriously.

"You'll learn better. Three or four good books *and* a bit of mystification, and people will take some notice. Putting a cat among the pigeons—I'm a great believer in that, because conventional people can't begin to cope. You're an example, Sheila, the minute you hear of something unorthodox you're helpless, you can't begin to cope. Always do what conventional people wouldn't do. It's the only way."

"Others manage without it," said Sheila.

"They haven't got along on negative resources for forty years, have they? Do you think you could have done?" He maintained his bantering tone.

Often, when boasting of his deceits, he sounded childlike

43

and innocent. He had a child's face: also, like many of the uninhibited, he had a child's lack of feeling. Much of his diablerie he performed as though he did not feel at all: and somehow one accepted it so.

But that was not all. There was a fibre in him which had brought him through a lifetime of begging, cajoling, using his arts on those he believed his inferiors. This fibre made him savage anyone who had been of use to him. It filled him with rancour that *anyone* should have power and money, when he had none. That afternoon he had been charming to Miss Smith, as though he considered her opinion as valuable as any of ours, or more so: he propitiated me because I had done nothing for him, and might even be an enemy: but to Sheila, who through the injustice of life had the power and will to befriend him, he could not help showing his teeth.

I was in a delicate position that afternoon. I should have liked to be brutal; but all I could safely do was to demonstrate that he ought to bear me in mind. For Sheila was not ready to cut her losses. It was not a matter of the money, which was trivial, nor of any feeling for him, which had not decided her in the first place and had turned to repulsion now. But her will had always been strong, and she had set it to do something for this man. He had turned out more monstrous than she reckoned on, but that was neither here nor there; her will would not let her go.

All I could do was listen while Robinson and Sheila discussed a manuscript, which he admired and she thought nothing of. He said goodbye to us at the top of the stairs, gleaming and deprecatory, like a host after a grand party. I was sure that, the instant the door closed behind him, he grinned at Miss Smith, congratulating himself on how he had ridden off the afternoon.

That summer, while I was reading the papers with an anxiety which grew tighter each month, Sheila paid less and less attention to the news. Her politics had once been like mine, she had hoped for and feared much the same things. But in the August and September of '38, when for the first time I began listening to the wireless bulletins, she sat by as though uninterested, or went out to continue reading a manuscript for Robinson.

On the day of Munich she disappeared without explanation in the morning, leaving me alone. I could not go out myself, because for some days I had been seized with lumbago, which had become a chronic complaint of mine, and which gave me nights so painful that I had to move out of our room during an attack. All that day of Munich, I was lying on a divan in what, when we first bought the house, had been Sheila's sitting-room; but since it was there that I had once told her I could stand it no longer, a decision I went back on within an hour, she no longer used it, showing a vein of superstition that I had not seen in her before.

Like those of our bedroom, the windows looked over the garden, the trees on the embankment road, the river beyond; from the divan, as the hours passed that day, I could see the tops of the plane trees against the blue indifferent sky.

The only person I spoke to from morning to late evening was our housekeeper, Mrs. Wilson, who brought me lemonade and food which I could not eat. She was a woman of sixty, whose face bore the oddity that a mild, seeping, life-long discontent had not aged, but had rather made it younger; the corners of her mouth and eyes ran down, her mouth was pinched, and yet she looked like a woman in early middle age whose husband was neglecting her.

Just after she had come up with tea, I heard her step on the stairs again, quick instead of, as usual, reproachfully laborious. When she entered her cheeks were flushed, her expression was humorous and attractive, and she said:

"They say there isn't going to be a war." She went on, repeating the word which was going through the streets, that the Prime Minister was off to Munich. I asked her to fetch me an evening paper. There it was, as she said, in the stop press news. I lay there, looking at the trees, which were now gilded by the declining sun, the pain lancinating my back, forgetting Sheila, lost in the fear of what would come, as lost as though it were a private misery.

About seven o'clock, when through the window the sky was incandescent in the sunset, Sheila's key turned in the lock downstairs. Quickly I took three aspirins, so as to be free from pain for half-an-hour. When she came she said, bringing a chair to the side of the divan:

"How have you been?"

I said, not comfortable. I asked how her day had gone. Not bad, she said. She volunteered the information (in my jealous days, I had learned how she detested being asked) that during the afternoon she had called at Maiden Lane. He still insisted that he would bring out a book in the spring. She did not guarantee it, she said, with a jab of her old realism.

I was impatient, not able to attend. I said: "Have you heard the news?"

"Yes."

"It's as bad as it can be."

Since tea-time I had wanted to talk to a friend who thought as I did. Now I was speaking to Sheila as I should have spoken years before, when she still had part of her mind free. It would have been a little surcease, to speak out about my fears.

"It's as bad as it can be," I repeated.

She shrugged her shoulders.

"Don't you think it is?" I was appealing to her.

"I suppose so."

"If you can have much hope for the future——"

"It depends how much the future interests you," said Sheila.

Her tone chilled me; but I was so desolate that I went on.

"One can't live like that," I cried.

Sheila replied:

"You say so."

As she stared down at me, with the sunset at her back, I could not make out her expression. But her voice held a brittle pity, as she said:

"Try and rest. Anyway, this will give us a bit of time."

"Do you want a bit of time on those terms?"

She said:

"It might give us time to get R.S.R. a book out."

It sounded like a frivolity, a Marie-Antoinettish joke in bad taste: but that would have been preferable. For she had spoken out of all that was left of her to feel, out of dread, obsessive will, the inner cold.

I shouted:

"Is that all you're thinking of, tonight of all nights?"

She did not speak again. She filled my glass with lemonade, and inspected the aspirin bottle to see that I had enough. For a time she sat silently beside me, in the room now taken over by the darkness. At last she said:

"Is there anything else I can do for you?"

I said no, and in poised, quiet steps she left me.

It was hot that night, and I did not sleep more than an hour or two. The attacks of pain kept mounting, so that I writhed on the bed and the sweat dripped off me; in the periods of respite, I lay with thoughts running through my mind, dark and lucid after the day's news, lucid until the next bout of pain. For a long time I did not think of Sheila. I was working out repetitively, uselessly, how much time there was, when the next Munich night would follow, what the choice would be. As the hours passed, I began to ask myself, nearer the frontier of sleep, how much chance there was that we should be left—no, not we, I alone—with a personal life? More and more as the morning came, the question took on dream-shapes but stayed there: if this happened or that, *what should I do with Sheila*?

I took it for granted that I was tied to her. In the past years when I faced, not just the living habit of marriage, but the thought of it, I knew that other men would have found it intolerable: that did not support me, for it made me recognise something harsher, that this was what my nature had sought out. Not because I took responsibility and looked after others: that was true but superficial, it hid the root from which the amiable and deceptive parts of my character grew.

The root was not so pretty. It was a flaw or set of flaws, which both for good and ill, shaped much of how I affected others and the way my life had gone. In some ways I cared less for myself than most men. Not only to my wife, but to my brother, to my friend Roy Calvert, to others, I devoted myself with a lack of self-regard that was, so far as it went, quite genuine. But deeper down the flaw took another shape. Had Sheila been thinking of it when, in our bedroom, she broke out about people helping others *for reasons of their own*?

At the springs of my nature I had some kind of pride or vanity which not only made me careless of myself but also prevented me going into the deepest human relation on equal terms. I could devote myself; that was all right; so long as I was not in turn understood, looked after, made to take the shames as well as the blessedness of an equal heart.

Thus, so far as I could see within, I had been in search of such a marriage as I found with Sheila—where I was protecting her, watching her face from day to day, and getting back no more interest, often indeed far less, than she would spend on her housekeeper or an acquaintance in a Chelsea pub. It was a marriage in which I was strained as far as I could bear it, constantly apprehensive, often dismally unhappy; and yet it left me with a reserve and strength of spirit, it was a kind of home.

There was a lot of chance, I knew, in human relations; one cannot have seen much unless one believed in chance; I might have been luckier and got into a relation less extreme; but on the whole, I had to say of myself what I should have said of others—in your deepest relations, there is only one test of what you profoundly want: it consists of what happens to you.

And yet, no one can believe himself utterly foredoomed. I was not ready to accept that I was my own prisoner. In the early morning, after the night of Munich, I recognised the question, which now formed itself quite clear: *what shall I do with Sheila?* interspersed among the shapes of the future. Once I had tried to leave her; I could not do so again. Often, though, I had let myself imagine a time in which I might be set free.

Now, in that desolate night, among the thoughts of danger, there entered the inadmissible hope, that somehow I should get relief from the strain of watching over her. In the darkness of the months to come, I might at least (I did not will it, but the hope was there) be freed from the sight of her neurosis. It could happen that I need be responsible no more. As the pain abated and the sky lightened I lay on the threshold of sleep, with the dream-thought that, throwing responsibility away, I should then find something better.

CHAPTER VI

FROWN UNDER THE BEDSIDE LAMP

FEW OF my acquaintances liked Sheila. Many men had been attracted to her and several had loved her, but she had always been too odd, too self-centred and ungiving, to evoke ordinary affection. As she grew older and the bones of her character showed through, that was more than ever true. Some of the helpless whom she was kind to idolised her, and so did those who worked for her, including Mrs. Wilson, who was the last person to express unconsidered enthusiasm. Apart from them, I had no one to talk to about her when the rumours began to spread; no one I knew in the Chelsea bars and parties would defend her, except one or two, like Betty Vane, who would do so for my sake.

That autumn, I could not discover how much the rumours were alive. I had the impression that after Sheila had confronted Robinson there had been a lull. But Robinson—it was only now that I realised it clearly—became so merry with gossip that he never let it rest for long; exaggerating, transmogrifying, inventing, he presented the story, too luscious to keep, to anyone who met him; everything became a bit larger than life, and I heard, through a chain of word-of-mouth which led back to him, that Sheila's private income was £4,000 a year, when in fact it was £700.

Thus I thought it likely that Sheila was still being traduced; watching her, I was convinced that she knew it, and that none of her attempts to forget herself had exposed her so. Sometimes, towards the end of the year, I fancied that she was getting tired of it. Even obsessions wear themselves out, I was thinking, just as, in the unhappiest love affair, there comes eventually a point where the forces urging one to escape unhappiness become infinitesimally stronger than those which immerse one in it.

In fact, Sheila's behaviour was becoming more than ever strange. She went out less, but she was not playing her records hour after hour, which was her final refuge. She seemed to have a new pre-occupation. Twice, returning home earlier than usual from Millbank, I heard her footsteps running over the bedroom floor and the sounds of drawers shutting, as though she had been disturbed by my arrival and was hiding something.

It was not safe to ask, and yet I had to know. Mrs. Wilson let fall that Sheila had taken to going, each morning, into the room we used as a study; and one day, after starting for the office, I came back as though by accident. Mrs. Wilson said that, following her new routine, Sheila was upstairs in the study. It was a room at the back of the house, and I went along the landing and looked in. Beside the window, which looked over the Chelsea roofs, Sheila was sitting at the desk. In front of her was an exercise book, an ordinary school exercise book ruled with blue lines; her head thrown back because of her long sight, she was looking at the words she had just written, her pen balanced over the page. So far as I could see from across the room, it was not continuous prose she was writing, nor was it verse: it looked more like a piece of conversation.

Suddenly she realised that the door was open, that I was there. At once she slammed the exercise book shut and pressed her hand on it.

"It's not fair," she cried, like an adolescent girl caught in a secret.

I asked her something neutral, such as whether I could change my mind and dine at home that night. "It's not fair," Sheila repeated, clutching her book. I said nothing. Without explanation she went across into the bedroom, and there was a noise of a drawer being unlocked and locked again.

But it did not need explanation. She was trying both to write and to keep it secret: was she thinking of Emily Brontë and Emily Dickinson? Had she a sisterly feeling for women as indrawn as herself? Usually, when we had spoken of them, she had—it was cool, I thought, coming from her— shown no patience with them, and felt that if they had got down to earth they might have done better.

Anyway, neither she nor I referred to her writing, until the night of the Barbican dinner. The Barbican dinner was one of the festivals I had to attend, because of my connection with Paul Lufkin. The Barbican was an organisation consisting largely of members of banks, investment trusts and insurance companies, which set out to make propaganda for English trade overseas. To this January dinner Lufkin was invited, as were all his senior executives and advisors, and those of his bigger competitors.

I would have got out of it if I could; for the political divide was by this time such that even people like me, inured by habit to holding their tongues, found it a strain to spend a social evening with the other side. And this was the other side. Among my brother and his fellow scientists, in the Chelsea pubs, in the provincial back streets where my oldest friends lived—there we were all on one side. At Cambridge, or even among Betty Vane's aristocratic relatives, there were plenty who, to the test questions of those years, the Spanish Civil War, Munich, Nazism, gave the same answers as I did myself. Here there was almost none.

I could hear my old master in Chambers, Herbert Getliffe, the rising silk, wise with the times as usual: he was singing in unison, as it were, and so were the active, vigorous, virile men round him: yes, Churchill was a menace and a war-monger and must be kept out at all costs: yes, war was getting less likely every day: yes, everything had been handled as well as it possibly could be handled, everyone knew we were ready to play ball.

I was frightened just as I had been on the night of Munich. I knew some of these men well: though they were less articulate than my friends, though they were trained to conform rather than not to conform, they were mostly able: they were tougher and more courageous than most of us: yet I believed that, as a class, they were self-deceived or worse.

Of all those I knew, there was only one exception. It was Paul Lufkin himself. He had taken his time, had tried to stay laodicean, but at last he had come down coldly among the dissidents. No one could guess whether it was a business calculation or a human one or both. There he sat, neat-headed, up at the benefactors' table, listening to the other bosses, impassively aware that they sneered about how he was trying to suck up to the Opposition, indifferent to their opinion or any other.

But he was alone, up among the tycoons: so was I, three or four grades down. So I felt a gulp of pleasure when I heard Gilbert Cooke trumpeting brusquely, on the opposite side of the table not far from me, telling his neighbours to make the most of the drinks, since there would not be a Barbican dinner next year.

"Why not?"

"We shall be fighting," said Gilbert.

"Let's hope it won't come to that," said someone.

"Let's hope it will," said Cooke, his face imperative and flushed. Men were demurring, when he brought his hand down on the table.

"If it doesn't come to that," he said, "we're sunk."

He gazed round with hot eyes: "Are you ready to see us being sunk?"

He was the son of a regular soldier, he went about in society, he was less used to being over-awed than the people round him. Somehow they listened, though he badgered and hectored them, though he was younger than they were.

He saw me approving of him, and gave a great impudent wink. My spirits rose, buoyed up by this carelessness, this comradeship.

It was not his fault that recently I had seen little of him. He had often invited me and Sheila out, and it was only for her sake that I refused. Now he was signalling comradeship. He called out across the table, did I know the Davidsons? Austin Davidson?

It was a curious symbol of alliance tossed over the heads of those respectable business men. Davidson was an art connoisseur, a member of one of the academic dynasties, linked in his youth with high Bloomsbury. No, I called out, I knew his work, of course, but not him. I was recalling to myself the kind of gibes we used to make a few years before about those families and that group: how they carried fine feelings so far as to be vulgar: how they objected with refined agony to ambition in others, and slipped as of right into the vacant place themselves. Those were young men's gibes, gibes from outside a charmed circle. Now they did not matter: Davidson would have been an ally at that dinner; so was Gilbert, brandishing his name.

When Gilbert drove me home I had drunk enough to be talkative and my spirits were still high. We had each been angry at the dinner and now we spoke out, Gilbert not so anxious as I about the future but more enraged; his fighting spirit heartened me, and it was a long time since I had become so buoyant and reassured.

In that mood I entered the bedroom, where Sheila was lying reading, her book near the bedside lamp, as it had been the evening we quarrelled over Robinson: but now the rest of the room was in darkness, and all I could see was the lamp, the side of her face, her arm coming from the shoulder of her nightdress.

I sat on my bed, starting to tell her of the purgatorial dinner—and then I became full of desire.

She heard it in my voice, for she turned on her elbow and stared straight at me.

"So that's it, is it?" she said, cold but not unfriendly, trying to be kind.

On her bed, just as I was taking her, too late to consider her, I saw her face under mine, a line between her eyes carved in the lamplight, her expression worn and sad.

Then I lay beside her, on us both the heaviness we had known often, I the more guilty because I was relaxed, because, despite the memory of her frown, I was basking in the animal comfort of the nerves.

In time I asked:

"Anything special the matter?"

"Nothing much," she said.

"There is something?"

For an instant I was pleased. It was some sadness of her own, different from that which had fallen on us so many nights, lying like this.

Then I would rather have had the sadness we both knew—for she turned her head into my shoulder, so that I could not watch her face, and her body pulsed with sobbing.

"What is the matter?" I said, holding her to me.

She just shook her head.

"Anything to do with me?"

Another shake.

"What then?"

In a desperate and rancorous tone, she said:

"I've been weak-minded."

"What have you done?"

"You knew that I'd been playing with some writing. I didn't show it to you, because it wasn't for you."

The words were glacial, but I held her and said, "Never mind."

"I've been a fool. I've let R.S.R. know."

"Does that matter much?"

"It's worse than that, I've let him get it out of me."

I told her that it was nothing to worry about, that she must harden herself against a bit of malice, which was the worst that could happen. All the time I could feel her anxiety like a growth inside her, meaningless, causeless, unreachable. She scarcely spoke again, she could not explain what she feared, and yet it was exhausting her so much that, as I had known happen to her before in the bitterness of dread, she went to sleep in my arms.

CHAPTER VII

TRIUMPH OF R. S. ROBINSON

WHEN Sheila asked Robinson for her manuscript back, he spent himself on praise. Why had she not written before? This was short, but she must continue with it. He has always suspected she had a talent. Now she had discovered it, she must be ready to make sacrifices.

Reporting this to me, she was as embarrassed and vulnerable as when she confessed that she had let him blandish the manuscript out of her. She had never learned to accept praise, except about her looks. Hearing it from Robinson she felt half-elated, she was vain enough for that, and half-degraded.

Nevertheless, he had not been ambivalent; he had praised with a persistence he had not shown since he extracted her promise of help. There was no sign of the claw beneath. It made nonsense of her premonition, that night in my arms.

Within a fortnight, there was a change. A new rumour was going round, more detailed and factual than any of the earlier ones. It was that Sheila had put money into Robinson's firm (one version which reached me multiplied the amount by three) but not really to help the arts or out of benevolence. In fact, she was just a dilettante who was supporting him because she wrote amateur stuff herself and could not find an easier way to get it published.

That was pure Robinson, I thought, as I heard the story— too clever by half, too neat by half, triumphant because he could expose the 'lie in life'. To some women, I thought also, it would have seemed the most innocuous of rumours.

To Sheila—I was determined she should not have to make the comparison. I telephoned Robinson at once, heard from his wife that he was out for the evening, and made an appointment for first thing next day. This time I meant to use threats.

But I was too late. Sitting in the drawing-room when I got home, Sheila was doing nothing at all. No book, no chess-men, not even her gramophone records—she was sitting as though she had been there for hours, staring out of the lighted room into the January night.

After I had greeted her and settled down by the side of the fire, she said:

"Have you heard his latest?"

She spoke in an even tone. It was no use my pretending. I said yes.

"I'm handing in my resignation," she said.

"I'm glad of that," I replied.

"I've tried as much as I can," she said, without any tone.

In the same flat, impassive voice, she asked me to handle the business for her. She did not wish to see Robinson. She did not care what happened to him. Her will was broken. If I could manage it, I might as well get her money back. She was not much interested.

As she spoke, discussing the end of the relation with no more emotion than last week's accounts, she pointed to the grate, where there lay a pile of ash and some twisted, calcined corners of paper.

"I've been getting rid of things," she said.

"You shouldn't have done," I cried.

"I should never have started," she said.

She had burned all, her own holograph and two type-scripts. But, against the curious farcical intransigence of brute creation, she had not found it so easy as she expected. The debris in the grate represented a long time of sitting before the fire, feeding in papers. In the end, she had had to drop most of the paper into the boiler downstairs. Even that night, she thought it faintly funny.

However, she had destroyed each trace, so completely that I never read a sentence of hers, nor grasped for certain what kind of book it was. Years later, I met the woman who had once been Miss Smith and Robinson's secretary, and she mentioned that she had glanced through it. According to her, it had consisted mostly of aphorisms, with a few insets like 'little plays'. She had thought it was 'unusual', but had found it difficult to read.

The morning after Sheila burned her manuscript, I kept my appointment with Robinson. In the Maiden Lane attic, the sky outside pressed down against the window; as I entered, Robinson switched on a single light in the middle of the ceiling.

"How are you, sir," he said. "I'm glad you've conquered that fibrositis, it must have made life miserable."

Courteous and also cordial, he insisted on putting me in the comfortable chair and fitting a cushion to ease the backache of six months before. His eyes were suspicious, but struck me as gay rather than nervous.

I began:

"I was coming to see you on my own account——"

"Any time you've got nothing better to do," said Robinson.

"But in fact I've come on my wife's."

"I haven't seen her for two or three weeks; how is she?"

"She wants," I said, "to finish any connection with you or what you call your firm or anything to do with you."

Robinson blushed, as he had done at our dinner party. That was the one chink in his blandness. Confidentially, almost cheerfully, he asked:

"Shouldn't you say that was an impulsive decision?"

He might have been a friend of years, so intimate that he knew what my life had been, enduring an unbalanced wife.

"I should have advised her to take it."

"Well," said Robinson, "I don't want to touch on painful topics, but I think perhaps you'll agree that it's not unreasonable for me to ask for an explanation."

"Do you think you deserve it?"

"Sir," he flared up, like a man in a righteous temper, "I don't see that anything in our respective positions in the intellectual world entitles you to talk to me like that."

"You know very well why my wife is quitting," I said. "You've made too much mischief. She isn't ready to stand any more."

He smiled at me sympathetically, putting his temper aside as though it were a mackintosh.

"Mischief?" he said.

"*Mischief*," he repeated, reflectively, like one earnestly weighing up the truth. "It would help me if you could just give me an example of what sort of mischief I'm supposed to be guilty of, just as a rough guide."

I said that he had spread slander about her.

"Remember," he said, in a friendly merry manner, "remember you're a lawyer, so you oughtn't to use those words."

I said that his slander about the book had sickened her.

"Do you really think," he said, "that a sane man would be as foolish as you make me out to be? Do you think I could possibly go round blackguarding anyone who was supporting me? And blackguarding her very stupidly, according to your account, because for the sum she lent me she could have published her book several times over. I'm afraid, I don't like to say it, but I'm afraid you've let Sheila's difficulties infect you."

For a second his bland reasonableness, his trick of making his own actions sound like a neurotic's invention, his sheer euphoria, kept me silent.

"Yes," he said. "I'm afraid you've let poor Sheila's

60

state infect you. I suppose it *is* the beginning of schizo-phrenia, isn't it?"

"I am not going to discuss my wife," I said. "And I don't think it profitable to discuss your motives——"

"As for her book," he said, "I assure you, it has real merit. Mind you, I don't think she'll ever become a professional writer, but she can say original things, perhaps because she's a little different from most of us, don't you know?"

"I've got nothing to say to you," I said. "Except to arrange how you can pay my wife's money back."

"I was afraid she might feel like that——"

"This is final," I said.

"Of course it is," said Robinson with his gay, whole-hearted laugh. "Why, I knew you were going to say that the very moment you came into the room!"

I had been strung up for a quarrel. It was a frustration to hear my words bounce back. If he had been a younger man, I might have hit him. As it was, he regarded me with sympathy, with humour in his small, elephantine eyes, the middle parting geometrically precise in his grandfatherly hair.

"You've done her harm," I said in extreme bitterness, and regretted the words as soon as they were out.

"*Harm?*" he enquired. "Because of her association with me? What kind of harm?"

He spread out his hands.

"But, as you said, this isn't the time or place to con-sider the troubles of poor Sheila. You came here to take her money out, didn't you? Always recognize the inevit-able, I'm a great believer in that. Don't you think it's time we got down to business?"

I had run into another surprise. As I sat beside his desk, listening to Robinson's summary of his agreement with Sheila and his present situation, I realised he was a man of unusual financial precision and, so far as I could judge, of honesty. It was true that, cherishing his own secretiveness, he concealed from me, just as he had originally concealed from Sheila, some of his sources of income and his expectations of money to come. Somehow he had enough money to continue in his office and to pay Miss Smith; meanwhile, he was postponing his first 'list' until the autumn; it struck me, was he glad of the excuse? Daydreaming, planning, word-spinning about the revival of past glories, that was one thing. Putting it to the test was another. Maybe he would like that date deferred.

No one could have procrastinated less, however, about repaying Sheila: he offered to write her a cheque for £300 that day, and to follow it with two equal instalments on June 1st and September 1st.

"Interest?" he asked, beaming.

"She wouldn't take it."

"I suppose she wouldn't," said Robinson with curiosity.

At once he proposed that we should go round to his solicitor's. "I never believe in delay," said Robinson, putting on a wide-brimmed hat, an old overcoat trimmed with fur at the collar and sleeves. Proud of his incisiveness, behaving like his idea of a business man (although it was as much like Paul Lufkin's behaviour as a Zulu's), he walked by my side through Covent Garden, the dignified little figure not up to my shoulder. Twice he was recognised by men who worked in the publishers' or agents' offices round about. Robinson swept off his grand hat.

"Good morning to you, sir," he cried affably, with a trace of patronage, just as R. S. Robinson, the coterie publisher, might have greeted them in 1913.

His face gleamed rosy in the drab morning. He looked happy. It might have seemed bizarre to anyone but him that he should have spent all his cunning on acquiring a benefactor, and then used equal ingenuity in driving the benefactor away. Yet I believed he had done it before, it was one of the patterns of his career. To him it was worth it. The pleasures of malice, the pleasures of revenge against one who had the unbearable impertinence to lean down to him—they were worth a bigger price than he had ever had to pay.

And more than that, I thought, as we sniffed the smell of fruit and straw in the raw air, Robinson walking with the assurance of one going to a reputable business rendezvous, it was not only the pleasure of revenge against a benefactor. There was something more mysterious which sustained him. It was a revenge, not against Sheila, not against a single benefactor, but against life.

When I reached home that afternoon, I heard the gramophone playing. That worried me; it worried me more when I found her not in the drawing-room, not in our bedroom, but in the sitting-room where I had spent the night of Munich and which to her was a place of bad luck. In front of her, the ash-tray must have held thirty stubs.

I began to say that I had settled with Robinson. "I don't want to hear anything about it," she said, in a harsh flat tone.

I tried to amuse her, but she said:

"I don't want to hear anything about it."

She put on another record, shutting out, not only the history of Robinson, but me too.

CHAPTER VIII

"YOU'VE DONE ALL YOU COULD"

IN THE summer, I no longer spent half my time away from
Sheila. We were waiting for the war to begin; I slept
each night in our bedroom, saw her waking and sleeping,
without break, as I had not done for years. As soon as war
came, I assumed that I should go on living beside her in the
Chelsea house, as long as one could foresee.

Those September nights, we were as serene, as near happy,
as ever in our marriage. I used to walk, not from Millbank
now but Whitehall, for I had already taken up my government job, all along the embankment, often at eight o'clock
and after; the air was still warm, the sky glowed like a
cyclorama; Sheila seemed glad to see me. She was even
interested in the work I was doing.

We sat in the garden, the night sounding more peaceful
than any peace-time night, and she asked about the Department, how much the Minister did, to what extent he was
in the pocket of his civil servants, just where I—as one of
his personal assistants—came in. I told her more of my own
concerns than I had for a long while. She laughed at me for
what she called my 'automatic competence', meaning that I
did not have to screw myself up to find my way about the world.

I was too much immersed in my new job to notice just
when and how that mood broke up. Certainly I had no
idea until weeks later that to herself she thought of a moment
of collapse as sharp as the crack of a broken leg—and she
thought also of as sharp a cause. All I knew was that, in the
well-being of September, she had, unknown to me, arranged
to join someone's staff on the first of January. It was work

that needed good French, which she had, and seemed more than usually suitable. She described it to me with pleasure, almost with excitement. She said:

"I expect it will turn out to be R.S.R. all over again," but she spoke without shadow. It was a gibe she could only have made in confidence and optimism.

Soon afterwards, not more than a fortnight later, I came home night following night to what seemed to me signs of the familiar strain, no different from what we each knew. I was disappointed the first time I came home to it; I was irritated, because I wanted my mind undistracted; I set myself to go through the routine of caring for her. Persuading her to leave her records and come to bed: talking to her in the darkness, telling her that, just as worse bouts had passed, so would this: discussing other people whose lives were riven by angst—it domesticated her wretchedness a little to have that label to pin on. It was all repetitive, it was the routine of consolation that I knew by heart, and so did she. Sometimes I thought you had to live by the side of one like Sheila to understand how repetitive suffering is.

All the time I was looking after her, absentmindedly, out of habit; it seemed like all the other times; it did not occur to me to see a deterioration in her, or how far it had gone. Not even when she tried to tell me.

One night, early in November, I came out of my first sleep, aware that she was not in her bed. I listened to her outside the door, heard a match strike. None of this was novel, for when she could not sleep she walked about the house smoking, considerate of me because I disliked the smell of tobacco smoke at night. The click of the bedroom door, the rasp of a match, the pad of feet in the corridor— many nights they had quietly woken me, and I did not get to sleep again until she was back in bed. This time it was no different, and according to habit I waited for her. The click of the door again: the slither of bedclothes, the spring of the bed. At last, I thought, I can go back to sleep: and contentedly, out of habit, called out—"All right?"

For an instant she did not answer; then her voice came: "I suppose so."

I was jerked back into consciousness, and again I asked: "*Are* you all right?"

There was a long pause, in the dark. At last a voice: "Lewis."

It was very rare for her to address me by my name.

I said, already trying to soothe her:

"What is it?"

Her reply sounded thin but steady:

"I'm in a pretty bad way."

At once I switched on my bedside lamp, and went across to her. In the shadow, for my body came between the light and her face, I could see her, pale and still; I put my arm round her, and asked what was the matter.

All of a sudden her pride and courage both collapsed. Tears burst from her eyes and, in the transformation of moments, her face seemed decaying, degenerate, almost as though it were dissolving.

"What is the matter?"

"I'm worried about January 1st."

She meant the job she had to take up that day.

"Oh, that!" I said, unable to keep down an edge of anti-climax, of sheer boredom.

I ought to have known that anything could be a trigger for her anxiety: but nothing, I knew also, was more boring than an anxiety one did not share.

"You must understand," she cried, for once making an appeal.

I tried to speak in the tone that she would trust. Soon— in those states she was easy to persuade—she trusted me as she had done before.

"You do see, don't you?" she cried, the tears stopping as she broke into speech that was incoherent, excited, little like her own. "The other day, three weeks ago next Monday, it was in the afternoon just after the post came, I realised that on January 1st I was going to get into the same state as I did over R.S.R. It is bound to happen, you do see that, don't you? There will be just the same kind of trouble, and it will all gather round me day after day."

"Look," I said, reasoning with her carefully, for long ago I had found the way that reassured her most, "I daresay there'll be trouble, but it won't be the same kind. There's only one R.S.R., you know."

"There's only one me," she said, with a splinter of detachment. "I suppose I was really responsible for the fiasco."

"Truly I don't think so," I said. "Robinson would have behaved the same to me."

"I doubt it," she said. "I've never done any good."

Her face was excited and pressing. "You must understand, as soon as I get among new people, I shall be caught in the same trap again."

I was shaking my head, but she broke out, very high:

"I tell you, I realised it that afternoon just after the post came. And I tell you, in the same second I felt something go in my brain."

She was trembling, although she was not crying any more. I asked her, with the sympathy of one who has heard it before and so is not frightened, about her physical symptoms. Often, in a state of anxiety, she had complained of hard bands constricting her head. Now she said that there had been continual pressure ever since that afternoon, but she would not describe the physical sensation that began it. I thought she was shy, because she had been exaggerating. I did not realise that she was living with a delusion, in the clinical sense. I had no idea, coaxing her, even teasing her, how much of her judgement had gone.

I reminded her how many of her fears had turned out nonsense. I made some plans for us both after the war. Her body was not trembling by this time, and I gave her a tablet of her drug and stayed by her until she went off to sleep.

Next morning, although she was not anxiety-free, she discussed her state equably (using her domesticating formula —'about twenty per cent angst today') and seemed a good deal restored. That evening she was strained, but she had a good night, and it was not for several days that she broke down again. Each night now, I had to be prepared to steady myself. Sometimes there were interludes, for as long as a week together, when she was in comfortable spirits, but I was tensed for the next sign of strain.

My work at the office was becoming more exacting; the Minister was using me for some talks face-to-face where one needed nothing else to think about and no tugs at the nerves; when I left Sheila in the morning, I wished that I were made so that I could forget her all through the day— but at some time, in the careful official conversation, a thought of her would swim between me and the man I was trying to persuade.

More than once, I found myself bitter with resentment against her. When we first married she had drained me of energy and nerve, and had spoiled my chance. Now, when I could least afford it, she was doing so again. That resentment seemed to exist simultaneously, almost to blend, with pity and protective love.

The first week in December, I was in the middle of a piece of business. One afternoon, about half-past five, when I was counting on working for an hour or two more, the telephone rang. I heard Sheila's voice, brittle and remote.

"I've got a cold," she said.

She went on:

"I suppose you couldn't come home a bit early? I'll make you some tea."

It was abnormal for her to telephone me at all, much less ask me to see her. She was so unused to asking that she had to make those attempts at the commonplace.

I took it for granted that something more was wrong, abandoned my work, and took a taxi to Chelsea. There I found that, although she was wretched and her tic did not leave her mouth, she had nothing new to say. She had fetched me home just to work over the moving belt of anxiety —the bits and pieces came round and round before us— Robinson, January 1st, her 'crack-up'. My impatience not quite suppressed, dully I said:

"We've been over all this before."

"I know it," she said.

"I've told you," I said mechanically, "worse things have passed, and so will this."

"Will it?" She gave a smile, half-trusting, half-contemptuous, then broke out:

"I've got no purpose. You've got a purpose. You can't pretend you haven't." She cried out: "I've said before, I've handed in my resignation."

I was tired of it, unable to make the effort of reassurance, irked that she had dragged me from the work I wanted to do. With the self-absorption that had now become complete, she dismissed all my life except the fraction of it I spent supporting her. We were sitting by the fire in the drawing-room. I heard myself using words that, years before, I had used in her old sitting-room. For there, in my one attempt to part from her, I had said that our life together was becoming difficult for me. Now I was near repeating myself.

"This is difficult for me," I said, "as well as for you."

She stared at me. Whether or not the echo struck her, I did not know. Perhaps she was too drawn into herself to attend. Or perhaps she was certain that, after all that had happened, all that had changed, I could no longer even contemplate leaving her.

"It is difficult for me," I said.

"I suppose it is," she replied.

On that earlier occasion, I had been able to say that for my own sake I must go. But now, as we both knew, I could not. While she was there, I had to be there too. All I could say was:

"Make it as easy for me as you can."

She did not reply. For a long time she gazed at me with an expression I could not read. She said, in a hard and final tone:

"You've done all you could."

CHAPTER IX

A GOODBYE IN THE MORNING

UP TO December 20th there was no change that I noticed. As I lived through those days they seemed no more significant than others. Later, when I tried to remember each word she and I said, I remembered also the signs of distress she showed about January 1st, and the new job. She was still too proud to ask outright, but she was begging me to find an excuse to get her out of it.

Otherwise she had fits of activity, as capricious as they used to be. She put on a mackintosh, in weather that was already turning into bitter winter, walked all day along the river, down to the docks, past Greenwich, along the mud-flats. When she got home, flushed with the cold, she looked as she must have done as a girl, after a day's hunting. She was cheerful that night, full of the enjoyment of her muscles; she shared a bottle of wine with me and fell asleep after dinner, a little drunk and happily tired. I did not believe in those flashes of cheerfulness, but also I did not totally believe in her distress. It did not seem, as I watched her, to have the full weight of her nature behind it.

Her moods fluctuated, not as my friend Roy Calvert's did in cycles of depression, but in splinters from hour to hour; more exactly, her moods could change within a single moment, they were not integral; sometimes she spoke unlike an integral person. But that had always been so, though it was sharper now. She still made her gibes, and, the instant she did so, I felt the burden of worry evanesce. This phase was nothing out of the ordinary, I thought, and we should both come through it, much as we had done for the past years.

In fact, I behaved as I had seen others do in crises, acting as though the present state of things would endure for ever, and occasionally, as it were with my left hand and without recognising it, showing a sense of danger.

One day I got away from my meetings and confided in Charles March, one of the closest friends of my young man-hood, who was at this time a doctor in Pimlico. I told him, in sharper tones than I used to myself, that Sheila was in a state of acute anxiety, and I described it: was it any use bringing in another psychiatrist? The trouble was, as he knew, she had consulted one before, and given him up with ridicule. Charles promised to find someone, who would have to be as clever and as strongwilled as she was herself, whom she might just conceivably trust. But he shook his head. "I doubt if he'll be able to do much for her. All he might do is take some of the responsibility off you."

On December 20th, Charles rang me up at the office and gave me a doctor's name and address. It happened to be the day I was bringing my first substantial piece of departmental business—the business from which Sheila had called me away a fortnight before—to an issue. In the morning I had three interviews, in the afternoon a com-mittee. I got my way, I was elated, I wrote a minute to my superior. Then I telephoned the doctor whom Charles had recommended; he was not at his surgery and would not be available for a fortnight, but he could see my wife in the first week in January, January 4th. That I arranged, and, with a throb of premonition, my own work shelved for a day or two, free to attend to her, I telephoned home.

I felt an irrational relief when she answered. I asked:

"How are you?"

"Much the same."

"Nothing's happened?" I asked.

"What could have happened?"

Her voice sharpened:

"I should like to see you. When shall you be here?"

"Nothing wrong since this morning?"

"No, but I should like to see you."

I knew her tone, I knew she was at her worst. I tried to coax her, as sometimes one does in the face of wretchedness, into saying that she was not so bad.

Flatly the words came to my ear:

"I'm not too bad to cope."

She added:

"I want to see you. Shall you be long?"

When I went into the hall, she was waiting there for me. She began to speak before I had taken my coat off, and I had to put my arm round her shoulders and lead her into the drawing-room. She was not crying, but I could feel beneath my hand the quiver of her fibres, the physical sign that frightened me most.

"It's been a bad day," she was saying. "I don't know whether I can go on. It's no use going on if it's too hard."

"It won't be too bad," I said.

"Are you sure?"

I was ready with the automatic consolation.

"Have I got to go on? Can I tell them I shan't be able to come on January 1st?"

That was what she meant, I had assumed, by 'going on'; she spoke like that, whenever she winced away from this ordeal to come, so trivial to anyone else.

"I don't think you ought," I said.

"It wouldn't matter much to them." It was as near pleading as she had come.

"Look," I said, "if you get out of this, you'll get out of everything else in the future, except just curling up into yourself, now won't you? It's better for you to come through this, even if it means a certain amount of hell.

F 73

When you put it behind you, all will be well. But this time you mustn't give up."

I was speaking sternly. I believed what I said; if she surrendered over this test, she would relapse for good and all into her neurosis; I was hoping, by making my sympathy hard, to keep her out of it. But also I spoke so for a selfish reason. I wanted her to take this job so that she would be occupied and so at least partially off my hands. In secret, I looked forward to January as a period of emancipation.

I thought of mentioning the doctor whom Charles March had recommended, and the appointment that I had made. Then I decided against.

"You ought to go through with it," I said.

"I knew you'd say that." She gave me a smile, not bitter, not mechanical, quite transformed; for a second her face looked youthful, open, spiritual.

"I'm sorry for giving you so much trouble," she said, with a curious simplicity. "I should have been luckier if I could have cracked up altogether, shouldn't I?" Her imagination had been caught by an acquaintance who had solved her problems by what they called a "nervous breakdown", and now seemed happy and at peace. "I couldn't pull that off somehow. But I ought to have been able to manage by myself without wearing you out so much."

As I listened I was moved, but, still trying to stiffen her nerve, I did not smile or show her much affection.

That night we played a couple of games of chess, and were in bed early. She slept quietly and next morning got up to have breakfast with me, which was unusual. Across the table her face looked more ravaged and yet more youthful without its makeup. She did not refer to what had been said the evening before; instead, she was talking, with amusement that seemed light and genuine, about my arrangements for the coming night. Gilbert Cooke had invited me to dinner at his club; getting back to Chelsea,

74

I said, in the blackout, having had a fair amount of drink, was not agreeable. Perhaps it would be better if I slept at my own club. How much should I have had to drink? Sheila wanted to know—with a spark of the inquisitiveness about male goings-on, the impudence that one saw sometimes in much younger women, high-spirited, not demure, but brought up in households without brothers.

On those light, teasing terms, we said goodbye. I kissed her and, in her dressing-gown, she came to the door as I went down the path. At the gate I waved, and standing with her arms by her sides, poised, erect and strong, she smiled. It was too far away to see her clearly, but I thought her expression was both friendly and jibing.

CHAPTER X

NO LETTER IN THE ROOM

AT White's that night, Gilbert Cooke and I had a convivial dinner. He had invited me for a specific reason and yet, despite his unselfconscious raids into other people's business, he could not confess this bit of his own until I helped him out. Then he was loose and easy, a man with an embarrassing task behind him; he ordered another bottle of wine and began to talk more confidentially and imperiously.

The favour he asked would not have weighed so heavy on most men. It appeared that he had been trying all ways to get into uniform, but he kept being turned down because he had once had an operation for mastoid. Gilbert was ashamed and sorry. He wanted to fight, with a lack of pretence that men of our age had felt twenty-five years before; in 1939 the climate, the social pressures, had changed; most other men I met in Gilbert's situation blessed their luck, but he felt deprived.

However, by this time, he had accepted his loss; since he could not fight, he wished to do something in the war. Stay with Paul Lufkin?

"Why does he want me to?" Gilbert Cooke enquired, with his suspicious, knowing, hot-eyed glance.

"Because you're useful to him, of course."

"No, he's thinking out something deeper than that. I'd give fifty quid to know just what."

"Why in God's name should he not want you to stay?"

"Haven't you realised he thinks about all of us five moves ahead?"

Gilbert's face was shining, as he filled his glass and pushed the bottle across. I did not realise what he wanted me to (which seemed to me conspiratorial nonsense), but instead I did realise another thing. Which was, that Gilbert, despite his independent no-man air in Paul Lufkin's company, was at heart more than normally impressionable: he gave Lufkin brusque advice, but in private thought he was a great man: so that Lufkin received the pleasures of not being flattered, and of being deeply flattered, at one and the same time.

But Gilbert, as well as being susceptible to personality, was a sincere and patriotic man. The country was at war, and with Lufkin, although Gilbert was hypnotised by the human drama, he was not doing anything useful. So this lavish bachelor dinner, this elaborate wind-up, led to nothing but a humble question, which he was too diffident to do more than hint at.

"You mean," I said, "that you'd like a job in a government department?"

"If they'd possibly have me."

"Why shouldn't they?"

"Oh, I was never up to their clan as a brain, I don't see why they should."

In fact, able active men of thirty-five, with decent academic careers, permanently exempt from call-up, were bound soon to be at a premium. I told him so.

"I'll believe that when I see it," said Cooke.

"They'd take you as a principal tomorrow."

"How could they think I was any use to them?"

A little drunk, half-irritated that he would not trust my judgement, half-touched by his modesty, I said:

"Look here. Would you like to work in my place?"

"You don't mean there would be a chance?"

"I can take the first step tomorrow."

Gilbert regarded me with bold eyes, determined to see

the catch in it, diffident about thanking me. From that instant he just wanted a comradely evening. Brandy by the fire: half-confidences: the stories, gilded at the edges, of youngish men on a happy alcoholic night. One thing struck me about Gilbert's stories. He was an adventurous, versatile man, always on the move: but he was meticulously pure in speech, and, although he spoke of women with liking, he did not talk openly of sex.

Next morning, in the breakfast room of my club, the coal-fire crackled and spurted: the unfolded newspapers glinted on the table under the light: in the street outside the pavement looked dark with cold. Although I had a headache, it was not enough to put me off my breakfast, and food was still good, so early in the war. I ate the kidneys and bacon, and, indulging my thirst, went on drinking tea; the firelight was reflected back from the grey morning mist outside the windows. Acquaintances came to the tables, opening their *Times*. It was all warmed and cared-for, and I enjoyed stretching out the minutes before I rang up Sheila. At a quarter-past nine, I thought, she would be getting up. In comfort, I drank another cup of tea.

When I got through to our house, the telephone burred out perhaps twenty times, but I was not anxious, thinking that Sheila must still be asleep. Then I heard Mrs. Wilson's voice.

"Who is it?"

I asked, was Sheila up.

"Oh, Mr. Eliot," came the thin, complaining voice.

"What's the matter?"

"Something's happened. I think you ought to come back straightaway, I think you must."

I knew.

"Is she all right physically?"

"No."

"Is she dead?"

78

"Yes."

"She's killed herself?"

"Yes."

I was sick with shock, with the first numbness; I heard myself asking:

"How did she do it?"

"It must have been her sleeping tablets, there's the empty bottle lying by the side of her."

"Have you called a doctor?"

"I'm afraid she's been dead for hours, Mr. Eliot. I only found her ten minutes ago, and I didn't know what to do."

I said that I would arrange everything, and be with her in half an hour.

"I'm very sorry about it myself. I was very fond of her, poor soul. It was a great shock for me, finding her," came Mrs. Wilson's voice, in a tone of surprise, aggrievement, injury. "It was a great shock for me."

At once I rang up Charles March. I must have a doctor whom I could trust, I thought. As I waited, it occurred to me that neither Sheila nor I had used a regular doctor in London. Apart from my lumbago, we had been physically healthy people.

Charles was out at a patient's. I left a message, saying that I needed him with extreme urgency. Then I went into the street and took a taxi home. In the freezing morning the desolate Park skimmed by, Exhibition Road, the knot of shop-lights by South Kensington Station. Twice the smell of the taxi's leather made me retch. I seemed at a distance from my own pain: somehow, dimly, numbly, I knew that grief and remorse were gnawing inside me, twisting my bowels with animal deprivation, with the sensual misery of loss. And also I felt the edge of a selfish and entirely ignoble fear. I was afraid that her suicide might do me harm; I shied from thinking of what kind of harm, but the superstitious reproach hung upon me, mingled with remorse. The fear was sharp, practical and selfish.

In the hall, Mrs. Wilson's eyes were bloodshot, and she squeezed her handkerchief and pressed it into the corner of one eye and then the other: but her manner had the eagerness, the zest, of one living close to bad news.

"She's not in the bedroom, Mr. Eliot," she whispered. "She did it in her old sitting-room."

I wondered whether it was a chance, or whether she had chosen it.

"Did she leave any letters?" I asked, and I also was near whispering.

"I couldn't see anything, I looked round, of course, but I couldn't see a piece of paper in the room. I went up with her tea, Mr. Eliot, and I knocked on the bedroom door, and no one answered, and I went in and there was no one there——"

Although Mrs. Wilson wished to follow me, I went upstairs alone. The sitting-room curtains were drawn, though I did not know by whom, it might have been by Mrs. Wilson a few minutes before. In the half-light I was struck by the dread that came on me as a child when I went into the room where my grandfather's body was stretched out. Before looking at her, I pulled the curtains open; the room stood bare to the leaden light. At last I forced my eyes towards the divan.

She was lying on her back, dressed in a blouse and skirt such as she wore in the house on an ordinary afternoon, her head a quarter turned towards the window. Her left hand was by her side and her right fell across her breast, the thumb wide apart from the fingers. The lines of her face were so softened by death that they had become only grazes, as though her living face had been photographed through muslin; her cheeks, which had never hollowed, now were as full as when she was a girl. Her eyes were open and enormous: on her mouth there was a defensive, deprecatory, astonished grin, exactly the grin she wore when she was taken at a loss and exclaimed 'Well, I'm damned'.

There was, just visible because of the tablets she had taken, a dried trickle of saliva down the side of her chin, as though she had dribbled in her sleep.

I stared for a long time, gazing down at her. However one read her expression, the moment of death seemed not to have been tragic or unhappy. I did not touch her; perhaps, if she had looked sadder, I should have done.

By the divan stood the bedside table, just as on the night of Munich, when she had placed my bottle of aspirin there for me. Now another bottle rested on the cherry wood, but empty and without its stopper, which she must have dropped on to the floor. Beside the bottle was a tumbler, containing about three fingers' depth of water, stale with the night's bubbles. There was nothing else at all. Into that room she brought nothing but her bottle and the glass of water.

I searched for a note as though I were a detective. In that room—in the bedroom—in my study—I studied the envelopes in the wastepaper baskets, looking for any line to her parents or me. In her handbag I found her pen unfilled. On her writing desk the paper was blank. She had gone without a word.

Suddenly I was angry with her. I was angry, as I looked down at her. I had loved her all my adult life; I had spent the years of my manhood upon her; with all the possessive love that I had once felt for her, I was seared because she had not left me a goodbye.

Waiting for Charles March, I was not mourning Sheila. I had room for nothing but that petty wound, because I had been forgotten; the petty wound, and also the petty fear of the days ahead. As I waited there, I was afraid of much, meeting the Knights, going to the office, even being seen by my friends.

CHAPTER XI

CLAUSTROPHOBIA IN AN EMPTY HOUSE

WHILE Charles March was examining her I went into the bedroom, where I gazed out of the window, aware of nothing but fears and precautions. The only recognition that I gave to Sheila was that my eyes kept themselves away from any glance at her bed, at the undisturbed immaculate bed.

There I stayed until Charles's step outside warned me. I met the concerned glance from his sharp, searching eyes, and we walked together to the study.

"This is bound to be a horror for you," he said. "And nothing that I or anyone else can say is going to alter that, is it?"

Nowadays Charles and I did not see each other often. When I first came to London as a poor young man to read in chambers, he had befriended me. We were the same age, but he was rich and had influential relatives. Since then he had changed his way of life, and become a doctor. When we met, the old intuitive sympathy sparked between us. But that morning he did not realise how little I was feeling, or what that little was.

"There is no doubt, I suppose?" I asked.

"You don't think so yourself?" he answered.

I shook my head, and he said:

"No, there's no doubt. None at all."

He added, with astringent pity:

"She did it very competently. She had a very strong will."

"When did she do it?" I had gone on speaking with neutrality. He was studying me protectively, as though he were making a prognosis.

"Some time last night, I think."

"Yes," I said. "I was out for the evening. I was having a cheerful time at a club, as a matter of fact."

"I shouldn't take that to heart, if I were you."

He leaned forward in his chair, his eyes brilliant in the dark room, and went on:

"You know, Lewis, it wasn't such an intolerable wrench for her to die as it would be for you or me. She wasn't so tied to life as we are. People are as different in the ways they die as in the ways they live. Some go out as though they were shrugging their shoulders. I imagine that she did. I think she just slipped out of life. I don't think she suffered much."

He had never liked her, he had thought her bad for me, but he was speaking of her with kindness. He went on: "You're going to suffer a lot more, you know."

He added:

"The danger is, you'll feel a failure."

I did not respond.

"Whatever you'd done or been, it wouldn't have helped her," he said, with energy and insistence.

"Anyway," I said, "that doesn't matter."

"It matters, if you're going to feel you've failed. And no one but yourself can be any good to you there."

Again I did not respond.

He gazed at me sternly: he knew that my emotions were as strong as his: he had not seen them dead before. He was using his imagination to help me, he did not speak for some time, his glance stayed hard and appraising as he reached a settlement in his own mind.

"The only thing I can do for you now is superficial, but it might help a little," he said, after a silence.

"What do you mean?"

"Does anyone else know about her?"

"Only Mrs. Wilson," I said.

"Would she keep quiet?"

"It's possible," I replied.

"If necessary, could you guarantee it?"

I did not reply at once. Then I said:

"If necessary, I think I could."

Charles nodded. He said:

"I expect it will make you just a little worse to have other people knowing about her death, I know it would me. You'll feel that your whole life with her is open to them, and that they're blaming you. You're going to take too much responsibility on yourself whatever happens, but this will make it worse."

"Maybe," I said.

"Well, I can save you that," he broke out.

He went on:

"It won't help much, but it will a little. I'm willing to sign a certificate that she died a natural death."

Charles was a bold man, who lived in close touch with moral experience. Perhaps he had that special boldness, that ability to act in moral isolation, that one found most commonly in men born rich. Between perjuring himself, which he would dislike more than most, and leaving me exposed he had made his choice.

I was not altogether surprised: in fact, in sending for him rather than for any of the doctors near, I had some such hope half-concealed.

I was tempted. Quickly I was running through the practical entanglements: if there was any risk to him professionally I could not let him run it. We had each been thinking of that, while he questioned me. Could I answer absolutely for Mrs. Wilson? Who else need know the truth? The Knights must, as soon as they arrived. But they would keep the secret for their own sakes.

I thought it over. As I did so, I had little insight into my own motives. It was not entirely, or even mainly, because of practical reasons or scruples about Charles's risk that I answered:

"It's not worth it."

"Are you sure?"

"Quite sure."

Charles went on persuading me until he was convinced that my mind was made up. Then he said that he was relieved. He left to enquire about the inquest, while I telephoned the Knights': I told Mrs. Knight the bare news and asked them to come that afternoon. She sounded reliable and active in the face of shock, but she cried: "I don't know how he'll get through it."

That same afternoon I had to go to a committee, among civil, sensible strangers.

Back in the house, blacked-out early on the December night, I could not stay still until the Knights came. Mrs. Wilson had gone out to shop, getting a meal ready for them, and I was alone in the empty house. Yet no house seemed empty while someone lay dead: the reverse was true, there was a claustrophobic pressure, although I had not visited the sitting-room again.

In my restlessness I turned over Sheila's books once more, re-read the letters in her desk, in the silly hope that I might find news of her. By a fluke, I did find just a little, not among her books or papers, but in her bag. Expecting nothing, I picked out her engagement diary and riffled through it; most of the pages shone bare, since the appointments with Robinson in January and February: since then, she had seen almost no one. But in the autumn pages I caught sight of a few written words—no, not just words, whole sentences.

It was an ordinary small pocket book, three inches by two, and she had scaled down her writing, which as a rule was elegant but had a long-sighted tallness. There were only seven entries, beginning in October, a week after the afternoon which she referred to as her 'crack-up'. As I read, I knew that she had written for herself alone. Some of the entries were mere repetitions.

November 4: Ten days since the sensation in my head. No good. No one believes me.

November 12: January 1 bad enough anyway. Seems hopeless after something snapped in head.

November 28: Told I must go on. Why should I? That's the one comfort, I needn't go on.

December 5: Bit better. Perhaps I can go on. It's easier, when I know I needn't.

Nothing more than that—but for the first time I knew how fixed her delusion was. I knew also that she had contemplated suicide for weeks past, had had it in her mind when I tried to hearten her.

Perhaps even when she first said she was handing in her resignation, that was a hint, as much as eight months ago. Had she intended me to understand her? But she was not certain, she had done no more than hint, even to herself. Had she been certain two nights before, when I told her again she must go on? Had she been certain next morning at breakfast, the last time I saw her alive, when she was making fun of me?

I heard Mrs. Wilson's step downstairs. I did not look at Sheila's writing any more: it was not to think, it was because of the claustrophobic pressure upon me in the house, that I went out of the front door and walked along the Embankment in a night as calm as the last night, as calm as when, quite untroubled, I had walked up St. James's Street with Gilbert Cooke. The sky was dark, so was the river, so were the houses.

CHAPTER XII

THE SMELL OF HERB TOBACCO

WHEN I got back to the house there was a sliver of
light between the black-out curtains of the drawing-
room; as soon as I stood inside the hall I heard a woman's
voice, Mrs. Knight's, raised, sustained, unrelenting. The
instant I entered the room, she stopped: there was a silence:
she had been talking about me.

Mr. Knight was sitting in an armchair by the fire, and she
had drawn up the sofa so as to be beside him. Her eyes
fixed on mine and did not budge, but his gazed into the
fire. It was he who spoke.

"Excuse me if I don't get up, Lewis," he said, still without
looking at me, and the polite whisper fell ominously into
the silent room. Still politely, he said that they had caught
an earlier train and I could not have expected them at this
time. His eyes had stayed hidden, but his expression was
pouched and sad. He said:

"Your housekeeper has shown us——"

"Yes."

The intimations of pain and sorrow, so weak all day,
quite left me. I felt nothing but guilt, and irrational fear.

"She left no word for anyone?"

"No."

"Not for you *or* us?"

I shook my head.

"I don't understand that. I don't understand *that*."

I wondered if he believed me, if he suspected that I had
destroyed a note. Certainly Mrs. Knight, suddenly set
loose, suspected it.

"Where were you last night?"

I replied that I was dining out—the jolly carefree evening came back to me.

"Why did you leave her? Hadn't you any consideration for her?"

I could not answer.

Why hadn't I looked after her? Mrs. Knight asked, angry and denouncing. All through our marriage, why had I left her to herself? Why hadn't I carried out what I promised? Why hadn't I taken the trouble to realise that she wanted looking after? Couldn't I have given her even a modicum of care?

"Oh no, he's done that," whispered Mr. Knight, with his eyes closed.

"You've left her *alone in this empty house*," Mrs. Knight went on.

"He's done as much as anyone could have." Mr. Knight spoke up, a little louder, defending me. She looked baffled, even frustrated, and began another attack.

"*Please*, my dearest," he ordered her in a loud voice, and she gave way. Then with the gentleness he always showed to her, he said, as though explaining:

"It is his affliction as well as ours."

Out of the corner of his eye he glanced at me, and murmured: "The last time I saw her"—he meant the visit eighteen months before—"I couldn't help thinking she was in a bad state. I believe I mentioned it, didn't I, Lewis, or did I just think it to myself? The last time I saw her. I wish that I had been wrong."

And yet, the fact that he had been perceptive, more perceptive than I or anyone else had been, gave him a vestigial comfort; even that night his vanity glowed for an instant.

"She shouldn't have done it," cried Mrs. Knight, in anger but with the only tears I had seen in her eyes.

"I have no comfort to give you, dearest," he said. "Or you either." Once more he was gazing into the fire, the

88

corner of his eyes sidling towards me. In my hearing he had not once spoken of the consolations of his religion. The room was quiet, all we heard was the ticking of the clock. Somehow we had passed into a patch of those doldrums which often lurk in the path, not only of a quarrel, but of any scene of violent feeling.

Breaking the quiet, Mrs. Knight asked whether there would have to be an inquest. I said yes. When? I told her that it was already arranged, for the following afternoon. Mr. Knight half-raised his lids with a speculative expression, looked as though he had something to say but had thought better of it. Then he mentioned casually: "Tomorrow afternoon? Not that I want anyone to give it a thought except my doctor, but it will presumably be a considerable strain on me."

"You've stood it well so far," said Mrs. Knight.

"If Ross (his doctor) were here, he would tell us it was dangerous," Mr. Knight continued. "I'm morally certain he would forbid it. But he won't have to know until he has to patch me up afterwards."

In a new kind of numbness I exclaimed:

"Never mind, don't take any risks. I can get through it by myself."

Mrs. Knight cried:

"No, we can't think of leaving you."

Mr. Knight muttered:

"I wouldn't willingly think of leaving you, it would throw all of it on to your shoulders——"

Mrs. Knight broke in: "We can't do it."

Mr. Knight went on: "One doesn't like to think of it, but Lewis, in case, in the remote case, that my wretched heart was getting beyond its degree of tolerance tomorrow afternoon, are you sure that you could if need be manage by yourself?"

So Mr. Knight, whose empathy was such that he knew more than most men both what my life with Sheila had been and what my condition was that night, was only anxious to escape and leave me to it: while Mrs. Knight, who blamed me for her daughter's unhappiness and death, felt in her fibres that they ought to stand by me in the end, give their physical presence if they could give nothing else. She felt it so primally that for once she gave up thinking of her husband's health.

There were those, among whom I had sometimes been one, who believed that, if she had not pampered his hypochondria, he would have forgotten his ailments half the time and lived something near a normal life. We were wrong. She had a rough, simple nature, full of animal force: but, despite her aggressiveness, she had always been, and was now as much as ever, under his domination. It was he who felt his own pulse, who gave the cry of alarm, and she who in duty and reverence echoed it. Even that night he could not subdue it, and for a few moments she was impatient with him.

In the end, of course, he got his way. She soon realised that the inquest would tax his heart more than she could allow; she became convinced that it was he who out of duty insisted on attending, and she who was obliged to stop him; she would have to forbid his doing anything so quixotic, even if I was prostrate without them.

As it was, I said that I would settle it alone, and they arranged to return home next morning. I did not mention Charles March's offer to give a false certificate, so that we could have avoided the inquest. I wondered how Mr. Knight would have reconciled his conscience, in order to be able to accept that offer.

In his labyrinthine fashion, Mr. Knight asked how much publicity we had to be prepared for. I shrugged it off.

"No," said Mr. Knight, "it will hurt you as much and more than us, isn't that true?"

It was, but I did not wish to admit it, I did not like the times that day when the thought of it drove out others.

Perhaps the war-news would be a blessing to us, Mr. Knight was considering. I said I would do my best with my press acquaintances. The Knights could go home next morning: I would do what could be done.

Relieved, half-resentful, half-protective, Mr. Knight began inquiring where I would sleep tomorrow night, whether I could take a holiday and get some rest. I did not want, I could not bear, to talk of myself, so I made an excuse and left them alone.

At dinner none of us spoke much, and soon afterwards, it must have been as early as nine o'clock, Mrs. Knight announced that she was tired and would go straight to bed. Of all women, she was the least well designed for subterfuges: she proclaimed her piece of acting like a blunt, embarrassed, unhappy schoolgirl. But I had no attention to spare for her; Mr. Knight was determined to speak to me in intimacy, and I was on guard.

We sat in the drawing-room, one each side of the fireplace, Mr. Knight smoking a pipe of the herb-tobacco which out of valetudinarian caution he had taken to years before. The smell invaded me and I felt a tension nearly intolerable, as though this moment of sense, the smell of herb tobacco, was not to be endured, as though I could not wait to hear a word. But when he did speak, beginning with one of his circuitous wind-ups, he astonished me: the subject he wanted to get clear before they left next day was no more intimate than the lease of the house.

When I married Sheila, I had had no capital, and Mr. Knight had lent us the money to buy a fourteen years' lease, which had been in Sheila's name. This lease still had six years to run, and Mr. Knight was concerned about the most business-like course of action. Presumably, after all that had happened, and regardless of the fact that the house was too large for a man alone, I should not wish to go on living there? If it were his place to advise me, he would advise against. In that case, we ought to take steps about disposing of the lease. Since the loan had been for Sheila's sake as well as mine, he would consider it wiped off, but perhaps I would think it not unreasonable, as he did himself, particularly as Sheila's own money would come to me under her will, that any proceeds we now derived from the lease should go to him?

Above all, said Mr. Knight, there was a need for speed. It might be possible to sell a house before the war developed: looking a few months ahead, none of us could guess the future, and any property in London might be a drug on the market. I had always found him one of the most puzzling and ungraspable of men, but never more so than now, when he took that opportunity to show his practical acumen. I promised to put the house in the agents' hands within a few days.

"I'm sorry to lay this on your shoulders too," he said, "but your shoulders are broad—in some ways——"

His voice trailed away, as though in the qualification he might be either envying me or pitying me. I was staring into the fire, not looking at him, but I felt his glance upon me. In a quiet tone he said:

"She always took her own way."

I did not speak.

"She suffered too much."

I cried out: "Could any man have made her happy?"

"Who can say?" replied Mr. Knight.

He was trying to comfort me, but I was bitter because that one cry had escaped against my will.

"May she find peace," he said. For once his heavy lids were raised, he was looking directly at me with sad and acute eyes.

"Let me say something to you," he remarked, his words coming out more quickly than usual, "because I suspect you are one of those who take it on themselves to carry burdens. Perhaps one is oneself, perhaps one realises the danger of those who won't let themselves forget."

For an instance his tone was soft, indulgent with self-regard. Then he spoke sharply: "I beg you, don't let this burden cripple you."

I neither would nor could confide. I met his glance as though I did not understand.

"I mean the burden of my daughter's death. Don't let it lie upon you always."

I muttered. He made another effort: "If I may speak as a man thirty years older, there is this to remember—time heals most wounds, except the passing of time. But only if you can drop the burdens of the past, only if you make yourself believe that you have a life to live."

I was gazing, without recognition, into the fire; the smell of herb tobacco wafted across. Mr. Knight had fallen silent. I reckoned that he would leave me alone now.

I said something about letting the house. Mr. Knight's interest in money did not revive; he had tried for once to be direct, an ordeal for so oblique a man, and had got nowhere.

For minutes, ticked off by the clock, again the only sound in the room, we stayed there; when I looked at him his face was sagging with misery. At last he said, after neither of us had spoken for a long while, that we might as well go to bed. As we went out to the foot of the stairs, he whispered: "If one doesn't take them slowly, they are a strain on one's heart."

I made him rest his hand on my shoulder, and cautiously, with trepidation, he got himself from tread to tread. On the landing he averted his eyes from the door of the room in which her body lay.

Again he whispered:

"Good night. Let us try to sleep."

CHAPTER XIII

A SMOOTH BEDCOVER

IT WAS three nights later when, blank to all feeling, I went into the bedroom and switched on the light. Blankly, I pulled off the cover from my own bed; then I glanced across at hers, smooth, apple-green under the light, undisturbed since it was made four days before. All of a sudden, sorrow, loss, tore at me like a spasm of the body. I went to the bed and drew my hands along the cover, tears that I could not shed pressing behind my eyes, convulsed in the ravening of grief. At last it had seized me. The bed was smooth under the light. I knelt beside it, and wave after wave of a passion of the senses possessed me, made me grip the stuff and twist it, scratch it, anything to break the surface, shining quietly under the light.

Once, in an exhausted respite, I had a curious relief. The week to come, some friends had invited us to dinner. If she had been alive, she would have been anxious about going, she would have wanted me to make excuses and lie her out of the evening, as I had done so many times.

Then the grief flooded through me again. In the derangement of my senses, there was no time to come: all time was here, in this moment, now, beside this bed.

I learned then, in that devastation, that one could not know such loss without craving for an after life. My reason would not give me the illusion, not the fractional hope of it —and yet I longed to pray to her.

PART II
THE SELF-DEFEATED

CHAPTER XIV

LOAN OF A BOOK

OUTSIDE the window, in the September sunshine, a couple of elderly men were sitting in deckchairs drinking tea. From my bed, which was on the ground floor of a London clinic, I could just see past them to a bed of chrysanthemums smouldering in the shadow. The afternoon was placid, the two old men drank with the peace of cared-for invalids; for me it was peaceful to lie there watching them, free from pain. True, Gilbert Cooke would be bringing me work, I should have to be on my feet by Thursday; but there was nothing the matter with me, I could lie idle for another twenty-four hours.

That day was Tuesday, and I had only entered the clinic on the previous Saturday afternoon. Since Sheila's death nearly two years before (this was the September of 1941) I had been more on the move then ever in my life, and the pain in my back had not been giving me much rest. It was faintly ludicrous: but, in the months ahead, I was going to be still more occupied, and it was not such a joke to think of dragging myself through meetings as I had been doing, or, on the bad days, holding them round my office sofa. It was not such a joke, and also it watered one's influence down: in any kind of politics, men listened to you less if you were ill. So I had set aside three days, and a surgeon had tried manipulating me under an anaesthetic. Although I was incredulous, it seemed to have worked. Waiting for Cooke that afternoon, I was touching wood in case the pain returned.

When Gilbert Cooke came in, he had a young woman with him whose name, when he made an imperious gobbled

97

introduction, I did not catch. In fact, taking from him at once some papers marked urgent, I only realised some moments afterwards, absent in my reading, that I had not heard her name. Then I only asked for it with routine politeness. Margaret Davidson. He had mentioned her occasionally, I recalled; she was the daughter of the Davidson whom he had talked of at the Barbican dinner and whom I had been surprised to hear that Gilbert knew.

I glanced up at her, but she had withdrawn to near the window, getting out of our way.

Meanwhile Gilbert stood by my bed, a batch of papers in his hand, haranguing me with questions.

"What have they been doing to you?"

"Are you fit for decent company at last?"

"You realise you must stay here until you're well enough not to embarrass everyone?"

I said I would take the committee on Thursday. He replied that it was out of the question. When I told him how I should handle that day's business he said that, even if I were fool enough to attend, I could not use those methods.

"You can't get away with it every time," he said, jabbing his thumb at me in warning. He stood there, his massive shoulders humped, his plethoric face frowning at me. After the fussy, almost maternal concern with which he looked after my health, as he had done since he came into my office, he turned brusquer still. He was talking to me like a professional no-man, just as he used to talk to Paul Lufkin. He did so for the same reason—because he regarded me as a success.

Working under me for nearly two years of war, Gilbert had seen me promoted; he had his ear close to the official gossip. He magnified both what I had done and what was thought of it, but it was true enough that I had made, in those powerful anonymous couloirs, some sort of reputation. Partly I had been lucky, for anyone as close to the

Minister as I was could not help but attract attention: partly, I had immersed myself in the job, my life simplified for the first time since I was a boy, with no one to watch over, no secret home to distract me.

To Gilbert, who had joined my branch soon after Sheila died, I now seemed an important man. As a consequence, he was loyal and predatory about my interests when I was not present, but face to face insisted on back-chat.

On the coming Thursday we should have to struggle with a problem of security. Some people in one of the 'private armies' of the time were busy with a project that none of us believed in; but they had contrived so to enmesh themselves in security that we could not control them. I knew about their project: they knew that I knew: but they would not talk to me about it. I told Gilbert that their *amour propre* might be satisfied if we went through a solemn minuet: they must be asked to explain themselves to the Minister, which they could not refuse to do: he would then repeat the explanation to me: then on Thursday both they and I could hint obliquely at the mystery.

It was the kind of silly tactic that any official was used to. I made some remark that it was dangerous to give secrets to anyone with exaggerated self-esteem: it was bad for business, and worse for his character.

I heard a stirring by the window. I looked at the young woman, who had been sitting quietly there without a word, and to my astonishment saw her face transfigured by such a smile that I felt an instant of ease, almost of expectancy and happiness. Never mind that my piece of sarcasm had been mechanical: her smile lit up her eyes, flushed her skin, was kind, astringent, lively, content.

Until that moment I had scarcely seen her, or seen her through gauze as one sees a stranger one does not expect to meet again. Perhaps I should have noticed that her features were fine-cut. Now I looked at her. When she was not smiling her face might have been austere, except for the accident that her upper lip was short, so that I could not help watching the delicate lines of her nostril and the peak of her lip. As she smiled her mouth seemed large, her face lost its fine moulding: it became relaxed with good nature and also with an appetite for happiness.

Looking at her, I saw how fine her skin was. She had used very little make-up, even on the lips. She was wearing a cheap plain frock—so cheap and plain that it seemed she had not just picked up the first in sight, but deliberately chosen this one.

As she sat by the window, her amusement drying up, she had a curious gaucheness, like an actor who does not know what to do with his hands. This posture, at the same time careless and shy, made her look both younger and frailer than she was in fact. The little I knew of her was collecting in my mind. She must be about twenty-four, I thought, twelve years younger than Gilbert or me. When she laughed again, and her head was thrown back, she did not look frail at all.

I smiled at her. I began to talk to her and for her. I was beating round for something to link us. She was working in the Treasury—no, she was not easy about the people or her job.

Acquaintances in Cambridge—we exchanged names, but no more.

How should I occupy myself tomorrow, I asked, staying here in this room?

"You oughtn't to do anything," she said.

"I'm not good at that," I replied.

"You ought to do as Gilbert tells you." She had taken care to bring him in, she broke the duologue, she smiled at him. But she spoke to me again: she was positive.

"You ought to rest all the week."

I shook my head; yet a spark had flashed between us.

No, I said, I should just have tomorrow to bask in and read—I was short of books, what would be best for the day in bed? She was quick off the mark.

"You want something peaceful," she said.

Not a serious novel, we agreed—not fiction at all, maybe —journals that one could dip into, something with facts in them. Which were the most suitable journals, Bennett's, Gide's, Amiel's?

"What about the Goncourts?" she asked.

"Just what I feel like," I said.

I asked, how could I possibly lay my hand on the books by tomorrow?

"I've got them at home," she said.

Suddenly the air held promise, danger, strain. I had not enough confidence to go ahead; I needed her to make the running, to give me the sign I longed for; I was waiting for her to say that she would bring a book, or send it to me. Yet I could feel, as she folded her fingers in her lap, that she was diffident too.

If it had been Sheila when I first knew her—some half-memory made me more constrained—she would not have given a thought that Gilbert had brought her into the room: she would have announced, in ruthlessness and innocence, that she would deliver the book next morning. But Margaret would not treat Gilbert so, even though their relation appeared to be quite slight. She was too good-mannered to give me the lead I sought. But, even if Gilbert had not been present, could she have done so? She was not only too gentle, but perhaps also she was too proud.

Looking at her, her head no longer thrown back, her eyes studying me, I felt that she had a strong will, but no more confidence that moment than I had myself.

It was Gilbert who snapped the tension off. He would arrange, he said, brusque and cheerful, to get the books

round to the clinic first thing next morning. Soon afterwards they left, Margaret saying goodbye from the door:
as soon as I heard their steps in the corridor, I was suffused
with happiness.

In a beam of evening sun which just missed my bed, the
motes were spinning. Outside it, in the twilight, I cherished
my happiness, as though by doing so I could stretch it out,
as though, by letting myself live in the moment of recognition between this young woman and me half an hour
before, I could stay happy.

Several times since Sheila's death, my eyes had lit up
at the sight of a woman, but I had not been able to free
myself enough, it had come to nothing. The qualms were
not buried; this could come to nothing too. But, just as
the old do not always or even most of the time feel old, so
someone whose nerve is broken can forget past disasters
and cherish the illusions of free will. I felt as free to think
of this young woman as if I had not met Sheila, as if I were
beginning.

It occurred to me that I had never been able to remember
my first meeting with Sheila. It was the second time I
could remember, her face already lined, handsome and
painted, at nineteen looking older than Margaret in the
middle twenties. Yes, I was comparing Margaret with
her, as I did when letting my imagination dwell on any
woman; it appeared that I had to make sure there was no
resemblance, to be convinced that anyone I so much as
thought of was totally unlike what I had known.

There was the same comparison in my mind as I thought
of Margaret's nature. She had enough spirit to be exciting—
but she seemed tender, equable, easy-going. An hour after
she had left, I was making day-dreams of her so.

That evening, lying in bed outside the beam of sunlight,
I basked in a kind of uncommitted hope; sometimes home-
sick images of the past filtered in, as well as the real past that

I feared. But I was happy with the illusion of free will, as though with this girl who had just left me bliss was mine if I chose it.

Nevertheless I need do nothing; I had admitted nothing to myself beyond recall; I could refrain from seeing her again without more than a spasm of regret and reproach for my own cowardice.

For that night, I could rest in an island of peace, hoarding my chance of bliss as I used to hoard sweets as a child, docketing them away in a bookshelf corner so that they were ready when I felt inclined.

CHAPTER XV

CONFIDENTIAL OFFER

STILL acting as though uncommitted, I invited Margaret and Gilbert Cooke together, three times that autumn. For me, there was about those evenings the suspense, the inadmissible charm, that abides in a period of waiting for climactic news, as it were an examination result, from which one is safe until the period is up. The meeting in a pub, where Gilbert and I went together from the office and found her waiting: the communiqués in the evening papers: the wartime streets at night: the half-empty restaurants, for London was not crowded that year: the times at dinner when we spoke of ourselves, the questions unspoken: the return alone to Pimlico in the free black night.

One evening in late November Gilbert had accompanied me out of the office for a drink in my club, as he often did. That day, as on most others, we went on discussing our work, for we were engrossed in it. Much of the time since Sheila's death, I had thought of little else: nor had Gilbert, intensely patriotic, caught up in the war. He had by now picked up some of the skills and language of the professional civil servants we were working with: our discussion that evening, just as usual, was much like the discussions of two professionals. I valued his advice: he was both tough and shrewd, and tactically his judgement was better than mine.

There was just one point, however, at which our discussion was not simply business-like. Gilbert had developed Napoleonic ambitions, not for himself, but for me: he saw me rising to power, with himself as second-in-command: he credited me with the unsleeping cunning he had once seen in Paul Lufkin, and read hidden meanings in moves that were quite innocent. Either as result or cause, his curiosity about my behaviour was proliferating so that I often felt spied upon. He was observant quite out of the ordinary run. He would not ask a disloyal question, but he had a gossip-writer's nose for information. I was fond of him, I had got used to his inquisitiveness, but lately it had seemed to be swelling into a mania.

We could be talking frankly about policy, with no secrets between us, when I happened to mention a business conversation with the Minister. A look, knowing and in-flamed, came into Gilbert's eyes: he was wondering how he could track down what we had said. He was even more zestful about my relations with the Permanent Secretary, Sir Hector Rose. Gilbert knew that the Minister wished me well; he was not so sure how I proposed to get on terms with Rose. About any official scheme, Gilbert asked me my intentions straight out, but in pursuit of a personal one he became oblique. He just exhibited his startling memory by quoting a casual remark I had made months before about Hector Rose, looked at me with bold, hinting eyes, and left it there.

So that I was taken unawares that night when, after we had settled a piece of work, he darted a glance round the bar, making certain no one had come in, and said:

"How much are you interested in Margaret?"

I should have been careful with anyone, with him more than most.

"She's very nice," I said.

"Yes?"

"She's distinctly intelligent."

Gilbert put down his tankard and stared at me.

"What else?"

"Some women would give a lot for her skin and features, don't you think?" I added: "I suppose some of them would say she didn't make the best of herself, wouldn't they?"

"That's not the point. Are you fond of her?"

"Yes. Aren't you?"

His face overcast and set so that one could see the double chins, Gilbert stared at the little round table on which our tankards stood. He said:

"I'm not asking you just for the fun of it."

With angry energy he was twisting into the carpet the heel of one foot, a foot strong but very small for so massive a man.

"I'm sorry," I said and meant it, but I could go no further. Ill-temperedly, he said:

"Look here, I'm afraid you might be holding off her because of me. I don't want you to."

I was saying something neutral, when he went on:

"I'm telling you not to worry. She'd make someone a wonderful wife, but it won't be me. I should slip away, whether you want to do anything about it or not."

He faced me with a fierce opaque gaze of one about to insist on giving a confidence.

"You're wondering why she wouldn't be the wife for me?"

He answered the question:

"I should be too frightened of her."

He had started the conversation intending to be kind, not only to me, but to Margaret. For he did not like the spectacle of lonely people: he could not help stirring himself and being a matchmaker. Yet, getting on towards forty, he was still a bachelor himself. People saw this self-indulgent, heavy-fleshed, muscular man, taking women out, dropping them, returning to his food and drink and clubs: and some, the half-sophisticated, wrote him down as a homosexual. They were crass. The singular thing was that Gilbert was better understood by less sophisticated persons; Victorian aunts who had scarcely heard of the aberrations of the flesh would have understood him better than his knowledgeable acquaintances.

In fact, if one forgot his inquisitiveness, he was much like some of his military Victorian forebears. He was as brave as those Mutiny soldiers, and like them good-natured, more than that, sentimental with his friends: and he could have been as ferocious as they were. His emotional impulses were strong beyond the normal, his erotic ones on the weak side. It was that disparity which gave him his edge, made him formidable and also unusually kind, and which, of course, kept him timorous with women.

He wanted to explain, he went on to tell me so over the little table in the bar, that he was frightened of Margaret because she was so young. She would expect too much: she had never had to compromise with her integrity: she had not seen her hopes fail, her spirits were still overflowing.

But, if she had been older and twice married, he would have been even more frightened of her—and would have given another reason just as eloquent and good.

CHAPTER XVI

FOG ABOVE THE RIVER

IN the week after that talk with Gilbert, I wrote twice to Margaret, asking her to come out with me, and tore the letters up. Then, one afternoon at the end of December, I could hold back no longer, but, as though to discount the significance of what I was doing, asked my secretary to ring up Margaret's office. "It doesn't matter if you don't find her," I said. "If she's not in, don't leave a message. It doesn't matter in the least." As I waited for the telephone to ring, I was wishing to hear her voice, wishing that she should not be there.

When she spoke, I said:

"I don't suppose you happen to be free tonight, do you?" There was a pause. "Yes, I am."

"Come and see me then. We'll go out somewhere."

"Lovely."

It sounded so easy, and yet, waiting for her that night in my flat in Dolphin Square, where I had moved after Sheila's death, I was nervous of what I did not know. It was not the nervousness that I should have felt as a younger man. I longed for an unexacting evening: I hoped that I could keep it light, with no deep investment for either of us. I wished that I knew more of her past, that the preliminaries were over, with no harm done.

Restlessly I walked about the room, imagining conversations, as it might have been in a day-dream, which led just where I wanted. The reading lamp shone on the backs of my books, on the white shelves; the room was cosy and confined, the double curtains drawn.

It was seven by my watch, and on the instant the door-bell buzzed. I let her in, and with her the close smell of the corridor. She went in front of me into the sitting-room, and, her cheeks pink from the winter night, cried: "Nice and warm."

When she had thrown off her coat and was sitting on the sofa, we had less to say to each other than on the nights we had dined *à trois*. Except for a few minutes in restaurants, this was the first time we had been alone, and the words stuck. The news, the bits of government gossip, rang like lead; the conversations I had imagined dropped flat or took a wrong turn; I felt she also had been inventing what she wanted us each to say.

She asked about Gilbert, and the question had a monotonous sound as though it had been rehearsed in her mind. When those fits and starts of talk, as jerky as an incompetent interview, seemed to have been going on for a long time, I glanced at my watch, hoping it might be time for dinner. She had been with me less than half an hour.

Soon after, I got up and went towards the bookshelves, but on my way turned to her and took her in my arms. She clung to me; she muttered and forced her mouth against mine. She opened her eyes with a smile: I saw the clear and beautiful shape of her lips. We smiled at each other with pleasure but much more with an overmastering, a sedative relief.

Although the lids looked heavier, her eyes were bright; flushing, hair over her forehead, she began to laugh and chatter. Enraptured, I put my hands on her shoulders.

Then, as if she were making a painful effort, her face became sharp and serious, her glance investigatory. She looked at me, not pleading, but screwing herself up to speak. She said:

"I want to ask you something. It's important."

Since I touched her, I had thought all was going as

I imagined it. She was pliant, my reverie was coming true at last. I was totally unprepared to see her face me, a person I did not know.

My face showed my surprise, my letdown, for she cried:

"You don't think I want to upset you, do you, now of all times?"

"I don't see why you should," I said.

"I've got to ask—before it's too late."

"What is it?"

"When you were with Sheila"—I had not talked much of her, but Margaret spoke as though she knew her—"you cared for her, I mean you were protecting her all the while. There wasn't any more to it, was there?"

After a pause, I said:

"Not much."

"Not many people could have done it," she said. "But it frightens me."

Again I did not want to speak: the pause was longer, before I said:

"Why should it?"

"You must know that," she said.

Her tone was certain, not gentle—my experience and hers might have been open before us.

"It wasn't a relationship," she went on. "You were standing outside all the time. Are you looking for the same thing again?" Before I had replied, she said: "If so——" Tears had come to her eyes. "It's horrible to say it, but it's no good to me."

Still crying, she said:

"Tell me. Are you looking for the same thing again?"

In my own time, in my own fashion, I was ready to search down into my motives. With pain, certainly with resentment, I knew I had to search in front of her, for her. This answer came slower even than my others, as though it had been dragged out. I said:

"I hope not." After a silence, I added:

"I don't think so."

Her face lightened, colour came back to her cheeks, although the tears still marked them. She did not ask me to repeat or explain: she took the words as though they were a contract. Her spirits bubbled up, she looked very young again, brilliant-eyed, delighted with the moment in which we both stood.

In a sharp, sarcastic, delighted voice, she said:

"No wonder they all say how articulate you are."

She watched me and said:

"You're not to think I'm rushing you. I don't want you bound to anything—except just that one thing. I think I could stand any tangle we get into, whatever we do—but if you had just needed someone to let you alone, just a waif for you to be kind to, then I should have had to duck from under before we start."

She was smiling and crying. "You see, I shouldn't have had a chance. I should have lost already, and I couldn't bear it."

She stroked my hand, and I could feel her shaking. She would have let me make love to her, but she had called on her nerves so hard that what she wanted most, for the rest of the night, was a breathing space.

Going out of the flat to dinner, we walked, saying little, as it were absently, along the embankment. It was foggy, and in the blackout, the writhing fog, our arms were round each other; her coat was rough under my hand, as she leant over the parapet, gazing into the high, dark water.

CHAPTER XVII

BUSINESS ON NEW YEAR'S DAY

ON the morning of New Year's Day, when I entered the Minister's office, he was writing letters. The office was not very grand; it was a cubby hole with a coal fire, the windows looking out over Whitehall. The Minister was not, at a first glance, very grand either. Elderly, slight, he made a profession of being unassuming. When he left the office he passed more unnoticed even than his civil servants, except in a few places: but the few places happened to be the only ones where he wanted notice, and included the Carlton Club and the rooms of the party manager.

His name was Thomas Bevill, and he was a cunning, tenacious, happy old man; but mixed with his cunning was a streak of simplicity that puzzled one more the closer one came. That morning of January 1, 1942, for instance, he was writing in his own round schoolboyish hand to everyone he knew whose name was in the Honours List.

No one was more hard-baked about honours than Bevill, and no one was more skilled in obtaining them for recipients convenient to himself. "Old Herbert had better have something, it'll keep him quiet." But when on New Year's Day the names came out, Bevill read them with innocent pleasure, and all the prizewinners, including those he had so candidly intrigued for, went up a step in his estimation. "Fifty-seven letters to write, Eliot," he said with euphoria, as though knowing that number in the Honours List reflected much credit both on them and him.

A little later his secretary came in with a message: "Mr. Paul Lufkin would be grateful if the Minister could spare time to see him, as soon as possible."

"What does this fellow want?" Bevill asked me.

"One thing is certain," I said. "He doesn't want to see you just to pass the time of day."

At that piece of facetiousness, Bevill gave a simple worldly chuckle.

"I expect he wants to know why his name isn't in the list this morning." His mind wandered back. "I expect he wants to be in next time."

To me, that did not sound in the least like Lufkin's style. He was after bigger prizes altogether; he was not so much indifferent to the minor rewards as certain they must come.

I had no doubt that he meant business; and I was anxious that we should find out what the business was, before the Minister received him. Make an excuse for today and prepare the ground, I said.

I did not want the Minister to get across Lufkin: even less did I want him to waffle. I had good reasons: Lufkin was rising to power, his opinion was one men listened to, and on the other hand Bevill's position was nothing like invulnerable. There were those who wanted him out of office. I had many reasons, both selfish and unselfish, for not giving them unnecessary openings.

However, the old man was obstinate. He had made such a technique of unpretentiousness that he liked being available to visitors at an hour's notice: he was free that morning, why shouldn't he see 'this fellow'? On the other hand, he was still suspicious about a personal approach on the Honours List and he did not want a tête à tête, so he asked me to be at hand, and, when Lufkin was shown in, remarked lightly:

"I think you know Eliot, don't you?"

"Considering that you stole him from me," Lufkin replied, with that off-hand edginess which upset many, but which bounced off the Minister.

"My dear chap," said Bevill, "we must try to make up for that. What can I do for you now?"

He settled Lufkin in the armchair by the fire, put on a grimy glove and threw on some coal, sat himself on a high chair and got ready to listen.

To begin with there was not much to listen to. To my surprise, Lufkin, who was usually as relevant as a high civil servant, seemed to have come with a complaint in itself trivial and which in any case was outside the Minister's domain. Some of his key men were being called-up: not technicians, whom the Minister could have interfered about, but managers and accountants. Take away a certain number, said Lufkin, and in a highly articulated industry you came to a critical point—efficiency dropped away in an exponential curve.

Bevill had no idea what an exponential curve was, but he nodded wisely.

"If you expect us to keep going, it doesn't make sense," said Lufkin.

"We don't just expect you to keep going, we rely on you," said Bevill.

"Well then."

"I don't mind telling you one thing," said Bevill. "That is, we mustn't kill the goose that lays the golden eggs."

He added:

"I can't promise anything, my dear chap, but I'll put in a word in the right quarter."

Uneasily I felt that they were under-rating each other. Bevill was an aristocrat; he had an impersonal regard for big business, but in his heart rarely liked the company of a business man. In Lufkin's presence, as in the presence of most others of the human race, Bevill could sound matey; he was not feeling so, he wanted to keep on amiable terms because that was the general principle of his life, but in fact he longed to bolt off to his club. While Lufkin, who had made his way by scholarships and joined his firm at seventeen, felt for politicians like Bevill something between envy and contempt, only softened by a successful man's respect for others' success.

Nevertheless, although he made Bevill uncomfortable, as he did most people, he was not uncomfortable himself. He had come for a purpose and he was moving in to it.

He said:

"There is one other point, Minister."

"My dear chap?"

"You don't bring us into your projects soon enough."

"You're preaching to the converted, you know. I've sown seeds in that direction ever since the war started— and I've still got hope that one or two of them may come home to roost."

The old man's quiff of hair was standing up, cockatoo-like; Lufkin gazed at him, and said:

"I'm glad to hear you say that, Minister." He went on, and suddenly he had brought all his weight and will into the words:

"I'm not supposed to know what you're doing at Barford. I don't know, and I don't want to know until it's time for me to do so. But I do know this—if you're going to get any results in time for this war, you ought to bring us in the instant you believe you can produce anything. Your people can't do big-scale chemical engineering. We can. We should have gone out of business if we couldn't."

"Well, *that's* a prospect that's never cost any of us an hour's sleep," said Bevill, gaining time to think, smiling with open blue eyes. In fact, the old man was worried, almost shocked. For Lufkin was speaking as though he knew more than he should. Barford was the name of the establishment where the first experiments on atomic fission had been started, nine months before; apart from the scientists on the spot, only a handful of people were supposed to have a glimmer of the secret, a few Ministers, civil servants, academic scientists, less than fifty in all. To Bevill, the most discreet of men, it was horrifying that even the rumour of a rumour should have reached Lufkin. Bevill never quite understood the kind of informal intelligence service that radiated from an industrialist of Lufkin's power; and he did not begin to understand that it was one of Lufkin's gifts, perhaps his most valuable one, to pick up hints that were floating through the technical air. For recognising others' feelings Lufkin had no antennae; but he had an extra set, more highly sensitised than those of anyone round him, for catching the first wave of a new idea.

That morning Bevill was determined to play for time, hiding behind his smoke-screen of platitudes like an amiable old man already a bit ga-ga. Even if the Barford project came off, even if they had to invoke the big firms, he was not sure whether he would include Lufkin. For the present he was not prepared to trust him, or anyone outside the secret, with so much as a speculation about Barford.

"My dear chap," he said, more innocent than a child, "I'm not feeling so inclined to count my chickens yet awhile, and believe me, if we don't mention any of these little games to our colleagues in industry, *or want anyone else to breathe a word about them*" (that was Bevill's way of telling a tycoon to keep his mouth shut), "it's because it is all Lombard Street to a china orange that they'll turn out to be nothing but hot air."

"I suggest that it's a mistake," said Lufkin, "to act on the basis that you're going to fail."

"No, but we think too much of you to waste your time——"

"Don't you think we're capable of judging that?"

"Your great company," said the Minister, "is doing so much for us already."

"That isn't a reason," replied Lufkin, deliberately losing his temper, "why you should leave us out of what may be the most important business you'll ever be responsible for."

The tempers of men of action, even the hard contrived temper of Lufkin, had no effect on Bevill, except to make him seem slightly more woolly. But he was now realising—it was my only reassurance that morning—that Lufkin was a formidable man, and that he would not be able to stonewall for ever. Expert in judging just how much protests were going to matter, Bevill knew that, if he consulted other firms before Lufkin's, there was certain to be trouble, and probably trouble of a kind that no politician of sense would walk into.

He knew that Lufkin was set in his purpose. It was not simply that, if the Barford project turned into hardware, there would be, not in a year, not during the war, but perhaps in twenty years, millions of pounds in it for firms like Lufkin's. It was not simply that—though Lufkin calculated it and wanted more than his share. It was also that, with complete confidence, he believed he was the man to carry it out. His self-interest did not make him hesitate, nothing would have seemed to him more palsied. On the contrary his self-interest and his sense of his own powers fused, and gave him a kind of opaque moral authority.

Throughout that interview with the Minister, despite the old man's wiliness, flattery and distrust, it was Lufkin who held the moral initiative.

CHAPTER XVIII

THE SWEETNESS OF LIFE

ON the ceiling, the wash of firelight brightened; a shadow quivered and bent among the benign and rosy light; there was the noise of a piece of coal falling, the ceiling flickered, faded, and then glowed. It might have been a holiday long forgotten or an illness in childhood, as I lay there in a content so absolute that it was itself a joy, not just a successor of joy, gazing up at the ceiling. In the crook of my arm Margaret's neck was resting; she too was gazing up.

Despite the blaze the air in the room was cold, for Margaret had to eke out her ration of coal, and the fire had not been lighted until we arrived. Under the bedclothes our skins touched each other. It was nine o'clock, and we had come to her room two hours before, as we had done often on those winter evenings. The room was on the ground floor of a street just off Lancaster Gate, and in the distance, through the cold wartime night, came the sough of traffic, washing and falling like the tide over a pebbly beach.

She was speaking, in spasms of talk that trailed luxuriously away, of her family, and how blissful and intimate they had been. Her hair on my shoulder, her hip against mine, that other bliss was close too; she had slipped into talking of it, once I had given her a cue. For I had mentioned, grumbling lazily in bed, that soon I should have some quite unnecessary exertion, since the Chelsea house I used to live in had been damaged in a raid the year before and its effective owner had begun pestering me with another list of suggestions.

"That's Sheila's father?" Margaret had said.

I said yes, for an instant disturbed because I had let the name creep in. Without any constraint, she asked:

"How did they get on?"

"Not well."

"No, I shouldn't have thought they would," she said.

Running through my mind were letters from the rectory, business-like, ingenious, self-pitying, assuming that my time was at Mr. Knight's disposal. Reflectively, Margaret was saying:

"It was different with me." She had always loved her father—and her sister also. She spoke of them, both delicately and naturally; she was not inhibited by the comparison with Sheila; she had brought it to the front herself.

Yet she too had rebelled, I knew by now—rebelled against her father's disbeliefs. It was not as easy as it sounded, when she told me their family life used to be intense and happy, and that anyone who had not known it so could not imagine what they had missed.

It was nine o'clock, and there was another hour before I need go out into the cold. By half-past ten I had to be back in my own flat in case the Minister, who was attending a cabinet committee after dinner, wanted me. I had another hour's grace in which I could hide in this voluptuous safety, untraceable, unknown. Though it was not only to be safe and secret that we came to her room rather than mine, but also because she took pleasure in it, because she seized the chance, for two or three hours among the subterranean airless working days, of looking after me.

I gazed at her face, her cheekbones sharp in the uneven light; she was relaxed because I was happy, just as I had seen her abandoned because she was giving me pleasure. Used as I was to search another's face for signs of sadness, I had often searched hers, unable to break from the habit, the obsession, sensitive beyond control that she might be miserable.

One night, not long before, this obsession had provoked a quarrel, our first. All that evening she had been subdued, although she smiled to reassure me; as we whispered in each other's arms, her replies came from a distance. At last she got up to dress, and I lay in bed watching her. Sitting naked in front of the looking-glass, with her back to me, her body fuller and less girlish than it appeared in clothes, she was brushing her hair. As she sat there, I could feel, with the twist of tenderness, how her carelessness about dress was a fraud. She made up little, but that was her special vanity; she had that curious kind of showing-off which wraps itself in the unadorned, even the shabby, but still gleams through. It was a kind of showing-off that to me contained within it some of the allure and mystery of sensual life.

In the looking-glass I saw the reflection of her face. Her smile had left her, the sweet and pleasure-giving smile was wiped away, and she was brooding, a line tightened between her eyebrows. I cried out:

"What's the matter?"

She muttered an endearment, tried to smooth her forehead, and said:

"Nothing."

"What have I done?"

I expected her moods to be more even than mine. I was not ready for the temper which broke through her.

She turned on me, the blood pouring up into her throat and cheeks, her eyes snapping.

"You've done nothing," she said.

"I asked you what was the matter."

"It's nothing to do with us. But it soon will be if you assume that you are to blame every time I'm worried. That's the way you can ruin it all, and I won't have it."

Shaken by her temper, I nevertheless pressed her to tell me what was on her mind. She would not be forced. Her

wiry will stood against mine. At last, however, seeing that
I was still anxious, with resentment she told me; it was
ludicrously hard for me to believe. The next day, she was
due to go to a committee as the representative of her branch,
and she was nervous. Not that she had ambition in her
job, but she felt humiliated if she could not perform credit-
ably. She detested 'not being equal to things'. She was,
as the civil servants said, 'good on paper', but when it
came to speaking in committee, which men like me had
forgotten could ever be a strain, she was so apprehensive
that she spent sleepless hours the night before.

It occurred to me, thinking her so utterly unlike Sheila
as to be a diametrical opposite, that I had for once caught
her behaving precisely as Sheila would have done.

After she had confided, she was still angry: angry that
I was so nervous about causing her unhappiness. It was
not a show of temper just for a bit of byplay; it had an edge
and foreboding that seemed to me, feeling ill-used, altogether out of proportion.

This night, as we lay together watching the luminescence
on the ceiling, the quarrel was buried. When I looked at
her face, the habit of anxiety became only a tic, for in her
eyes and on her mouth I saw my own serenity. She was
lazier than usual; as a rule when I had to make my way
back to my telephone at Dolphin Square, she accompanied
me so as to make the evening longer, though it might mean
walking miles in the cold and dark; that night, stretching
herself with self-indulgence, she stayed in bed. As I said
goodnight I pulled the blankets round her, and, looking
down at her with peace, saw the hollow of her collar-bone
shadowed in the firelight.

CHAPTER XIX

TWO SISTERS

IT was not until a Saturday afternoon in May that Margaret could arrange for me to meet her elder sister. At first we were going for a walk in the country, but a despatch-box came in, and I had to visit the Permanent Secretary's office after lunch. As I sat there answering Hector Rose's questions, I could see the tops of the trees in St. James's Park, where I knew the young women were waiting for me. It was one of the first warm days of the year and the windows were flung open, so that, after the winter silence in that office, one seemed to hear the sounds of spring.

Before Rose could write his minute to the Minister, he had to ring up another department. There was a delay, and as we sat listening for the telephone Rose recognised the beauty of the afternoon.

"I'm sorry to bring you back here, my dear chap," he said. "We ought to be out in the fresh air." Disciplined, powerful, polite, he did not really mind; but he was too efficient a man to stay there working for the sake of it, or to keep me. He worked fourteen hours a day in wartime, but there was nothing obsessive about it; he just did it because it was his job and the decisions must be made. The only thing obsessive about him was his superlative politeness. That afternoon, with Margaret and her sister outside in the Park, Rose many times expressed his sorrow and desolation at taking up my time.

He was forty-five that year, one of the youngest of heads of departments, and looked even younger. His eyes were heavy-lidded and bleached blue, his fair hair was smoothed back. He was one of the best-thought-of civil servants of his day. I had much respect for him, and he some for me, but our private relation was not comfortable, and while we were waiting for the telephone call we had nothing spontaneous to say to each other.

"I really am most exceedingly sorry," he was saying. The words sounded effusive and silly: in fact he was the least effusive and silly of men, and, of those I knew, he was with Lufkin the one with most aptitude for power. Since the war began he had been totally immersed in it, carrying responsibility without a blink. It was a lesson to me, I sometimes thought, about how wrong one can be. For, in the great political divide before the war, it was not only Lufkin's business associates who were on the opposite side to me. Bevill, the old aristocratic handyman of a politician, had been a Municheer: so had Rose and other up-and-coming civil servants. I had not known Rose then: if I had done, I should have distrusted him when it came to a crisis. I should have been dead wrong. Actually, when war came, Bevill and Rose were as whole-hearted as men could be. Compared with my friends on the irregular left, their nerves were stronger.

Rose continued to apologise until the call came through. Then, with remarkable speed, he asked me for one fact and wrote his comment to the Minister. He wrote it in the form of a question: but it was a question to which only a very brash minister could have given the wrong answer.

"Ah well," said Rose, "that seems to conclude your share in the proceedings, my dear Eliot. Many many many thanks. Now I hope you'll go and find some diversions for a nice Saturday afternoon."

His politeness often ended with a malicious flick: but this was just politeness for its own sake. He was not interested in my life. If he had known, he would not have minded: he was not strait-laced, but he had other things to speculate about.

Released into the Park, I was looking for Margaret— among the uniforms and summer frocks lying on the grass, I saw her, crowded out some yards away from our rendez-vous. She was stretched on her face in the sunshine, her head turned to her sister's, both of them engrossed. Watching the two faces together, I felt a kind of intimacy with Helen, although I had not spoken to her. Some of her expressions I already knew, having seen them in her sister's face. But there was one thing about her for which Margaret had not prepared me at all.

Sitting erect, her back straight, her legs crossed at the ankles, she looked smart: unseasonably, almost tastelessly smart in that war-time summer, as if she were a detached observer from some neutral country. The black dress, the large black hat, clashed against that background of litter, the scorched grass, the dusty trees.

She was twenty-nine that year, four years older than Margaret, and she seemed at the same time more poised and more delicate. In both faces one could see the same shapely bones, but whereas in Margaret's the flesh was firm with a young woman's health, in her sister's there were the first signs of tightness—the kind of tightness that I had seen a generation before among some of my aunts, who stayed cared for too long as daughters and settled down at Helen's age to an early spinsterhood. Yet Helen had married at twenty-one, and Margaret had told me that the marriage was a happy one.

They were so engrossed that Margaret did not notice me on the path. She was talking urgently, her face both alive and anxious. Helen's face looked heavy, she was replying in a mutter. Their profiles, where the resemblance was clearest, were determined and sharp. I called out, and Margaret started, saying, "This is Lewis."

At once Helen smiled at me; yet I saw that it was an effort for her to clear her mind of what had gone before. She spoke one or two words of formal greeting. Her voice was lighter than Margaret's, her speech more clipped; but she intimated by the energy with which she spoke a friendliness she was too shy, too distracted, to utter.

As I sat down—"Be careful," she said, "it's so grimy, you have to take care where you sit."

Margaret glanced at her, and laughed. She said to me: "We were clearing off some family business."

"Dull for other people," said Helen. Then, afraid I should think she was shutting me out, she said quickly, "Dull for us, too, this time."

She smiled, and made some contented-seeming remark about the summer weather. Only a trace of shadow remained in her face; she did not want me to see it, she wanted this meeting to be a successful one.

Yet each of the three of us was tongue-tied, or rather there were patches of silence, then we spoke easily, then silence again. Helen might have been worrying over her sister and me, but in fact it was Margaret who showed the more concern. Often she looked at Helen with the clucking, scolding vigilance that an elder sister might show to a beloved younger one, in particular to one without experience and unable to cope for herself.

As we sat together in the sunshine, the dawdling feet of soldiers and their girls scrabbling the path a few yards away, Helen kept being drawn back into her thoughts; then she would force herself to attend to Margaret and me, almost as though the sight of us together was a consolation. Indeed, far from worrying over her sister, she seemed happiest that afternoon when she found out something about us. Where had we met, she had never heard? When exactly had it been?

Shy as she was, she was direct with her questions, just as

I had noticed in other women from families like theirs. Some of the concealments which a man of my kind had learned, would have seemed to Helen, and to Margaret also, as something like a denial of integrity. Helen was diffident and not specially worldly: but, if Margaret had hidden from her that she and I were living together, she would have been not only hurt but shocked.

For minutes together, it pulled up her spirits, took her thoughts out of herself, to ask questions of Margaret and me: I believed that she was making pictures of our future. But she could not sustain it. The air was hot, the light brilliant; she sat there in a brooding reverie.

CHAPTER XX

A DARKENING WINDOW

HOPING that Helen might talk to her sister if they were alone, I left them together in the Park, and did not see Margaret again until the following Monday evening. She had already told me over the telephone that she would have to dine with Helen that night: and when we met in a Tothill Street pub Margaret said straight away:

"I'm sorry you had to see her like this."

"I like her very much," I said.

"I hoped you would." She had been looking forward for weeks to my meeting with Helen: she wanted me to admire her sister as she did herself. She told me again, anxious for me to believe her, that Helen was no more melancholy than she was, and far less self-centred.

"No one with any eyes would think she was self-centred."

"It's such an awful pity!" she cried.

I asked her what it was.

"She thought she was going to have a child at last. Then on Saturday she knew she wasn't."

"It's as important as that, is it?" I said. But she had told me already how her sister longed for children.

"You saw for yourself, didn't you?"

"How much," I asked, "is it damaging her marriage?"

"It's not. It's a good marriage," she said. "But still, I can't help remembering her when she was quite young, even when she was away at school, she used to talk to me about how she'd bring up her family."

She was just on the point of going away to meet Helen when Betty Vane came in.

As I introduced them, Betty was saying that she had telephoned the office, got Gilbert Cooke and been told this was one of my favourite pubs—meanwhile she was scrutinising Margaret, her ears sharp for the tone in which we spoke. Actually Margaret said little: she kept glancing at the clock above the bar: very soon she apologised and left. It looked rude, or else that she was deliberately leaving us together: it meant only that, if she had had to seem off-hand to anyone, she would make sure it was not to her sister.

"Well," said Betty.

For an instant I was put out by the gust of misunderstanding. I made an explanation, but she was not accepting it. She said, her eyes friendly and appraising:

"You're looking much better, though."

I had not seen her for some time, though now I was glad to. When Sheila died, it had been Betty who had taken charge of me. She had found me my flat, moved me out of the Chelsea house; and then, all the practical help given and disposed of, she got out of my way; she assumed I did not want to see her or anyone who reminded me of my marriage. Since then I had met her once or twice, received a couple of letters, and that was all.

Unlike most of our circle, she was not working in London, but in a factory office in a Midland town. The reason for this was singular: she, by a long way the most loftily born of my friends, was the worst educated; in the schoolroom at home she had scarcely been taught formally at all; clever as she was, she did not possess the humblest of educational qualifications, and would have been hard-pushed to acquire any.

Here she was in the middle thirties, opposite me across the little table in the pub, her nose a bit more peaked, her beautiful eyes acute. She had always liked her drink and now she was putting down bitter pint for pint with me: she did not mention Sheila's name or any trouble she had seen me through, but she enjoyed talking of the days past; she had a streak of sentiment, not about any special joy, but just about our youth.

There was a haze of home-sickness over us, shimmering with pleasure, and it stayed as we went out to eat. Out to eat better than I had eaten all that year, for Betty, even though she was not living in London, kept an eye on up-and-coming restaurants; she took as much care about it, I thought, as a lonely, active and self-indulgent man. Thus, at a corner table in Percy Street, we questioned each other with the content, regard, melancholy and comfort of old friends—edged by the feeling, shimmering in the home-sick haze, that with different luck we might have been closer.

I enquired about the people she was meeting and what friends she had made, in reality enquiring whether she had found a lover or a future husband. It sounded absurd of me to be euphemistic and semi-arch, as circuitous as Mr. Knight, to this woman whom I knew so well and whose own tongue was often coarse. But Betty was coarse about the body—and about her emotions as inhibited as a schoolgirl. She just could not utter, I knew from long ago, anything that she felt about a man. Even now, she sounded like a girl determined not to let herself be teased. Yes, she had seen a lot of people at the factory: "Some of them are interesting," she said.

"Who are they?"

"Oh, managers and characters like that."

"Anyone specially interesting?" I was sure she wanted to talk.

"As a matter of fact," she blurted out, "there's someone I rather like."

I asked about him—a widower, a good deal older than she was, moderately successful.

"Of course," I said, "you've never met people of that kind before."

"He's a nice man."

"It sounds all right," I said affectionately.

"It might be all right," she said with a touch of the hope she never quite lost, with absolute lack of confidence.

"My dear, I beg you," I broke out, "don't think so little of yourself."

She smiled with embarrassment. "I don't know about that——"

"Why in God's name shouldn't it be all right?"

"Oh well," she said, "I'm not everyone's cup of tea."

She spoke out firmly. She was relieved to have confessed a little, even in such a strangulated form. She shut up, as though abashed at her own outpouringness. Sharply, she began to talk about me. In a moment she was saying:

"What about that girl who rushed out of the pub?"

"I met her last autumn," I replied.

"Is it serious?"

"Yes, it is."

Betty nodded.

She said, in a companionable, almost disapproving tone:

"You have had such a rotten time. This isn't another of them, is it?"

"Far from it."

She stared at me.

"It would be nice," she said, her voice going suddenly soft, "if you could be happy."

She added: "There's no one who deserves it more."

In the restaurant corner, the air was warm with a sentimental glow. Betty was a realistic woman: about herself, realistic to an extent that crippled her: to most people she did not give the benefit of the doubt. But about me her realism had often been blurred, and she thought me a better man than I was.

How much better than I was—I could not avoid a glint of recognition an hour after. I had gone glowing from the restaurant to Margaret's room, where she was talking to Helen. When I arrived they were happy. Helen's spirits had revived; like Margaret, she did not give up easily. I gathered she had been to a doctor; and then she refused to talk further that evening of her own worry. When I came in, it was clear that they had been talking instead—with pleasure and amusement—about Margaret and me.

In the midsummer evening, the folding door between Margaret's bedroom and sitting-room was thrown open; their chairs were opposite each other round the empty grate in the sitting-room, which in the winter we had never used. Outside in the street, still light although it was getting on for ten, children were playing, and just across the area, close to the window and on a level with our chairs, passed the heads and shoulders of people walking along the pavement. It might have been the 'front room' of my childhood.

In it, Helen, dressed with the same exaggerated smartness as in the Park, looked more than ever out of place. I thought for an instant how different they were. Despite her marriage, despite her chic, something of my first impression of her lingered, the touch of the clever, delicate, and spinsterish. And yet they had each the same independence, the same certainty that they were their own judges, bred in through the family from which Margaret, more than her sister, had rebelled, bred in each one just as much as the mole over the hip which she had told me was a family mark. About Helen there was nothing of Margaret's carelessness; and yet in other ways so unlike her sister, Margaret, who rejoiced in giving me pleasure, who had the deep and guiltless sensuality of those women to whom giving pleasure is a major one, answered just as deliberately for herself.

"You oughtn't to live like this, you know," Helen said, glancing about the room, "it is really rather messy. Miles says you'd do far better——"

"Oh, Miles," Margaret said. "He would." They were speaking of Helen's husband, whom they both appeared to regard with a kind of loving depreciation, as though they were in some way leagued in a pact to save him from himself. Yet from what I had heard he was a successful man, amiable, self-sufficient, regarding responsibility as a kind of privilege. "It's lucky he chose the right one of us."

"Very lucky," said Helen, "you would have made him quite miserable." When she spoke of him her face grew tender, content. It was a maternal contentment: like a warm-hearted and dutiful child, he gave her almost all she desired.

Margaret smiled back at her, and for a second I thought I saw in her face a longing for just such a contentment, just such a home; ordered, settled, the waiting fire, the curtains drawn against the night.

"It wouldn't have been my sort of thing," she said.

It was at this moment that I felt my talk with Betty, which had left me in such a glow, had suddenly touched a trigger and released a surge of sadness and self-destruction.

It seemed like another night, drinking with Betty, going home to Sheila—not a special night, more like many nights fused together, with nothing waiting for me but Sheila's presence.

That night lay upon this. I was listening to Margaret and Helen, my limbs were heavy, for an instant I felt in one of those dreams where one is a spectator but cannot move.

When Margaret had talked, earlier that evening, of the children her sister wanted, she was repeating what she had told me before; and, just as before, she was holding something back.

I had thought, when I saw them together in that room half an hour before, that, unlike in so much, they were alike in taking their own way. But they were alike at one other point. It was not only Helen who longed for children;

132

Margaret was the same. Once we had spoken of it, and from then on, just as tonight, she held back. She did not wish me to see how much she looked forward to her children. If she did let me see it, it would lay more responsibility upon me.

Listening to them, I felt at a loss with Helen because she was confident I should make her sister happy.

When she got up to go, I said how much I had enjoyed the evening. But Margaret had been watching me: after seeing her sister to the door, she returned to the empty sitting-room and looked at me with concern.

"What is the matter?" she said.

I was standing up. I took her in my arms and kissed her. Over her head, past the folding doors, I could see the bed and the windows beyond, lit up by the afterglow in the west. With an effort, disproportionately great, I tried to throw off the heaviness, and said:

"Isn't it time we talked too?"

"What about?"

"We ought to talk about us."

She stood back, out of my arms, and looked at me. Her eyes were bright but she hesitated. She said:

"You don't want to yet."

I went on:

"We can't leave it too long."

For an instant her voice went high.

"Are you sure you're ready?"

"We ought to talk about getting married."

It was some instants before she spoke, though her eyes did not leave me. Then her expression, which had been grave, sharp with insight, suddenly changed: her face took on a look of daring, which in another woman might have meant the beginning of a risky love affair.

"No," she said. "I want you. But I want you in your freedom."

That phrase, which we had just picked up, she used to make all seem more casual to us both. But she was telling me how much she knew. She knew that, going about in high spirits, I still was not safe from remorse, or perhaps something which did not deserve that name and which was more like fear, about Sheila. That misery had made me morbidly afraid of another; Margaret had more than once turned her face away to conceal the tears squeezing beneath her eyelids, because she knew that at the sight of unhappiness I nowadays lost confidence altogether.

She accepted that, just as she accepted something else, though it was harder. It was that sometimes I did not have fear return to me with the thought of Sheila, but joy. Cheated by memory, I was transported to those times—which had in historical fact been negligible in the length of our marriage—when Sheila, less earthbound than I was, had lifted me off the earth. Cheated by memory, I had sometimes had that mirage-joy, that false-past, shine above a happy time with Margaret, so that the happiness turned heavy.

She knew all that; but what she did not know was whether I was getting free. Was I capable of a new start, of entering the life she wanted? Or was I a man who, in the recesses of his heart, manufactured his own defeat? Searching for that answer, she looked at me with love, with tenderness, and without mercy for either of us.

"Don't worry," she said, putting her arms round me, "there's plenty of time."

She muttered, her head against my chest:

"I'm not very patient, you know that now, don't you? But I will be."

Below my eyes her hair was smooth; the window had darkened quickly in the past minutes; I was grateful to her.

CHAPTER XXI

THE ACQUIESCENT VERSUS THE OPAQUE

THROUGH the spring and summer, the Minister had been able to go on stalling with Paul Lufkin. The Barford project had run into a blind alley, it looked likely that there would be no development in England, and nothing for the industrialists to do. All of which was true and reasonable, and Lufkin could only accept it; but he was alert when, in the autumn, a new rumour went round. It was that a fresh idea had sprung up at Barford, which some people, including Bevill himself, wanted to invest in.

As usual, Lufkin's information was something near accurate. None of us was certain whether Barford would be saved or the scientists sent to America, but in October the struggle was going on; and while we were immersed in it, Lufkin did not visit the Minister again but out of the blue invited me to dinner.

When I received that note, which arrived a week before the decision over Barford was to be made, I thought it would be common prudence to have a word with Hector Rose. So, on an October morning, I sat in the chair by his desk. Outside the window, against a windy sky, the autumn leaves were turning. Even by his own standards Hector Rose looked spruce and young that day—perhaps because the war news was good, just as in the summer there had been days when, tough as he was, he had sat there with his lips pale and his nostrils pinched. The flower bowl was always full, whatever the news was like; that morning he had treated himself to a mass of chrysanthemums.

"Well, my dear Eliot," he was saying, "it's very agreeable to have you here. I don't think I've got anything special, but perhaps you have? I'm very glad indeed to have the chance of a word." I mentioned Lufkin's invitation. In a second the flah-flah dropped away—and he was listening with his machine-like concentration. I did not need to remind him that I had, not so long ago, been a consultant for Lufkin, nor that Gilbert Cooke had been a full-time employee. Those facts were part of the situation; he was considering them almost before I had started, just as he was considering Lufkin's approaches to the Minister.

"If our masters decide to persevere with Barford"— Rose spoke as though some people, utterly unconnected with him, were choosing between blue or brown suits: while he was totally committed on Barford's side, and if the project survived he would be more responsible, after the scientists, than any single man—"if they decide to persevere with it, we shall have to plan the first contact straightaway, that goes without saying.

"We shall have to decide," added Rose coldly, "whether it is sensible to bring Lufkin in."

He asked:

"What's your view, Eliot? Would it be sensible?"

"So far as I can judge, it's rather awkward," I said. "His isn't obviously the right firm—but it's not out of the question."

"Exactly," said Rose. "This isn't going to be an easy one."

"I think most people would agree that his firm hasn't got the technical resources of the other two——" I named them.

"What has Lufkin got?"

"I'm afraid the answer to that is, Lufkin himself. He's much the strongest figure in the whole game."

"He's a *good chap*," said Hector Rose incongruously. He was not speaking of Lufkin's moral nature, nor his merits as a companion: Rose meant that Lufkin was a panto-crator not dissimilar from himself.

He stared at me.

"My dear Eliot," he said, "I'm sure it's unnecessary for me to advise you, but if you do decide that he is the right man for us, then of course you're not to feel the least embarrassment or be too nice about it. The coincidence that you know something about him—the only significance of that is, that it makes your judgement more valuable to us. It's very important for us not to fall over backwards and, for quite inadequate reasons, shirk giving the job to the right man, that is, if we finally decide that he does turn out to be the right man."

I was a little surprised. No one could have doubted that Hector Rose's integrity was absolute. It would have been high farce to try to bribe him; he assumed the same of me. Nevertheless, I expected him to be more finicky about the procedure, to talk about the necessity of justice not only being done, but being seen to be done. In fact, as the war went on and the state became more interleaved with business, civil servants like Rose had made themselves tougher-minded; nothing would get done if they thought first how to look immaculate.

In the same manner, when I asked whether I might as well let Lufkin entertain me, Rose replied: "The rule is very simple, my dear Eliot, and it remains for each of us to apply it to himself. That is, when some interested party suddenly becomes passionately desirous of one's company. The rule is, do exactly as you would if the possibility of interest did not exist. If you wouldn't normally accept an invitation from our excellent friend, don't go. If you would normally accept, then do go, if you can bear it. I can't say that I envy you the temptation," said Rose, whose concept of an evening out was a table for two and a bottle of claret at the Athenaeum.

When I came to spend the evening at Lufkin's, I would have compounded for a table for two myself. As in the past when I was one of his entourage, I found his disregard of time, which in anyone else he would have bleakly dismissed as 'oriental', fretting me. In his flat at St. James' Court, his guests were collected at eight o'clock, which was the time of the invitation, standing about in the sitting-room drinking, nine of us, all men. Lufkin himself was there, standing up, not saying much, not drinking much, standing up as though prepared to do so for hours, glad to be surrounded by men catching his eye. Then one of his staff entered with a piece of business to discuss: and Lufkin discussed it there on the spot, in front of his guests. That finished, he asked the man to stay, and beckoned the butler, standing by the dinner table in the inner room, to lay another place. Next, with the absence of fuss and hurry of one in the middle of a marathon, which he showed in all his dealings, he decided to telephone: still standing up, he talked for fifteen minutes to one of his plants.

Meanwhile the guests, most of whom were colleagues and subordinates, stood up, went on drinking and exchanged greetings to each others' wives. "Give my regards to Lucille." "How is Brenda?" "Don't forget to give my love to Jacqueline." It went on, just as it used when I attended those dinners, and men heartily enquired after Sheila and sent messages to her: not that they knew her, for, since she never went to a party, they could only have met her for a few minutes, and by accident. But, according to their etiquette, they docketed her name away and afterwards punctiliously enquired about her, as regularly as they said good evening. No doubt most of those husband-to-husband questions that night, so hearty, so insistent, were being asked about women the speakers scarcely knew.

THE ACQUIESCENT VERSUS THE OPAQUE

It was nearly half-past nine when Lufkin said: "Does anyone feel like eating? I think we might as well go in."

At the crowded table Lufkin sat, not at the head, but in the middle of one side, not troubling to talk, apparently scornful of the noise, and yet feeling that, as was only right, the party was a success. There was more food and drink than at most wartime dinners: I thought among the noise, the hard male laughter, how little any of these men were giving themselves away. Orthodox opinions, collective gibes, a bit of ribbing—that was enough to keep them zestful, and I had hardly heard a personal remark all night. It made me restless, it made me anxious to slither away, not only to avoid conversation with Lufkin, but also just to be free.

The walls pressed in, the chorus roared round me: and, in that claustrophobia, I thought longingly of being alone with Margaret in her room. In a kind of rapturous day-dream, I was looking forward to marrying her. In the midst of this male hullabaloo my confidence came back. I was telling myself, almost as one confides, brazenly, confidently and untruthfully to an acquaintance on board ship, that it was natural I should trust myself so little about another marriage after the horror of the first.

Listening to someone else's history, I should not have been so trustful about the chances of life. Thinking of my own, I was as credulous as any man. Sitting at that table, responding mechanically and politely to a stranger's mono-logue, I felt that my diffidence about Margaret was gone.

When one of Lufkin's guests said the first goodnight, I tried to go out with him. But Lufkin said: "I've hardly had a minute with you, Eliot. You needn't go just yet."

That company was good at recognising the royal com-mand. Within a quarter of an hour, among thanks and more salutations to wives, the flat was empty, and we were left alone. Lufkin, who had not stirred from his chair as he received the goodbyes, said:

"Help yourself to another drink and come and sit by me."

I had drunk enough, I said. As for him, he always drank carefully, though his head was hard for so spare and unpadded a man. I sat in the chair on his right, and he turned towards me with a creaking smile. We had never been intimate, but there was a sort of liking between us. As usual, he had no small talk whatsoever; I made one or two remarks, about the war, about the firm, to which he said yes and no. He started off:

"Quite frankly, I still don't like the way Barford is being handled."

He said it quietly and dryly, with a note of moral blame that was second nature to him.

"I'm sorry about that," I said.

"It's no use being sorry," he replied. "The thing is, we've got to get it right."

"I'm at a bit of a disadvantage," I said, "not being able to say much about it."

"You can say quite enough for the purpose."

I asked straight out:

"How much do you know?"

"I hear," Lufkin replied, in his bluntest and most off-hand tone, "that you people are wasting your own time and everyone else's debating whether to shut the place up or not."

"I hope they'll come down in favour," I said, feeling my way. "But I'm by no means sure."

"In that case you're losing your grip," Lufkin gave a cold, jeering smile. "*Of course* they'll keep it going."

"Why do you say that?"

For a second I did not put it past him to have inside knowledge, but he answered:

"No one ever closes a place down. Governments can't do it; that's one of the things that's wrong with them." He went on:

"No, you'd better assume that they'll keep it ticking over. But not putting enough behind it, blowing hot and cold the whole wretched time. That's what I call making the worst of both worlds."

"You may be right," I said.

"I've been right before now," he said. "So it won't be much satisfaction."

In his negotiations Lufkin made much use of the charged silence, and we fell into one now. But it was not my tactic that night to break it; I was ready to sit mute as long as he cared. In time he said: "We can assume they're going to hopelessly underestimate their commitment, and unless someone steps in they'll make a mess of it. The thing is, we've got to save them from themselves."

Suddenly his eyes, so sad and remote in his hard, neat, skull-like head, were staring into mine, and I felt his will, intense because it was canalised into this one object, because his nature was undivided, all of a piece.

"I want you to help," he said.

Again I did not reply.

He went on: "I take it the decisions about how this job is done, and who makes the hardware, are going to be bandied about at several levels."

Lufkin, with his usual precision and realism, had made it his business to understand how government worked; it was no use, he had learned years before, to have the entrée to cabinet ministers unless you were also trusted by the Hector Roses and their juniors.

"I'm not prepared to let it go by default. It's not my own interests I'm thinking of. It's a fourth class risk anyway, and, so far as the firm goes, there's always money for a good business. As far as I go myself, no one's ever going to make a fortune again, so it's pointless one way or the other. But I've got to be in on it, because this is the place where I can make a contribution. That's why I want your help."

It sounded hypocritical: but Lufkin behaved just as he had to Bevill the previous New Year's Day, not altering by an inch as he talked to a different man, just as stable and certain of his own motives. It sounded hypocritical, but Lufkin believed each word of it, and that was one of his strengths.

For myself, I could feel a part of me, a spontaneous part left over from youth, which sympathised with him and wanted to say yes. Even now the temptation was there—one that Lufkin had never felt. But, since I was a young man, I had had to learn how, in situations such as this, to harden myself. Just because I had to watch my response, which was actually too anxious to please, which wanted to say yes instead of no, I had become practised at not giving a point away: in a fashion different from Lufkin's, and for the opposite reasons, I was nearly as effective at it as he was himself.

That night, I still had not decided whether I ought to throw in my influence, such as it was, for him or against him.

"I can't do much just yet," I said. "And if I tried it would certainly not be wise."

"I'm not sure I understand you."

"I've been associated with you," I told him, "and some people will remember that at the most inconvenient time. You can guess the repercussions if I overplayed my hand——"

"What would you say, if I told you that was cowardly?"

"I don't think it is," I said.

For his own purposes, he was a good judge of men, and a better one of situations. He accepted that he would not get further just then and, with no more ill grace than usual, began to talk at large.

"What shall I do when I retire?" he said. He was not inviting my opinion; his plans were as precise as those he sent to his sales managers, although he was only forty-eight; they were the plans such as active men make, when occasionally they feel that all their activity has done for them is carve out a prison. In reality Lufkin was happy in his activity, he never really expected that those plans would come about—and yet, through making them, he felt that the door was open.

As I heard what they were, I thought again that he was odder than men imagined; he did not once refer to his family or wife; although I had never heard scandal, although he went down to his country house each weekend, his plans had been drawn up as though she were dead.

"I shall take a flat in Monaco," he announced briskly. "I don't mean just anywhere in the principality, I mean the old town. It isn't easy to get a place there for a foreigner, but I've put out some feelers."

It was curious to hear, in the middle of the war.

"What ever shall you do?" I said, falling into the spirit of it.

"I shall walk down to the sea and up to the Casino each day, there and back," he said. "That will give me three miles walking every day, which will do for my exercise. No man of fifty or over needs more."

"That won't occupy you."

"I shall play for five hours a day, or until I've won my daily stipple, whichever time is the shorter."

"Shan't you get tired of that?"

"Never," said Lufkin.

He went on, bleak and inarticulate:

"It's a nice place. I shan't want to move, I might as well die there. Then they can put me in the Protestant cemetery. It would be a nice place to have a grave." Suddenly he gave a smile that was sheepish and romantic. In a curt tone, as though angry with me, he returned to business.

"I'm sorry," he put in as though it were an aside, "that

you're getting too cautious about the Barford project. Cold feet. I didn't expect yours to be so cold."

I had set myself neither to be drawn nor provoked. Instead I told him what he knew already, that at most points of decision Hector Rose was likely to be the most influential man—and after him some of the Barford technicians. If any firm, if Lufkin's firm, were brought in, its technicians would have to be approved by the Barford ones. Lufkin nodded: the point was obvious but worth attending to. Then he said, in a cold but thoughtful tone:

"What about your own future?"

I replied that I simply did not know.

"I hear that you've been a success at this job—but you're not thinking of staying in it, there'd be no sense in that."

I repeated that it was too early to make up my mind.

"Of course," said Lufkin, "I've got some right to expect you to come back to me."

"I haven't forgotten that," I said.

"I don't understand all you want for yourself," said Lufkin. "But I can give you some of it."

Looking at him, I did not know whether it was his harsh kindness, or a piece of miscalculation.

CHAPTER XXII

MENTION OF A MAN'S NAME

WAKING, I blinked my eyes against the light, although it was the dun light of a winter afternoon. By the bedside Margaret, smiling, looked down on me like a mother.

"Go to sleep again," she said.

It was Saturday afternoon, the end of a busy week; the day before, Barford's future had been settled, and, as Lufkin had forecast, we had got our way. Soon, I was thinking, lying there half-asleep in Margaret's bed, we should have to meet Lufkin officially——

"Go to sleep again," she said.

I said that I ought to get up.

"No need." She had drawn an armchair up to the bed, and was sitting there in her dressing-gown. She stroked my forehead, as she said:

"It's not a sensible way to live, is it?"

She was not reproaching me, although I was worn out that afternoon, after the week's meetings and late nights, dinner with Lufkin, dinner with the Minister. She pretended to scold me, but her smile was self-indulgent, maternal. It was pleasure to her to look after anyone; she was almost ashamed, so strong was that pleasure, she tried to disparage it and called it a lust. So, when I was tired and down-and-out, any struggle of wills was put aside, she cherished me; often to me, who had evaded my own mother's protective love, who had never been cared for in that sense in my life, it was startling to find her doing so.

Yet that afternoon, watching her with eyes whose lids still wanted to close, letting her pull the quilt round my shoulders, I was happy, so happy that I thought of her as I had at Lufkin's, in her absence. For an interval, rare in me, the imagination and the present flesh were one. It must go on always, I thought, perhaps this was the time to persuade her to marry me.

She was gazing down at me, and she looked loving, sarcastic, in charge.

No, I thought, I would not break this paradisal state; let us have it for a little longer; it did not matter if I procrastinated until later that night, or next week, so long as I was certain we should be happy.

Thus I did not ask her. Instead, in the thickness of near-sleep, in the luxury of fatigue, I began gossiping about people we knew. Her fingers touching my cheeks, she joined in one of those conspiracies of kindness that we entered into when we were at peace, as though out of gratitude for our own condition we had to scheme to bring the same to others. Was there anything we could do for Helen? And couldn't we find someone for Gilbert Cooke? We were retracing old arguments, about what kind of woman could cope with him, when, suddenly recalling another aspect of my last talk with Lufkin, I broke out that Gilbert might soon have a different kind of problem on his hands.

I explained that, like me, he would be engaged in the negotiations over which firm to give the contract to—which, now that the decision had gone in favour of the project, was not just a remote debating point but something we should have to deal with inside a month. Just as Lufkin was too competent not to know my part in the negotiations, so he would know Gilbert's; it might be small, but it would not be negligible. And Gilbert, after the war, would certainly wish to return to Lufkin's firm: would he be welcome, if he acted against Lufkin now?

I told Margaret of how, right at the end of our tête-à-tête, when we were both tired and half-drunk, Lufkin had let fly his question about my future, and I still could not be sure whether it was a threat. Gilbert might easily feel inclined to be cautious.

Margaret smiled, but a little absently, a little uncomfortably, and for once brushed the subject aside, beginning to talk of a man she had just met, whose name I had not heard. He was a children's doctor, she said, and I did not need telling how much she would have preferred me to live such a life. The official world, the corridors of power, the dilemmas of conscience and egotism—she disliked them all. Quite indifferent to whether I thought her priggish, she was convinced that I should be a better and happier man without them. So, with a touch of insistence, she mentioned this new acquaintance's work in his hospital. His name was Geoffrey Hollis; perhaps it was odd, she admitted, that so young a man should devote himself to children. He was as much unlike Gilbert as a man could be, except that he also was a bachelor and shy.

"He's another candidate for a good woman," she said.

"What is he like?"

"Not much your sort," she replied, smiling at me.

Years before, each time Sheila had thrown the name of a man between us, I had been pierced with jealousy. She had meant me to be, for, in the years before we married and I loved her without return, she was ruthless, innocent and cruel. What had passed between us then had frightened me of being jealous, and with Margaret, though sometimes I had watched for it, I had been almost immune.

Nevertheless, the grooves of habit were worn deep. Hearing of Hollis, even though her face was holding nothing back, I wished that I had asked her to marry me half an hour before, when there was not this vestigial cramp keeping me still, when I had not this temptation, growing out of former misery and out of a weakness that I was born with, to retreat into passiveness and irony.

I was gazing at her, sitting by the bedside in the cold and browning light. Slowly, as her eyes studied mine, her mouth narrowed and from it edged away the smile of a loving girl, the smile of a mother. Upon us seeped—an instant suddenly enlarged in the rest and happiness of the afternoon—the sense of misunderstanding, injustice, illimitable distance, loss.

In time she said, still grave:

"It's all right."

"Yes," I answered.

She began to smile again and asked, putting Gilbert's dilemma aside, what I was going to do about Lufkin and how much I minded. She had never pressed me before about what I should choose to do when the war ended. I could break with the past now, there were different ways of earning a living ahead of me, she had been content to leave it so; but now in the half-light, her hands pressing mine, she wanted me to talk about it.

CHAPTER XXIII

GIGANTESQUE

THE Minister tended to get irritated with me when there was an issue which he had to settle but wished to go on pretending did not exist. His manner remained matey and unpretentious but, when I had to remind him that the Barford contract must be placed within a fortnight, that two major firms as well as Lufkin's were pressing for an answer, Bevill looked at me as though I had made a remark in bad taste.

"First things first," he said mysteriously, as though drawing on fifty years of political wisdom, the more mysteriously since in the coming fortnight he had nothing else to do.

In fact, he strenuously resented having to disappoint two or three influential men. Even those like me who were fond of the old man did not claim that political courage was his most marked virtue. To most people's astonishment, he had shown some of it in the struggle over Barford; he had actually challenged opinion in the Cabinet and had both prevailed and kept his job; now that was over, he felt it unjust to be pushed into more controversy, to be forced to make more enemies. Enemies—old Bevill hated even the word. He wished he could give the contract to everyone who wanted it.

Meanwhile, Sir Hector Rose was making up his own mind. The secret Barford file came down to me, with a request from Rose for my views on the contract.

It did not take me much time to think over. I talked to Gilbert, who knew the inside of Lufkin's firm more recently than I did. He was more emphatic than I was, but on the same side. It was an occasion, I decided without worry, to play safe both for my own sake and the job's.

So at last I did not hedge, but wrote that we ought not to take risks; this job did not need the special executive flair that Lufkin would give it, but hundreds of competent chemical engineers, where the big chemical firms could outclass him; at this stage he should be ruled out.

I suspected that Rose had already come to the same opinion. All he committed himself to, however, were profuse thanks on the telephone and an invitation to come myself, and bring Cooke, to what he called 'a parley with Lufkin and his merry men'.

The 'parley' took place on a bitter December morning in one of the large rooms at the back of our office, with windows looking out over the Horse Guards towards the Admiralty: but at this date most of the glass had been blown in, the windows were covered with plasterboard, so that little light entered but only the freezing air. The chandeliers shone on to the dusty chairs: through the one sound window the sky was glacial blue: the room was so cold that Gilbert Cooke, not over-awed enough to ignore his comfort, went back for his greatcoat.

Lufkin had brought a retinue of six, most of them his chief technicians; Rose had only five, of whom a Deputy Secretary, myself and Cooke came from the Department and two scientists from Barford. The Minister sat between the two parties, his legs twisted round each other, his toes not touching the ground; turning to his right where Lufkin was sitting, he began a speech of complicated cordiality. "It's always a pleasure, indeed it's sometimes the only pleasure of what they choose to call office," he said, "to be able to sit down round a table with our colleagues in industry. You're the chaps who deliver the goods and we know a willing horse when we see one and we all know what to do with willing horses." The Minister continued happily, if a trifle obscurely; he had never been a speaker, his skill was the skill of private talks, but he enjoyed his own speech and did not care whether he sounded as though his head were immersed in cotton-wool. He made a tangential reference to a 'certain project about which the less said the better', but he admitted that there was an engineering job to be done. He thought, and he hoped Mr. Lufkin would agree, that nothing but good could accrue if they all got together round the table and threw their ideas into the pool.

Then he said blandly, with his innocent old man's smile, "But now I've got to say something which upsets me, though I don't expect it will worry anyone else."

"Minister?" said Lufkin.

"*I'm afraid I must slip away,*" said Bevill. "We all have our masters, you know." He spoke at large to Lufkin's staff. "You have my friend Lufkin, and I'm sure he is an inspiring one. I have mine and he wants me just on the one morning when I was looking forward to a really friendly useful talk." He was on his feet, shaking hands with Lufkin, saying that they would never miss him with his friend and colleague, Hector Rose to look after them, speaking with simple, sincere regret at having to go, but determined not to stay in that room five minutes longer. Spry and active, he shook hands all the way round and departed down the cold corridor, his voice echoing briskly back, "Goodbye all, goodbye all!"

Rose moved into the chair. "I think the ceremonies can be regarded as having been properly performed," he said. "Perhaps it would set us going if I try to clear the air." For once he was not at his most elaborately polite. I felt certain it was only just before the meeting that he had heard of the Minister's intention to flit. But his statement was as lucid and fair as usual, and no one there could have guessed whether he was coming down for or against Lufkin. There was just one single job to be performed, he said; not much could be said, but, to make possible some kind of rational exchange, he took it on his own responsibility to tell Lufkin's technicians a bare minimum. There was no money in it; the Government would pay as for a development contract. Further, the best expert opinion did not think this method economically viable in peacetime.

"So that, whoever we ask to take this job on, we are not exactly conferring a benefit on them."

"It is a matter of duty," said Lufkin, sounding hypocritical and yet believing every word. "That's why I'm prepared to undertake it."

"You could do it, with your existing resources?"

Lufkin replied: "I could do it."

When he spoke like that, off handedly but with confidence and weight, men could not help but feel his power, not just the power of position, but of his nature.

For some time the parties exchanged questions, most of them technical: how long to build a plant in Canada, how pure must the heavy water be, what was the maximum output. Listening, I thought there was an odd difference between the civil servants and the businessmen. Lufkin's staff treated him with extreme, almost feudal deference, did not put questions on their own account, but made their comments to him. Whereas the civil servants, flat opposite to the others' stereotype of them, spoke with the democratic air of everyone having his say, and as though each man's opinion was as worth having as Sir Hector Rose's.

This was even true of John Jones. Jones was over fifty, had just become a Deputy Secretary, and would not go further. The wonder to me was that he had gone so far. He had a pleasant rosy-skinned face, an air of one about to throw away all constraint and pretence and speak from the bottom of his heart. But when he did speak, it was usually in praise of some superior.

Yet even he kept at least a tone of independence and like many in the Department called Rose, the least hearty of men, by his Christian name, which would have been not so much improper as unthinkable from Lufkin's subordinates towards the boss.

Sitting by me, sprawled back in his chair but with his chins thrust into his chest, Gilbert Cooke had been making a noise as though half sniffing, half grunting to himself. As the discussion went on, he sniffed more impatiently, ceased to sprawl back as though in the bar at White's, and hunched himself over the committee table, a great stretch of back filling out the vicuna coat.

"I don't understand something you said," he suddenly shot out across the table to Lufkin.

"Don't you?" Lufkin twitched his eyebrows.

"You said you can do it with your existing resources."

"I did."

"You can't, you know, if by resources you include men, which you've got to."

"Nonsense." Lufkin shrugged it off and was speaking to Rose, but Gilbert interrupted.

"Oh no. For the serious part of this job you've only got three groups of men you can possibly use, the ——'s and ——." Rapidly, inquisitively, Gilbert was mentioning names, meaningless to most people there. He said:

"You've got no option, if you're not going to make a hash of this job, you've got to transfer eighty per cent of them. That means taking them off your highest priority jobs, which other Departments won't bless any of us for, and you'll come rushing to us demanding replacements which we shall have to extract from other firms. It is bound to make too much havoc whatever we do, and I don't see rhyme or reason in it."

Lufkin looked at the younger man with a sarcastic, contemptuous rictus. They knew each other well: often in the past it had surprised me that they were so intimate. Within a few moments both had become very angry, Lufkin in cold temper, Gilbert in hot.

"You are talking of things you know nothing about," said Lufkin. Furiously Gilbert said:

"I know as much as you do."

Then, his temper boiling over, he made a tactical mistake; and to prove that he remembered what he had known about the business four years before, he insisted on producing more strings of names.

Recovering himself, sounding irritated but self-contained, Lufkin said to Rose: "I don't see that these details are likely to help us much."

"Perhaps we can leave it there, can we, Cooke?" Rose said, polite, vexed, final.

Lufkin remarked, as though brushing the incident aside: "I take it, all you want from me about personnel is an assurance that I've got enough to do the job. I can give you that assurance."

Rose smoothly asked:

"Without making any demands on us for men, either now or later?"

Lufkin's face showed no expression. He replied: "Within reason, no."

"What is reason?" Rose's voice was for an instant as sharp as the others.

"I can't commit myself indefinitely," said Lufkin calmly and heavily, "and nor can any other man in my position."

"That is completely understood, and I am very very grateful to you for the statement," said Rose, returning to his courtesy. With the same courtesy, Rose led the discussion away. The morning went on, the room became colder, several times men stamped their numbing feet. Rose would not leave an argument unheard, even if his mind was made up at the start. It was well after one o'clock when he turned to Lufkin.

"I don't know how you feel, but it seems to me just possible that this is about as far as we can go today."

"I must say, I think we've covered some ground," said John Jones.

"When do we meet again?" said Lufkin.

"I shall, of course, report this morning's proceedings to my master." Rose said the word with his customary ironic flick; but he was not the man to scurry to shelter. Unlike the Minister, he did not mind breaking bad news. Indeed, under the ritual minuet, he did it with a certain edge. "I'm sure he will want to go into it further with you. Perhaps you and he, and I think I might as well be there, could meet before the end of the week? I can't anticipate what we shall arrive at as the best course for all of us, but it seems to me just possible—of course I am only thinking aloud—that we might conceivably feel that we are making such demands on you already that we should not consider it was fair to you to stretch you in a rather difficult and unprofitable direction, just for the present at least. We might just conceivably suggest that your remarkable services ought to be kept in reserve, so that we could invoke them at a slightly later stage."

I wondered if Lufkin recognised that this was the end. At times his realism was absolute: but, like other men of action, he seemed to have the gift of switching it off and on at will. Thus he could go on, hoping and struggling, long after an issue was settled; and then stupefy one by remarking that he had written the business off days before. At that moment he was speaking to Rose with the confidence and authority of one who, at a break in a negotiation, assumed that he will with good management get his way.

The same evening Gilbert came into my office. It was about the time I was leafing through my in-tray, packing up for the night; it was about the time that, the year before, when he and I and Margaret used to go out together, he habitually called in and sat waiting for me.

For months past he had not done so. Often, when I lunched with him or when we walked in the Park afterwards, he jabbed in a question about me and Margaret, led up to traps where I had to lie or confide; he knew her, he knew her family and acquaintances, it could not be a secret that she and I spent many evenings together, but, taking that for granted, I responded to him as though there were nothing else of interest to tell.

Seeing him loom there, outside the cone of light from the desk lamp, I felt very warm to him.

"Well," I said, "we shouldn't have won without you."

"I don't believe anyone was listening to my piece," Gilbert replied. It rang mock-shy, like someone wanting praise for a drawing-room turn. In fact, it was genuine. Gilbert found it hard to credit that men paid attention to him.

Then he gave the hoarse high laugh one often hears from very strong, fleshy, active men.

"Damn it, I enjoyed it," he cried.

"What exactly?"

"I enjoyed throwing a spanner into the works!"

"You did it all," I told him.

"No, I just supplied the comic act."

He had no idea that his courage was a support to more cautious people. I wanted to reassure him, to tell him how much I admired it. So I said that I happened to be going out that night with Margaret: would he care to come too?

"I'd love it," said Gilbert.

Without concealment, he did love it, sitting between us

156

at the restaurant. Although he was so large a man he seemed to be burrowing between us, his sharp small eyes sensitive for any glance we exchanged. He enjoyed his food so much that he automatically raised his standard of living, for men obscurely felt that they owed him luxury they would never aspire to themselves; even that night, right in the middle of the war, I managed to stand him a good bottle of wine. It was freezing outside, but the nights had been raidless for a long time; in London it was a lull in the war, the restaurant was crowded and hot, we sat in a corner seat and Gilbert was happy. He infected me, he infected Margaret, and we basked in his well-being.

Suddenly, towards the end of the meal, with eyes glistening he said to me:

"I've stolen a march on you."

"What have you been up to?"

"I've been inside a house you might be interested in."

I shook my head.

"The house of a family that means something to you," said Gilbert, knowing, hot-eyed, imperious. Then he said, gazing straight at Margaret:

"*Nothing to do with you.*"

For an instant, I wondered whether he had met the Knights.

"Who is it?" I asked.

"Put him out of his misery," said Margaret, also on edge.

"He ought to be able to guess," said Gilbert, disappointed, as though his game were not quite a success.

"No," I said.

"Well, then," Gilbert spoke to Margaret. "He's got a new secretary. I've found out about her young man and his family. I've had tea with them."

It was such an anti-climax that I laughed out loud. Even so, the whole performance seemed gigantesque. It was true that I had a new secretary, a young widow called Vera

Allen: I did not know anything about her life. Gilbert told us that she was in love with a young man in the office, whose family he had tracked down.

When Gilbert described the visit, which he had planned like a military operation, his curiosity—for that alone had driven him on—made him appear more gigantesque, at times a little mad. Telling us with glee of how he had traced their address, made an excuse for an official visit to Kilburn, called at the house, found they were out, traced them to a pub and persuaded them to take him home for a pot of tea, he was not in the slightest gratifying a desire to go slumming. He would have gone off on the same chase if the young man's father had been a papal count.

Gilbert's inquisitiveness was so ravening that he was as happy, as unceremonious, wherever it led him, provided he picked up a scrap of human news. Having an evening pot of tea with this young man's parents, he felt nothing but brotherliness, except that hot-eyed zest with which he collected gossip about them, Helen, her marriage, perhaps at fourth-hand about Margaret and me.

"You are a menace," said Margaret, but with indulgence and a shade of envy for anyone who could let himself rip so far.

When we went out from the restaurant into the bitter throat-catching air, we were still happy, all three of us. Gilbert continued to talk triumphantly of his findings and, walking between us, Margaret took his arm as well as mine.

CHAPTER XXIV

MILD WIND AFTER A QUARREL

ROSE worked fast after the meeting, and within a fortnight the contract was given to one of Lufkin's rivals. During that fortnight, several of the Minister's colleagues were rumoured to have gone to dinner at St. James's Court; the Minister's own position was precarious and some of those colleagues did not wish him well. But, once the contract was signed, I thought it unlikely that Lufkin would waste any more time intriguing against the old man. Lufkin was much too practical a person to fritter himself away in revenge. For myself, I expected to be dropped for good, but no worse than that. Lufkin cut his losses, psychological as well as financial, with a drasticness that was a taunt to more contemplative men.

With that business settled and my mind at ease, I walked early one Saturday afternoon along the Bayswater Road to Margaret's flat. It was mid-December, a mild wet day with a south west wind; the street, the park, lay under a lid of cloud; the soft mild air blew in my face, brought a smell from the park both springlike and rich with autumnal decay. It was a day on which the nerves were quite relaxed, and the mild air lulled one with reveries of pleasures to come.

For a couple of days I had not seen Margaret; that morning she had not telephoned me as she usually did on Saturday, but the afternoon arrangement was a standing one, and relaxed, comfortable with expectancy, I got out the latchkey and let myself into her room. She was sitting on the stool in front of her looking-glass: she did not get up or look round: the instant I saw her reflection, strained and stern, I cried:

"What is the matter?"

"I have something to ask you."

"What is it?"

Without turning round, her voice toneless, she said:

"Is it true that Sheila killed herself?"

"What do you mean?"

Suddenly she faced me, her eyes dense with anger.

"I heard it last night. *I heard it for the first time.* Is it true?"

Deep in resentment, I stood there without speaking. At last I said:

"Yes. It is true."

Few people knew it; as Mr. Knight had suggested that night we talked while Sheila's body lay upstairs, the newspapers had had little space for an obscure inquest; I had told no one.

"It is incredible that you should have kept it from me," she cried.

"I didn't want it to hang over you——"

"What kind of life are we supposed to be living? Do you think I couldn't accept anything that has happened to you? What I can't bear is that you should try to censor something important. I can't stand it if you insist on living as though you were alone. You make me feel that these last twelve months I have been wasting my time."

"How did you hear?" I broke out.

"We've been pretending——"

"How did you hear?"

"I heard from Helen."

"She can't have known," I cried out.

"She took it for granted that I did. When she saw I didn't, what do you think it was like for both of us?"

"Did she say how she'd heard?"

"How could you let it happen?"

Our voices were raised, our words clashed together.

"Did she say how she'd heard?" I shouted again.

"Gilbert told her the other day."

She was seared with distress, choked with rage. And I felt the same sense of outrage; though I had brought the scene upon myself, I felt wronged.

Suddenly that desolation, that dull fury, that I wanted to visit on her, was twisted on to another.

"I won't tolerate it," I shouted. Over her shoulder I saw my face in her looking-glass, whitened with anger while hers had gone dark.

"I'll get rid of him. I won't have him near me."

"He's fond of you——"

"He won't do this again."

"He's amused you often enough before now, gossiping about someone else."

"This wasn't a thing to gossip about."

"It's done now," she said.

"I'll get rid of him. I won't have him near me."

I said it so bitterly that she flinched. For the first time she averted her glance: in the silence she backed away, rested an arm on the window sill, with her body limp. As I looked at her, unseeing, my feelings clashed and blared—protests, antagonism, the undercurrent of desire. Other feelings swept over those—the thought of Gilbert Cooke spying after Sheila's death, searching the local paper, tracking down police reports, filled my mind like the image of a monster. Then a wound re-opened, and I said quietly:

"There was someone else who went in for malice."

"What are you talking about?"

In jerky words, I told her of R. S. Robinson.

"Poor Sheila," Margaret muttered, and then asked, more gently than she had spoken that afternoon: "Did it make much difference to her?"

"I've never known," I said. I added:

"Perhaps not. Probably not."

Margaret was staring at me with pity, with something like fright; her eyes were filling with tears; in that moment we could have come into each other's arms.

I said:

"I won't have such people near me. That is why I shall get rid of Gilbert Cooke."

Margaret still stared at me, but I saw her face harden, as though, by a resolution as deliberate as that on the first evening we met alone but more painful now, she was drawing on her will. She answered:

"You said nothing to me about Robinson either, or what you went through then."

I did not reply. She called out an endearment, in astonishment, in acknowledgment of danger.

"We must have it out," she said.

"Let it go."

After a pause she said, her voice thickening:

"That's too easy. I can't live like that."

"Let it go, I tell you."

"No."

As a rule people thought her younger than she was, but now she looked much older. She said:

"You can't get rid of Gilbert."

"I don't think that anything can stop me."

"Except that it would be a wrong and unfair thing to do. And you are not really so unfair."

"I've told you my reason," I cried.

"That's not your reason. You're lying to yourself."

My temper was rising again. I said:

"I'm getting tired of this."

"You're pretending that Gilbert was acting out of malice, and you know it isn't true."

"I know more of men like Gilbert than you ever will. And I know much more of malice."

"He's been perfectly loyal to you in every way that matters," she said, conceding nothing. "There's no excuse on earth for trying to shift him out of your office. I couldn't let you do it."

"It is not for you to say."

"It is. All Gilbert has done is just to treat you as he treats everyone else. Of course he's inquisitive. It's all right when he's being inquisitive about anyone else, but when he touches you—you can't bear it. You want to be private, you don't want to give and take like an ordinary man." She went on: "That's what has maddened you about Gilbert. You issue bulletins about yourself, you don't want anyone else to find you out." She added: "You are the same with me."

Harshly I tried to stop her, but her temper was matching mine, her tongue was cooler. She went on: "What else were you doing, hiding the way she died from me?"

I had got to the pitch of sullen anger when I did not speak, just stood choked up, listening to her accusations.

"With those who don't want much of you, you're unselfish, I grant you that," she was saying. "With anyone who wants you altogether, you're cruel. Because one never knows when you're going to be secretive, when you're going to withdraw. With most people you're good," she was saying, "but in the end you'll break the heart of anyone who loves you.

"I might be able to stand it," she was saying, "I might not mind so much, if you weren't doing yourself such harm."

Listening to her, I was beyond knowing where her insight was true or false. All she said, her violence and her love, broke upon me like demands which pent me in, which took me to a breaking point of pride and anger. I felt as I had done as a boy when my mother invaded me with love, and at any price I had, the more angry with her because of the behaviour she caused in me, to shut her out.

163

"That's enough," I said, hearing my own voice thin but husky in the confining room, as without looking at her I walked to the door.

In the street the afternoon light was still soft, and the mild air blew upon my face.

CHAPTER XXV

CATCH OF BREATH IN THE DARKNESS

SOON I went back to her, and when we took Helen out to dinner in January, we believed that we were putting a face on it, that we were behaving exactly as in the days of our first happiness. But, just as subtle bamboozlers like R. S. Robinson waft about in the illusion that their manoeuvres are impenetrable, whereas in fact they are seen through in one by the simplest of men—so the controlled, when they set out to hide their moods, take in no one but themselves.

Within a few weeks, Helen rang me up at the office saying that she was in London for the day, and anxious to talk to me. My first impulse was to put her off. It was uneasily that I invited her to meet me at a restaurant.

I had named the Connaught, knowing that of all her family she was the only one who liked the atmosphere of the opulent and the smart. When I arrived there, finding her waiting in the hall, I saw she was on edge. She was made up more than usual, and her dress had a rigid air of stylishness. She might like the atmosphere, but she could not help the feeling that she had been brought up to despise it; perhaps the slight edge of apprehension, of unfamiliarity, with which, even after all these years, she was troubled whenever she entered a world which was not plain living and high thinking, was one of its charms for her. She did not, as Betty Vane did, take it for granted; for her it had not lost its savour. But added to this temperamental unease, was uneasiness at what she had to say to me.

Sheltered in a corner in the inner dining-room, she did not speak much. Once, as though apologising for her shyness, she gave me a smile like her sister's, at the same time kind and sensuous. She made some remark about the people round us, commented admiringly on a woman's clothes, then fell into silence, looking down at her hands, fiddling with her wedding-ring.

I asked her about her husband. She replied as directly as usual, looking a little beyond my face as if seeing him there, seeing him with a kind of habitual, ironic affection. I believed that she had known little of physical joy.

Suddenly she raised her eyes, which searched mine as Margaret's did. She said:

"You'd like it better if I didn't speak."

"Perhaps," I said.

"If I thought I could make things worse, I wouldn't come near either of you—but they're as bad as they can be, aren't they?"

"Are they?"

"Could things be worse, tell me?"

"I don't think it's as bad as that."

To Margaret and me, holding to each other with the tenacity that we each possessed, truly it did not seem so bad: but Helen was watching me, knowing that words said could not be taken back, that there are crystallisations out of love, as well as into it. She knew of my deception over Sheila's suicide: did she think that this was such a crystallisation? That as a result Margaret could not regain her trust?

"You know, Lewis, I mind about you both."

"Yes, I know that."

It was easy, it was a relief, to reply with her own simplicity.

"When I first saw you together," she said, "I was so happy about it."

"So was I." I added: "I think she was too."

"I know she was.

166

"I thought you had been lucky to find each other, both of you," she was saying. "I thought you had both chosen very wisely."

She leant towards me.

"What I'm afraid of," she broke out, quietly and clearly, "is that you are driving her away."

I knew it, and did not know it. Margaret was as tenacious as I was; but she was also more self-willed, and far less resigned. In a human relation she was given to action, action came as naturally and was as much a release as in a more public setting it came to Paul Lufkin or Hector Rose. Sometimes I felt that, although her will was all set to save us, she was telling herself that soon she must force the issue. Once or twice I thought I had detected in her what I had heard called 'the secret planner', who exists in all of us often unrecognised by ourselves and who, in the prospect of disaster, even more so in the prospect of continuing misery, is working out alternative routes which may give us a chance of self-preservation, a chance of health.

"There's still time," said Helen, and now she was nerving herself even harder, since there was a silence to break, "to stop driving her away." She pulled on her left glove and smoothed it up to the elbow, concentrating upon it as if its elegance gave her confidence, made her the kind of woman with a right to say what she chose.

"I hope there is."

"Of course there is," she said. "Neither of you will ever find the same again, and you mustn't let it go."

"That is true for me. I am not sure it's true for her."

"You must believe it is."

She was frowning, speaking as though I were obtuse.

"Look, Lewis," she said, "I love her, and of course I'm not satisfied about her, because what you are giving each other isn't enough for her, you know that, don't you? I love her, but I don't think I idealise her. She tries to be good, but I don't think she was given the sort of goodness that's easy and no trouble. She can't forget herself enough for that, perhaps she wants too many different things, perhaps she is too passionate."

She was not using the word in a physical sense.

"And you—you wouldn't do for everyone, would you, but you can match her all along the line, you're the one person she needn't limit herself with, and I believe that's why it was so wonderful for her. She'd be lucky to have a second chance.

"I don't think that she'd even look for one," Helen went on. "But I wasn't thinking mainly of her."

Helen's tone was for a second impatient and tart, she was in control of herself: and I was taken aback. All along I had assumed that she had forced herself to tax me for Margaret's sake. "I think it's you who stand to lose," she said. "You see, she wouldn't expect so much again, and so long as she found someone to look after, she could make do with that."

I thought of the men Margaret liked, the doctor Geoffrey Hollis, other friends.

"Could you make do?" Helen asked insistently.

"I doubt it."

After Helen's intervention I tried to hearten both Margaret and myself. Sometimes I was hopeful, I could show high spirits in front of her: but my spirits were by nature high, despite my fears. I had lost my judgement: sometimes I remembered how Sheila had lost hers, I remembered the others I had seen at a final loss, the unavailing and the breakdowns: now I knew what it was like.

I tried to bring her back, and she tried with me. When I was with her, she made-believe that she was happy, so as to fight the dread of another sadness, the menace of a recurrent situation. I wanted to believe in her gaiety, sometimes I did so: even when I knew she was putting it on for my sake.

One evening I went to her, the taxi jangling in the cold March light. As soon as I saw her, she was smiling, and on the instant the burden fell away. After we had made love, I lay there in the dark, in the quiet, comforted by a pleasure as absolute as any I had known. Drowsily I could shake off the state in which, somewhere deep among my fears, she took the place of Sheila. At first I had seemed to pick her out because she was so unlike; yet of late there had been times in which I saw Sheila in my dreams and knew that it was Margaret. I had even, not dreaming but in cold blood, discovered points of identity between them; I had gone so far as to see resemblances in Margaret's face.

I was incredulous that I could have thought so, feared so, as I lay there with her warm against my arms.

In the extreme quiet I heard a catch of her breath, and another. At once I shifted my hand and drew it lightly over her cheek: it was wet and slippery with tears.

The last hour was shattered. I looked down at her, but we had no fire that night, the room was so dark that I could scarcely see her face, even for the instant before she turned it further from me.

"You know how easily I cry," she muttered. I tried to soothe her; she tried to soothe me.

"This is a pity," she said in anger: then she cried again.

"It doesn't matter," I said mechanically. "It doesn't matter."

I could not find the loving kindness to know that for her physical delight was a mockery, when there was this distance between us.

I had no self-knowledge left. I felt only uselessness and what seemed like self-contempt. Walking with her in the park later that night, I could not speak.

CHAPTER XXVI

FROM THE LAST LIGHT TO THE FIRST

WHEN she walked with me across the Park that night, and on other nights in the weeks that followed, the cold spring air taunted us; often we hoped that all would come well, that we should have confidence in each other again.

Then, one morning in May, I heard of Roy Calvert's death. He had been my closest friend: though my friendships with George Passant and Charles March and my brother had been strong, this was different in kind. I had come to know him when I was most distracted about Sheila; he had seemed the most fortunate of men, he had given me sympathy more penetrating than anyone else's, but he too was afflicted, with a melancholy that in the end made his life worthless. I had tried to support him; for a while, perhaps, I was some use, but not for long. Now he was dead, and I could not get away from my sadness. It stayed like smoked glass between me and the faces in the streets.

In the past two years I had seen him little, for he was flying in the Air Force, and, though Margaret and he knew what the other meant to me, they had never met. Yet it was true that each had disliked the sound of the other's name. Roy was not fond of women of character, much less if they had insight too; if I were to marry again, he would have chosen for me someone altogether more careless, obtuse and easy-going.

In return she suspected him of being a poseur, a romantic fake without much fibre, whose profundity of experience she mostly discounted and for the rest did not value. In her heart, she thought he encouraged in me much that she struggled with.

At the news of his death she gave no sign, so far as I could see through the smear of grief, of her dislike, and just wanted to take care of me. I could not respond. I was enough of an official machine—as I had been in the weeks after Sheila's death—to be civil and efficient and make sharp remarks at meetings: as soon as I was out of the office I wanted no one near me, not even her. I recalled Helen's warning; I wanted to pretend, but I could not.

It did not take her long to see.

"You want to be alone, don't you?" she said. It was no use denying it, though it was that which hurt her most. "I'm less than no help to you. You'd better be by yourself."

I spent evenings in my own room, doing nothing, not reading, limp in my chair. In Margaret's presence I was often silent, as I had never been with her before. I saw her looking at me, wondering how she could reach me, clutching at any sign that I could give her—and wondering also whether all had gone wrong, and if this was the last escape.

On a close night, near mid-summer, the sky not quite dark, we walked purposelessly round the Bayswater streets and then crossed over to Hyde Park and found an empty bench. Looking down the hollow towards the Bayswater Road we could see the scurf of newspapers, the white of shirts and dresses in couples lying together, shining out from the grass in the last of the light. The litter of the night, the thundery closeness: we sat without looking at each other: each of us was alone, with that special loneliness, containing both guilt and deprivation, containing also dislike and a kind of sullen hate, which comes to those who have known extreme intimacy, and who are seeing it drift away. In that loneliness we held each other's hand, as though we could not bear the last token of separation.

She said quietly, in a tone of casual gossip, "How is your friend Lufkin?"

We knew each other's memories so well. She was asking me to recall that once, months before, when we were untroubled, we had met him by chance, not here, but on the path nearer the Albert Gate.

"I haven't seen him."

"Does he still feel misunderstood?"

Again she was making me recall. She had taught me so much, I told her once. She had said: "So have you taught me." Most of the men I talked to her about had never come near her father's world: she had not realised before what they were like.

"I'm sure he does."

"*Snakes-in-the-grass.*" It was one of Lufkin's favourite exclamations, confronted with yet another example, perpetually astonishing to him, of others' duplicity, self-seeking, and ambition. Margaret could not believe that men so able could live cut off from their own experience. It had delighted her, and, searching that night for something for us to remember, she refound the phrase and laughed out loud.

For a while we talked, glad to be talking, of some of the characters I had amused her with. It was a strange use for those figures, so grand in their offices, so firm in their personae, I thought later, to be smiled over by the two of us, clutching on to the strand of a love-affair, late at night out in the park.

We could not spin it out, we fell back into silence. I had no idea of how the time was passing, now that the night had come down. I could feel her fingers in mine, and at last she called my name, but mechanically, as though she were intending an endearment but was remote. She said:

"A lot has happened to you."

She did not mean my public life, she meant the deaths of Sheila and Roy Calvert.

"I suppose so."

"It was bound to affect you, I know that."

"I wish," I said, "that I had met you before any of it happened."

Suddenly she was angry.

"No, I won't listen. We met when we did, and this is the only time together we shall ever have."

"I might have been more——"

"No. You're always trying to slip out of the present moment, and I won't take it any more."

I answered sullenly. The present moment, the existent moment—as we sat there, in the sultry darkness, we could neither deal with it nor let it be. We could not show each other the kindness we should have shown strangers: far less could we allow those words to come out which, with the knowledge and touch of intimacy, we were certain could give the other a night's peace. If she could have said to me, it doesn't matter, leave it, some day you'll be better and we'll start again—If I could have said to her, I will try to give you all you want, marry me and somehow we shall come through—But we could not speak so, it was as though our throats were sewn up.

We stayed, our hands touching, not tired so much as stupefied while the time passed: time not racing hallucinatorily by, as when one is drunk, but just pressing on us with something like the headaching pressure of the thundery air in which we sat. Sometimes we talked, almost with interest, almost as though we were going out for the first time, for the first meal together, about a play that ought to be seen or a book she had just read. After another bout of silence, she said in a different tone:

"Before we started, I asked what you wanted from me."

I said yes.

"You said, you didn't want anything one-sided, you didn't want the past all over again."

I replied: "Yes, I said that."

"I believed you," she said.

Over Park Lane the sky was not so densely black, there was a leaden light just visible over the roofs. The sight struck more chilly than the dark had been. The midsummer night was nearly over. She asked:

"It looks as though we have come to a dead end?"

Even then, we wanted to hear in each other the sound of hope.

174

CHAPTER XXVII

VIEW OF A SWINGING DOOR

WITHOUT seeing Margaret again I went off travelling on duty, and it was a fortnight before I returned to London. The day I got back, I found a note on my desk. Margaret had telephoned, would I meet her that evening in the foyer of the Café Royal? At once I was startled. We had never gone there before, it was a place without associations.

Waiting, a quarter of an hour before the time she fixed, I stared at the swinging door and through the glass at the glare outside. The flash of buses, the dazzle of cars' bonnets, the waft of the door as someone entered but not she—I was at the stretch of waiting. When at last the door swung past and showed her, minutes early, I saw her face flushed and set; but her step, as she came across the floor, was quick, light and full of energy.

As she greeted me her eyes were intent on mine; they had no light in them, and the orbits had gone deeper and more hollow.

"Why here?" I broke out.

"You must know. I hope you know."

She sat down: I had a drink ready, but she did not touch it.

"I hope you know," she said.

"Tell me then."

She was speaking, so was I, quite unlike the choked hours in the park: we were speaking at our closest.

"I am going to get married."

"Who to?"

"Geoffrey."

"I knew it."

Her face at the table came at me in the brilliant precision of a high temperature, sharp edged, so vivid that sight itself was deafening.

"It is settled, you know," she said. "Neither of us could bear it if it wasn't, could we?"

She was speaking still with complete understanding, as though her concern for me was at its most piercing, and mine for her; she was speaking also as one buoyed up by action, who had cut her way out of a conflict and by the fact of acting was released.

I asked:

"Why didn't you write and tell me?"

"Don't you know it would have been easier to write?"

"Why didn't you?"

"I couldn't let you get news like that over your breakfast and by yourself."

I looked at her. Somehow, as at a long distance, the words made me listen to what I was losing—it was like her, maternal, irrationally practical, principled, a little vain. I looked at her not yet in loss, so much as in recognition.

She said: "You know you've done everything for me, don't you?"

I shook my head.

"You've given me confidence I should never have had," she went on. "You've taken so many of the fears away."

Knowing me, she knew what might soften the parting for me.

Suddenly she said:

"I wish, I wish that you could say the same."

She had set herself to be handsome and protective to the end, but she could not sustain it. Her tears had sprung out. With a quick, impatient, resolved gesture, she was on her feet.

"I hope all goes well with you."

The words, doubtful and angry in their tone, heavy with her concern, were muffled in my ears. They were muffled, like a sad forecast, as I watched her leave me and walk to the door with a firm step. Not looking back, she pushed the door round, so hard that, after I had lost sight of her, the empty segments sucked round before my eyes, sweeping time away, leaving me with nothing there to see.

PART III

CONDITION OF A SPECTATOR

CHAPTER XXVIII

A CHANGE OF TASTE

AFTER Margaret gave me up, I used to go home alone when I left the office on a summer evening. But I had plenty of visitors to my new flat, people I cared for just enough to be interested to see, friendly acquaintances, one or two protégés. For me they were casual evenings, making no more calls on me than a night's reading.

Sometimes, in the midst of a long official gathering, I thought, not without a certain enjoyment, of how baffled these people would be if they saw the acquaintances with whom I proposed to spend that night. For now I had been long enough in the office to be taken for granted: since the Minister lost his job, I did not possess as much invisible influence as when I was more junior, but in official eyes I had gone up, and the days were stable, full of the steady, confident voices of power. Then I went home from one of Hector Rose's committees, back to the dingy flat.

Just after Margaret said goodbye, I had to move out of the Dolphin block and, not in a state to trouble, I took the first rooms I heard of, in the square close by. They took up the ground floor of one of the porticoed Pimlico houses; the smell of dust was as constant as a hospital smell; in the sitting-room the sunlight did not enter, even in high summer, until five o'clock. In that room I listened to the acquaintances who came to see me; it was there that Vera Allen, my secretary, suddenly broke out of her reserve and told me of the young man whom Gilbert had identified. He seemed to love her, Vera cried, but he would neither marry nor make love to her. That was, on the surface, a story commonplace enough, in contrast to some of the others which came my way.

Of my old friends, the only one I saw much of was Betty Vane, who came in to make the flat more liveable, just as she had busied herself for me after Sheila's death. She knew that I had lost Margaret: about herself she volunteered nothing, except that she had left her job and found another in London, leaving me to assume that she and I were in the same state.

Irritable, undemanding, she used to clean up the room and then go with me round the corner to the pub on the embankment. Through the open door the starlings clamoured: we looked at each other with scrutiny, affection, blame. We had been friends on and off for so long, and now we met again it was to find that the other had got nowhere.

When she or any other visitor let herself out last thing at night, there was likely to be a pad and scuffle outside my door and a soft, patient, insidious knock. Then round the door would insinuate a podgy shapeless face, a great slack heavy body wrapped in a pink satin dressing-gown. It was Mrs. Beauchamp, my landlady, who lived on the floor above mine and who spent her days spying from her room above the portico and her nights listening to steps on the stairs and sounds from her tenants' rooms.

One night, just after Betty had left, she went through her routine:

"I was just wondering, Mr. Eliot, I knew you won't mind me asking, but I was just wondering if you had a drop of milk?"

The question was a matter of form. With each new tenant, she cherished a hope of heart speaking unto heart, and, as the latest arrival, I was going through the honeymoon period. As a matter of form, I asked her if she could manage without the milk for that night's supper.

"Ah, Mr. Eliot," she breathed, a trifle ominously, "I'll do what I can."

Then she got down to business.

"That was a very nice young lady if you don't mind me saying so, Mr. Eliot, that seemed to be coming to see you when I happened to be looking down the street tonight, or at least, not exactly young as some people call young, but I always say that none of us are as young as we should like to be."

I told her Betty was younger than I was: but as she thought me ten years older than my real age, Mrs. Beauchamp was encouraged.

"I always say that people who aren't exactly young have feelings just the same as anyone else, and sometimes their feelings give them a lot to think about, if you don't mind me saying so, Mr. Eliot," she said, with an expression that combined salacity with extreme moral disapproval. But she was not yet satisfied.

"I shouldn't be surprised," she said, "if you told me that that nice young lady had come of a very good family."

"Shouldn't you?"

"Now, Mr. Eliot, she does or she doesn't. I'm sorry if I'm asking things I shouldn't, but I like to feel that when anyone does the same to me I don't send them away feeling that they have made a *faux pas*."

"As a matter of fact she does."

"Breeding will out," Mrs. Beauchamp exhaled.

The curious thing was, she was an abnormally accurate judge of social origin. The derelicts who visited me she put down to my eccentricity: the respectable clerks from the lower middle classes, like Vera Allen and her Norman, Mrs. Beauchamp spotted at once, and indicated that I was wasting my time. Of my Bohemian friends, she detected precisely who was smart and who was not.

She went on to tell me the glories of her own upbringing, the convent school—'those dear good nuns'—and of Beauchamp, who was, according to her, entitled to wear *seventeen distinguished ties*. Improbable as Mrs. Beauchamp's autobiography sounded when one saw her stand oozily in the doorway, I was coming to believe it was not totally untrue.

Whenever I answered the telephone in the hall, I heard a door click open on the next floor and the scuffle of Mrs. Beauchamp's slippers. But I could put up with her detective work, much as I used, before he touched a nerve, to put up with Gilbert Cooke's.

All this time, since the day when he told Margaret's sister of the suicide, I had been meeting Gilbert in the office; I talked business with him, even gossiped, but I had not once let fall a word to him about my own concerns. He was the first to notice signs of anyone withdrawing, but this time I was not sure that he knew the reason. I was quite sure, however, that he had discovered the break with Margaret, and that he was expending some effort to observe how I was living now.

Coming into my office one evening in the autumn, he said imperiously and shyly:

"Doing anything tonight?"

I said no.

"Let me give you dinner."

I could not refuse and did not want to, for there was no pretence about the kindness that brimmed from him. As well as being kind, he was also, I recognised once more, sensitive: he did not take me to White's, since he must have imagined—the last thing I should have mentioned to anyone, to him above all—how I linked our dinner there with the night of Sheila's death. Instead, he found a restaurant in Soho where he could order me one or two of my favourite dishes, the names of which he had stored away in that monstrous memory. He proceeded to bully me kindly about my new flat.

"It's near the Dolphin, isn't it?" (He knew the address.) "It's one of those 1840'ish houses, I suppose. Not much good in air raids, you must move out if they start again," he said, jabbing his thumb at me. "We can't let you take unnecessary risks."

"What about you?" I said. His own flat was at the top of a ramshackle Knightsbridge house.

"It doesn't matter about me."

Brushing my interruption aside, he got back to the subject, more interesting to him, of my living arrangements.

"Have you got a housekeeper?"

I said I supposed that one could call Mrs. Beauchamp that.

"Doesn't she make you comfortable?"

"Certainly not."

"I don't know," he cried impatiently, "why you don't do something about it!"

"Don't worry yourself," I said, "I genuinely don't mind."

"What is she like?"

I wanted to warn him off, so I smiled at him, and said: "To put it mildly, she's just a bit inquisitive."

When I had spoken I was sorry, since it suddenly struck me as not impossible that Gilbert would find occasion to have a tête-à-tête with Mrs. Beauchamp. For the moment, however, he laughed, high-voiced, irritated with me.

The meal went on agreeably enough. We talked official shop and about the past. I thought again, everything Gilbert said was his own, in his fashion he was a creative man. He was being lavish with the drink, and now there was half-a-bottle of brandy standing before us on the table. It was a long time since I had drunk so much. I was cheerful, I was content for the evening to stretch out. As I was finishing some inconsequential remark I saw Gilbert leaning over the table towards me, his big shoulders hunched. His eyes hot and obsessive, he said:

"I can tell you something you've been waiting to know."

"Never mind," I replied, but I was taken off guard.

"Have you seen Margaret since she got married?"

"No."

"I suppose you wouldn't!" He laughed, satisfied, on top. "Well, you needn't get too bothered about her. I think she'll be all right."

I wanted to cry out, 'I don't intend to listen', just as I had avoided going near anyone who knew her or even hearing the date of her wedding. The only news I had not been able to escape was that she was married. I wanted to shout in front of Gilbert's inflamed eyes—'I can stand it, if I don't hear'. But he went on: Geoffrey Hollis had taken a job at a children's hospital, they were living at Aylesbury.

"I think she'll be all right," said Gilbert.

"Good."

"He's head over heels in love with her, of course."

"Good," I said again.

"There is one other thing."

"Is there?" I heard my own voice dull, mechanical, protecting me by thrusting news away.

"She's going to have a child."

As I did not reply, he continued:

"That will mean a lot to her, won't it?"

"Yes."

"Of course," said Gilbert, "she can't have started it more than a month or two——"

While he was talking on, I got up and said that I must have an early night. There were no taxis outside, and together we walked up Oxford Street: I was replying to his chat affably if absently: I did not feel inimical; I already knew what I was going to do.

The next morning I sat in my office thinking of how I was going to say it, before I asked Vera Allen to fetch Gilbert in. He slumped down in the easy chair beside my desk, relaxed and companionable.

"Look," I said, "I want you to transfer to another branch."

On the instant he was braced, his feet springing on the floor, like a man ready to fight.

"Why?"

"Will it do any good to either of us to answer that?"

"You just mean, that you want to get rid of me, after four years, without any reason, and without any fuss?"

"Yes," I said. "I mean that."

"I won't accept it."

"You must."

"You can't force me."

"I can," I replied. I added: "If necessary, I shall." I was speaking so that he would believe me. Then I added in a different tone:

"But I shan't have to."

"Why do you think you can get away with it?"

"Because I need you to go to make things easier for me."

"Good God," cried Gilbert, his eyes angry and puzzled, "I don't think I deserve that."

"I've got great affection for you, you know that," I said. "You've been very good to me in all kinds of ways, and I shan't forget it. But just now there are parts of my life I don't want to be reminded of——"

"Well?"

"While you're about, you can't help reminding me of them."

"How do you mean, I can't help it?"

"You can see."

Hotly, angrily, without self-pity or excuse, Gilbert said: "It's my nature. You know how it is."

I knew better than he thought; for in my youth I had been as tempted as most men by the petty treachery, the piece of malice warm on the tongue at a friend's expense, the kind of personal imperialism, such as he had shown the night before, in which one imposes oneself upon another. Even more I had been fascinated by the same quicksands in other men. As to many of us when young, the labile, the shifting, the ambivalent, the Lebedevs and the Fyodor Karamazovs, had given me an intimation of the depth and wonder of life. But as I grew up I began to find it not only unmagical, but also something like boring, both in others and myself. At the age when I got rid of Gilbert Cooke I found it hard to imagine the excitement and attention with which, in my young manhood, I had explored the transformation-scene temperament of an early friend. As I got near forty, my tastes in character had changed, I could not give that attention again. If I had still been able to, I could have taken Gilbert as an intimate friend.

CHAPTER XXIX

FIRST INTERVIEW OF GEORGE PASSANT

WHEN I told Rose that I wished to transfer Gilbert Cooke, I had an awkward time.

"Of course, I have only a nodding acquaintance with your dashing activities, my dear Lewis," said Rose, meaning that he read each paper word by word, "but I should have thought the present arrangement was working reasonably well."

I said that I could see certain advantages in a change.

"I must say," replied Rose, "that I should like to be assured of that."

"It would do Cooke good to get a wider experience——"

"We can't afford to regard ourselves as a training establishment just at present. My humble interest is to see that your singular and admirable activities don't suffer." He gave his polite, confident smile. "And forgive me if I'm wrong, but I have a feeling that they will suffer if you let Master Cooke go."

"In many ways that's true," I had to say in fairness.

"I shouldn't like us to forget that he showed a certain amount of moral courage, possibly a slightly embarrassing moral courage, over that Lufkin complication last year. I scored a point to his credit over that. And I have an impression that he's been improving. He's certainly been improving appreciably on paper, and I've come to respect his minutes."

As usual, Hector Rose was just. He was also irritated that I would not let him persuade me. He was even more irritated when he learned how I proposed to fill Gilbert's place. For, finding me obstinate, and cutting the argument short, he admitted that they could probably give me an 'adequate replacement'; it was the end of 1943, there were plenty of youngish officers invalided out, or a few capable young women 'coming loose'.

No, I said, I would not take a chance with anyone I did not know through and through; the job was going to get more tangled, and parts of it were secret; I wanted someone near me whom I could trust as I did myself.

"I take it that this specification is not completely in the air, and you have some valuable suggestion up your sleeve?"

I gave the name: George Passant. The man who had most befriended me in my youth, although I did not tell Rose that. He had been working as a solicitor's managing clerk in a provincial town for twenty years. The only point in his favour in Rose's eyes was that his examination record was of the highest class.

Further, I had to tell Rose that George had once got into legal trouble, but had been found innocent.

"In that case we can't count it against him." Rose was showing his most frigid fairness, as well as irritation. He dismissed that subject, it was not to be raised again. But sharply he asked me what proofs 'this man' had given of high ability. His lids heavy, his face expressionless, Rose listened.

"It isn't an entirely convincing case, my dear Lewis, don't you feel that? It would be much easier for me if you would reconsider the whole idea. Will you think it over and give me the benefit of another word tomorrow?"

"I have thought it over for a long time," I replied. "If this job"—I meant, as Rose understood, the projects such as the headquarters administration of Barford which came in my domain—"is done as it needs to be done, I can't think of anyone else who'd bring as much to it."

"Very well, let me see this man as soon as you can."

Just for that instant, Hector Rose was as near being rude as I had heard him, but when, three days later, we were waiting to interview George Passant, he had recovered himself and, the moment George was brought in, Rose reached heights of politeness exalted even for him.

"My dear Mr. Passant, it is really extremely good of you, putting yourself to this inconvenience just to give us the pleasure of a talk. I have heard a little about you from my colleague Eliot, whom I'm sure you remember, but it is a real privilege to have the opportunity of meeting you in person."

To my surprise George, who had entered sheepishly, his head thrust forward, concealing the power of his chest and shoulders, gave a smile of delight at Rose's welcome, immediately reassured by a display of warmth about as heartfelt as a bus conductor's thanks.

"I don't get to London very often," said George, "but it's always a treat."

It was a curious start. His voice, which still retained the Suffolk undertone, rolled out, and, as he sat down, he smiled shyly at Rose but also man-to-man. They were both fair, they were both of middle height, strongly built, with massive heads; yet, inside that kind of structural resemblance, it would have been hard to find two men more different.

Even spruced up for the interview, George looked not so much untidy as dowdy, in a blue suit with the trouser legs too tight. His shoes, his tie, separated him from Rose as much as his accent did, and there was not only class, there was success dividing them. George, never at his ease except with protégés or women, was more than ever fiddling for the right etiquette in front of this smooth youngish man, more successful than anyone he had met.

Sitting down, he smiled shyly at Rose, and of all the contrasts between them that in their faces was the sharpest.

At forty-six Rose's was blankly youthful, the untouched front of a single-minded man, with eyes heavy and hard. George, three years younger, looked no more than his age; he was going neither grey nor bald; but there were written on him the signs of one who has found his temperament often too much to manage; his forehead was bland and noble, his nose and mouth and whole expression had a cheerful sensual liveliness—except for his eyes, which, light blue in their deep orbits, were abstracted, often lost and occasionally sad.

With the practised and temperate flow of a civil service interview, Rose questioned him.

"I wonder if you would mind, Mr. Passant, just helping us by taking us through your career?"

George did so. He might be shy, but he was lucid as always. His school career: his articles with a Woodbridge solicitor——

"Forgive me interrupting, Mr. Passant, but with a school record like yours I'm puzzled why you didn't try for a university scholarship?"

"If I'd known what they were like I might have got one," said George robustly.

"Leaving most of us at the post," said Rose with a polite bow.

"I think I should have got one," said George, and then suddenly one of his fits of abject diffidence took him over, the diffidence of class. "But *of course* I had no one to advise me, starting where I did."

"I should hope that we're not wasting material like you nowadays, if you will let me say so."

"More than you think." George was comfortable again. He went on about his articles: the Law Society examinations: the prizes: the job at Eden and Martineau's, a firm of solicitors in a midland town, as a qualified clerk.

"Where you've been ever since. That is, since October 1924," put in Rose smoothly.

"I'm afraid so," said George.

"Why haven't you moved?"

"You ought to be told," said George, without any embarrassment, "that I had an unpleasant piece of difficulty ten years ago."

"I have been told," said Rose, also without fuss. "I can perfectly well understand that trouble getting in your way since—but what about the years before?"

George answered: "I've often asked myself. Of course I didn't have any influence behind me."

Rose regarded him as though he wanted to examine this lack of initiative. But he thought better of it, and dexterously switched him on to legal points. Like many high-class civil servants, Rose had a competent amateur knowledge of law; I sat by, without any need to intervene, while George replied with his old confidence.

Then Rose said: most countries recruit their bureaucracy almost exclusively from lawyers: our bureaucracy is not fond of them: who is right? It was a topic which Rose knew backwards, but George, quite undeterred, argued as though he had been in Permanent Secretaries' offices for years: I found myself listening, not to the interview, but to the argument for its own sake: I found also that Rose, who usually timed interviews to the nearest two minutes, was letting this over-run by nearly ten. At last he said, bowing from the waist, as ceremonious as though he were saying goodbye to Lufkin or an even greater boss:

"I think perhaps we might leave it for the moment, don't you agree, Mr. Passant? It has been a most delightful occasion and I shall see that we let you know whether we can possibly justify ourselves in temporarily uprooting you——"

With a smile George backed out, the door closed, Rose

looked not at me but out of the window. His arms were folded on his chest, and it was some moments before he spoke.

"Well," he said.

I waited.

"Well," he said, "he's obviously a man of very high intelligence."

In that respect, Rose in half an hour could appreciate George's quality more than his employer in the solicitors' firm, who had known him half a lifetime. He went on:

"He's got a very strong and precise mind, and it's distinctly impressive. If we took him as a replacement for Cooke, on the intellectual side we should gain by the transaction."

Rose paused. His summing-up was not coming as fluently as usual.

He added: "But I must say, there seems to be altogether too much on the negative side."

I stiffened, ready to sit it out.

"What exactly?"

"Not to put too fine a point on it, a man of his ability who just rests content in a fourth-rate job must have something wrong with him."

A stranger, listening to the altercation which went on for many minutes, would have thought it business-like, rational, articulate. He might not have noticed, so cool was Rose's temper, so long had I had to learn to subdue mine, that we were each of us very angry. I knew that I had only to be obstinate to get my way. I could rely on Rose's fairness. If George had been an impossible candidate, he would have vetoed him. But, although Rose felt him unsuitable and even more alien, he was too fair to rule him out at sight.

That being so, I should get George if I stuck to it; for this was the middle of the war, and I was doing a difficult job. In peace-time, I should have had to take anyone I was given. Rose had been trained not to expect to make a personal choice of a subordinate, any more than of an office chair: it offended him more, because mine was nothing but a personal choice. It was war-time, however; my job was regarded as exacting and in part it was abnormally secret. In the long run I had to be given my head. But I knew that I should have to pay a price.

"Well, my dear Lewis, I am still distinctly uneasy about this suggestion. If I may say so, I am slightly surprised that you should press it, in view of what I have tried, no doubt inadequately, to explain."

"I wouldn't do so for a minute," I replied, "if I weren't unusually certain."

"Yes, that's the impression you have managed to give." For once Rose was letting his bitter temper show. "I repeat, I am surprised that you should press the suggestion."

"I am sure of the result."

"Right." Rose snapped off the argument, like a man turning a switch. "I'll put the nomination through the proper channels. You'll be able to get this man started within a fortnight."

He glanced at me, his face smoothed over.

"Well, I'm most grateful to you for spending so much time this afternoon. But I should be less than honest with you, my dear Lewis, if I didn't say that I still have a fear this may prove one of your few errors of judgement."

That was the price I paid. For Rose, who in disapproval invariably said less than he meant, was telling me, not that I might turn out to have made an error of judgement, but that I had already done so. That is, I had set my opinion against official opinion beyond the point where I should have backed down. If I had been a real professional, with a professional's ambitions, I could not have afforded to. For it did not take many 'errors of judgement'—the most minatory phrase Rose could use to a colleague—docketed in that judicious mind, to keep one from the top jobs. If I became a professional, I should have the future, common enough if one looked round the Pall Mall clubs, of men of parts, often brighter than their bosses, who had inexplicably missed the top two rungs.

I did not mind. When I was a young man, too poor to give much thought to anything but getting out of poverty, I had dreamed of great success at the Bar; since then I had kept an interest in success and power which was, to many of my friends, forbiddingly intense. And, of course, they were not wrong: if a man spends half of his time discussing basketball, thinking of basketball, examining with passionate curiosity the intricacies of basketball, it is not unreasonable to suspect him of a somewhat excessive interest in the subject.

Yet, over the last years, almost without my noticing it, for such a change does not happen in a morning, I was growing tired of it: or perhaps not so much tired, as finding myself slide from a participant into a spectator. It was partly that now I knew I could earn a living in two or three different ways. It was partly that, of the two I had loved most, Sheila had ignored my liking for power, while Margaret actively detested it. But, although I believed that Margaret's influence might have quickened the change within me, I also believed it would have happened anyway.

Now that I felt a theme in my life closing, I thought it likely that I had started off with an interest in power greater than that of most reflective men, but not a tenth of Lufkin's or Rose's, nothing like enough to last me for a lifetime. I expected that I should keep an eye open for the manœuvres of others: who will get the job? and why? and how? I expected also that sometimes, as I watched others installed in jobs I might once have liked, I should feel regret. That did not matter much. Beneath it all, a preoccupation was over.

As it vanished step-by-step, so another had filled its place.

But this other was genuine; I had been clear about it, although I had had to push it out of sight, even when I was a child. I had known that sooner or later I should have some books to write; I did not worry about it; I was learning what I had to say. In trouble, that knowledge had often steadied me, and had given me a comfort greater than any other. Even after Margaret left me, in the middle of the war, when I was too busy to write anything sustained, nevertheless I could, last thing at night, read over my notebooks and add an item or two. It gave me a kind of serenity; it was like going into a safe and quiet room.

After the cold parting with Rose I went to my own office, where George was sitting by the window smoking a pipe.

"That will be all right, barring accidents," I told him at once.

"He was extraordinarily nice to me," said George enthusiastically, as though the manner of his reception by Rose was much more important than the prosaic matter of the result.

"You'd expect him to be civil, wouldn't you?"

"He was extraordinarily nice to me, right from the minute I went in," said George, as though he had anticipated being tripped up inside the door.

I realised that George had not speculated on why Rose and I had been discussing him for so long. He was not given to meeting danger half way; he had been happy, sitting by my window, looking down into Whitehall, waiting for me to bring the news. He was happy also, later that evening, as we walked through the streets under a frigid moon, though not in the way I was. I was happy that night because it took me back through the years to the time when he and I walked the harsher streets of the provincial town, George making grandiose plans for me, his brightest protégé—to the time which seemed innocent now, before

I met Sheila, to those years in the early twenties when the world outside us seemed innocent too.

It was unlikely that George gave a thought to that past, for he was not in the least a sentimental man. No, he was happy because he enjoyed my company, my company as a middle-aged man in the here and now: because he had been received politely by an important person: because he saw work ahead on which he could stretch himself: because he was obscurely scoring against all the people who had kept him dim and unrecognised so long: and because, in the moonlit night, he saw soldiers and women pairing off in the London streets. For George, even in his forties, was one of those men who can find romantic magnificence in sex without trappings; the sight of the slit of light around the nightclub door, and he was absentminded with happiness; his feet stumped more firmly on the pavement, and he cheerfully twirled his stick.

CHAPTER XXX

SPECTATOR'S PARADISE

WE WERE busy that winter sketching out a new project, and on many nights George Passant and my secretary worked later than I did at the office and then went on to my flat to get a draft finished. At the flat they met some of my acquaintances; George, whose eyes brightened at the sight of Vera Allen, did not know what had happened to me, nor speculate much about it.

It would not have occurred to him that I was getting consolation from being a looker-on. It would have occurred to him even less that, just occasionally, when I was listening, trying to give sensible advice, there came thoughts which I had to use my whole will to shut out. In that rational, looking-on, and on the whole well-intended existence, I would suddenly have my attention drained away, by something more actual than a dream, in which a letter was on the way from Margaret, asking me to join her.

George would have believed none of that. To him I appeared quieter and more sober than I used to be, but still capable of high spirits. He assumed that I must have some secret source of satisfaction, and often, if we were left alone in the flat, he would say with an air of complacence, correct and smug:

"Well, I won't intrude on your private life."

Then he would walk happily off up the square, twiddling his stick and whistling.

On the nights she came home with us, Vera Allen used to leave when she thought George was still occupied, so that he would not have an excuse to walk with her to the bus.

He remained good-humoured and aware of her until one evening, when they arrived at the flat half an hour before me, there was a constraint between them so glaring that it was almost tactless not to refer to it. That evening it was George who left first.

When I heard his steps clumping defiantly along the pavement, I gazed with amusement at Vera. She was standing up ready to hand me papers, not showing any tiredness after the night's work, her figure neat and strong as a dancer's. It was that figure which made her seem so comely, for her face, with the features flattened and open, was not beautiful, was scarcely even pretty; yet behind the openness of her expression, there was some hint—often I had thought it illusory, but that did not matter—of hidden hopes which tempted men, which made a good many speculate on how surprising she might be in one's arms. But most men, unlike George, knew it was futile.

She was a simple, direct and modest young woman. Although she was only twenty-seven, her husband had been killed four years before. Now she was in love again, with an absolute blinkered concentration of love, so that she seemed to breathe and eat only as means to the end of having Norman to herself. They were not lovers, but she had not a second's recognition of the flesh to spare for any other man. She was—as far as I could guess about her—both passionate and chaste.

I smiled at her. She trusted me now. I asked:

"What's the matter with Mr. Passant?"

Vera's eyes, clear and unblinking, met mine: there might have been a tinge of colour on her cheeks and neck, as she considered.

"I should have thought he was a little highly strung, Mr. Eliot."

She paused, like a politician issuing a statement, and added:

"Yes, he is *on the highly strung side*. I don't think I can put it better than that."

I nearly told her I did not think she could have put it worse. Vera, although not sophisticated, was also not coy: but she had a knack of finding insipid words which satisfied herself though no one else, and then of gripping on to them as though they were so many umbrellas. Highly strung. From now on she would firmly produce that egregious phrase whenever George was mentioned. What did it mean? Amorising, importunate, randy, gallant? Something like that: I doubted if she had made a distinction, or could recognize at sight the difference between a violently sensual man like George and some of her flirtatious hangers-on. She just put them impartially aside. For a woman of her age, she was curiously innocent.

But there was one authority who did not regard her so. Soon after I had asked her about George—she would not give away any more—I let her out, and, as I was returning along the hall-passage to my room, heard an excited, insinuating voice from the next landing.

"Mr. Eliot! Mr. Eliot!"

"Yes, Mrs. Beauchamp?" I called out irritably. I could not see her, this was early in 1944, the black-out was still on, and the only light was from the blue-painted bulb in the hall.

"I must have, that is if you can spare the time of course, I must have a little private word *entre nous*."

I went up the stairs and made her out, in the spectral light, standing outside her own closed door.

"I think I must tell you, Mr. Eliot, I'm sure I shouldn't be doing my duty if I didn't."

"Don't worry too much."

"But I do worry when it's my duty, Mr. Eliot, I'm the biggest worrier I've ever met."

It was clear that I had not yet found a technique for dealing with Mrs. Beauchamp.

"You see, Mr. Eliot," she whispered triumphantly, "before you came in this evening the door of your room just happened to be open and I just happened to be going upstairs, actually I had just been doing a bit of shopping, not that I should ever think of looking in your room if I didn't hear a noise, but I thought, I know Mr. Eliot would want me to pay attention to that, I know you would, Mr. Eliot, if you'd seen what I'd seen."

"What did you see?"

"Always respect another person's privacy, Major Beauchamp used to say," she replied. "I've always done my best to live up to that, Mr. Eliot and I know you have," she added puzzlingly as though I, too, had sat under Major Beauchamp's moral guidance.

"What did you see?"

"*Ecrasez l'infame*," said Mrs. Beauchamp.

In a whisper, fat-voiced and throbbing, she broke out: "Oh, I'm sorry for that poor friend of yours, poor Mr. Passant!"

This seemed to me an absurd let-down; to imagine that George, having been turned down, was going out heart-broken into the night, was too much even for Mrs. Beauchamp.

"He'll get over it," I said.

"I'm sure I don't quite follow you," she replied virtuously.

"I mean, Mr. Passant won't worry long because a young woman doesn't feel free to have dinner with him."

Speaking to Mrs. Beauchamp I often found myself, as if hypnotized by her example, becoming more and more genteel.

"If it were only that!"

Dimly, I could perceive her hands clasped over her vast unconfined bust.

"Oh, if only it were that!" She echoed herself.

"What else could it be?"

"Mr. Eliot, I've always been afraid you'd think too well of women. A gentleman like you is always apt to, I know you do if you don't mind my saying so, you put them on a pedestal and you don't see their feet of clay. So did Major Beauchamp and I always prayed he'd never have reason to think different, because it would have killed him if he had and I hope it never will you, Mr. Eliot. That secretary of yours, I don't like to speak against someone who you are so good to, but I'm afraid I have had my eyes on her from the start."

That did not differentiate Vera sharply from any other woman who came to the house, I thought.

"Looking as though butter wouldn't melt in her mouth," said Mrs. Beauchamp with a crescendo of indignation. She added: "*Cherchez la femme!*"

"She's a friend of mine, and I know her very well."

"It takes a woman to know another woman, Mr. Eliot. When I looked into the room tonight, with the door happening to be open and hearing that poor man cry out, I saw what I expected to see."

"What in God's name was that?"

"I saw that young woman, who's so nice and quiet when she wants to be with gentlemen like you, like a ravening beast seeking for whom she may devour."

"What are you wanting to tell me?" I said. "Do you mean that Mr. Passant was trying to seduce her, or that she was encouraging him, or what?"

"Nice people talk about men seducing women," Mrs. Beauchamp remarked in an oozing, saccharine whisper. "Nice people like you, Mr. Eliot, can't believe that it's the other way round, it's not even six of one and half a dozen of the other, you should have seen what I saw when I was going up those stairs!"

"Perhaps I should."

"No, you shouldn't, I should have kept your eyes away from that open door."

"Now what was it?"

"It's only that I don't like to tell you, Mr. Eliot."

But Mrs. Beauchamp could not hold back any longer.

"Because I saw that young woman, at least I suppose she'd call herself a young woman, and even from where I was I could see that she was crammed with the lust of the eye and the pride of life, I saw her standing up with her arms above her head, and offering herself with the light full on, ready to gobble up that poor man, and he was cowering away from her, and I could see he was shocked, he was shocked to the soul. If that door hadn't been open, Mr. Eliot, I don't like to imagine what she would have been doing. As it was, it was a terrible thing for me to have to see."

I suppose she must have seen something: what the scene had actually been, I could not even guess. Just for an instant, such was the mesmerism of her gothic imagination, I found myself wondering whether she was right—which, the next day in cold blood, I knew to be about as probable as that I myself should make proposals to Mrs. Beauchamp on the landing outside her door. I could make no sense of it. It was conceivable that Vera had been slapping George's face, but though George was awkward he was not brash, he was slow moving until he was certain a woman wanted him. Anyway, they had somehow planted themselves in a moment of farce; and when I saw them in the office, Vera tweeded and discreet, George bowing his great head over the papers, I should have liked to know the answer.

Constraint or no constraint, they had to work at close quarters, for we were occupied more intensely and secretly than before on a new project. It was in fact not so much a new project, as an administrator's forecast of what was to be done if the Barford experiment succeeded. It happened to be the kind of forecast for which the collaboration of George and me might have been designed. George was

204

still out of comparison better than I was at ordering brute facts: within weeks, he had comprehended the industrial structures on which we had to calculate with an accuracy and speed that only two men I knew could have competed with, one of those two being Hector Rose. On the other hand, George lacked what I was strong in, a sense of the possible, the nose for what not to waste time thinking about. It was I who had to pick my way through conferences with Lufkin and other firms' equivalents of Lufkin.

When I had to negotiate with Lufkin, he was as reasonable as though our previous collision had never occurred. For my part I realised that I had been quite wrong in keeping him out: we should have gained three months if the first contract had gone to him. No one held it against me: it had been one of those decisions, correct on the surface, for which one gathered approval instead of blame. Yet I had not made a worse official mistake. It was clear enough now that, if the Barford project came off, we should be fools to keep Lufkin out again.

When, in the late spring, I delivered my report to Rose, he first expressed his usual mechanical enthusiasm:

"I must thank you and congratulate you, if you will allow me, my dear Lewis, I do thank you most warmly for doing this job for us."

I was so used to his flourishes, taking the meaning out of words, that I was surprised when he said, in his rarer and dryer tone:

"This looks about the best piece of work you've done here."

"I think it may be," I said.

"It really does suggest that we can see our way through the next three years without looking unnecessarily imbecile. It really does look as though we might possibly do ourselves some good."

He was meaning high praise, the plan seemed to him realistic; and that was praise from a master.

Very pleased, I replied: "I don't deserve much of the credit."

"May I enquire who does?"

"Passant has done at least sixty per cent of the job and probably nearer seventy per cent."

"My dear Lewis, that's very handsome of you, but I don't think you need indulge in quite such excessive magnanimity."

He was smiling, polite, rigid, closed.

"It's perfectly true," I said, and described what George had done. Patient as always, Rose heard me out.

"I am very much obliged to you for that interesting example of job analysis. And now, my dear chap, you must allow others the pleasure of deciding just how much credit is due to you and how much to your no doubt valuable acquisition."

Meanwhile George walked about with a chuff smile, complacent because he knew the merit of his work, complacent because he was certain it was recognised. For years he had endured being underestimated and, now that at last he was among his intellectual equals, he felt certain that he would get his due. At one time that impervious optimism had annoyed me, but now I found it touching, and I was determined to make Rose admit how good he was. For Rose, however antagonistic to George, would think it his duty to give him a fair deal.

Oblivious of all this, George went happily about, although, after his first weeks in London, he did not accompany me on reflective bachelor strolls at night. An absent-minded, unfocused look would come into his eyes as we took our after office drink and, like a sleep-walker, he would go out of the pub, leaving me to walk back to Pimlico alone.

Curiously enough, it was from Vera, wrapped in her own emotions, neither observant nor gossipy, that I received a hint. One evening in May, as she came in for the last letters of the day, she stared out of the window with what —it was quite untypical of her—looked like a simper.

"We don't seem to be seeing as much of Mr. Passant, do we?" she said.

"Haven't you?"

"Of course not," she flushed. She went on:

"Actually, there's a story going about that he has found someone who is keeping him busy."

When she told me, it sounded both true and the last thing one would have expected. For the girl who was taking up George's time was a typist in another department, virginal, obstinate, and half his age; their exchanges seemed to consist of a prolonged argument, suitable for the question-and-answers of an old-fashioned women's magazine, of whether or not he was too old for her. Even to Vera, it seemed funny that George should be so reduced; but, so the story ran, he was captivated, he was behaving as though he were the girl's age instead of his own. No one would have thought he was a sensualist; he was only eager to persuade her to marry him. I remembered how he had tried to get married once before.

"Isn't it amusing?" said Vera, with fellow-feeling, with a lick of malice. "I say good luck to him!"

I was thinking, with a spectator's impatience, that she and George would have been well matched. She might be dense, or humourless, or self-deceiving, but George would have minded less than most men, and underneath it she was as strong as he was. Instead, she had found someone who it seemed could give her nothing, which was a singular triumph for the biological instinct. Now, to cap it all, George was doing the same. Yet she was totally committed, and so perhaps was he. Speculating about them both, I felt extreme curiosity, irritation, and a touch of envy.

CHAPTER XXXI

ANNOUNCEMENT IN A NEWSPAPER

INTO my dusty bedroom, where the morning light was reflected on the back wall, Mrs. Beauchamp entered with the breakfast tray at times which tended to get later. Breakfast itself had reached an irreducible minimum, a small pot of tea and a biscuit.

"I do what I can, Mr. Eliot," said Mrs. Beauchamp, not apologetically but with soft and soothing pride.

While she stood there, as though expecting congratulations, and then paddled about on the chance of more exposures of human wickedness, I picked up the newspaper. Each morning, gripped by an addiction I could not control, like one compelled to touch every pillarbox in the street, I had to run my eye down the column of Births, searching for the name of Hollis. After Gilbert's final piece of gossip, this habit had taken hold of me long before Margaret's child could possibly be born: and, each morning I did not find the name, I felt a superstitious relief and was ready to pander to Mrs. Beauchamp.

One morning in May—we were waiting for the invasion, there was a headline on the outside of *The Times*—I was giving way to the addiction, the routine tic, scanning through the 'H's' before I opened the paper.

The name stood there. It stood there unfamiliar, as it might be in an alphabet like Russian, which I did not easily read and had to spell out. Margaret. A son.

"Anything interesting, Mr. Eliot?" came Mrs. Beauchamp's unctuous voice, as from the end of an immense room.

"Nothing special."

"There never is, is there?"

"An old friend of mine has just had a child, that's all."

"There was a time when I should have liked a little one, Mr. Eliot, if I may put it like that. But then when I saw what they grew up into, I must say I thought I'd had a blessing in disguise."

When I got rid of her, I read the notice meaninglessly time and time again, the paper still unopened. Despite my resolutions, I could not drive the thought down, the thought of seeing her. I wrote a note, in words that were no different from when I used to write to her, to say I had read the news.

I knew the wisdom of those who cut their losses: how often had I advised others so? Don't meet, don't write, don't so much as hear the name: come to terms, give your imagination to others, dismiss the one who has gone. That was what I had set myself, mainly for my own sake, perhaps with a relic of responsibility for her. It was not much help to remember it now; then at last I managed to tear the letter up.

Walking along the square, I was trying to domesticate the news. She would be very happy: even if she had not been happy without qualification before, which I did not wish to think of, this would make up for it. Maybe her children would become more important than her husband. That might have been so with me. Then as I thought of her, with detachment and almost with pleasure, the possessive anger broke through, as though my stomach had turned over and my throat stopped up. This child ought to have been mine.

I was trying to domesticate the news, to think of her gently as though we had known each other a long time before; she would be an over careful mother, each mistake she made with the child she would take to heart; she did not believe so much in original endowment as I did, she believed that children were a bit more of a blank sheet; the responsibilities would weigh on her, would probably age her—but, with children, she would not think that her life was wasted.

As I thought of her gently, the anger stayed underneath. With an attention more deliberate than before, I set myself to squeeze interest out of the people round me. It was then I really got to know the predicament of Vera and Norman. Towards the end of the summer, when the flying bombs stopped and we could talk in peace, they visited me together several times: and then Norman took to coming alone.

When I first saw them together, I thought that beside her he was insignificant. He was small, with a sallow, delicate face; he had been unfit for the Army and had stayed in his civil service job which, like Vera, he had entered at sixteen. He seemed to have nothing to say, although his expression was sensitive and fine; when I tried to lead him on, throwing out casts about books or films, I found he was as uncultivated as she. They went to dances, listened to a little music, walked in the country at week-ends; they were each earning about £400 a year, which to them meant comfort, and their lives were oddly free from outside pressure. To me, remembering the friends in my young manhood, whose origins were similar to theirs, Vera's and Norman's whole existence, interests and hopes seemed out of comparison more tame.

Even Vera, who was brimful of more emotion than she seemed to understand, was chiefly pre-occupied in Norman's company that night with the unrewarding problems of my domestic arrangements. Why should I live in such discomfort?

"It's not logical," she said.

I told her that it would not make much difference to me.

"I'm not convinced about that," she said.

I told her that it was sometimes a psychological help not to give a thought about how one lived.

Vera shook her head.

"You'd be just as independent in a proper service flat," she said.

She had missed the point, but I saw Norman looking at me.

"You want someone to run the place for you," said Vera. She added:

"Please don't think I'm saying anything against Mrs. Beauchamp. She's as kind as anyone you'll ever get, I knew that the first time I saw her. Of course, she's the motherly type."

I was thinking, Vera was as unperceptive about people as anyone I knew, when suddenly I was distracted by a smile from Norman, a smile which, loving and clear-eyed, reflected precisely the same thought. It was a smile of insight. Suddenly I took to him. I felt a sharper sympathy with him than I could with her.

I encouraged him to come and see me, although I soon knew what I was letting myself in for; most of the time it was hard work.

As I knew him better, I discovered that my impressions had been right, it was true that he had a natural understanding of others: more than that, he often made me feel that he was genuinely good. But that understanding and goodness seemed to be linked in him, as I had known them once or twice before, with a crippling infirmity. He was a neurotic; he was beset by anxiety, so that he could barely cope with his life.

Much as I liked him, honestly as I wished to do my best for him and Vera and see them happy, I found it a tax to listen to the unwindings of an anxiety neurosis, which nearly always to an outsider seemed mechanical and tedious, for hours an evening and for evenings on end. Once he was started on his 'condition', as he called it, it was a joke at my expense that I had once thought him inarticulate. Yet, if my listening was any good to him, I had to continue.

I did not know whether I was any use to him, except that anyone ready to listen and not disapprove gave him an hour or two's relief. He had been to doctors, spending a disproportionate amount of his pay for years, but now he had lost hope in them. He gained hope, though, with a neurotic's fitfulness, as I told him a few sensible platitudes: that he wasn't unique, that plenty of others—more than he thought—didn't find themselves easy to live with. I had not done much better than he had, I told him; he ought to be warned by my example, and not give way to his nature. Otherwise he would find himself living as a looker-on, self-indulgent and alone.

The better I knew him, though, the more I liked him and the less I thought of his chances. By the end of the year, when he was repeating to me the stories that I knew by heart, I was coming to believe that he was too far gone.

One night in December, not long after Norman had left me, Mrs. Beauchamp's head came ectoplasmically round the door. She had not made the instantaneous appearance with which she greeted the departure of a woman visitor; it must have been ten minutes since the door clicked to, but I was still sitting in my chair.

"You're looking tired, if you don't mind me saying so," she whispered.

I felt it: to be any support to Norman, one needed to have one's patience completely under control, to show no nerves at all.

"I'll tell you what I'm going to do," she said. "I'm going to find you just a little something to eat, which I'd invite you to have upstairs, if I had got my place quite ship-shape, which I haven't been able to."

Although I was hungry, I regarded Mrs. Beauchamp with qualified enthusiasm. These fits of good nature were spontaneous enough, and had no motive except to cheer one up—but in retrospect she admired them, realised how she had performed services right outside the contract, and so felt justified in lying in bed an hour later.

Mrs. Beauchamp returned into my room with a tin of salmon, a loaf of bread, two plates, one fork and one knife.

"If you don't mind me cleaning the cutlery after you've had a little snack," she said. "Somehow I haven't been able to manage all the washing-up."

Thus I got through my salmon, and then sat by while Mrs. Beauchamp munched hers. Despite the shiny look of enjoyment on her face she felt obliged to remark:

"Of course, it isn't the same as fresh."

Suddenly I was reminded of my mother, to whom fresh salmon was one of the emblems of the higher life which she had so proudly longed for.

"But I like to think of you having something tasty last thing at night. I hope you don't mind me saying so, but I do my best, Mr. Eliot."

She looked at me with an expression at the same time invulnerable, confident and ingratiating.

"Some do their best and *some don't*, Mr. Eliot," she whispered. "That's why it's so unfair on people like you and me, if I may say so of both of us, who really set themselves out to do their best. Do you think anyone appreciates us? Do you think so?"

Mrs. Beauchamp was becoming more excited: as she did so her expression stayed firm and impassive, but her eyes popped, and her cheeks became more shiny: her voice sank into a more insidious whisper.

I shook my head.

"When I think of the help that you try to give people—and so do I, if you don't mind me saying so, in my own

way, without pushing myself forward—when I think of the
help we give, and then what certain persons *do*! Sometimes
I wonder if you ever let yourself realise what those people
do, Mr. Eliot."

She went on whispering:

"I scarcely dare think of it."

Her voice became still more hushed:

"If we looked out of that window, Mr. Eliot, we could
see the windows on the other side of the Square. Have
you ever thought what we should see *if we pulled the blinds*?
It's terrible to think of. Sometimes I fancy what it would
be like if I became invisible, like the man in the film, and
had to go and stand in all the rooms in the Square, one
after another, so that I should be there in the corner and
couldn't help seeing what people do."

Mrs. Beauchamp, day-dreaming of a voyeuse's paradise,
seeping herself into invisibility, sat enormous in her pink
satin, cheeks flaming and eyes dense.

"If I had to watch all that, Mr. Eliot," she said, "I
doubt if I should ever be the same again."

I said that I was sure she would not be.

"Rather than do what some people do," she said, "I'd
stay as I am for ever with my own little place upstairs,
looking after myself as well as I can, and doing my best
for my tenants and friends, if you don't mind me calling
you that, Mr. Eliot. People may laugh at me for doing my
best, but they needn't think I mind. Some of them don't
like me, you don't have to pretend, Mr. Eliot, I'm not such
a softy as I look and I tell you they don't like me. And
I don't mind that either. If a person does her best it doesn't
matter what people think of her. I expect they believe I'm
lonely. But I am happier than they are, Mr. Eliot, and
they know it. No one's ever said—there's poor old Mrs.
Beauchamp, she wants someone to look after her, she's
not fit to live by herself."

It was quite true. No one had thought of her so.

"I shouldn't be very pleased if anyone did say that," Mrs. Beauchamp remarked in a whisper, but with ferocity. Then affable, glutinous again, she said:

"What I say is, the important thing is to grow old with dignity. I know you will agree with me, Mr. Eliot. Of course, when I come to the evening of my life, and I don't regard myself as quite there yet, if some decent good man had the idea that he and I might possibly join forces, then I don't say I should turn down the proposition without thinking it over very, very seriously."

CHAPTER XXXII

OUTSIDE THE HOUSE

ON an evening in May, just after the German war had ended, Betty Vane called on me. I had seen little of her during the spring: once or twice she had rung up, but I had been busy with Vera or Norman or some other acquaintance; Betty, always ready to believe she was not wanted, had been put off. Yet she was one of the people I liked best and trusted most, and that evening when she came in, bustling and quick-footed, I told her that I had missed her.

"You've got enough on your hands without me," she said.

It sounded ungracious. She had never been able to produce the easy word. She was looking at me, her eyes uncomfortable in her beaky face.

She said curtly:

"Can you lend me fifty pounds?"

I was surprised, for a moment—because previously when she was hard-up I had pressed money on her and she would not take it. She was extravagant, whenever she had money she splashed it round: she was constantly harassed about it, she lived in a clutter of card debts, bills, pawnshops, bailiffs. Hers was, however, the poverty of someone used to being dunned for a hundred pounds when behind her there were trusts of thousands. She had invariably refused to borrow from me, or from anyone who had to earn his money. Why was she doing so now? Suddenly I realised. Bad at easy words, bad at taking favours, she was trying to repay what I had just told her: this was her way of saying that she in turn trusted me.

As she put my cheque into her bag, she said in the same curt, forbidding tone:

"Now you can give me some advice."

"What is it?"

"It involves someone else."

"You ought to know by now that I can keep quiet," I said.

"Yes, I know that."

She went on awkwardly:

"Well, a man seems to be getting fond of me."

"Who is he?"

"I can't tell you." She would say nothing about him, except that he was about my own age. Her explanation became so constrained as to be almost unintelligible—but now she was speaking of this man 'liking her', of how he wanted to 'settle down' with her. Every time she had confided in me before, it had been the other way round.

"What shall I do?" she asked me.

"Do I know him?"

"I can't tell you anything about him," she replied.

"You're not giving me much to go on," I told her.

"I'd like to tell you the whole story, but I can't," she said, with the air of a little girl put on her honour.

I was thinking, a good many men were frightened of her, she was so sharp-eyed and suspicious, her self-distrust making her seem distrustful of others. But when she let herself depend on anyone her faith was blind.

"Do you love him?" I asked her.

Without hesitation, straight and confiding, she replied: "No."

"Do you respect him?" For her, no relation would be tolerable without it. This time she hesitated. At last she said: "I think so."

She added:

"He's a curious man."

I looked at her. She smiled back, a little resentfully.

"On the face of it," I said, "I can't possibly say go ahead, can I? But you know more than I do."

"I've not been exactly successful so far."

"I just don't see what the advantages are. For you, I mean."

For the first time that evening she gazed at me with affection.

"We're all getting on, you know. You're nearly forty, and don't you forget it. I was thirty-seven this March."

"I don't think that's a good reason."

"We haven't all got your patience."

"I still don't think it's a good reason for you."

She gave a cracking curse.

"I haven't got all that to look forward to," she said.

She was so unsure of herself that she had to break in, before I could reply:

"Let's skip it. Let's go to a party."

A common acquaintance had invited her, she wanted to take me. In the taxi, on the way to Chelsea, she was smiling with affection, the awkwardness had gone, the resented confidence; we might have just met, I might have been giving her a lift to a party, each of us pleasurably wondering whether anything would come of it. After all the years she had gone to parties, she still had the flush, the bright eye, the excited hope that something, someone, might turn up.

As soon as we arrived at the studio, I saw a man I knew; pushing into the corner of the room, he and I stood outside the crowd and he told me about a new book. While I was listening, I caught a voice from the window-seat behind us. From the first words, I recognised it. It was R. S. Robinson's.

He was sitting with his back to me, his beautiful hair shining silver, his neck red. Listening to him was a woman of perhaps thirty, who looked intelligent, amiable and plain. It was soon clear that she had recently published a novel.

"I have to go back a long way to find a writer who opens the window of experience to me as you do," he was saying. "Not that you do it all the time. Sometimes you're rather tantalising, I must tell you. Sometimes you give me the sensation that you are opening a window but not running up the blinds. But at your best, in those first thirty pages—I have to go back a long way. Who do you think I have to go back to?"

"You're making too much of it," came the woman's voice, abashed, well-bred.

"I have to go back a long way." Robinson was speaking with his old authority, with the slightly hectoring note of one whose flattery is rejected and who has to double it: "Beyond my dear Joyce—I'm not telling you that your achievement is equal to his, but I do say your vision is nearer to the springs of life. I have to go back beyond him. And beyond poor old Henry James. Certainly beyond George Eliot. They can say what they like, but she was heavy as porridge most of the time, and porridgy writers have to be much greater than she was. Those first pages of yours aren't porridgy at all, they're like one's first taste of first-class *pâté*. I have to go back a bit beyond her, why I don't mind going back to—you won't guess who——"

"Do tell me."

"Mrs. Henry Wood."

Even then, flattering her for his own purposes, he could not resist that piece of diablerie, that elaborate let-down. She sounded a modest woman, but there was disappointment and mild protest in her voice: "But she was nothing like so good as George Eliot."

Robinson rapidly recovered himself.

"George Eliot had all the talent in the world, and not a particle of genius. Mrs. Henry Wood had very little talent and just a tiny vestige of the real blessed thing. That's what people ought to have said about you, and believe me it's the most important thing that can be said about any writer. I should like to have the responsibility of making them say it about you. Does anyone realise it?"

"No one's ever told me."

"I always say it takes an *entrepreneur* with a bit of his own genius to recognise a writer who has it too. That's why it's a providential occasion, you and I meeting here tonight. I should like to put over another piece of the real thing before I die. I'm absolutely sure I could do it for you."

"What firm is yours, Mr. Robinson?"

Robinson laughed.

"At present I can't be said to have a firm. I shall have to revive the one I used to have. Haven't you heard of R. S. Robinson?"

She looked embarrassed.

"Oh dear," he said, with one of his bursts of hilarious honesty, "if you'd been at a party like this twenty-five years ago and hadn't heard of me, I should have left you and gone to find someone interesting. But you will hear of R. S. Robinson's again. We're going to do things together, you and I. I assure you, we're bound to put each other on the map."

Then I tapped him on the arm. He looked up to see who I was. With complete good humour he cried:

"Why, it's Lewis Eliot! Good evening to you, sir!"

I smiled at the young woman, but Robinson, sparkling with cunning, did not intend me to talk to her. Instead, he faced into the room, and said, either full of hilarity or putting on a splendid show of it:

"Is this a fair sample of the post-war spirit, should you say?"

I broke in:

"It's a long time since I met you last."

Robinson was certain that I was threatening his latest plan, but he was not out-faced. He had not altered since the morning I recovered Sheila's money; his suit was shabby and frayed at the cuffs, but so were many prosperous men's after six years of war. He said to the young woman, with candour, with indomitable dignity:

"Mr. Eliot was interested in my publishing scheme a few years ago. I'm sorry to say that nothing came of it then."

"What have you been doing since?" I asked.

"Nothing much, sir, nothing very much."

"What did you do in the war?"

"*Nothing at all.*" He was gleeful. He added:

"You're thinking that I was too old for them to get me. Of course I was, they couldn't have touched me. But I decided to offer my services, so I got a job in—(he gave me the name of an aircraft firm)—and they subsidised me for four years and *I did nothing at all.*"

The young woman was laughing: he took so much delight in having no conscience that she also felt delight. Just as Sheila used to.

"How did you spend your time?" she asked.

"I discovered how to be a *slow clerk*. Believe me, no one's applied real intelligence to the problem before. By the time I left, I could spin a reasonable hour's work out into at least two days. And that gave me time for serious things, that is, thinking out the programme you and I were talking about before Mr. Eliot joined us."

He grinned at me with malicious high spirits, superiority and contempt.

"I suppose you've been doing your best for your country, sir?" Just as I remembered him, he felt a match for any man alive.

I enquired:

"Have you got a job now?"

"Certainly not," said Robinson.

I wondered if, with his bizarre frugality, he had saved money out of his wages at the factory. Then I spoke across him to his companion:

"I don't think we've been introduced, have we?"

Soon after I heard her name I left them, to Robinson's surprise and relief. I left them with Robinson's triumphant "Good evening to you, sir" fluting across the room, and muttered to Betty that I was slipping away. Alone in that room, she knew that something had gone wrong for me; disappointed after the promise of the early evening, she could read in my face some inexplicable distress.

"I'm sorry," she whispered.

She was right. I had been upset by the sound of the young woman's name. As soon as I heard it, I knew she was a cousin of Charles March's. She was likely, therefore, to be a woman of means, and in fact Robinson would not be pouring flattery over her if she were not. But that did not matter; it would be easy to pass word to Charles about Robinson; it was not for her sake that I left the party, went out into Glebe Place, turned down towards the Embankment, and, without realising it, towards the house I had lived in years before. I was not driven so because of anything that happened at that party; no, it was because, for the first time for years, my grief over Sheila had come back, as grinding as when, after her death, I went into our empty room.

At the first murmur of Robinson's voice, I had felt a presentiment; listening to what otherwise might have amused me, I had been rigid, nails against my palms, but still impervious, until, when I asked the young woman her name, the reply set loose a flood of the past. Yet I had only heard that name before in circumstances entirely undramatic, having nothing to do with Sheila or her death: perhaps Charles March had mentioned it in the days we saw each other most often, before either of us had married, walking about in London or at his father's country-house. That was all; but the flood that name set loose drove me down the dark turning of Cheyne Row towards the river.

Down Cheyne Row the windows were shining, from the

pub at the Embankment corner voices hallooed; I was beset as though I were still married and was going through the back streets on my way home.

I was not seeing, nor even remembering: it was not her death that was possessing me: it was just that, walking quickly beside the bright houses, their windows open to the hot evening breeze, I had nothing but a sense of failure, loss, misery. The year before, when I received bad news, fresher and more sharply wounding, the news of Margaret's child, I could put a face on it, and make myself shove the sadness away. Now this older sadness overcame me: my stoicism would not answer me. I felt as I had not done since I was eight years old, tears on my cheeks.

Soon I was standing outside the house, which, since I left it in the spring after Sheila died, I had not been near, which I had made détours not to see. Yet the sight dulled my pain, instead of sharpening it. One outer wall had been blasted down, so that, where Mrs. Wilson used to have her sitting-room, willowherb was growing, and on the first floor a bath jutted nakedly against the cloud-dark sky. The light from an Embankment lamp fell on the garden-path, where grass had burst between the flags.

Gazing up at the house, I saw the windows boarded up. Among them I could pick out those of our bedroom and the room next door. In that room Sheila's body had lain. The thought scarcely touched me, I just looked up at the boards, without much feeling, sad but with a kind of hypnotised relief.

I did not stay there long. Slowly, under the plane trees, past the unpainted and sunblistered houses, I walked along the Embankment to my flat. The botanical gardens were odorous in the humid wind, and on the bridge the collar of lights was shivering. Once the thought struck me: had I come home? Was it the same home, from which I had not been able to escape? The lonely flat—how different was it from the house I had just stood outside?

CHAPTER XXXIII

PATHOLOGY OF SPECTATORS

DURING the rest of that year, I was on the edge of two dramas. The first was secret, known only by a handful of us, and was going to overshadow much of our lives; it was the result of those meetings of old Bevill's early in the war, of the intrigues of Lufkin and the science of men like my brother; it was the making of the atomic bomb. The second was public, open each morning for a week to anyone who read newspapers, and important to not more than half a dozen people of whom, although I did not fully realise it till later, I was one.

Innocent, tossed about by blind chance, Norman Lacey, and through him Vera, lost their privacy that autumn— for Norman's father was tried at the Old Bailey. If he was guilty, the crime was a squalid one; but the after-effects of the trial ravaged those two, so that for a time I thought that Norman at least would not recover. What they went through, how she was strong enough to carry them both, was a story by itself—but for me, the lesson was how poorly I myself behaved.

Norman and Vera asked help from me, help which would be embarrassing, and possibly a little damaging, for me to give. They looked to me to go into court with a piece of evidence which could do neither them, nor Norman's father, any practical good, and might do me some practical harm. It was evidence so trivial that no lawyer would have subpœnaed me to give it. All it did in effect was to show that I knew them well; clutching at any hope, they had a sort of faith that my name might protect them.

It was the kind of demand which, had it come from an acquaintance, I should have evaded with a clear conscience. I had taken some responsibility for these two; they thought I had given them intimacy, could I just shut it off when otherwise I had to accept the consequences?

As soon as I had smelt the danger ahead of them, I had wanted excuses to absent myself. It was a dilemma I did not like, any more than I liked my own feelings. I did what I had not done for years, and asked advice. I did not want worldly advice; I longed for Margaret's; indeed, one night I read through the Hollises in the London directory, wondering whether they might have returned to the town, knowing that I had a true reason for writing to her, knowing also that it was a pretext. At last I went with my trouble to George Passant.

A few months past, the young woman he had been pursuing with such adolescent ardour had closed their years of argument and gone back home. She had refused to marry him; she had refused to sleep with him; and George, comically frustrated for a man of passion, seemed to an observer to have got nothing out of it. But that was not what he thought. "It's been a magnificent affair!" he cried, as though his gusto had mysteriously slipped into the wrong groove. As he grew older, he seemed to luxuriate more and more in his own oddity.

Nevertheless when on an autumn night we went into the Tothill Street pub and I confessed the story, he was surprisingly prosaic.

"It would be absolutely ridiculous for you to take the slightest risk," he said.

I had told him my relations with Vera and Norman as accurately as I could. I had also told him of the police investigations, which I could confide to no one else: with George, however uproarious his own life was being, any secret was safe.

As he listened to me, he looked concerned. It occurred to me that he took pride in my public reputation. He did not like to see me rushing into self-injury as he might have done himself: he had always had a streak of unpredictable prudence: that evening, he was speaking as sensibly as Hector Rose.

"If you could make any effective difference to the old man's (Lacey's) chance of getting off, then we might have to think again," said George, "though I warn you I should be prepared to make a case against that too. But that question doesn't arise, and there is obviously only one reasonable course of action."

George ordered pints of beer, facing me with his aggressive optimism, as though the sane must triumph.

"I'm not so sure," I said.

"Then you're even more incapable of reason than I ever suspected."

"They'll feel deserted," I said. "Especially the young man. It may do him a certain amount of harm."

"I'm afraid," said George, "I can't take into account every personal consequence of every action. Particularly as the poor chap's going to have such harm done him anyway that I can't believe your demonstrating a little common sense would matter a button in the general catastrophe."

"There's something in that," I replied.

"I'm glad you're showing signs of recognition."

"But I took them both up," I said. "It's not so good to amuse myself with them when they're not asking anything —and then not to stand by them now."

"I can't admit that they've got the slightest claim on you." George's voice rose to an angry shout. He pulled down his waistcoat and, his tone still simmering, addressed me with a curious formality.

"It's some considerable time since I have spoken to you on these matters. I should like to make it clear that everyone who has had your friendship has had the best of the bargain. I am restricting myself to talking of your friendships, I had better emphasise that. With some of your women, I couldn't give you such a testimonial. So far as I can make out, you treated Margaret Davidson badly and stupidly. I shouldn't be surprised if the same weren't true of Betty Vane and others. I expect you ought to reproach yourself over some of those."

I was thinking, George was not so inattentive as he seemed.

"But I don't admit that anyone alive has any right to reproach you about your friendships. I should like to see anyone contradict me on that point," said George, still sounding angry, as though he were making a furious debating speech. But his face was open and heavy with affection. "I can work it out, I might remind you that I can work it out as well as anyone in London, exactly what you've given to those two. You've been available to them whenever they've wanted you, haven't you?"

"Yes."

"You've never protected yourself, have you? You've let them come to you when you've been tired and ill?"

"Sometimes."

"You've let them take precedence over things you enjoy. You've kept away from smart parties because of them, I should be surprised very much if you haven't."

I smiled to myself. Even now, George kept a glittering image of 'smart parties' and of the allure they must have for me. Yet he was exerting his whole force, he was speaking with a thumping sweetness.

"I know what you've given them. A good many of us can tell from personal experience, and don't forget my experience of you goes back further than the others. Sometimes I've thought that you haven't the faintest idea of how people appreciate what you've done for them. I should like to inform you that you are known to be a preposterously unselfish friend. I have the best of reasons for knowing it."

George was a human brother. He fought with his brother men, he never wanted to be above the battle. He did not understand the temptation, so insidious, often so satisfying to men like me, of playing God: of giving so much and no more: of being considerate, sometimes kind, but making that considerateness into a curtain with which to shut off the secret self I could not bear to give away. Some of what he said was true: but that was because, in most of the outward shows of temperament, what one loses on the swings one gains on the roundabouts. Because I had been so tempted to make myself into a looker-on, I asked little of those I was with. I was good-natured, sometimes at a cost to myself, though not at a fundamental cost. I had become unusually patient. I was fairly tolerant by temperament, and the curve of my own experience made me more so. Judged by the ordinary human standards, I was interested and reliable. All that, I had gained—it was what George saw, and it not quite negligible—by non-participation. But what was George did not see was that I was being left with a vacuum inside me instead of a brother's heart.

In the end, I gave the evidence. I tried to accept my responsibility to Vera and Norman as though I felt it. So far as the gossip reached me, I did not lose much; although I did not recognise it for months to come, I gained something.

That winter, sitting alone in my room, I thought often of myself as I had done on the night of Munich; but I had learned more of myself now, and disliked it more. I could not help seeing what had gone wrong with me and Margaret, and where the profound fault lay. It could have seemed the legacy that Sheila had left me: that was an excuse; the truth was meaner, deeper, and without any gloss at all. It was the truth that showed itself in my escape into looking-on. I knew now how much there was wrong with those who became spectators. Mr. Knight was a spectator of the world of affairs, because he was too proud and diffident to match himself against other men: and I could see how his pride-and-diffidence was as petty as vanity, he would not match himself because they might see him fail. Superficially, unlike Mr. Knight, I was not vain: but in my heart, in my deepest relations, it was the same with me.

There was another comparison distinctly less congenial. There was someone else who looked on, and felt lifted above ordinary mortals as she did so. Mrs. Beauchamp—yes, we had something in common. Yes, Mr. Knight and she and I were members of the same family.

Lonely in that first winter of peace, I thought of how joyful Margaret and I had been at first, and how towards the end I had gone to her, the taxi racketing in the steely light, guilt beating on me like rain upon the window. I could understand more of it now. First I had tried to make her into a dream image, a kind of anti-Sheila: then I had transformed her into Sheila come again: I had been afraid to see her as she was, just herself, someone whose spirit was as strong as mine.

Although I did not know it, I was gaining something.

Just as, when Margaret at last admitted defeat about our relation, I had seen in her a secret planner devising (almost unknown to herself) a way out—so now, myself defeated, disliking what I had come to, the secret planner began to work in me.

Often, when a branch of one's life has withered, it is others who first see the sap rise again. One is unconscious of a new start until it is already made: or sometimes, in the same instant, one knows and does-not-know. Perhaps when, believing myself pre-occupied over Vera and Norman, I furled through the telephone directory for Margaret's address, I was already committing myself to a plan which might re-shape my life; perhaps, months earlier, when I stood outside the house of my first marriage and thought I had no hope of any other home, hope was being born.

Perhaps I knew and did-not-know. But, in fact, the first signs of the secret planner which I observed, as though I were watching an intruder and a somewhat tiresome one, were a little absurd. For all of a sudden I became discontented with my flat at Mrs. Beauchamp's. Instead of being able to put up with anything, I could scarcely wait to make a change. Restlessly, quite unlike myself, I called on agents, inspected half a dozen flats in an afternoon, and took one before night. It was on the north side of Hyde Park, just past Albion Gate, and too large for me, with three bedrooms and two sitting-rooms, but I told myself that I liked the view over the seething trees, over the Bayswater Road, along which I used to walk on my way to Margaret.

That night, for the first time, I was in search of Mrs. Beauchamp and not she of me. I rapped on her door, rattled the letter-box, called her name, but, although I did not believe that she was out, got no reply. So I left a note and, feeling that her technique was well-proved and that I might pay her a last compliment by copying it, sat with the door open listening for her steps. Even then I did not hear her until the scuffle of her slippers was just outside my door.

"Mr. Eliot, I found your little letter saying that you wanted to speak to me," she whispered.

I asked if she had been out, knowing for certain that she could not have been.

"As a matter of fact, I haven't, Mr. Eliot," she said. "To tell you the honest truth, I've been getting so worried about the catering that I just can't sleep until daylight, and so I have been allowing myself a little doze before I have to set about my bit of an evening meal."

Whatever she had been doing, I believed it was not that. Her expression was confident, impenetrable, wide-awake.

'Catering' meant getting my morning tea, and her remark was a first move towards stopping it.

"I'm sorry to drag you down," I said.

"It's part of my duty," she replied.

"I thought I ought to tell you at once," I said, "that I shall have to leave you soon."

"I'm very sorry to hear you say that, Mr. Eliot." She gazed at me with a firm glance, disapproving, almost inimical, but also a little pitying.

"I shall be sorry to go."

I said it as a civility: oddly, Mrs. Beauchamp compelled civility, it was impossible to suggest to her what I thought of her and her house.

"I shall be sorry to go," I repeated. Then I felt a pang of genuine, ridiculous, irrational regret.

"No one has to live where they don't want to, Mr. Eliot."

Her expression showed no diminution of confidence. If I felt a pang of sadness, she had never appeared less sad. Others might find any parting a little death, but not Mrs. Beauchamp.

"If you don't mind me asking, after the little talks we've had when you've been lonely and I was trying to cheer you up," her tone was soft as ever, perhaps a shade less smooth, "but if you don't mind me asking, I was wondering if you intended to get married again?"

"I haven't been thinking of it."

"Well then, that's something, and, without pushing in where I'm not welcome, that's the wisest thing you've said tonight or for many a long night, Mr. Eliot. And I hope you'll remember me if any woman ever gets you in her clutches and you can't see a glimpse of the open door. *Never notice their tears*, Mr. Eliot."

After that exhortation, Mrs. Beauchamp said briskly: "Perhaps we ought to have a little chat about the catering,

Mr. Eliot, because you'll be here another two or three weeks, I suppose."

Most people, on being given notice, served their time out with a good grace, I was thinking: in fact, they were more obliging in that last fortnight than ever before. But Mrs. Beauchamp's was a tough nature. She had decided that making my morning tea was too much for her; the fact that I was leaving soon did not weaken her. In a good-natured whisper she told me that I should get a nice breakfast, much nicer than she had been able to do for me, over in Dolphin Square. She looked at me with a sly, unctuous smile.

"Well, Mr. Eliot, I'm sure you'll live at better addresses than this, if I may say so. But, though I suppose I'm not the right person to tell you and it doesn't come too well from me, I just can't help putting it to you, that a lot of water will have to flow under the bridges, before you find a place where you'll be as much at home."

CHAPTER XXXIV

CONFIDENTIAL OFFER IN REVERSE

WHEN I decided to take up again with Gilbert Cooke, I knew what I was doing. Or at least I thought I did. I had left open no other line of communication with Margaret; he would have news of her; I had to hear it. Beyond that, my foresight was cut off.

So I telephoned to his new office late on a May afternoon. Was he free that night? His voice was stiff. No, he was not certain. Yes, he could find time for a quick meal. Soon we were walking together across the Park; under the petrol-smell of a London summer there was another, mixed from the grass and the wall-flowers, sharpened by the rain. It brought back walking in London as a student, the smell of the Park promising and denying, taunting to a young man still chaste.

Massive beside me, his light feet scuffing the ground, Gilbert was saying little: unless I asked a question, his lips were squashed together under the beaky nose. I had forgotten that he was proud. He was not prepared to be dropped and then welcomed back. I had forgotten also that he was subtle and suspicious.

He did not believe that I suddenly wanted him for his own sake. He guessed that I was after something, perhaps he had an inkling of what it was. He was determined not to let me have it.

Yet he could not resist letting me know that he still had his ear to the ground. As we climbed the Duke of York's Steps he said, out of the blue:

"How's the new flat?"

Q   233

I said—irked that he could still surprise me—all right.

"Is it going to work?"

"I think so."

"It'll be all right if the old lady gets better or worse. Because if she gets worse the agents will have to put someone else in. But it's going to be fatal if she stays moderately ill."

His information was accurate. Mine was one of four service flats, looked after by a manageress; within the last fortnight, she had gone to bed with a heart-attack.

"It's pretty adequate," I said, as though apologising for myself.

"I don't know about that," said Gilbert.

Like other apolaustic men, he had the knack of making one's living arrangements sound pitiful. I felt obliged to defend mine.

"It's *better* anyway," Gilbert conceded. "I grant you that, it's better."

Although he had dropped into speaking of my physical comforts with his old concern, he would not volunteer a word about any common friends, anyone I might be interested in, let alone Margaret. The May night, the petrol-smell, the aphrodisiac smell: as we walked he talked more, but it was putting-off, impersonal talk, deliberately opaque.

As I watched him, stretched out in a leather armchair at my club, just as he had been the night he offered to stand down over Margaret, his body was relaxed but his eyes shone, unsoftened, revengeful. There was nothing for me but to be patient. I set myself to speak as easily as when he was working for me. How was he? What was happening to him? What was he planning for his future? He did not mind answering. It gave him a pleasure edged with malice to go on elaborating about his future, knowing that I was getting nowhere near my object. But also, I thought, he was in a difficulty and glad of an opinion. Now that the

234

war was over, he could not settle what to do. Perhaps the civil service would keep him; but, if he had the choice, he would prefer to return to Lufkin.

"The trouble is," said Gilbert, "I don't believe for a second he'll have me."

"Why shouldn't he?"

"What about the bit of fun-and-games when I slipped one under his ribs?"

"It was fair enough."

"Paul Lufkin has his own idea on what's fair. Opposing him isn't included."

"I got in his way as much as you did," I said, "and I'm on definitely good terms with him now."

"What's that in aid of?" said Gilbert. He added:

"The old thug will never have me back. I wish to God he would."

"Why do you want to go back so much?"

He said something about money, he said that he might be marrying at last. At that moment he was speaking cordially, even intimately, his face flushed in the clubroom half-light; I believed that the mention of marriage was not a blind, I even wondered (he kept all clues from me) who the woman might be.

I said: "As I told you a minute ago, I get on well with Paul Lufkin nowadays. Better than I used to, if it comes to that. Will you let me feel out the ground about you?"

"Why should you?" His glance was suspicious, and at the same time hopeful.

"Why not?"

He cupped his hands round the tankard on the table.

"Well," he said, with a hesitating, unwilling pleasure, "if it's not too much of an infliction, I should be damned relieved if you would."

The room, not yet lit up, was cool as a church in the summer evening, but Gilbert glowed in his chair: other men had gone up to dinner and we were left alone. He glowed, he swallowed another pint of beer, in the chilly room he seemed to be exuding warmth; but that was all he gave out. Although he had accepted my offer, he was returning nothing.

I was thinking: I should have to play his game, and bring in her name myself. It meant a bit of humiliation, but that did not matter; what did matter was that he would see too much. It was a risk I ought not to take. As I bought myself a drink, I asked:

"By the way, have you seen Margaret lately?"

"Now and again."

"How is she?"

"Is there anything wrong with her?" His eyes were sparkling.

"How should I know?" I replied evenly.

"Isn't she much as you'd expect?"

"I've quite lost touch."

"Oh." He was briskly conversational. "Of course, I've kept my eye on all of them, I suppose I see them once every two months, or something like that." He was spinning it out. He told me, what I knew from the newspapers, that Margaret's mother had died a year before. He went on to say, with an air of enthusiasm and good-fellowship:

"Of course, I've seen quite a lot of Helen and her husband. You did meet him, didn't you? He's a decent bird——"

"Yes, I met him," I said. "When did you see Margaret last?"

"It can't have been very long ago."

"How was she?"

"I didn't notice much change."

"Was the child all right?"

"I think so."

I broke out:

"Is she happy?"

"Why shouldn't she be?" Gilbert asked affably. "I should have thought she had done as well as most of us. Of course you can't tell, can you, unless you've known someone better than I ever did Margaret?"

He knew, of course, how my question had been wrung out of me. He had been waiting for something like it: I might as well have confided straight out that I still loved her. But he was refusing to help. His mouth was smiling obstinately and his eyes, merry and malicious, taunted me.

CHAPTER XXXV

SIMPLE QUESTION ON TOP OF A BUS

I HAD to honour my offer to Gilbert, and I arranged to call on Paul Lufkin. When I arrived at the Millbank office, where in the past he had kept me waiting so many stretches of hours and from which I used to walk home to Sheila, he was hearty. He was so hearty that I felt the curious embarrassment which comes from the spectacle of an austere man behaving out of character.

Some of his retinue were waiting in the ante-room but I was swept in out of turn, and Lufkin actually slapped me on the back (he disliked physical contact with other males) and pushed out the distinguished visitors' chair. Now that I was, in his eyes, an independent success, a power in my own right though still minor compared to him, he gave me the appropriate treatment. The interesting thing was, he also truly liked me more.

He said: "Well, old chap, sit down and make yourself comfortable."

He was sitting at his own desk, showing less effects of the last years than any of us, his handsome skull face un-ravaged, his figure still as bony as an adolescent's.

"Believe it or not," he went on, "I was thinking of asking you to come to one of my little dinner parties.

"We must fix it," he said, still acting his impersonation of heartiness. "We've had some pretty jolly parties in our time, haven't we?"

I responded.

"There's a secret I was going to tell you. But now you've given me the pleasure of a visit"—said Lufkin with an entirely unfamiliar politeness—"I needn't wait, I may as well tell you now."

I realised that he was delighted to have me sitting there. He wanted someone to talk to.

"As a matter of fact," he said, "these people want to send me to the Lords."

'These people' were the first post-war labour government, and at first hearing it sounded odd that they should want to give Lufkin a peerage. But although he was one of the most eminent industrialists of his day, he had, with his usual long-sightedness, kept a foot in the other camp. He had never been inside the orthodox conservative party: he had deliberately put some bets on the other side, and since 1940 that policy had been paying off.

In private his politics were the collectivist politics of a supreme manager, superimposed on—and to everyone but himself irreconcilable with—a basis of old-fashioned liberalism.

"Shall you go?"

"I don't see any good reason for turning them down. To tell you the honest truth, I think I should rather like it."

"Your colleagues won't."

I meant what he must have thought of, that his fellow-bosses would regard him as a traitor for taking honours from the enemy.

"Oh, that will be a nine days' wonder. If I'm useful to them, they'll still want me. And the minute I'm not useful they'll kick me, whether I've got a coronet or not."

He gave a savage, creaking chuckle.

"Most of them would give their eyes for one, anyway. The main advantage about these tinpot honours—which I still think it's time we got rid of—" he put in, getting it both ways, as so often, "isn't the pleasure they cause to the chaps who get them: it's the pain they cause to the chaps who don't."

He was very happy, and I congratulated him. I was pleased: he was as able in his own line as anyone I knew, in the world's eye he had gone the furthest, and I had an inexplicable liking for him.

I enquired what title he would choose.

"Yes, that's the rub," said Lufkin.

"Haven't you settled it?"

"I suppose it will have to be the Baron Lufkin of somewhere or other. Lord Lufkin. It's a damned awful name, but I don't see how I can hide it. It might be different if I believed in all this flummery. It would have been rather fun to have a decent-sounding name."

"Now's your chance," I teased him, but he snapped:

"No. We're too late for that. It's no use rich merchants putting on fancy dress. It's damned well got to be Lord Lufkin."

He had the shamefaced, almost lubricious, grin of a man caught in a bout of day-dreaming. He had been writing down names on his blotter: Bury St. Edmunds was his birthplace, how would Lord St. Edmunds look? Thurlow, Belchamp, Lavenham, Cavendish, Clare, the villages he knew as a boy: with his submerged romanticism, he wanted to take a title from them. He read them out to me.

"Pretty names," he said, inarticulate as ever. That was all the indication he could emit that they were his Tansonville, his Méséglise, his Combray.

"Why not have one?" Just for once I wanted him to indulge himself.

"It's out of the question," he said bleakly.

I thought he was in a good mood for my mission. I said I had a favour to ask him.

"Go ahead."

"I should like to talk to you about Gilbert Cooke."

"I shouldn't." Instantaneously the gracious manner—finger-tips together, Lufkin obliging a friend—had broken up. All at once he was gritty with anger.

As though not noticing him, I tried to put my case: Cooke had done well in the civil service, he was highly thought of by Hector Rose and the rest——

"I don't think we need waste much time on this," Lufkin interrupted. "You mean, you're asking me to give Cooke his job back?"

"I wanted you to hear——"

"That's what it boils down to, isn't it?"

I nodded.

"Well, my answer is short and simple. I wouldn't pay Cooke in washers."

It was no use. Implacable, tied up in his anger, as rude as I had seen him, he cut me short.

When I reported the answer to Gilbert, he said:

"That's burnt it." His face flushed, he went on:

"I never ought to have let him get the smallest blasted bleat from my direction, I never ought to have let you go near the man. There it is!

"Well," he said defiantly, "I'd better make sure that the chaps here want me. I've always said that in business you've either got to be a tycoon or a born slave, and damn it, I'm not either. I once told P.L. that."

"What did he say?"

"Offered me a three-year contract."

On his disappointment Gilbert put a dashing face; when he turned it towards me it was still pursed with comradely malignance. I fancied that, whether I brought him good news or bad from Lufkin, he would not have relented. He had so often relished letting slip a piece of gossip, but he was relishing even more holding on to one.

Before I could search for another link with Margaret there happened what at the time seemed a wild coincidence, a thousands-to-one-against chance. One Saturday morning, thinking nothing of it, I was rung up by old Bevill, who, after a period of what he himself described as 'the wilderness', had returned to Whitehall as chairman of the atomic energy project. He was just off to the country for the weekend, he said: he had a 'little job' he wanted to 'unload' on to me: would I mind going with him as far as Charing Cross?

In the circumstances, I thought he might have risen to a taxi: but no, Bevill stood at the bus stop, briefcase in hand, bowler hat on head, getting a modest pleasure out of his unpretentiousness. At last we mounted a bus, the top deck of which was empty, so that Bevill, instead of waiting until the platform at Charing Cross, was able to confide.

"I'm being chased, Lewis," he said, looking over his shoulder to make sure no one was coming up, and somehow giving the impression that he was really on the run.

"Who by?"

"People who always know better than anyone else," the old man replied. "I don't know about you, Lewis, but I don't like people who're always positive you're wrong and they're right. Particularly intellectuals, as I believe they're called nowadays, or else have the impertinence to call themselves. The nigger in the woodpile is, they can make a hell of a lot of noise."

"What do they want?"

"Do you remember that fellow Sawbridge?" The question was rhetorical; old Bevill, my brother and the Barford scientists, Hector Rose and I were not likely to forget Sawbridge, who had not long since been sent to jail for espionage.

The bus in front of us disappeared out of Whitehall with a swishing scarlet flash: we were stopped at the traffic lights, and Bevill stared up at Nelson's statue.

"Now that chap up there, *he* was a different kettle of fish from Sawbridge. You can't make me believe he would have betrayed his country." In action, the old man could be as capable and cynical as most men: in speech he could be just as banal.

"You can't make me believe he would have had any use for intellectuals," Bevill went on darkly. "Kicked them in the pants, that's what he would have done."

As we curved round Trafalgar Square, Bevill told me that some people unspecified were asking 'silly questions' about the trials of the atomic spies: why had they all pleaded guilty, why were the prison terms so long?

"Long," said Bevill. "If you ask me, they were lucky to get away with their necks.

"But I tell you, Lewis," he went on, more like his patient political self, "some people are asking questions, all in the name of civil liberties if you please, and we don't want any more questions than we can help because of the effect on our friends over the other side. And so it may be a case where a bit of private conversation can save a lot of public fuss, even if it does seem like eating humble-pie."

He gave a furtive grin, and said:

"That's where you come in, my lad."

"You want me to talk to them?"

"No, Lewis, I want you to listen to them. Listening never did any of us any harm, and talking usually does," said Bevill, in one of his Polonian asides. "Someone's got to listen to one of those fellows, and you're the man for the job.

"You see," said Bevill, staring uncomplainingly down at a traffic block, "they might trust you, which they'd never begin to do with Rose or me. They'd never get it out of their heads that I was an old die-hard who didn't understand what they were talking about and didn't care a kipper for what was bothering them. And I'm not sure," said Bevill, with his customary realism and humility, "I'm not sure that they'd be far wrong."

"Who is it," I asked, marking down a tiresome, tricky,

but not important date for the following week, "that you want me to see?"

"One of those fellows who write about pictures," Bevill replied, pointing intelligently at the National Gallery. "His name is Austin Davidson. I expect you've heard of him."

"Yes, I have."

"Somehow he gave the impression, or someone else did, that he knew you. Do you know the fellow, Lewis?"

"I've never met him."

"I suppose he's one of those chaps who makes a painter's reputation and then gets his share of the takings when the prices go up," said Bevill, with a simple contempt that he would not have thought of applying to a politician or even a businessman. But I was not paying attention to that accusation, which was about the last that, from Davidson's eminence, he could ever have imagined being uttered against himself, casually but in cold blood. Instead, staring down at the pavement artist in front of the Gallery, hearing old Bevill bring out the name of Margaret's father, I was full of an instantaneous warmth, as though I were completely relaxed and could count, so delectably sharp were they, the leaves of grass on the verges down below.

"Are you positive you haven't met the chap?" Bevill was enquiring.

"Quite."

"Well, I got the impression, if I'm not muddling things, that he gave me to understand, or he may have said so to Rose, that you'd be very acceptable as someone to talk to. And that suggests to me that you'd be able to keep those fellows from making any more fuss."

The bus started, and Bevill was peering through the window, trying to see the clock on Charing Cross.

"I needn't tell you," he said cheerfully, "not to tell them anything they oughtn't to know."

CHAPTER XXXVI

READING-LAMP ALIGHT IN A PEACEFUL ROOM

HEARING that Davidson was to be given a private explanation, George Passant stormed with fury.

"If one of my relations," he cursed, "had been uncomfortable about the Sawbridge case or any other blasted case, are you going to tell me that that old sunket Bevill would have detailed a high civil servant to give them an interview? But this country doesn't use the same rules if you come from where I did instead of bloody Bloomsbury."

It was a long time since I had heard George explode with the radical fervour of his youth.

"I suppose," he said, "you don't feel inclined to tell this man there's no reason on God's earth why he should get special treatment."

I said no.

"Your proper answer to these people," George cried, "when they come begging favours, is Doctor Johnson's to Lord Chesterfield."

I was not sure what obscure grievance George was hugging on my behalf.

"Bloody Bloomsbury": George's swear-words crackled out with 'Bloomsbury' after each one. George's political passions were still rooted in the East Anglian earth, where his cousins were farm labourers: like most rooted radicals, he distrusted upper-class ones, he felt they were less solid men than reactionaries such as old Bevill.

Then he simmered down and said, with a bashful friendliness: "Well, there's one thing, I'm glad this didn't happen when you were still thinking about Margaret. It would have been a bit embarrassing." He added comfortably: "That's all over and done with, at any rate."

Two days later, not waiting for his name to be called out, Davidson walked, head bent, across the floor of my office. He was not looking at me or Vera Allen or anyone or anything: he was so shy that he would not glance up, or go through any formula of introduction.

As he sat in the armchair I could see his grey hair, of which a quiff fell over his forehead, but not his face. He was wearing an old brown suit, and his shirt-sleeves were so long that they covered half his hands; but, among that untidiness, I noticed that the shirt was silk. He said, without any preamble at all, self-conscious and brusque:

"You used to be a lawyer, didn't you?"

I said yes.

"How good were you?"

"I should never," I replied, "have been anything like first-class."

"Why not?"

Despite his awkwardness, he was a man to whom one did not want to give a modest, padded, hypocritical answer.

"It's the sort of career," I said, "where you've got to think of nothing else, and I couldn't manage it."

He nodded, and then, for a second, looked up. My first impression of his face was how young it was. At that time he was in his middle sixties, but his skin, under layers of sunburn, was scarcely lined—except that his neck had the roughness of an ageing man's. My second impression was of a curious kind of beauty. Each of his daughters had inherited his fine bones; but Davidson's face, at the same time delicate and sculptured, had an abstract beauty which theirs missed. His eyes, quite unlike Margaret's, which were transparent and light, shone heavily—pigmented, deep sepia brown, opaque as a bird's.

As he looked up, for an instant his face broke into a grin.

"That's not entirely to your discredit," he said. Soon he was looking at his knees again, and saying: "You're said to know about this Sawbridge business, is that true?"

"Yes."

"You really do know about it, you haven't just seen the papers?"

I began: "I was present when he was first appointed——" and again Davidson gave an evanescent grin.

"That sounds good enough. No wonder you've got your reputation as a picker. It would be simplest if you told me about it from there."

So I told the story, from the time Sawbridge entered Barford after three years' research in an Oxford laboratory: the first suspicion that he was passing information to a Russian agent, as far back as 1944: the thicker suspicion, a year later: the interrogation, in which my brother, who had been his scientific leader, took a part: his confession, arrest and trial.

All the time I was speaking Davidson did not stir. His head was bent down, I was addressing myself to his grey hair, he moved so little that he might not have heard at all, and when I finished he remained immobile.

At last he said: "As an expositor, with Maynard Keynes marked at 100, your score is about 75. No, considering the toughness of the material, I put you up to 79." After that surprising evaluation he went on:

"But none of what you tell me is satisfactory—is it? —unless I can get answers to three questions."

"What are they?"

"To begin with, is this young man really guilty? I don't mean anything fancy, I just mean, did he perform the actions he was charged with?"

"I have no doubt about that."

"Why haven't you any doubt? I know he confessed, but I should have thought the one thing we've learned in the

last ten years is that in suitable circumstances almost anyone can confess to almost anything."

"I hadn't any doubt long before he confessed."

"You had some other evidence?"

He looked up, his face troubled, stern, and suspicious.
"Yes."

"What was it?"

"It was intelligence information. I'm not free to tell you
more than that."

"That doesn't seem specially reassuring."

"Look——" I started, stumbled over his name and finally
said uneasily 'Mr. Davidson', as though I were going to
my first dinner party and was not sure which fork to use.
It was not that he was older; it was not that he was a man
of liberal principle, disapproving of me; it was simply that
I had loved his daughter, and some odd atavistic sense
would not let me address him unceremoniously by his
name.

When I had got over my stuttering I told him that most
intelligence secrets were nonsense, but that some weren't:
some ways of collecting information any government had
to keep tight, so long as we had governments at all: this
was a case in point.

"Isn't that extremely convenient?" said Davidson.

"It must seem so," I said. "Nevertheless it's true."

"You're certain of that?"

"Yes," I said.

Again he looked at me. As though satisfied, he said:

"Accepting that, then, I come straight on to the next
question. Why did he plead guilty? If he hadn't, from what
you've just said he'd have had you all in difficulties——"

I agreed.

"Then why did he?"

"I've often wondered," I said, "and I've got no explanation at all."

"What I want to be convinced of," said Austin Davidson, "is that there were no unfair threats—or unfair inducements as far as that goes—before he was tried."

Once more I did not resent the words, they were too impersonal for that. Instead of replying with official palaver, I was searching for the literal truth. I said that, after Sawbridge was arrested, my firsthand knowledge ended but I thought it very unlikely that anything unfair had been done.

"Why do you think that?"

"I've seen him since, in prison. And if there had been anything of the sort, I can't imagine why he shouldn't complain. It isn't as though he's been converted. He's still a communist. If he had anything to complain of, I don't think he'd be excessively considerate about our feelings."

"That's a genuine point," said Davidson. I could feel he was believing me, as he continued:

"Well, I've only one more question. Fourteen years seemed to most of us a savage sentence. Was there any influence from government or your official people to suggest that he ought to be made an example of?"

"On that," I replied, "I know no more than you do."

"I should like to know what you think."

"I should be astonished if there were anything said directly," I said. "The most that can have happened is that judges like all the people round them are affected by a climate of thought."

Staying very still, Davidson did not speak for some time, until, throwing back his forelock like a boy, he said: "Well, I don't think there's any more you can tell me, and I'm glad to have found someone who could speak straight."

He continued: "So on the whole you are happy about the Sawbridge business, are you?"

He might have meant it as a formal ending, but I was suddenly provoked. I had not enjoyed defending the

R   249

establishment: but I was also irked by the arrogance of men of decent feeling like Davidson, who had had the means to cultivate their decent feelings without the social interest or realism to imagine where they led. I spoke sharply, not like an official. I finished up:

"You ought not to think that I like what we've done. Or a good many other things we're having to do. People of my sort have only two choices in this situation, one is to keep outside and let others do the dirty work, the other is to stay inside and try to keep off the worst horrors and know all the time that we shan't come out with clean hands. Neither way is very good for one, and if I had a son I should advise him to do what you did, and choose a luckier time and place to be born."

It was a long time since I heard my own temper running loose. Davidson was looking at me with a friendly and companionable frown.

"Yes," he remarked, "my daughter said you must be feeling something like that.

"I asked her about you," he went on casually, and added, with a simplicity that was at the same time arrogant and pure: "I've never fancied myself at judging people when I first meet them. So I have to find out about them in my own fashion."

For a fortnight I was immersed in that kind of comfort which is like a luxurious cocoon as one delays before a longed-for and imminent fate, which I had also known after my first meeting with Margaret. I was still not calculating; I, who had calculated so much, went about as though the machine had been switched off; now that I had a card of re-entry into the Davidson family, I still felt the future free.

I still felt so, when I wrote a note to Davidson, telling him I had a little more information about the Sawbridge case, if he chose to call. He did call: he seemed satisfied: afterwards we walked together down Victoria Street. It was a blazing hot day, people were walking in the shade, but Davidson insisted on keeping to the other side.

"We mustn't miss a second of this sun," he said, as though it were a moral axiom.

He walked with long strides, his head down, his feet clumpingly heavy on the pavement for so spare a man. His shirt sleeves hung beneath his cuffs, over-long and unbuttoned. Shabby as he was, passers-by noticed him; he was the most striking and handsome figure in the street. I thought how like that shabby carelessness was to Margaret's.

Suddenly he said:

"I'm giving a show at my house next week." A private view, he explained, for two young painters. "Would that interest you?"

"Very much," I said. I said it eagerly, without any guard.

Not looking at me, Davidson lolloped along.

"Wait a minute," he said. "Do you know anything about pictures? It's a waste of your time and mine if you don't, don't you know."

"I know a little."

"You're not bluffing, are you?"

"I don't think so."

"I'd better ask you a few questions."

There and then, in Victoria Street in the sweating sunshine, as we passed offices of consultant engineers, Davidson gave me a brisk viva. Embarrassed, anxious to pass, doing my best, I nevertheless felt a twinge of amusement, as a comparison struck me. To Davidson, whose taste had no use for concealments, this was a matter to be cleared up in the open; it was just a question of whether I was equipped to look at pictures or not; there were no overtones, no other motives, on his side or mine.

It did not occur to him that I was snatching at the chance to meet his daughter again. Yet he was a man who, so I had heard and I had no reason to doubt it, had once been well-known for his love-affairs. Sheila's father, the Reverend Laurence Knight, had been a faithful husband, living obscurely all his life in a country vicarage: yet, in Davidson's place, he would have known precisely what I was after, not now, when it was easy to see, but within minutes of our first meeting. Mr. Knight, incidentally, would have tantalised me and then found some excuse for holding back the invitation.

Davidson did not go in for any flourishes: he just formed his opinion, and announced:

"You'd never have made a living at it, don't you know."

I was in suspense; I agreed.

"It might just be worth your while to come along," he said, staring at the pavement in front of him. "But only just."

Waiting in my flat on the evening of the private view I saw the sky over Hyde Park turn dark, sodden with rain to come. Standing by the window, I kept glancing at my watch, although it was still not time to leave, and then gazed out again over the trees into the leaden murk. Then I looked back into the room. On the little table by the sofa the reading lamp was gleaming, and a book which I had left open shone under the light.

It was peaceful, it had never seemed so peaceful. For an instant I wanted to stay there, and not go out. It would be easy to stay; I need only telephone and make an apology, in that party I should not be missed, the significance I was giving it was my own invention, and besides myself no living person knew. I looked at the lamp and the sofa, with a stab almost of envy.

Then I turned back to the window, reading my watch, impatient that it was still not time to go.

PART IV

THE UNDETACHED

CHAPTER XXXVII

SMELL OF LEAVES IN THE RAIN

IN the hall of Davidson's house the brightness, clashing with the noise of the party within, took me aback; it was Davidson himself who came to greet me.

"You decided it was worth while, did you?" he asked.

As I was putting my coat down, he said:

"I met someone who knew you this morning." He gave the name of an elderly acquaintance. "She was anxious to get in touch with you. I'd better hand this over before I forget." It was a card with an address and telephone number.

I asked if it could wait, but Davidson had discharged his commission and was not interested any more.

"If you *fancy yourself* at the telephone, there's one under the stairs," he said. He spoke in a severe minatory voice, as though telephony were a difficult art, and it was presumptuous on my part to pretend to have mastered it. In fact Davidson, who was so often the spokesman of the modern, whose walls were hung with the newest art, had never come to terms with mechanical civilisation. Not only did he go deaf if he put a receiver to his ear: even fountain pens and cigarette lighters were white-man's magic which he would have no dealings with.

While I was making my call, which turned out to be of no possible importance, I was by myself listening to the continuum of noise from the unknown rooms. I felt a prickle of nervousness not, it seemed, because Margaret might be there, but just as though I had ceased to be a man of forty, experienced at going about amongst strangers: I felt as I might have done when I was very young.

When at last I went in I stayed on the outskirts of the room trying to put myself at ease. I looked away from the pictures, from the unknown people, out through the window to a night so dark, although it was only nine o'clock in July, that the terrace was invisible: in the middle distance twinkled the lamps along Regent's Park. Down below the window lights, the pavement was bone-white, the rain had still not fallen.

Then I walked round the room, or rather the two rooms which, for the show, had had their dividing doors folded. There must have been sixty or seventy people there, but apart from Davidson, alert and unpompous among a knot of young men, I did not see a face I knew. Along one long wall were hung a set of non-representational paintings, in which geometrical forms were set in a Turnerian sheen. Along the other were some thickly-painted portraits, not quite naturalistic but nearly so. Trying to clamp myself down to study them, I could not settle to it.

I found myself falling back into the refuge I had used at twenty. I used to save my self-respect by the revenges of my observation, and I did so now. Yes, most of the people in these rooms were different animals from those one saw at Lufkin's dinners or round the committee tables with Hector Rose: different animals in an exact, technical sense: lighter-boned, thinner, less heavily muscled, their nerves nearer the surface, their voices more pent-in: less exalting in their bodies' strength than so many of Lufkin's colleagues—and yet, I was prepared to bet, in many cases more erotic. That was one of the paradoxes which separated these persons from the men of action; I thought of acquaintances of mine in Lufkin's entourage who walked with the physical confidence, the unselfconscious swagger, of condottieri; but it was not they who were driven, driven to obsession by the erotic life, but men as it might be one or two I saw round me that night, whose cheeks were sunken and limbs shambling, who looked, instead of bold and authoritative like Lufkin's colleagues, much younger than their years.

Soon someone recognised me, and, opposite one of the non-representational patterns, I was caught up in an argument. In a group of five or six I was the oldest man, and they treated me with respect, one even called me 'sir'. It was an argument such as we knew by heart in those years, about the future of abstract art. I was talking with the fluency of having been through those tricks before, talking with the middle-aged voice, the practised party voice. They called me 'sir', they thought me heterodox, they were not as accustomed to debating or so ready for shock tactics. None of them knew that, five minutes before, I had been nervous and lost.

All the time I was arguing, I was staring over them and past them, just as though I were a young man on the make, looking out at a party for someone more useful than his present company. I had seen no sign of her, but, as the minutes seeped on, I could not keep my glance still.

At last I saw her. She came out of the crowd by the wall opposite ours and further down the room; she was speaking to a woman, and she spread out her hands in a gesture I had often seen, which suddenly released her animation and gaiety. As she talked my glance was fixed on her: it was many instants before her eyes came my way.

She hesitated in front of a neglected picture and stood there by herself. A young man at my side was speaking insistently, heckling me with polite questions. She was walking towards us. As she came inside our group, the young man halted his speech.

"Go on," said Margaret.

Someone began to introduce me to her.

"We've known each other for years," she said, protectively and gently. "Go on, I don't want to interrupt."

As she stood, her head bent down and receptive, I saw

her for an instant as though it were first sight. Excitement, a mixture of impatience and content, had poured into my nerves—but that seemed disconnected from, utterly uncaused by, this face which might have been another stranger's. Pale, fine rather than pretty, just missing beauty, lips and nostrils clean-cut, not tender until she smiled—it was an interesting face, but not such a face as in imagination I admired most, not even one that, away from her, I endowed her with.

Then the first sight shattered, as I thought she had changed. Five years before, when I had first met her, she could have passed for a girl: but now, at thirty, she looked her full age. Under the light, among the dark hair glinted a line of silver; her skin which, with her blend of negligence and subfusc vanity she used to leave untouched, was made up now, but there were creases round her mouth and eyes. Suddenly I remembered that when I knew her there were some broken veins just behind her cheekbones, odd for so young and fine-skinned a woman; but now under the powder they were hidden.

Standing in the middle of this group she was not embarrassed, as she would have been once. She rested there, not speaking much nor assertively, but a woman among a crowd of younger men: now there was no disguising her energy, her natural force.

The light seemed brighter on the eyes, the pictures further away, the crowd in the room noisier, voices were high around me, questions came at me, but I had dropped out of the argument. Once, glancing at Margaret, I met her eyes: I had not spoken to her alone. At last the group moved on, and we were left just for an instant isolated, no one listening to us. But now the chance had come, I could not speak: the questions I wanted to ask, after three years of silence, would not come to the tongue, I was like a stutterer needing to bring out his dreaded consonant. We gazed at each other, but I could not utter. The silence tightened between us.

Foolishly I creaked out some remark about the pictures, asking how she liked them, as banal a question as though she was a boring acquaintance with whom I had to make my ration of conversation. In the midst of that nonsense my voice broke away from me, and I heard it sound intense, intimate and harsh.

"How are you?"

Her tone was kinder, but just as edged: "No, how are you?"

Her eyes would not leave mine. Each willed the other to answer first; I gave way.

"I haven't much to tell you," I said.

"Tell me what there is."

"It could be worse."

"You've always been ready to bear it, haven't you?"

"No, my life isn't intolerable," I said, trying to tell her the precise truth.

"But what?"

"There's not much in it," I replied.

"Yes, I was afraid so."

"Were you?"

"People often talk about you, you know."

The crowd pressed upon us, they parted me from her, although before we had to talk at large, she was muttering about something she wished for me. She had begun to say it with an impatient, eager smile.

As I was speaking to the newcomers, I noticed a tall youngish man detach himself from another group and whisper to Margaret, who was glancing in my direction.

She looked tired, she seemed to be wanting to go home, but soon she beckoned to me.

"You haven't met Geoffrey, have you?" she said to me.

He was a couple of inches taller than my six feet, very

thin, long-handed and long-footed; he was thirty-five, goodlooking in a lantern-jawed fashion, with handsome eyes and deep folds in his cheeks. The poise of his head was arrogant, other men would judge him pleased with his looks; but there was nothing arrogant about him as we shook hands, he was as short of conversation as I had been with Margaret a few minutes before, and just as I had opened imbecilely about the pictures, so did he. He had known about me and Margaret long before he married her; now his manner was apologetic, quite unlike his normal, so I fancied, as he asked my opinion of the pictures, in which his interest was, if possible, less than mine.

Margaret said they must be going soon, Helen would be waiting up for them.

"That's my sister-in-law," Geoffrey explained to me, still over-embarrassed, over-considerate. "She's sitting in with the infant."

"She still hasn't any of her own?" I asked Margaret. I recalled the times when, joyful ourselves, we had arranged her sister's well-being, the conspiracies of happiness. Margaret shook her head:

"No, poor dear, she had no luck."

Geoffrey caught her eye, and he said, in what I took to be his confident doctor's voice:

"It's a thousand pities she didn't get some sensible advice right at the beginning."

"But yours is well?" I spoke to both of them, but once more I was asking Margaret.

It was Geoffrey who replied.

"He's all right," he said. "Of course, if you're not used to very young children, you might get him out of proportion. Actually, for general development, he'd certainly be in the top ten per cent of two year olds, but probably not in the top five."

His tone was exaggeratedly dry and objective, but his

eyes were innocent with love. He went on, with the pretence of objectivity which professionals believe conceals their pride:

"Only yesterday, it's simply an example, he took a flash lamp to pieces and put it together again. Which I couldn't have done at the age of four."

Conscious of Margaret's silence, I expressed surprise. Geoffrey's tone changed, and as he spoke to me again I thought I heard something hard, jaunty, almost vindictive:

"You'd better come and see him for yourself."

"No, he wouldn't enjoy it," said Margaret quickly.

"Why shouldn't he come for lunch, then he can inspect the boy?"

"It would be very inconvenient for you." Margaret spoke straight to me.

I replied to Geoffrey:

"I'd like to come."

Soon afterwards, sharply, Margaret said again that they must be going home. I walked with them out of the room, into the hall, where, through the open door, we could hear the rain pelting down. Geoffrey ran out to bring the car round, and Margaret and I stood side by side staring out into the dark terrace, seeing the rain shafts cut through the beam of light from the doorway. On the pavement the rain hissed and bounced; the night had gone cool; a clean smell came off the trees, making me feel for an instant calm when, knowing nothing else for certain, I knew I was not that.

Neither of us turned towards the other. The car came along the kerb, veils of rain shimmering across the head-lights.

"I shall see you then," she said, in a flat, low voice.

"Yes," I said.

CHAPTER XXXVIII

SIGNIFICANCE OF A QUARREL

AS I sat between Margaret and Geoffrey Hollis at their dining-table, I wanted to speak amiably to him.

Outside the sun was shining, it was a sleepy middle-of-the-day; no one was to be seen in the Sumner Place gardens; the only sound, through the open windows, was the soporific sweep of buses along the Fulham Road. I had only arrived a quarter of an hour before, and we spoke, all three of us, as though we were subdued by the heat. Geoffrey was sitting in a shirt open at the neck, and Margaret in a cotton frock; we ate boiled eggs and salad and drank nothing but iced water. In between times Geoffrey and I exchanged polite curiosity about our working days.

In the dining-room, which was like a pool of coolness after the streets, all we said sounded civil. I was hearing what it meant to be a children's doctor, the surgery hours, the hospital rounds, the proportion of nights he could expect a call. It was useful, it was devoted, it was no more self-indulgent than the meal he ate. Nor was the way he talked about it. He had admitted that in some respects he was lucky. "Compared with other doctors anyway," said Geoffrey. "Any other sort of doctor is dealing with patients who by and large are going to get worse. With children most of them are going to get better. It gives it quite a different flavour, you see, and that's a compensation."

He was provoking me: it was enviable, it was admirable. I wanted to prove it wasn't.

Suspicious of myself, I changed the subject. Just to keep the conversation easy, I asked him what he thought of some news from the morning's paper.

"Oh yes," he said indifferently, "a parent who came in mentioned it."

"What do you think?"

"I haven't any idea."

"It's pretty plain, isn't it?"

"Maybe," he replied. "But, you see, I haven't read a morning paper."

"Are you as busy as all that?" I tried to be companionable.

"No," he said, with pleasure, tilting his head back like someone who has taken a finesse. "It's a matter of general policy. Twelve months ago we decided not to take a daily paper. It seemed to me that far more days than not, it was going to make me slightly miserable without any gain to anyone, and with just conceivably a fractional loss of efficiency to myself. In any case I don't believe in adding to the world's stock of misery, even if it's through my own. So we decided the sensible course was to stop the paper."

"I couldn't do that," I broke out.

"Quite seriously," said Geoffrey, "if a lot of us only bit off what we could chew, and simply concentrated on the things we can affect, there'd be less tension all round, and the forces of sweetness and light would stand more chance."

"I believe you're dangerously wrong," I said.

Again he was provoking me; the irritation, which would not leave me alone at that table, was jagging my voice; this time I felt I had an excuse. Partly it was that this kind of quietism was becoming common among those I knew, and I distrusted it. Partly Geoffrey himself seemed to me complacent, speaking from high above the battle; and, like many people who led useful and good lives, even like many who had a purity of nature, he seemed insulated by his self-regard.

Suddenly Margaret spoke to me.

"He's absolutely right," she said.

263

She was smiling, she was trying to speak easily, as I tried to speak to Geoffrey, but she was worried and angry.

"Why do you say that?"

"We've got to deal with things that are close enough to handle," she said.

"I don't believe," I said, getting angrier, "that you can cut yourself off from the common experience around you. And if you do, I am sure you lose by it."

"Lose by it how?"

"Lose by it as a person. Just like very optimistic people who shut off anything that is painful to see. I should have thought you'd diminish yourself unless you suffer your sufferings as well as enjoy your joys."

Margaret gave a smile half malicious, as though gratified that my temper had gone higher than hers.

"The trouble," she said, "with the very realistic men who live in this world, like you, is that they're so hopelessly unpractical when it comes to the point. You don't think Geoffrey's realistic, but he's so much more practical than you are that you don't begin to start. He likes dealing with children and he likes being happy. Hasn't it occurred to you that no one except you worries whether they're 'diminishing themselves' or not?"

I was getting the worst of it; I could not overbear her— I was hurt because she had taken his side with such an edge.

In return, I found myself talking to hurt.

I reminded her that I had never been comfortable about recipes for the good life—like those of her father's friends twenty years before—which depended on one's being an abnormally privileged person.

"To be honest," I looked at Geoffrey and then at her, "yours doesn't seem to me a great improvement. Your whole attitude would be unthinkable unless you happened to have one of the very few jobs which is obviously benevolent and unless both of you happened to come from families who were used to doing good rather than having good done to them."

"Lewis," she called out my name for the first time for three years, but furiously, "that's quite unfair!"

"Is it?" I asked her, watching the flush mount from her neck.

"Well, I wouldn't deny," said Geoffrey, with exasperating fairness and a contented, judicious smile, "that there may be something in it."

"Do you really say that I patronise anyone?" she cried.

"With individuals, no, I shouldn't say so. But when you think about social things, of course you do."

Her eyes were dark and snapping; her cheeks were flushed; it was as I remembered her when angry, the adrenalin was pumping through her, all pallor had left her and she looked spectacularly well.

"I must say," Geoffrey remarked pacifically, "I'm inclined to think he's right."

"I suppose you'll say I'm a snob next?" Her eyes, still snapping, were fixed on me.

"In a rarefied sense, yes."

Geoffrey reminded her that it was half-past one, time to give Maurice his meal. Without speaking, her shoulders set with energy, with anger against me, she took the tray and led us to the nursery.

"There he is," said Geoffrey, as I got my first glance at the child.

His pen was just outside a strong diagonal of sunlight; sitting with his back to the bars, like an animal retreating at the zoo, he was slowly tearing a magazine to pieces. I had only my brother's boy to compare him with, and despite what I had heard of his manual precocity, I could not see it. I just saw him tearing up the paper with that solemn,

s   265

concentrated inefficiency characteristic of infants, which made his hand and elbow movements look like those of a drunken man photographed in slow motion.

I did not go up to him, but went on watching as, after Margaret spoke to him, he continued obsessively with his task. He was, and the sight wounded me though I had prepared for it, a most beautiful child. The genes had played one of their tricks, and had collected together in him the best looks of parents and grandparents, so that already, under the india-rubber fat, one could pick out the fine cheekbones of his mother and the poise of his father's neck. It was easy to imagine him as a young man, dark, indrawn, hard to approach and gaining admirers just because of that.

Margaret was telling him that his meal was ready, but he replied that he did not want it.

"What do you want?" she asked, with that matter-of-fact gentleness she showed to a lover.

The little boy was gripping a ping-pong ball, and, as soon as she lifted him from his pen, he began to lam it at a looking-glass over the mantelpiece, and then at a picture near the cot.

Geoffrey left, to fetch something missing from the tray, but the boy paid no notice, and went on throwing the ball. As he let fly, I was scrutinising the boneless movement of his shoulder, as fluid as though he were double-jointed. Margaret said to me:

"It's a nice way for him to be."

"Isn't he rather strong?" I asked.

She was smiling at me, the quarrel smoothed away by the animal presence of her son. As she stood with him thigh-high beside her, she could not conceal—what at her father's party she remained silent about, when Geoffrey was so voluble—her passion for the child. It softened and filled out her face, and made her body lax. Pained again as by

266

the boy's good looks, I knew that I had not seen her look more tender.

"It's nice for him just to chuck himself about," she said.

I caught her meaning. Like many of the sensitive, she had wished often, especially before she gained the confidence that she could make a man happy, that her own childhood had been less refined, had been coarser and nearer the earth.

I put in a remark, to let her know I understood. She smiled again: but Maurice began shouting, violent because she was talking away from him.

While he had his meal I remained outside the circle of attention, which was lit by the beam of sun gilding the legs of the high chair. Geoffrey sat on one side, Margaret in front, the child facing her with unflickering eyes. After two or three spoonfuls he would not eat until she sang; as I listened, it occurred to me that, when I had known her, I had not once heard her singing voice. She sang, her voice unexpectedly loud and deep; the child did not take his eyes off her.

The robust sound filled the room: Geoffrey, smiling, was watching the boy: the beam of sunlight fell on their feet, as though they were at the centre of a stage, and the spotlight had gone slightly off the mark.

The meal was over, Geoffrey gave the child a sweet, for an instant the room went dead quiet. They were still sitting with the sunlight round their feet, as Margaret gazed at her son, either unselfconscious or thinking she was not observed. Then after a moment she raised her head, and I felt rather than saw, for I had looked away, that her glance had moved from the child to me. I turned towards her: her eyes did not fall, but her face went suddenly sad. It was only for a second. She gazed again at the little boy, and took his hand.

It had only been for a second, but I knew. I should have

known before, when we parted after her father's party, certainly when she quarrelled with me in defence of Geoffrey at the dining-table, if I had not desired it too much: I knew now that she was not free of me, any more than I of her.

In the hot room, noisy now with the boy's demands, I felt, not premonition, not responsibility, not the guilt that would have seemed ineluctable if I had seen another in my place, but an absolute exaltation, as though, all in one move, I had joy in my hands and my life miraculously simple. I did not recognise any fear mixed with the joy, I just felt happy and at one.

CHAPTER XXXIX

ILLUSION OF INVISIBILITY

IT WAS a September afternoon when I was waiting, for the first time since her marriage, to meet Margaret alone. It was the day on which I had been helping to interview Gilbert Cooke. Half an hour before I was due at our rendezvous he entered, having already heard from Hector Rose that he was safe.

"So I diddled them, did I?" he said, not so much with pleasure as a kind of gloating triumph: which was the way in which he, who did not expect much success, greeted any that came to him. Actually, this was more than a success, for in fact, though not in form, it settled his career for life. Hector Rose was deciding his final judgement on each of the men in the Department who wished to be established in the service; once a week, a committee of four of us sat and interviewed; George Passant's turn would arrive soon.

"It can't come unstuck now, can it?" Gilbert said, flushed, his eyes bloodshot. I told him that Rose's nomination would have to be accepted.

"Damn it," cried Gilbert, "I never reckoned on finishing up as a civil servant."

"What did you reckon on?" I knew he would scarcely be able to answer: for in his career he had always been a curiously vague and unself-seeking man.

"Oh," he said, looking badgered, "there was a time when I thought I might make something of it as a soldier. That was before the doctors did me in the eye. And then I thought I might collect some cash with that old shark

Lufkin. I don't know. But the last thing I should ever have dreamt of was finding myself here for good. To tell you the honest truth," he burst out, "I should never have credited that I was clever enough!"

Oddly, in a certain restricted sense, he was not: he had nothing of the legalistic accuracy and lucidity of the high-class civil servant: the deficiency would stop him going very far, as Rose and the others had agreed that day: he would most likely get one rung higher and stop there.

Nevertheless, he had put up a good performance before those men so different from himself. He was so little stiff that Rose felt his own stiffness soften, and enjoyed the sensation: sometimes his refusal to stay at a distance, his zest for breathing down one's neck, made him paradoxically welcome to correct and buttoned natures. Hector Rose and his colleagues did not over-value him much; they were too experienced, and their judgment too cool for that; they were probably right to keep him; but still, there was no doubt that, if the decision had been a closer thing, he had the advantage that respectable men liked him.

I wondered what they would have thought, if they had guessed at his wilder activities. For instance, it would have startled them to know that, sitting in my office that afternoon, I—after being a friend for a dozen years and his boss for several—was frightened of him. Frightened, that is, of his detective work. I did not dare let out a hint that I was slipping away for tea. Even then I was still nervous of his antennae, as though they might pick up the secret in the air.

Thus, sweating and fretted, I was late when at last I reached the café opposite St. James's Park tube station. Margaret was sitting there, stubs of cigarettes in the ash-tray. She looked anxious, but unreproachful and glad.

"I'll tell you why I was late," I said.

"It doesn't matter, you're here now."

"No, I'd better tell you." I could not have got away from Gilbert, I explained, without the danger of his finding out that I was meeting her.

"Oh well," she said. She spoke as though she had not admitted to herself the thought of concealment. At the same moment, her face was flushed with happiness and a kind of defiant shame. Firmly, she began to ask me what I had been doing.

"I told you, nothing that matters."

"No," she said, still with energy and animation, "I don't even know where you're living. You know much more about me than I do about you."

I told her what I was busy with. I said that I was not held any longer by the chessboard of power: I had gone as far as I intended in the official life.

"I thought so," she said with pleasure, understanding my present better than my past.

"I am not sure that it would have happened but for you."

"It would," she said. The cups of tea steamed, a cigarette end smouldered against the metal ash-tray, the smell was acrid: I saw her as though the smoked glass of care had been snatched from in front of my eyes. Twenty minutes before I had been on edge lest anyone, as it might be Gilbert, should pass the window and see us sitting there. Now, although we were smiling at each other and our faces would have given us away to an acquaintance, I felt that secrets did not matter, or more exactly that no one could notice us; I had been taken by one of those states, born of understanding, desire and joy, in which we seem to ourselves anonymous and safe. It was a state which I had seen dangerous to discreet men going through an illicit love-affair, when suddenly, in a fugue of astonished bliss, such a man can behave as if he believed himself invisible.

Her hand was on the table, and I touched her fingers. We had made love together many times, we had none of that surprise to come: but, at the touch, I shivered as though it were a complete embrace.

"Let me talk to you," I said.

"Can't we leave it?" she cried.

"Can we?"

"It'd be better to leave it, just for a while." She spoke in a tone I had not heard—it held both joy and fear, or something sharper than fear.

"I used to be pretty expert at leaving things just for a while," I said, "and it wasn't an unqualified success."

"We're peaceful now," she broke out.

She added:

"When a thing is said, we can't come back where we are."

"I know it." There was a hush. I found myself trying to frame the words, just as when she first forced me on that evening years before—with an inarticulateness more tormenting to one used to being articulate, with the dumbness I only knew when I was compelled to dredge my feelings. "It is the same with me," I said at length, "as when I first met you."

She did not move or utter.

"I hope," I said, the words dragging out, "it is the same with you."

She said: "You don't hope: you know."

The room was dark; in the street the sun had gone out. She cried—her voice was transformed, it was light with trust, sharp with the curiosity of present joy:

"When were you certain it was the same with you?"

"Some time ago."

"Was it that night at my father's?"

"If not before," I answered. "I've thought of you very much. But I was afraid my imagination might be cheating me."

"What time that night?"

272

"I think when you were standing there, before we spoke."

I asked: "When were you certain?"

"Later."

She added: "But I wanted you to come that night."

"If we hadn't met again there, we should have soon," I said.

"I talked about you to my father. I lied to myself, but I was trying to improve the chances of meeting you——"

"You needn't worry, I should have seen to it that we did."

"I'm not worrying," she said. "But I wanted to tell you that we're both to blame."

To both of us, blame seemed remote or rather inconceivable; the state of happiness suffused us with its own virtue.

We said no more except chit-chat. Yes, when she could get Helen to look after the child again, she would let me know. It was time for her to go. We went out into the street, where the light had that particular density which gives both gentleness and clarity to the faces of passers-by. The faces moved past us, softly so it seemed, as I watched Margaret put her foot on the taxi-step and she pressed my hand.

CHAPTER XL

HAPPINESS AND MAKE-BELIEVE

IN THE same café a week later Margaret sat opposite me, her face open and softened, as though breathing in the present moment. When I first met her I had been enraptured by her capacity for immediate joy, and so I was now. There had been none of the dead blanks of love between us, such as a man like me might have run into. Once there had been struggle, resentment and dislike, but not the dead blank.

In the aura from the table lamp, she was smiling. Outside the window the afternoon light was muted, so that on the pavement faces stood out with a special delicacy. She took the sight in, content and rapacious, determined to possess the moment.

"It's like last week," she cried. "But last week it was a few shades darker, wasn't it?"

We had not much time. She would have to be home by six, to let her sister go. With a mixture of triumph, humility and confusion she had told Helen that it was I she was meeting.

She was not used to lying, I thought. She had not before done anything unstraightforward or that caused her shame.

She was happy sitting there opposite me. But I knew that she was, to an extent and for the first time, making believe. What she had replied, when I had declared myself the week before, was true. As we talked, she felt a joy she could not restrain: together, we were having an intimation of a life more desirable than we had known. But I knew

274

that for her, though not for me, it was not quite real. It was a wonderful illusion; but the reality was when she got back to her husband and the child.

In a marriage unhappier than hers, I could not forget how, returning to Sheila in the evening, I gained just one recompense, a feeling of moral calm: and I was sure that in Margaret's own home, in a marriage which was arid but for the child, it was just that moral calm which she knew. It came upon her when she went home after our meeting, at the first sight of the child. It did not so much wipe away the thought of our meeting as make it seem still delectable but unreal.

It was that which I had to break. I did not want to: we were in a harmony that seemed outside of time: we could go on talking as though it were a conversation more serene than any the most perfect marriage could give, with no telephone bell, no child's voice, to interrupt. But my need was too great, I could not leave it there.

Once more I was dredging for what I had to say.

"When I told you," I began, "that it was the same with me, there is one difference."

"Is there?" She said it with doubt and reluctance.

I went on:

"In our time together you were right and I was wrong."

"That doesn't matter."

"Yes, it does, because there is a difference now. I hope I've changed a little in myself, I know I've changed in what I want."

Her eyes were as brilliant as when she was angry: she did not speak.

I said:

"I want for us exactly what you always did."

"I never thought I should hear you say that!"

She had cried out with joy: then, in an instant, her tone was transformed.

275

"Other things have changed too," she said.

She looked straight at me, and asked:

"Are you sure?"

In a time so short that I could not measure it, her mood had flickered as I had never seen in her, from triumphant joy to bitterness and shame, and then to concern for me.

"No," she broke out, "I take that back, I shouldn't have said it. Because you couldn't have done this unless you were sure."

"I'm sure of what I want," I repeated. "As I say, I hope I have changed in myself, but of that I can't be sure, it's very hard to know what's happening in one's own life."

"That's rather funny, from you." Again her mood had switched, she was smiling with affectionate sarcasm. She meant that, herself used to being in touch with her own experience, she had discovered the same in me. On the surface so unlike, at that level we were identical. Perhaps it was there, and only there, that each of us met the other half of self.

"Once or twice," I said, "I've woken up and found my life taking a course I'd never bargained on. Once upon a time I thought I knew the forces behind me pretty well—but now it seems more mysterious than it used to, not less. Isn't that so with you?"

"It may be."

She added:

"If it is, it's frightening."

"For me, it's made me less willing to sit down to——"

I stumbled for a moment.

"Sit down to what?"

"To my own nature: or anyway the side of it which did us both such harm."

"It wasn't all your doing," she said.

I answered:

"No, not all. I agree, I won't take all the responsibility, not more than I have to."

We fell into a silence, one of those doldrums that sometimes take over in a mutual revelation, just as in a scene of violence.

She began, in a manner gentle and apparently realistic: "If it were possible for us to start again, you'd look very foolish, wouldn't you? Especially to those who know our story."

I nodded.

"It would seem inconceivably foolish at the best," she said.

"They'd have a certain justice," I replied.

"You haven't had much practice at looking foolish, have you? Have you begun to imagine how humiliating it would be? Particularly when people think you're so wise and stable?"

"I can ride that," I said.

"It might not be so nice."

She went on:

"Those who love you would blame poor Sheila—and those who don't would say there'd always been something wrong with you and now you've come out into the open and shown it."

"One's enemies are often righter than one's friends."

"They're not. That's the sort of remark that sounds deep and is really very shoddy." She said it with love.

The café was emptying, our time was running out. She said, in a sharp, grave tone:

"But what they would think of you, perhaps you're right, that's not the real point. The real point is, you've not had much practice at behaving badly, have you?"

I said:

"I've done bad things."

"Not like what this would be."

"The way I behaved to you before," I said, "was worse than anything I have to do now."

"This way," she said, "you know what you would be asking me to do." She meant—do harm to others, act against her nature and beliefs.

"Do you think I haven't faced that?"

She said:

"I was not absolutely sure."

Yet, though she seemed to be speaking realistically, there was a haze of happiness round her, and me also. Incongruously I recalled the night when Lufkin, at the height of his power, indulged a romantic dream of retiring to Monaco. She too was speaking of a future that in her heart she did not expect to see. Usually her spirit was nakeder than mine: for once it was the other way about. Her face, her skin, her eyes were happy: yet she was levitated with something like the happiness of a dream.

I did not doubt that, in my absence, she would have to listen again to what I had said.

Once more she spoke gently, reasonably, intimately.

"If we could make a new start, I should be afraid for you."

"I need it——"

"You'd know," she said, "you've just said you know, what it would mean for me to come to you. You'd be committed more than anyone ought to be. If things ever went wrong, and it might be harder for you day by day than you could possibly foresee, then I'm afraid you'd feel obliged to endure for ever."

"You can't be much afraid," I said.

"I should be, a little."

She could keep her words honest, so could I—while, with the lamp on the table between us, our hopes were expanding, sweeping us with them into a gigantic space of well-being. Our hopes no longer had any connection with the honest, doubting words we said.

CHAPTER LXI

END OF AN EPOCH

AFTER that second meeting, and before we could contrive another, a chance to be unclandestine came along, for we were invited to the same wedding-party. In itself, the occasion would have been startling enough: when I saw the invitation I felt fooled. The party was to announce the marriage that had taken place, weeks before, in secret— the marriage of Gilbert Cooke and Betty Vane.

As I walked along the river to the house they had borrowed for the night, a house near Whistler's, which in those years had become just a place to be hired, I was both elated, because of Margaret, and faintly sad, self-indulgently in tune with the autumn night. It was drizzling and warm, the leaves slippery on the pavement, the smell of must all round; it was an autumn night which held more sensual promise than the spring.

I was not thinking much about Betty and Gilbert. When I first heard the news I had been piqued because she had not confided in me. Maybe she had, it occurred to me, a year or more ago: more likely than not, this was what she meant by her chance to settle down. Should I have told her that I did not believe the marriage could work? She was so shrewd, she would know what I felt without my saying it. I knew too well, however, that the shrewd and clear-sighted, if they are unhappy and unsettled and lonely enough, as she was, can delude themselves at least as much as, perhaps more than, less worldly people.

Yet, as I went towards the party, the lights from the windows shimmering out into the drizzle, I was aware of other thoughts drifting through my mind, as though this marriage were an oddly final thing. For me it seemed to call out time, it was the end of an epoch. I had known them each so long, Betty for nearly twenty years. We had seen in each other youth passing, causes dribbling out, hopes cutting themselves down to fit our fates: our lives had interleaved, we had seen each other in the resilience of youth's flesh, on and off for years we had, in the other's trouble, helped pick up the pieces. Now we saw each other when the covers and disguises were melting away, when the bones of our nature were at last showing through.

Our life of the 'thirties, our wartime life, was over now. Somehow the gong sounded, the door clanged to, more decisively through her marriage than through any fatality to those who touched me to the roots—through her, who was just a comrade, someone I had been fond of without fuss.

In the house, the first person I recognised was old Bevill, drinking a glass of champagne at the bottom of the stairs and talking to a pretty girl. The downstairs rooms were already full of people, and I had to push my way upstairs to reach the main origin of noise. As I passed him, Bevill told me that Gilbert and his wife were 'up above'. He said:

"I always wondered when our friend would succumb. Do you know, Lewis, I've been married forty-eight years. It makes you think."

The old man was radiant with champagne and the company of the young. He began to tell us the story about Betty Vane's father—"We were at school together, of course. We never thought he'd come into the title, because there was that cousin of his who went off his head and stayed off his head for thirty years. So it didn't look much of a cop for Percy Vane. We didn't call him Percy, though, we called him Chinaman Vane—though I haven't the faintest idea why, he didn't look like a Chinaman, whatever else they could say about him."

This incongruity struck Bevill as remarkably funny, and his bald head flushed with his chortles: he was content to stand in the hall without inserting himself into the grander circles of the party. But there were others who were not: the main room upstairs was packed with immiscible groups, for Gilbert and Betty had invited guests from all the strata they had lived among. There was Lord Lufkin and some of his court, from Gilbert's business past: acquaintances from Chelsea before the war, the radicals, the ill-fitting, the lumpen-bourgeoisie.

There were a good many civil servants, among them Hector Rose, for once at a disadvantage, abnormally uncomfortable and effusively polite, detesting the sight of any society except in the office and the club. There was George Passant, moving about alone, with that expression unfocused, reverie-laden, absently smiling, which at this time more and more came over him in the proximity of women. There were Gilbert's relatives, many of them soldiers, small-headed, thin, gravel-voiced. There were Betty's, the younger women talking in the curious distorted Cockney of their generation of the upper-class, huddled together like a knot of scientists at the British Association anxious not to be interrupted by camp-followers.

In all those faces there was only one I looked for. Soon I discovered her, listening but not participating at the edge of a large circle, her eyes restlessly looking out for me. As at her father's, we met alone in the crowd.

"That's better," she said.

"I wish I could have brought you," I said.

"I was touching wood, I didn't like to ask for you."

She was excited; as she lit a cigarette, there was a tremor in her fingers.

"Who have you been talking to?"

"Oh, I haven't got as far as that." She was laughing, not only with excitement, but at herself. Even now that she was grown-up, she was still shy. If this had been an ordinary party, not a cover for the two of us to meet, she would still have had to brace herself to cope: though, when once she had started, she revelled in it.

"We're here, anyway, and that's lucky," I said.

"It is lucky," she replied with an active, restless smile.

I was just telling her that soon we could slip away downstairs and talk, when Betty herself joined us.

"Lewis, my dear. Won't you wish me luck?"

She held out her arms, and I kissed her cheek. Then, bright-eyed, she glanced at Margaret.

"I don't think we've met, have we?" said Betty.

"You have," I was putting in, when Betty went on:
"Anyway, I'm sorry, but will you tell me who you are?"

It sounded at best forgetful, it sounded also rude, for Betty's manner to a stranger was staccato and brusque. Yet she was the least arrogant of women, and I was at the same time astonished by her and upset to see Margaret wilt.

"My name," she said, with her chin sunk down, "is Margaret Hollis."

"Oh, now I know," cried Betty. "You used to be Margaret Davidson, didn't you?"

Margaret nodded.

"I've heard my husband talk about you."

With the same heartiness, the same apparent lack of perception, Betty went on with meaningless gossip, not caring that Margaret and I were looking strained. Yes, her husband Gilbert was a friend of Margaret's sister Helen, wasn't he? Yes, Gilbert had spoken about Helen's husband. At last Betty broke off, saying to Margaret:

"Look, there are some people here who I want you to meet. I'll take you along straightaway."

Margaret was led off. I had to let her go, without protecting her. It was a bitterness, known only to those in llicit love, not to be able to be spontaneous. I was reckoning how much time I had to allow before I could take her away.

Meanwhile, myself at a loss, I looked round. Gilbert, high-coloured, was surveying his guests with bold, inquisitive eyes. They were the collection of acquaintances of half-a-lifetime; I expected his detective work was still churning on; but I was thinking again, as I had done walking to the house, how this was some sort of end. For Gilbert who, despite his faults, or more precisely because of them, cared as little for social differences as a man can do, had travelled a long way through society, just as I had myself, in the other direction.

So had Betty: the unlucky mattered, politics mattered, friends mattered and nothing else. When I had first met them both, it had seemed to us all self-evident that society was loosening and that soon most people would be indifferent to class. We had turned out wrong. In our forties we had to recognise that English society had become more rigid, not less, since our youth. Its forms were crystallizing under our eyes into an elaborate and codified Byzantinism, decent enough, tolerable to live in, but not blown through by the winds of scepticism or individual protest or sense of outrage which were our native air. And those forms were not only too cut-and-dried for us: they would have seemed altogether too rigid for nineteenth-century Englishmen. The evidence was all about us, even at that wedding party: quite little things had, under our eyes, got fixed, and, except for catastrophes, fixed for good. The Hector Roses and their honours lists: it was a modern invention that the list should be systematised by civil service checks and balances: they had ceased to be corrupt and unpredictable, they were now as hierarchically impeccable as the award of coloured hats at the old Japanese Court. And I did not believe that I was seduced by literary resonances when I imagined that

Betty Vane's and Thomas Bevill's relatives were behaving like Guermantes.

Just as the men of affairs had fractionated themselves into a group with its own rules and its own New Year's Day rewards, just as the arts were, without knowing it, drifting into invisible academies, so the aristocrats, as they lost their power and turned into ornaments, shut themselves up and exaggerated their distinguishing marks in a way that to old Bevill, who was grander than any of them, seemed rank bad manners, and what was worse, impolitic. But old Bevill belonged to a generation where the aristocracy still kept some function and so was unselfconscious: in his time it was far more casual, for example, where you went to school; when he told his anecdote about Percy Vane, the school they were both attending was not Eton; yet it was to Eton, without one single exception in the families I knew, that they sent their sons, with the disciplined conformity of a defiant class. With the same conformity, those families were no longer throwing up the rebels that I had been friendly with as a young man; Betty Vane and Gilbert Cooke had no successors.

Looking round their wedding-party, I could not shake off a cliché of those years, this was the end of an epoch; I should have liked the company of those who could see one beginning.

A twitch at my arm, and Betty was glancing up at me.

"All right?" she said.

"Are you?" Angrily, I wanted to ask why she had been rude to Margaret: but once more I had to calculate.

"Yes, my dear."

"I never thought of this happening to you."

"I can manage it," she said. It was not just her courage and high spirits: she meant it.

She broke off sharp: "I'm sorry I had to cart her off. But people were watching you."

"Does that matter?" I replied blank-faced.

"You ought to know."

"What do you expect me to know?"

"So long as you realise that people were watching you."

"I see."

"That's all I can do for you now," said Betty.

She was, of course, warning me about her husband. It removed my last doubt that she might not know him right through, and on her account I was relieved. She was too loyal to say more, perhaps this was the one crack in her loyalty I should ever see, and she only revealed it because she thought I was running into danger. She had done me so many good turns; I was touched by this last one.

And yet, I could not be sure why she had been so uncivil to Margaret. It had not been necessary, not even as a ruse. At their only other encounter, she had thought Margaret rude: was she getting her own back? Or had she genuinely forgotten Margaret's face? No one had indulged less in petty spite—just for a second, had she been doing so?

Just as I had got out of the room, on the balcony on my way downstairs to Margaret, someone intercepted me. For minutes I was pegged there, the glasses tinkling on the trays as they were carried past, the noise climbing in amplitude and pitch, Gilbert leaning from the door and taking note.

Over the banisters, when I broke away, I saw Margaret standing about down below.

"I feel a bit badgered," I said as soon as I reached her, all tension leaving me.

"So do I."

"Still, we're here, and it's worth it."

She called out my name, quietly but with all her force, more of an endearment than any could be. Her expression was brilliant, and until she spoke again I totally misread it.

"Isn't it?" I cried.

In the same quiet and passionate tone, she said:

"We're deceiving ourselves, aren't we?"

"About what?"

"About us."

"I've never been so sure," I said.

"It's too late. Haven't we known all along it's too late?"

"I haven't."

"I'm just not strong enough," she said. I had never known her ask for pity before.

"You will be," I said, but I had lost my nerve.

"No. It's too late. I knew it, tonight. I knew it," she said.

"We can't decide anything now." I wanted to soothe her.

"There's nothing to decide." She used my name again, as though that was all she could tell me.

"There will be."

"No, it's too hard for me."

"Come out with me——"

"No. Please get me a taxi and let me go home."

"We shall have to forget all this."

For an instant I heard my voice hard.

"There's no future in it," she cried, using the slang flatly instead of her own words. "Let me go home."

"I shall speak to you tomorrow."

"It will be cruel if you do."

Guests were passing us on their way out, and looking at her, knowing that she was near breaking-point, I could do nothing. I called out to the porter and asked him to find a cab. She thanked me, almost effusively, but I shook my head, my eyes still on her, trying to make my own choice, trying not to be crippled by the habits of defeat, the recurrent situations, the deepest traps within me.

CHAPTER XLII

APPARENT CHOICE

LISTENING the next afternoon to George Passant talking of his future, I said nothing of mine. For months, almost for years, since my resolve about Margaret began to form, I had not hinted even at a hope, except to her; but it was not only secretiveness that kept me reticent with George, it was something like superstition. For I had telephoned Margaret that morning, insisting that we should meet and talk it out, and she had given way.

"Assuming that I'm kept in this department, which I take it is reasonable, then I may as well plan on living in London for the rest of my life," said George.

His interview was arranged for a fortnight hence; and George, with the optimism which he had preserved undented from his youth, through ill-luck and worse than ill-luck, took the result for granted.

"I haven't any idea," I said—it was true, but I could not help being alarmed by George's hubris—"what Rose intends to do about you."

"Whatever we think of Rose," George replied comfortably, "we have to admit that he's a highly competent man."

"His personal choices are sometimes odd."

"I should have said," George was unaffected, "that he paid some attention to justice."

"I don't deny that," I said. "But——"

"In that case we're reasonably entitled to consider that he's pretty well informed of what I've done here."

"Within limits that's probably so."

"You're not going to tell me," George was getting argumentative, "that a man as competent as Rose isn't going to see a certain slight difference in effectiveness between what I've done here and what some of those other nice young gentlemen from upper-class Bastilles (George meant public schools) have twittered about trying to do. Take old Gilbert. He's not a bad chap to have a drink with, he's always been exceedingly pleasant to me, but God preserve my eternal soul, I can shift more in an afternoon than Gilbert can manage dimly to comprehend in three weeks' good hard slogging."

"You're preaching to the converted," I said.

"Well, if you're handsome enough to concede that simple point," George replied, "you can perhaps understand why I don't propose to indulge in unnecessary worry."

Yet I, who was upset by George's kind of hope, lived with my own: I found it driving me almost as though I were obeying another person's instructions: I found it driving me, a little absurdly, to talk to a lawyer about divorce. Just as it was slipping out of control, I asserted some caution, even more absurdly: so that, setting out to talk to a lawyer, I did not go to one of the divorce experts whom I had known when I was practising at the Bar, but instead, as though avoiding going under a ladder at the last minute, just paid as it were a friendly call on my old master Herbert Getliffe.

The morning was dark: murk hung over the river, and in chambers the lights were on. It might have been one of the autumn mornings nearly twenty years before, when I sat there, looking out of the window, with nothing to do, avid for recognition, bitter because it would not come. But I felt no true memory of that past: somehow, although I had not revisited the place for years, no trigger released the forces of past emotion, my sense of faint regret was general and false. No trigger clicked, even when I read the list of names at the foot of the staircase, a list where my own name had stood as late as the end of the war: Mr. Getliffe, Mr.

288

W. Allen . . . they had been there before my time. No trigger clicked, even when I went into Getliffe's room, smelt the tobacco once so familiar, and met the gaze of the bold, opaque and tricky eyes.

"Why, it's old L.S.," said Herbert Getliffe, giving me his manly, forthright handshake. He was the only man alive who called me by my initials: he did it with an air both hearty and stern, as though he had just been deeply impressed by a code of gravitas. In fact, he was a man of immense cunning, mercurial and also impressionable. His face was flat and rubbery, his lips red and, despite himself, even in his most magisterial acts there was an imp not far from his eyes. When I had worked in his chambers he had treated me with a mixture of encouragement and lavish unscrupulousness: since then we had kept an affection, desultory and suspicious, for each other. Even now, it surprised me that he was one of the more successful silks at the common law bar: but that was the fact.

I had only seen him once or twice since the night of the Barbican dinner before the war, when I went home to Sheila drunk and elated. I asked how he was getting on.

"It would be ungrateful to grumble," he replied in a stately fashion. "One manages to earn one's bread and butter"—as usual, he could not keep it up, and he winked—"*and* a little piece of cake."

"What about you, L.S.?" He was genuinely curious about others, it was one of his strengths. "Every time I hear about you, you seem to be flourishing."

Yes, I said things had gone comparatively well.

"You go from power to power, don't you? Backstairs secrets and gentlemen in little rooms with XYZ after their names, all clamping collars round our necks," he said, with a kind of free association. He broke out:

"There was a time when I used to think you'd become an ornament here." He grinned: "In that case, just about this year of grace we should have begun to cut each other's throats."

"I'm sure we should," I said.

Getliffe, his mood changing within the instant, looked at me in reproach.

"You mustn't say those things, L.S. You mustn't even think them. There's always room at the top and people like you and me ought to help each other.

"Do you know," he added in a whisper, "that just now one has to turn down cases one would like to take?"

"Too busy?"

"One's never too busy for a thousand smackers," said Getliffe frowning: he was, unexpectedly so after the first impression he made, one of the most avaricious of men.

"Well then?"

"One comes to a stage when one doesn't want to drop any bricks."

He was coy, he repeated his allusion, looked at me boldly like a child expecting to be caught out, but would not explain. Then I realised. There would be vacancies on the Bench soon, Getliffe was in the running, and throughout his whole career he would have sacrificed anything, even his great income, to become a judge. As he sat there that morning I thought I was seeing him almost on top of his world, Getliffe *in excelsis*, one of the few men I had ever seen in sight of all he wanted. It was to him at that moment that I had to let my secret out.

"Herbert," I mentioned it casually, "I may want, it isn't certain but I may, a bit of advice about a divorce case."

"I thought your poor wife was dead," Getliffe replied, and his next words overlay the first: "I'm very sorry to hear it, L.S."

"I may want some professional advice about how to get it through as painlessly as possible."

"*I've* always been happily married," Getliffe reproved me. "I'm thankful to say that the thought of divorce has never come into either of our heads."

"Anyone would like to be in your position," I told him. "But——"

"I always say," Getliffe interrupted, "that it takes a sense of humour to make a success of marriage. A sense of humour, and do-unto-others—especially *one other*—as-you-would-they-should-do-unto-you. That's what it takes."

"Some of us aren't quite as lucky."

"Anyway," said Getliffe, suddenly curious, "what position are you in?"

I knew that, although tricky, he was also discreet. I told him that I had known a woman, whose name did not matter at present, before her marriage: she had been married under four years and had a child not yet three: now she and I had met again, and wished to get married ourselves.

"Well, L.S., I've got to tell you what I think as man-to-man, and I've got to tell you that your decent course is to get out."

"No, I shan't do that," I said.

"I've thought of you as a fellow-sinner, but I've never thought of you as heartless, you know."

He looked at me without expression, and for an instant his tricks, his moral indignation and boasting dropped away: "Tell me, old chap, is this desperately important for you?"

I said the one word: "Yes."

"I see." His tone was kind.

"Well," he said, "it's no use saying any more about what I think. I can tell you the best chap to go to, of course, but you probably know that yourself. But, if you must, I should go to —— Do you know that he's pulling in £20,000 a year these days? It's a very easy side of the profession,

L.S., and sometimes one wishes that one hadn't started off with one's principles."

"At this stage," I said, "I doubt if he could say anything that you and I don't know. You see, the woman I want to marry has nothing to complain of from her husband."

"Will he play? Between you and me and these four walls, I shouldn't if I were in his shoes."

"It wouldn't be reasonable to ask him, even if we felt able to," I replied. "He happens to be a doctor."

Getliffe regarded me with a hot-eyed, flustered look:

"Tell me, L.S., are you co-habiting with her?"

"No."

I was not sure that he believed me. He was, at one and the same time, deeply religious, prudish and sensual: and, as a kind of combined result, he was left with the illusion that the rest of mankind, particularly those not restrained by faith, spent their whole time in unregulated sexual activity.

Recovering from his excitement, he became practical about legal ways and means, which I was conversant with, which normally I should have found tiresome or grittily squalid, but which that morning gave me a glow of confidence. The smoke-dark sky, the reading-lamp on Getliffe's desk, the tobacco smell: the hotel evidence we should want: the delay between the suit being filed and the hearing: the time-lag before the decree absolute: as I discussed them, I had forgotten how much I had invented, talking to Getliffe. It sounded down-to-earth, but for me it was the opposite.

The next afternoon, the November cloud cap still lay low over the town, and looking out from my flat, past the reflection of the lamp in the window whose curtains were not drawn, I saw the Park prematurely grey. Each instant I was listening for the lift outside, for Margaret for the first time had promised to come to me there. She was not yet due, it was only ten to four, but I had begun to listen for her early. With five minutes still to go, I heard the grinding and cranking of the antique machine, and went out on to the dark landing. The lights of the lift slowly moved up; there she was in the doorway, her cheeks pink from the cold air, hands tucked inside her fur coat, her eyes brilliant as though she were relaxed at being in the warm.

Straightaway she came into my arms, the fur comforting under my palms as I held her. After we had kissed, but while she was still close to me, she said: "I've thought about being with you."

She added:

"It's been a long time."

As she took off her coat her movements were assured, flowing and without nerves: she was enjoying herself; she was so different from the woman who had left me at the party that I was both delighted and taken aback. Somehow I felt that, high as her spirits were, they were still deluding her.

Sitting on the sofa, she held out her feet to the electric fire, and I took my place beside her and put my arm round her. It was all as simple, as domestic, as though we had never parted.

"I'm sorry about that night," she said.

"I was afraid."

"You needn't have been."

"I didn't believe it was the end."

"It's not so easy to end as all that, is it?" she said, with a sarcastic smile but her eyes light.

"I hope it's not," I said. "I don't only hope it, but I think it."

"Go on thinking it," she cried, leaning back against my arm.

We were both looking across the room towards the windows, where, the sky having darkened and closed in, we saw nothing but the images of the room's lights. We were each in that state—and we knew it in the other—which was delectable and deceptive, lazy on the tide of unadmitted desire.

"I don't want to move," she said.

It was some time, it might only have been seconds, before she made herself sit straight and look at me. She had the air of positive resolve which comes to one when cutting through a tangle. She had gone through nights, just as I had, when all seemed simple: then next morning the tangle was unresolvable again. That afternoon, she had come feeling all was clear.

"Whatever we do, it isn't going to be easy, is it?" she said.

"No."

"I mean," she went on, "nothing can be easy when we have so many people to think of."

I was not ready to reply, when she reiterated:

"It isn't only ourselves, there are two others I'm bound to care for."

"You don't think I've forgotten about Geoffrey and the child, do you?"

"You can't ask me to hurt either of them. I'll do anything for you if I don't have to hurt them. I'm all yours."

Her face was passionate and self-willed. She said:

"That's the proposition I've got to make. We've got to hide it. I never thought I should want to hide anything, but I'll do it for you, I'll do it because I need you. It will take some hiding, I shall have to let Helen into it so that I can get away, I shan't be able to come to you more than once or twice a week, but that will make up for everything. It'll rescue us, we can go on for ever, and we're luckier than most people ever will be in their lives."

The sight of the flush on her cheeks, usually so pale, excited me.

I went to the fireplace. As I looked down at her, I had never wanted her more. I was seized with memories of taking her, the words we had muttered; I was shaken by one memory, a random one, not specially ecstatic, of lifting her naked in front of a looking-glass, which came from so deep as to be almost tactile.

I was thinking also how perfectly it would suit me to have her as my mistress, a relation which would give me the secretive joy I doted on, make no new claims on me, leave me not struggling any more to reshape my life.

It seemed as near a choice as I had had.

I heard my own voice, thick and rough:

"No."

"Why not?"

"It must be all or nothing."

"How can it be either?"

"It must be."

"You're asking too much."

"Have you begun to think," I asked, "what a secret affair would mean to you? It would have its charm to start with, of course it would, everyone who's lived an open life always hankers after concealments and risks. But you'd soon get over that, and then you'd find it meant lies upon lies. Corroding every other relation you had in order to sustain one that you began to dislike more and more. You haven't been used to playing confidence tricks. It would mean for you that you'd never behave again as you like to behave——"

"I dare say it would mean all that," she said. "But, if it avoids pain for others, do you think I should be put off?"

My hand gripping the mantelpiece, I said as simply as I could:

"It would not avoid pain for me."

"I was afraid of that."

"I don't mean jealousy, I mean deprivation. If I took you on your terms, I should lose what I want most of all.

I'm not thinking of you at all now, I'm just thinking of myself."

"I'm glad," she said.

"I want you to be with me all the time. I believe we shall be happy, but I can't promise it. But you know it better than anyone will ever do, I'm not good at living face-to-face with another human being. Unless you're with me I shall never do it."

As I spoke, she had bent her head into her hands, so that I could only see her hair.

"I can't be sad, I can't be," she said at last. "But I don't see that there is a way through."

She looked up, her eyes lucid, and said:

"I can't get out of talking to you about Geoffrey, though you won't like it."

"Go on," I replied.

"I don't want to make it too dramatic. I'm fond of him, but I'm not driven to him as I am to you. I'm not even sure how much he depends on me——"

"Well then."

"It may be a good deal. I must tell you this, I used to hope it was."

She went on:

"I don't know him, I never have done, as well as I do you. I don't know how strong his feelings are. His senses are strong, he enjoys himself very easily, he's inclined to be impatient with people who don't find life as easy as he does."

She wanted to believe that that was all. She was trying not to give herself the benefit of the doubt. The words she said—just as when we first met secretly in the café—were honest. But once again her hopes, and mine also, were stronger than the words. She wanted to believe that he did not need her much. I wanted to believe it too.

Then she burst out—"He's never done a thing to me or said a thing to me that isn't as considerate as it could be.

He's not given me a single bad hour to hold against him. How can I go to him and say, 'Thank you, you've been good to me, now for no reason that I can possibly give you I intend to leave you cold.'"

"I am ready to speak to him," I said.

"No," she said violently. "I won't be talked over."

For an instant, temper, something deeper than temper, blazed from her eyes. She smiled at me:

"I'm sorry," she said. "I wish I could be angry with him, and it makes me angry with you instead."

"As for talking me over," she added, "he might not mind, he might regard it as civilised. But you and I aren't civilized enough for that."

"I will do anything to bring him to the point," I said.

"Not that."

"Then will you?"

"After what I've said, you oughtn't to ask me."

As I stood by the mantelpiece in the bright room, watching her on the sofa, the curtains still not drawn and the winter sky black above the Park, the air was heavy between us, heavy in a way no tenderness could light.

"Do you think I like you having the harder part?" I said.

"I'll do anything but that."

"It's our only hope."

"I beg you," she said, "let's try my way."

It was a long time before, in the heavy thudding air, I could reply.

"No," I said.

CHAPTER XLIII

VISIT FROM A WELL-WISHER

ONE afternoon in the following week, when I was still in suspense, my secretary came into the office and said that Mr. Davidson was asking to see me. Behind my papers, for I was busy that day, I welcomed him, apprehensive of the mention of Margaret's name which did not come.

I was incredulous that he had dropped in just because he was in tearing spirits and liked my company.

"Am I interrupting you?" he said, and chuckled.

"That's an unanswerable question," he broke out. "What does one say, when one's quite openly and patently in the middle of work, and some ass crassly asks whether he's interrupting you?"

"Anyway," I said, "this can all wait."

"The country won't stop?" With a gesture as lively as an undergraduate's, he brushed the quiff of grey hair off his forehead. "You see, I'm looking for someone to brag to. And there's no one else in this part of London whom I can decently brag to, at least for long enough to be satisfactory."

He had just, calling at the Athenaeum, received the offer of an honorary degree, not from his own university but from St. Andrews. "Which is entirely respectable," said Davidson. "Of course, it doesn't make the faintest difference to anything I've tried to do. If in twenty years five people read the compositions of an obsolete critic of the graphic arts, it won't be because some kind academic gentleman gave him an LL.D. In fact, it's dubious whether critics ought to get any public recognition whatever. There's altogether too much criticism now, and it attracts altogether too much esteem. But still, if any criticism is going to attract esteem, I regard it as distinctly proper that mine should."

I smiled. I had witnessed a good many solid men receive honours, men who would have dismissed Davidson as bohemian and cranky: solid men who, having devoted much attention to winning just such honours, then wondered whether they should accept them, deciding, after searching their souls, that they must for their wives' and colleagues' sakes. By their side, Austin Davidson was so pure.

"The really pressing problem is," said Davidson, "to make sure that all one's acquaintances have to realise the existence of this excellent award. They have a curious tendency not to notice anything agreeable which comes one's way. On the other hand, if someone points out in a very obscure periodical that Austin Davidson is the worst art critic since Vasari, it's quite remarkable how everyone I've ever spoken to has managed to fix his eyes on that.

"Of course," Davidson reflected happily, "I suppose one would only be kept completely cheerful if they had a formula to include the name in most public announcements. Something like this. 'Since the Provost and Fellows of Eton College have been unable to secure the services of Mr. Austin Davidson, they have appointed as Headmaster . . .' Or even 'Since H.M. has not been successful in persuading Mr. Austin Davidson of the truths of revealed religion, he has elevated to the See of Canterbury. . . .'" He was so light-hearted, I did not want to see him go, the more so as I knew now he had detected nothing about Margaret and me. A few months before, I had been hyperæsthetised for the opposite reason, hoping to hear him bring out her name.

Enjoying himself, he also did not want to part. It was getting too late for tea in the cafés near Whitehall, and

Davidson drank little: so I suggested a place in Pimlico, and, as Davidson had a passion for walking, we started off on foot. He lollopped along, his steps thudded on the dank pavement; his fancies kept flicking out. When we passed the dilapidated rooms-by-the-hour-or-night hotels of Wilton Road, he jerked with his thumb at one, a little less raffish, with it door shut and the name worse for wear over the fanlight.

"How much should I have to pay you to spend a night there?"

"You pay the bill too?"

"Certainly I pay the bill."

"Well then, excluding the bill, three pounds."

"Too much," said Davidson severely, and clumped on.

I had wanted to escape that meeting, and it turned out a surprise: so did another which I did not want to escape—with his daughter Helen. When she telephoned and said, not urgently so far as I could hear, that she would like to see me, I was pleased: and I was pleased when I greeted her on the landing of my flat.

It was years since I had seen her; and, as soon as I could watch her face under my sitting-room light, I wondered if I should have guessed her age. She was by now in her late thirties, and her cheeks and neck were thinning; her features, which had always had the family distinction without her sister's bloom, had sharpened. Yet, in those ways passing or already passed into scraggy middle-age, she nevertheless had kept, more than any of us, the uncovered-up expression of her youth: she had taken on no pomp at all, not even the simple pomp of getting older: there was nothing deliberate about her, except for the rebellious concern about her clothes, which, I suspected, had by now become automatic, even less thought-about than Margaret's simplicity. Her glance and smile were as light as when she was a girl.

"Lewis," she said at once, "Margaret has told me about you two."

"I'm glad of it."

"Are you?" She knew enough about me to be surprised: she knew that, holding this secret, I would not have shared it with my own brother, intimate though we were.

"I'm glad that someone knows whom we can trust."

Staring at me over the sofa-head, Helen realised that I meant it, and that this time, unlike all others, the secrecy was pressing me in. The corners of her eyes screwed up: her mouth was tart, almost angry, with the family sarcasm.

"That's not the most fortunate remark ever made," she said.

"What do you mean?"

"I wasn't very anxious to come to see you today."

"Have you brought a message from her?" I cried.

"Oh, no."

For an instant I was relieved; she was more tense than I was.

"Margaret knows that I was coming here," she said. "And I believe she knows what I was going to say."

"What is it?"

She spoke fast, as though beset until she had it out: "What you're planning with Margaret is wrong."

I gazed at her without recognition and without speaking. After a time, she said, quite gently, now she had put the worst job behind her:

"Lewis, I think you ought to answer for yourself."

"Ought I?"

"I think so. You don't want to frighten me off, do you? You've done enough of that with other people, you know."

I had always had respect for her. After a pause, I said:

"You make moral judgements more easily than I do."

301

"I dare say I overdo it," said Helen. "But I think you go to the other extreme. And that has certain advantages to you when you're planning what you're planning now."

"Do you think I'm specially pleased with myself about it?"

"Of course you're worried." She studied me with her sharp bright eyes. "But I don't know, I should have said you seemed much happier than you used to be."

She went on:

"You know I wish you to be happy, don't you?"

"I know," I said.

"And I wish it for her too," said Helen.

Suddenly, across the grain of feeling, she smiled.

"When a woman comes to anyone in your predicament and says 'Of course, I wish both of you well, I couldn't wish anyone in the world better, *but*——' it means she's trying to break it up. Quite true. But still I love her very much, and I was always fond of you."

There was a silence.

She cried out, sharp, unforgiving:

"But the child's there. That's the end of it."

"I've seen him——" I began.

"It didn't stop you?"

"No."

"I can't understand you." Then the edge of her voice turned away. "I'm ready to believe that you and she could make something more valuable for each other than she and Geoffrey ever could. I always hoped that you'd get married in the first place."

She said:

"But just because you're probably right for each other, just because you're capable of being good to and for each other, you can't go back to it now."

For the first time I was irritated and confused, I stumbled to find an answer in her own terms.

302

"You can't," she said, pushing my retort aside, "take the slightest risk about the child. It's not only for his sake, it's for hers, because you know what it would mean for her, if anything went wrong with him."

"I'm not afraid that anything would go wrong."

"You can't take the risk." She went on:

"If things didn't go right for the child, then it wouldn't matter if you felt it wasn't your fault and that he'd never have coped anyway. What do you think she would feel?"

She said:

"She must see this as well as I do. I can't understand her."

I began to answer her. Whatever Margaret and I did, I said, there was no way open of behaving as we wished to behave. Each of us knew the responsibilities, I said.

"If anything went wrong with him, she'd never forgive herself."

"Whether she does——"

"It would be there, coming between you, for the rest of your lives," Helen said.

"I've imagined even that," I replied.

"You've no right to do it," she burst out. I had been forcing down anger, but hers had broken loose.

"You must let us answer for ourselves," I said.

"That's too easy," she cried. She was gentler than her sister; I had not seen violent temper released in her before. "I'd better tell you now, if you go ahead with this, I won't give either of you the slightest help, I won't make things easier for you by half an hour."

"Do you hope that will change our minds?"

"I hope so very much," she said. "If I can stop her coming to you, I shall do it."

I tried to control myself, and meet her case.

As I spoke, I was thinking that in Helen maternal love was stronger beyond comparison than any other. It was her

unassuageable deprivation that she had not had children
and she still went from doctor to doctor. She had the
maternal devotion of a temperament emotional but sexually
cool; she could not but help feel that the love for a child wa
measured on the same plane as sexual love.

To Margaret that would have been meaningless. Fo
her, those loves were different in kind. Almost as materna
as her sister, she had scarcely spoken to me about the boy
and yet all along she had been thinking what Helen had
just threatened us with. Her feeling for the child wa
passionate. It had more ferocity than Helen's would have
had, yet it could not cancel out that other feeling which
pulled her as it were at right angles—that feeling which
unlike Helen's idea of it, was at root neither gentle no
friendly, that feeling which, although it contained an ele
ment of maternal love, was in totality no nearer to tha
love than it was to self-destruction or self-display.

Helen's insight was acute, I was thinking; she had learn
more than most, and all she said about human actions yo
could trust—unless they were driven by sex. Then it wa
as though the drawing-pins had worked loose, the drawing
pins which fitted so accurately when she charted a descrip
tion of a nephew sucking up to an aunt. Suddenly, if she
had to describe sexual feeling, the paper was flapping
she was not hopelessly far away but the point never quite
fitted. Somehow she sketched out friendships and trust and
a bit of play and imagined that was sexual love. I remembered
how many observers I had listened to and read, whose
charts flapped loose exactly as hers did—observers wicked
as well as high-minded, married as well as Jane Austens
men and women. Often their observations sounded cosy
when you were not in trouble, but when you were they migh
as well have been nonsense verse.

Yet I could not shrug off Helen's warning about the
child. When I was younger, I might have thought that,

by explaining to myself why she felt so deeply, I was explaining it away. Now I could not delude myself so conveniently.

I had to answer something to which there was no straight answer, telling her that for my part I would accept the penalties and guilt, and that I believed the tie between us would bear what the future laid upon it.

I had made up my mind, I told her: I did not know whether Margaret would come to me, but I was waiting for her.

CHAPTER XLIV

SECOND INTERVIEW OF GEORGE PASSANT

NEXT morning after breakfast—the sky over the Park was so brilliant in November sunshine that I hushed the give-away words, the secret irked me more—I rang up Margaret: I had to tell her of my conversation with her sister, without softening any of her sister's case.

"I knew she was against us," came Margaret's voice.

"She said nothing that we hadn't thought," I said, reporting Helen's words about the child.

"Perhaps we should have told each other."

"It has made no difference."

"I never expected her to be so much against us." There was a note of rancour in Margaret's tone, a note almost of persecution, very rare in her. Anxiously, I thought that the weeks of deception were wearing her down: they had begun to tell on me, who was better adapted for them: in so many ways she was tougher, and certainly braver, than I was, but not in this.

I said that we must meet. No, there was no one to look after the child. Tomorrow? Doubtful.

"We must settle it," I said, for the first time forcing her.

"It will be easier next week."

"That's too long."

The receiver went dead, as though we had been cut off. Then she said a word and stopped. She, usually so active, could not act: she was in a state I also knew, when it was easier to think of disrupting one's life, so long as the decision were a week ahead, than to invent an excuse to go for a walk that afternoon.

At last: "Lewis." Her voice had the hardness, the hostility of resolve. When I replied, it came again: "I'll go for tea to my father's on Friday, you can call and find me there."

For the moment relieved, waiting for the Friday which was two days ahead, I arrived at Whitehall in the dazzling morning: odd, it struck me sometimes, to arrive there after such a scene, to meet one's colleagues with their shut and public faces, and confront them with one's own.

That particular morning, as it happened, was not routine: I had to go straight to Rose's room, where I was required for two interviews, of which the second was to be George Passant's.

On Rose's desk chrysanthemums bulged from the vases, the burnt smell bit into the clean, hygienic air, along with Rose's enthusiastic thanks to me for sparing time that morning, which in any case I was officially obliged to do.

"Perhaps we might as well get round the table," he said, as usual punctual, as usual unhurried. The two others took their places, so did I, and the first interview began. I knew already—I had heard Rose and Jones discuss the man—that the result was not in doubt. He was an ex-regular officer who had entered the department late in the war, and they agreed—his work had not come my way—that he was nowhere near the standard of the administrative class.

Polite, patient, judicious, Rose and the others questioned him, their expressions showing neither encouragement nor discouragement, neither excessive interest nor dismissal. They were all three sensible at judging men, or at least at judging men as creatures to do business with. They were on their own ground, selecting for the bureaucratic skills in which not only Rose, but also the youngest of the three, Osbaldiston, was expert.

The third was John Jones, who was now Sir John and a year off retirement: still looking handsome and high-coloured, and as though bursting with a heterodox opinion, a revelation straight from the heart, but after forty years of anxiety to please hypnotized by his own technique, unable to take his eye away from watching Rose's response. Rose found him agreeable: granted Jones's modest degree of talent, he had got on a good deal better as a snurge than he would have done as a malcontent, and it was romantic to think otherwise: but, when it came to serious business, his view did not count with Rose by the side of Osbaldiston's, who was twenty-five years younger.

Osbaldiston, a recent arrival, was an altogether more effective man. Unlike Rose or Jones, he had not started in a comfortable professional family, and socially he had travelled a long way, further than me or my friends: born in the East End, a scholarship, Oxford, the civil service examination. In the Treasury he had fitted so precisely that it seemed, though it was not, a feat of impersonation: Christian names, the absence of jargon, the touch of insouciant cultivation carried like a volume in the pocket— they all sounded like his native speech. Long, thin, unworn, he seemed to many above the battle and a bit of a dilettante. He was as much above the battle as a Tammany boss and as much a dilettante as Paul Lufkin. He was so clever that he did not need to strain, but he intended to have Rose's success and more than Rose's success. My private guess was that he was for once over-estimating himself: nothing could prevent him doing well, one could bet on his honours, one could bet that he would go as high as Jones—but perhaps not higher. It might be that, in the next ten years when he was competing with the ablest, he would just lack the weight, the sheer animal force, to win the highest jobs.

The first interview closed in courtesies from Rose to the candidate. As the door closed, Rose, without expression, looked round the table. Osbaldiston at once shook his head: I shook mine, then Jones shook his.

"I'm afraid the answer is no," said Rose, and without any more talk began writing on the nomination form.

"He's a nice chap," said Osbaldiston.

"Charming," said Jones.

"He's been quite useful within his limits," said Rose, still writing.

"He's got a service pension of seven hundred pounds, as near as makes no matter," said Osbaldiston. "He's forty-six, and he's got three children, and it's a bit of a fluke whether he collects another job or not. What I can't see, Hector, is how on those terms we're going to recruit an officer corps at all."

"It's not our immediate pigeon," replied Rose from his paper, "but we shall have to give it a bit of thought." The curious thing was, I knew that they would.

"Well," said Rose, signing his name, "I think we'll have Passant in now."

When George entered, he wore a diffident, almost soapy smile, which suggested that, just as on his first appearance in the room, he expected to be tripped up inside the door. As he sat in the vacant chair, he was still tentatively smiling: it was not until he answered Rose's first question that his great head and shoulders seemed to loom over the table, and I could, with my uneasiness lulled, for an instant see him plain. His forehead carried lines by now, but not of anxiety so much as turbulence. Looking from Osbaldiston's face and Rose's to George's, one could see there the traces of experiences and passions they had not known—and yet also, by the side of those more disciplined men, his face, meeting the morning light, seemed mysteriously less mature.

Rose had begun by asking him what he considered his 'most useful contribution so far' to the work of the Department.

"The A—job I'm doing now is the neatest," said George, as always relishing the present, "but I suppose that we

got further with the original scheme for Tube Alloys"
(that is, the first administrative drafts about atomic energy).

"Would you mind running over the back history, just
to get your part and the Department's part in something like
perspective?" Rose inquired with unblinking politeness.
"Perhaps you'd better assume that our colleague here"—
he looked at Osbaldiston—"is pretty uninformed about
the early stages, as he wasn't in at the beginning."

"Perhaps you'd better," said Osbaldiston offhandedly.
"Though as a matter of fact I've done some of my home-
work since."

Starting to enjoy himself, George gave the history of the
atomic energy project from the time he entered the office.
Even to me, his feat of memory was fantastic; my own
memory was better than most, I had been as close to this
stuff as he had, but I could not have touched that display
of recapitulation. I could feel that, round the table, they
were each impressed, and all took for granted that it was
unthinkable for him to give a date or a paper fact wrong.
But he was a shade too buoyant, and I was not quite easy.
It was partly that, unlike Osbaldiston, he had not taken
on a scrap of protective coloration; given the knowledge,
he would have made his exposition in the identical manner,
in the same hearty voice, when I first met him in a
provincial street twenty-five years before. And also—this
made me more uneasy—he had not put our part in the
project in exact proportion: we had been modestly
important, but not quite so important as he thought.

George was beaming and at ease. Jones, who I knew
liked him, put in some questions about method which might
have been designed to show George at his most competent.
George's answer was lucidly sober. Just then it seemed to
me unthinkable that any body of men, so fair-minded as
these, could reject him.

Jones had lit a pipe, so that the chysanthemum smell no

310

onger prevailed over the table; outside the windows at
ur back, the sun must have been brilliant to make the room
o light. Rose continued with the interview: present work?
ow much could be dispensed with? One answer business-
ke, another again too buoyant and claiming too much,
ne third fair and good. At all interviews Rose was more
han ever impassive, but he gave a slight acquiescent nod:
o at once did Jones.

Then, as though lackadaisically, Osbaldiston spoke.
"Look here," he said to George, "there's something we
re bound to have at the back of our minds, and it's far
etter to have it in the open, I should have thought. You're
bviously an intelligent chap, if I may say so. But with due
espect you don't seem to have done much with your life
ntil you got dragged here by the war, and then you were
orty-three already. It's bound to strike all of us as curious.
Vhy was it? Can you give us some sort of lead?"

George stared at him.

"I'm afraid," George said, with diffidence, "that I didn't
et much of a start."

"Nor did a lot of us, you know."

"I've got to make it clear that my family was very poor."

"I bet it wasn't as poor as mine." Osbaldiston made
point of not being snobbish about his origin. It was for
hat reason that he was more pressing about George's
ack of ambition than Rose had been in the first interview
hree years ago.

"And of course," said George, "everyone at school
hought that becoming a solicitor's clerk was a step up in the
vorld for me, a bit above my station, as a matter of fact.
No one ever pointed out, even if they knew, which I'm
nclined to doubt, that there was anything else open to me."

"I suppose schools were worse in your time," said
Osbaldiston. "And afterwards you were with your firm,
Eden and Martineau, for over twenty years and I take it

311

the job is still open for you—I confess I'm still puzzled tha
you didn't see your way out."

"Perhaps I didn't give it as much attention as other
might have done, but at first there were things whic
interested me more. Somehow the right chance neve
seemed to present itself——"

"Bad luck," said Osbaldiston casually, but they wer
looking at each other with incomprehension, the youn
man who, wherever you put him, knew how the successfu
world ticked, George who was always a stranger there.

Osbaldiston told Rose that he had no more questions
punctiliously Rose asked George if he had anything mor
he wished to tell us. No, said George, he thought he ha
been given a very full hearing. With a curious unobsequiou
and awkward grace, George added:

"I should like to say that I am grateful for your considera
tion."

We listened to George's footsteps down the corrido
When they had died away, Rose, again without expressio
and in a tone utterly neutral, said:

"Well, what do you think of him?"

Quick off the mark and light-toned, Osbaldiston said
"At any rate, he's not a nobody."

"I thought he interviewed rather well," said Jones.

"Yes. He had his ups and downs," said Osbaldiston
"On the whole he interviewed much as you'd expect. H
showed what we knew already, that there's something i
him."

Rose said nothing, while Osbaldiston and Jones agree
that George's mind was powerful, that he would have don
well in any academic course. If he had sat for the competitiv
examination as a young man at the regulation age, he woul
have got in comfortably, Osbaldiston reflected, and had a
adequate career.

"What do you think, Hector?" Jones enquired.

Rose was still sitting silent, with his arms folded on his chest.

"Perhaps he would," he said after a pause. "But of course that isn't the point. He's not a young man now, he's a middle-aged one of forty-seven, and I think it's fair to say a distinctly unusual one."

"I'm inclined to think," Rose added, his face blank, "that the answer this time isn't immediately obvious."

At once, I knew what I was in for. Indeed, I had known it while Rose sat, politely listening to the other's views, non-committal in his quietness. For, in the long run, the decision was his: the rest of us could advise, argue, persuade: he would listen to the sense of opinion, but his was the clinching voice. Though it did not sound like it, though the manners were egalitarian and not court manners, this was as much a hierarchy as Lufkin's firm, and Rose's power that morning, concealed as it was, was as free as Lufkin's.

The only chance was for me to match will against will. He had opposed George's entry right at the beginning; Rose was not the man to forget his own judgements. In that one impartial comment of his, I could hear him believing inflexibly that he had been right.

Yet within the human limits he was a just man: and, screwing myself up for the argument, there were some fears which I could wipe away. I could rely on it that he would not mention George's prosecution fourteen years before: he had been acquitted, that was good enough. I could also rely on it that neither he nor the others would be much put off by rumours of George's womanising. Compared with those three round the table that morning, not many men, it struck me afterwards, would have been so correct, un-inquisitive, unbiased.

"It might help us," said Rose, "if Lewis, who has seen more of Passant's work than any of us, would give us his views. I'm very anxious," he said to me, "that you should feel we've been seized of all the information we ought to have."

Addressing myself to Rose, I made my case. Probably I should have made it more fluently for anyone but George. I was not relaxed, I had to force myself into the professional idiom.

I described his work, trying to apportion his responsibility, remembering that to Rose it would not seem right if I did not also demarcate my own. I said that he was a man of immense capacity. It was true—I was straining not to overstate my case—that his immediate judgment was not always first-class, he hadn't the intuitive feel for what could or could not be done. But he had two qualities not often combined—zest for detail and executive precision, together with a kind of long-term imagination, a forecaster's insight into policy. In the area between detail and the long term, he was not so good as our run-of-the-mill administrators: but nevertheless his two qualities were so rare that he was more valuable than any of them.

I had been talking on the plane of reason, but I heard my own voice harsh, emphatic without helping the sense.

"We're most grateful to you for that piece of exposition, my dear Lewis. We really are very, very much obliged to you."

Jones sucked at his pipe: one could feel him sniffing dissension in the air: he said:

"I imagine that, if old Passant didn't get established, he'd just go straight back to those solicitors and it wouldn't be any terrific hardship for him."

"He'd be about £200 a year better off with us," said Osbaldiston, "but you can knock some of that off for living in London."

"I wonder whether it would be really a kindness to establish him?" Jones was meditating. "Because he's obviously an unusual man, as Hector says, but with the

314

best will in the world we can't do much for him. He'd have to begin as a principal and he's nearly fifty now, and at his age he couldn't possible go more than one step up. That's not much for someone who really is a bit of a fellow in his own way."

"It may not be much, but he wants it," I burst out.

"All that is off the point," said Rose, with untypical irritation. "We're not required to say what is good for him or what isn't, and we're not concerned with his motives. He's applied to be established, and he's got a right to apply, and our business starts there and ends there. The only conceivable point we have got to decide is whether on his merits we ought to recommend him. I suggest," he said, recapturing his politeness but with a flick in his tone, "that we shall find the problem quite sufficiently intricate without introducing any psychological complications."

"I'm not sure," said Osbaldiston, "that I can see a strong enough reason for not having him."

"Do you see one, Hector?" asked Jones.

"Aren't you making very heavy weather of it?" I said, thinking the time for caution had gone. "Here's a man everyone agrees to have some gifts. We're thinking of him for a not desperately exalted job. As a rule we can pass people, like Cooke for example, without half this trouble. Does anyone really consider that Cooke is a quarter as competent as Passant?"

"I didn't want to give my opinion," said Rose smoothly and slowly to Jones, "before I had some indication of what you others thought. I still don't want to rush things, but perhaps this is a reasonable time to sketch out the way my mind's been tending. As for your question, Lewis, I don't consider that we've been making unduly heavy weather of this business. We want to see that this man gets fair treatment: and we also don't want to take an unjustified risk for the Department. It isn't entirely easy to reconcile those

315

two objectives. I'm inclined to think that you slightly, not very greatly, but perceptibly, exaggerate Passant's mental qualities, but I won't quarrel with the view that he is a distinctly better mind than Cooke, for example, or, as far as that goes, than most of the ordinary principals in the Department. I think I remember saying much the same thing when I first saw him. On the other hand, that doesn't entirely persuade me that keeping him wouldn't be a mildly regrettable risk where the Department stands to lose slightly more than it stands to gain. After all, if we keep Passant, we gain a principal in some ways rather better than the average, in some ways, as you very properly pointed out, Lewis, rather worse. And at the same time we take on a definite hazard, not of course a serious one or one likely to materialize in fact, but the kind of hazard that you can't escape if you commit yourself to a man of, I don't want to do him an injustice but perhaps I can reasonably say, powerful, peculiar and perhaps faintly unstable personality. There's bound to be a finite chance that such a man wouldn't fit in for his remaining thirteen years or whatever it is. There's a finite chance that we should be making trouble for ourselves. There might just possibly be some row or commotion that wouldn't do us any good. I don't think that it is responsible to take those risks for the sake of an appointment at this level. I think I should conceivably have come down in Passant's favour if we were able to consider him for something more senior. He's the sort of man, in fact, who might have been far less trouble as a cabinet minister than he'd be in the slightly more pedestrian ranks of the administrative service."

"Well," said Jones, "I don't think any one could add much to a summing up like that."

While there had seemed a doubt, Osbaldiston had been as painstaking as Rose himself. Now he tilted back his chair, and sounded more than ever offhand.

"Agreed," he said, as if anxious not to waste any more time. "Though perhaps it's a pity that we didn't catch the chap young."

"In that case, with your approval," Rose remarked, "I propose to report on him to the Commission in terms something like this. I'll send you a draft. But I propose to say that he has filled a principal's place here quite up to standard form, and in one or two respects better than standard form. That we consider him intellectually well up to the level of the administrative class. But that at his age, bearing in mind certain features of his personality, we shouldn't feel entirely easy about fitting him into the Department as an established man."

"It might be a friendly thought," said Jones, and he was speaking with good nature, "to tell him to withdraw and not fag to go up to the Commission. Because there will be nothing they can do but say no."

"I agree," said Rose.

I began, keeping my voice down, still seeming reasonable, to open the argument again, but in a moment Osbaldiston broke in:

"It's no use going over old ground."

"I really don't think it's very profitable," said Rose.

Then I lost my temper. I said they were too fond of the second-rate. I said that any society which deliberately made safe appointments was on the way out.

"I'm sorry that we can't carry you with us, Lewis." Rose's eyes were cold, but he was keeping his own temper.

"You do not realise your own prejudices," I cried.

"No, this isn't at all profitable and we must agree to differ." Rose spoke with exaggerated calm. "You've had more experience in selecting men than any of your colleagues. As you know, I for one have often been guided by you. But you'd be the first to admit that no man can be infallible. And even very wise people sometimes seem no more infallible than the rest of us, the nearer they get toward home."

He had permitted himself that last arctic flick. Then leaning back in his chair, his face smooth, he said:

"Well, I think that is all for this morning. Thank you all very, very much for sparing your valuable time. Thank you, John. Thank you, Douglas. Thank you *very* much, Lewis."

Back in my room, I stared out into the sun-bright White hall with the gauze of anger, of something like anxiety, or despondent restless bitterness in front of my eyes. It was the state that I used to know more often, that I had lived in during my worst times. It was a long while since I had been so wretched.

It had come pretty easy, it had not given me much regret to slip out of the struggles of power—as a rule I did not mind seeing the places of power filled by the Osbaldistons, those who wanted them more. But that morning, gazing blankly down at the sunny street, I was wretched because I was not occupying them myself. Then and only then I could have done something for George and those like him.

The men I sat with in their offices, with their moral certainties, their comfortable, conforming indignation which never made them put a foot out of step—they were the men who managed the world, they were the people who in any society came out on top. They had virtues denied the rest of us: I had to give them my respect. But that morning I was on the other side.

CHAPTER XLV

FRIGID DRAWING-ROOM

IN Whitehall the fog was dense: it was a little whiter, I
could make out the lights in the shop-fronts, as the taxi
nosed up Baker Street. By the time we reached Regent's
Park, the pavements were clear to the view as far as the
glowing ground-floor windows. Trying to damp down
expectation, I was soothed by the fog shutting me in: instead
of the joggle of the taxi, the reminder of adult expectations
to which one did not know the end, I felt the sheer cosiness
of a childhood's winter afternoon.

Whatever my expectations had been, I was surprised
when I entered Davidson's study. For Margaret smiled at
me, without much trace of trouble: Davidson did not look
up: they were playing a game. In the fireplace stood a
teapot, cups, a plate of crumpets, but on Davidson's side
the tea had a skin on it. The crumpet's butter was solid.
He was leaning, his face still distinguished even though his
mouth was open with concentration, over the board. So far
as I could pick up at a glance, the board was homemade,
something like a chess board but not symmetrical and with
at least three times the number of squares on the base line:
at some points there appeared to be blanks and hazards.
They were using ordinary chessmen, but each had some
extra pieces, together with small boxes whose function I
did not begin to understand.

As I looked at Margaret's face, it seemed to me that I
remembered returning to the house in Chelsea, finding
Sheila staring with psychotic raptness at her chessmen: it
was not a jab of pain, it was more like the pleasure (the

exact converse of the Dantesque misery) with which, in the company of someone whom one safely loves, one looks in at a place where one has been miserable.

"She said that you might be coming," said Davidson without preamble, gazing up under his eyebrows and then back at the board.

I said, "Just for a few minutes", but Davidson ignored me. "You'll have to play, of course," he said sternly. "It's a much better game with three."

It was, in fact, a war game which Davidson had perversely invented while he and his friends were pacifists in 1914–18. So far as I could judge, who envisaged the game stretching on, the three of us kept speechless there, it was elaborate but neat, crisp because he had a gift for concepts: Davidson wanted to explain it to me in all its beauties, irritated because I did not seem to be attending. I did not even pay enough attention, Davidson indicated, to the names of the two sides. They were Has-beens and Humbugs. The Has-beens were the side Davidson was commanding: their officers were chosen from his allies, associates and teachers, for Davidson, with his usual bleak honesty, knew critical fashion when he saw it. The other side was picked from Davidson's irremovable aversions, among them D. H. Lawrence, Jung, Kierkegaard; various Catholic intellectuals and Communist art critics had places as brigadiers.

I did not know enough about the game to lose on purpose. All I knew was that Davidson would never get bored with it.

I could not even guess whether Margaret was willing to break the peace-of-the-moment.

Just then she was threatening one of her father's rooks, who stood for an academic philosopher known to all three of us.

"He oughtn't to be on your side anyway," said Margaret. Davidson studied the battle-plan.

"Why shouldn't he?" he said without attention.

"He's going to be the next convert, or so the Warden says."

"The Warden," Davidson remarked, still pre-occupied with his move, "is a good second-class liar."

At last he guarded the rook, and was able to gather together the conversation—"he (the philosopher) is about as likely to be converted as I am. He's a perfectly sensible man."

"And you couldn't say fairer than that, could you?"

Davidson smiled: he liked being teased by his daughter: it was easy to feel how he had liked being teased, perhaps still did, by other women.

"He was always perfectly sensible," he said.

"However did you know?"

"I don't remember him ever saying anything really crass," said Davidson.

"But you all said the same things," said Margaret. "I always wondered how you could tell each other apart."

It was the first time I had seen her alone with her father. I had heard her talk of him very often, but never to him: and now I listened to her sounding gay and very much his daughter. Although I should have known better, I was surprised.

It was true that she felt something stronger than dislike for the beliefs of her father and his friends, and still more for their unbeliefs. She had been passionately convinced ever since she was a child that their view of life left out all that made men either horrible or splendid.

And yet, seeing her with her father, upset because I wanted nothing but to speak to her alone, I had to notice one thing—that she was proud of him. Her language was more like his than mine; in some ways her nerves were too.

I noticed something else, as I tried to calculate when the game might end—that she was disappointed for him. By the standards of his friends, he, who in his youth had been one of the most glittering of them, had not quite come off. He was no sort of creative person, he was not the critic that some of them had been. He had no illusion about it: at times, so Margaret divined, he had suffered because of it, and so did she. She could not help feeling that, if she had been a man, she would have been stronger than he. That protest, born of their relation or edged by it, had been too deep for me to see, in our first time together. I imagined her as other people did: all they imagined was true, she was loving, she was happy to look after those she loved—it was all true: but it was also true (and the origin of much that she struggled with) that her spirit was as strong as her father's or mine, and in the last resort did not give an inch to either of us.

The game continued. Repeatedly Margaret was glancing at me, until suddenly, as though screwing herself to the threshold edge, she said:

"I want to talk to Lewis for a minute."

It was Davidson's move, and with a faint irritation he nodded. In an instant I followed Margaret into the hall; she led me into the drawing-room, which was dark except for a dim luminescence from the street lamp outside, bleared by the fog: the room struck chilly, but her cheek, as my fingers touched it, was hot, and I could feel my own skin flushed. She switched on a light: she looked up at me, and, although we were alone in the long room, although there was no one else in the house except Davidson, her voice was faint.

"Don't worry," she said.

"That's easy to say."

"No, it's not easy to say." She had roused herself. Her face was wide open: it might have been smiling or in pain.

"I tell you," she cried, "there's no need to worry!"

I exclaimed.

"Do you believe me?" she cried.

"I want to believe you."

"You can." Then she added, in a matter-of-fact but exhausted tone:

"I'll do it."

She went on:

"Yes, I'll tell him."

We were standing in the corner of the frigid room. I felt for an instant the rip of triumph, then I shared her tiredness. It was the tiredness which comes after suspense, when the news may be good or bad: suddenly the good news comes, and in the midst of exaltation one is so light-headed with fatigue that one cannot read the letter through. I felt that happiness had sponged my face, taking away care like the smell of soap in the morning: I saw her face, also washed with happiness.

We stood quiet, our arms round each other: then I saw there was another purpose, a trouble, forming underneath the look of peace.

She said:

"I'll tell him. But you must wait a little."

"I can't wait any longer."

"You must be patient, just this once."

"No, you must do it straightaway."

"It's not possible," she cried.

"It's got to be."

I was gripping her shoulders.

"No," she said, looking at me with knowledge of us both, "I don't want you to, it would be bad. I promise you, it won't be long."

"What are you waiting for?" To my bewilderment, she replied in a tone sounding like one of her aunts, astringent, cynical:

"How often have I told you," she said, "that if you're

going to hurt anyone, it's no use being timidly considerate over the time you choose to do it?

"I always told you," she could not leave it alone, "that you did more harm by trying to be kind. Well, there's nothing like practising what one preaches."

She was trapped, so that she could not bring herself to tell the truth to Geoffrey, or even mildly upset him. By a minor irony, the reason was as prosaic as some which had from time to time determined my own behaviour. It happened that Geoffrey was within a fortnight of sitting his examination for Membership, that is, his qualification as a specialist. It happened also that Geoffrey, so confident in general, was a bad and nervous examinee. She had at least to coax him through, take care of him for this last time: it meant dissimilating, which to her was an outrage, it meant not acting, which was like an illness—and yet not to look after him, just then, when he was vulnerable, would mean a strain she could not take.

"If you must," I agreed at last.

She was relieved, she was abandoned to relief. Soon this would be behind us, she said. Then, as though at random, she cried:

"Now I want to do something."

"What?"

"I want us to go and tell my father."

Her cheeks and temples had coloured, her eyes were bright with energy, her shoulders were thrown back. She led me back through the house, her steps echoing excitedly in the empty hall, until we threw open the door of the study where her father, his beautiful head sunk on his chest, was staring with a mathematician's intensity at the board.

"I've got something to tell you," she said.

He made a cordial but uninterested noise.

"You'll have to listen. Or have I got to write you a letter about it?"

Reluctantly he looked up, with intelligent, brilliant, opaque eyes. He said:

"If you're going to disturb the game, I hope it isn't something trivial."

"Well. Lewis and I want to get married."

Davidson looked blank-faced. He seemed to have had no intimation whatsoever of the news: she might have been telling him that she had just seen a brontosaurus.

"Do you, by God?" he said.

Then he became convulsed with laughter.

"Perhaps you were within your rights to disturb the game. No, I can't say that the news is entirely trivial."

"I haven't told Geoffrey yet," she said. "I can't for a little while. I don't know whether he'll let me go."

"He'll have to," said Davidson.

"It may be difficult."

"I should have thought he was a moderately civilised man," he replied. "In the long run, one's got no choice in these things, don't you know?"

She would have preferred her father not to be quite so casual: but telling him had given her the pleasure of action. It was a joy to let us be seen in another's eyes.

For once her father's glance had not dropped; he looked at her with a sharp, critical, appreciative smile, and then at me.

"I'm quite glad," he said.

I said:

"You ought to be prepared for some unpleasantness. We shall be giving anyone who wants plenty to get hold of."

"Anyone who wants," he replied indifferently, "is welcome to it, I should have thought."

I supposed he did not know our story, but went on:
"Even well-wishers are going to find it slightly bizarre."

"All human relationships are slightly bizarre unless one

is taking part," said Davidson. "I don't see why yours is any more so than anyone else's."

He went on:

"I've never known a situation where it was worth listening to outsiders."

He was the last man to talk for effect: he meant it. It was a kind of contempt which was much more truly aristocratic than that of Betty Vane's relatives: it was the contempt of an intellectual aristocracy, who never doubted their values, least of all in sexual matters: who listened to each other, but not at all to anyone outside. Sometimes—it had often alienated his daughter—his lack of regard for opinion implied that those outside the magic ring might as well belong to another species. But, in times of trouble, it made him inflexible, one to whom the temptations of disloyalty did not exist.

"As a general rule and nonsense apart," he said, "when people are in your position the only help of any conceivable good is practical."

With a surprisingly brisk and executive air, he asked: "Are you all right for money?"

It sounded more surprising, for Davidson, who had never got acclimatised to fountain-pens or telegrams, seemed the most unpractical of men. In fact, the concentration he applied to art-history or to home-made games went also into his investments and he had been consistently and abnormally successful with them.

I told him that money was not a problem. Still executive he said:

"I've known it to be useful to have somewhere to live where people don't expect to find you. I could arrange to let you have this house for six months."

Margaret said she might take him at his word. She would want somewhere to live with the child until we could be married.

326

Davidson was satisfied. He had no more to contribute. Once more he studied his daughter's face with pleasure, then his eyes dropped to their habitual level. Although he did not openly suggest that we should finish the game, his glance began to stray towards the board.

CHAPTER XLVI

LAST TRAIN TO A PROVINCIAL TOWN

EACH morning, as I telephoned Margaret, the winter sky heavy over the trees outside, I heard her forcing her voice to hearten me. At last, so near the time when I trusted her to come to me, I was jealous. I could not stand the thought of her life from day to day, I had to switch my imagination off. I could not stand the thought of her keeping his spirits up; I went through those prosaic miseries of the imagination in which one is tormented by the hearth-glow of another's home, even if it is an unhappy home.

I told myself her part was the harder, but I began to be frightened of the telephone, as though it did nothing but force me to think of her home, of the two of them together.

As we talked, I never inquired about the exact date of his Membership. It was partly that I was trying to keep my side of the bargain, she was to choose her time: but it was also that I did not want to know, either that or anything else about him.

Christmas passed. On a morning just as I was getting ready to ring her up, the telephone bell rang. I heard her voice, though it was distorted and forced.

"It will be all right."

"You've told him?" I cried.

"Yes, I've told him."

"Is all well?"

"All will be well." She was crying.

"When?"

"Soon."

"Very soon?" I burst out.

She said:

"For a long time he wouldn't believe it."

"When shall I fetch you?"

"I had to make him believe me."

"The sooner I'm with you——"

"He can't understand why this has happened to him."

"Has he accepted it?"

"Yes, but he's bitter."

She had deceived herself when we talked of him, she was saying. I replied, if that was true, I had deceived myself as much. Then crying, sometimes dragged back to the night just past (for they had talked right through it) she was asking, as she had not done before, for me to reassure her, to tell her what we should give each other.

When would she come to me? Not that day, she said, in a tone that made me feel there was one last way in which she was trying to look after him. Not that day, but the next.

"At last," she said, in a tone neither sad nor young.

That same evening, I was having a drink with George Passant, who had served his final day at the office and was returning to the provincial town by the last train. We met in a public house, for George had not adapted himself to clubs: there he sat by the fire, enjoying himself as comfortably as in our youth. I told him again, as I had done many times, how angry I was with the Department, and how I still uselessly thought of methods by which I might have presented the case better.

"It was a nuisance," said George. "But anyway I had three interesting years, I wouldn't have been without them for the world."

Somehow he could still draw a line across the past, regard it with an invulnerable optimism as though it had happened to someone else.

"The more I think of it," said George, with a complacent smile, "the better it seems. I've had three remarkably interesting years and done some work which I know the value of better than anyone else. The value in question is incidentally considerable. In the process I've been able to estimate the ability of our hierarchical superiors and there's no danger that I shall be tempted to get them out of proportion. And also I've managed to seize the opportunity for a certain amount of private life. Which all constitutes a pretty fair return for a very minor bit of humiliation."

When he first heard that he had been rejected, he had broken into a comminatory rage, cursing all who had ever been in authority over him, all officials, all members of the new orthodoxy, all who conspired to keep him in the cold. But very soon he had been exaggeratedly reasonable, pointing out "Of course, I couldn't expect anything different . . ." and he would produce some ingenious, highly articulated and quite unrealistic interpretation of why Rose, Jones and Osbaldiston found it necessary to keep him out.

So now he sat comfortably by the fire, drinking his beer, proving to me that he was not damaged.

"All I hope is that you invite me up here pretty regularly," said George. "In future, an occasional visit to London will be essential to my well-being."

It might have been some new night-spot he had discovered: it might have been the balm, mysterious to all but himself, of meeting successful acquaintances: probably it was both, but I did not attend, for I had meant to tell him my news and this was the opening.

"Of course," I said.

I had listened while Margaret, rejoicing in candour had broken our secret to her father. Myself, I had not said anything, open or implicit, even to my brother or to a friend as old as George—except when, to my own astonishment, I came out with it to Getliffe. Even with George tha

330

night I did not wish to talk: I still wanted to be timid with fate: I found myself speaking with an obliqueness I could not quite control.

"Next time you come," I said, "there's just a faint possibility that I may not be alone."

"I'll give you plenty of notice," said George obtusely.

"I mean, I may have someone in my flat."

George chuckled.

"Oh well, she won't be there for ever."

"As a matter of fact," I said, "it's not quite inconceivable, of course, it's too early to say——"

George was puzzled. He had not often heard me so incoherent; he had not heard me anything like so incoherent twenty years before, when my friends and I told glorious stories of fornications we had not yet in fact committed. At last I made it clear enough, and he was on his feet towards the bar, saying in a great voice: "Well, this is a new start, and I'm damned if we don't have a celebration!"

Superstitiously I tried to stop him, but he turned on me: "Is this a new start or isn't it?"

"I hope it is."

"Don't sit on the blasted fence. Of course it is, and I'm not going to be done out of celebrating it."

George continued in that state of noisy argumentative well-being until, when he had drunk more, he said:

"There's a certain beautiful symmetry in the way we stand tonight. You're just coming out of your old phase of existence—just at the precise moment that I am neatly returning to mine."

He laughed out loud, not rancorously, not enviously, but with a curious pleasure, pleasure it seemed in the sheer pattern of events. He was a happy man: he always had been, but was growing even happier in middle age, when it seemed to all external eyes that he had totally failed. As he said, he was returning to his old existence, to the

provincial town, to the firm of solicitors, where he would
continue not as partner but as managing clerk: and there
one would have bet that night, George first to do so, he
would stay for the rest of his life. But he breathed in a
happiness that begins to visit some in middle age: it was the
happiness which comes to those who believe they have lived
according to their nature. In George's own view he had
been himself, he had lived as himself, more than anyone
round him. He blamed his external calamities to that
cause and still thought—partly as a consolation, partly
because in the happiness of his senses it seemed true—that
he had had the best of the bargain.

With five minutes to go before the last train left, we
arrived at St. Pancras. I told George, as we walked down the
platform in the cold, the red lights smeared out by an erup
tion of sulphur smoke, that this was the identical train I
used to catch, going home from London after eating dinner
at the Inn. But George's capacity to respect the past, never
large, was full up for one night. He merely said absently
"I expect you did," and instead gazed with absorption into
a first-class carriage. There a fat, high-coloured, pursy man
of about thirty, elegantly dressed, was waving a finger
with stern, prissy disapproval at a companion, seedy, cheer
ful-looking and twenty years older. As we left them to it
George, gazing out under the dome, into the smoky dark
yelled with laughter.

"It might have been me!" he shouted. "It might have
been me! That young chap is like A——"

Whistles were blowing, the train was ready to leave
London, and he was thinking of nothing but his internal joke

"Like A——," he cried, looking down at me from the
window. "Like A—— expecting me to sympathise because
he's hard pressed on three thousand a year. And immediately giving me advice on how much I ought to save out
of eight hundred."

CHAPTER XLVII

MIDDLE OF THE NIGHT

THE ROOM was dark as I woke up: at the edge of the curtains lurked the fringes of luminescence which, with a kind of familiar comfort, told me that it was the middle of the night. I felt happy; at the same time I was taking ease and comfort, not only from the familiar fringe of light, but also from a scent in the bedroom which was strange there. Basking, I stretched and sat up, looking down at Margaret asleep. In the dimness I could just make out her face, turned into the pillow, one arm thrown above her head, the other trailing at her side. She was fast asleep, and, when I bent and put my mouth to her shoulder, the warm flesh did not move, her breathing did not so much as catch, went on slow and steady in the relaxed air.

Often in the past months I had woken up, seen the fringe of light round the window curtains, had become conscious of my worries about her and known that it would be a long time before I got off to sleep again. Now I was rested; I had only to turn over—it was odd to look into the darkness with nothing on my mind, to sleep as deeply as she was sleeping.

Just then it was a luxury to stay awake. I got out of bed and went towards the door, which we had left open so that we could hear a sound from the child's room: he, too, was peacefully asleep. Walking quietly through the dark rooms, I felt there was no resistance between me and the air, just as I had sometimes felt on warm evenings in the streets of towns. Yes, I could think of the problems ahead of us, many of them the same problems over which I had worried

333

through the broken nights: but I thought of them without worry, almost without emotion, as though they were there to be picked up. Perhaps that was a state, it seemed to me later, in which men like Lufkin or Rose lived much of their lives.

Standing by the sitting-room window I looked down at the road, where the lights of cars kept giving form to the bushes by the park edge. The cars and lorries went by below: above them, the lamps suspended over the middle of the road swung in the night wind: watching them, I was happy without resistance. I had woken into a luminous happiness, and it stayed with me.

PART V

ANOTHER HOMECOMING

CHAPTER XLVIII

BIRTH OF A SON

WAITING in the dark bedroom I heard Margaret's steps as she returned to bed. I asked if anything was the matter, and in a matter-of-fact whisper she told me to cover my eyes, she was going to switch on the light.

Then she said:

"Well, it's no use saying that I hope I'm not going to disturb you." Her tone was sarcastic and calm. For an instant, not calm myself, I nevertheless recalled her father laughing at me in the same tone, one afternoon when he interrupted my work at the office.

"I'm pretty certain," she said, "that it's coming early."

She was a fortnight from her time, and I was startled.

"No," she said, "it's nothing to upset you. I'm quite glad."

She sounded so happy, above all so calm, that I could not help respond. What could I do for her, I asked?

"I think it might be as well to ask Charles March to come round."

Charles March, who had moved to a practice north of the Park, had looked after her during her pregnancy: when we were waiting for him after I had telephoned, I told Margaret, trying to match her nerve, that I only seemed to meet him at the crises of my life.

"This isn't a bad one, though," she said.

"I touch wood more than you do," I replied.

"You are superstitious, aren't you?" she said. "When I first noticed it, I couldn't believe it. And I daren't ask you, because I thought I must be wrong."

337

I had drawn the curtains. Outside the window a red-brick parapet solidified the first morning sunshine: below and beyond were gardens misty, washed-out in the dawn, but the glaring bricks glowed near, a starling stood immobile on the wall, harshly outlined as if it were cardboard.

Margaret was sitting up in bed, pillows behind her, twitting me not only to give me reassurance, but also because she was steady-hearted and full of a joy I could not share. For her the child was living now, something to love.

As Charles March examined her, and I stood gazing down from the sitting-room into the Park, I felt afraid for her because we were happy. I was afraid for the child because I wanted it. I had a special reason for fear, as Charles March had told me that we ought not to have another.

Down below, the first bus sped along in the milky light. Since she came to me, we had been happy. Beforehand, we had both taken it for granted that to reshape a life took effort, humility and luck; I did not know whether I could manage it. That we should stay together, was certain: in the world's eyes we should bring it off, but we should judge ourselves by what we saw in each other's. Up to now we had been blessed.

In a true relation—I had evaded it for so long—one could not absent oneself, one could not be above the battle, one fought it out. It was hard for me to learn, but we were able to know each other so. Only in one aspect, I thought, had she found me absenting myself—and only she would have perceived it. She perceived it when she saw me with her boy, Maurice, Geoffrey's child; for with him I was not natural, I did not let myself go. I was well disposed to him through conscience, not through nature, and she knew it. I was as considerate as I could be, but that was my old escape, turning myself into a benevolent spectator.

It made us more than ever anxious for children of our own.

BIRTH OF A SON

After we married, in the late summer of the year she came to me, which was 1947, four months passed before she conceived. She had watched me play with the little boy during those months: he liked me because I was patient and more even-tempered than she was. When she became pregnant she felt happiness for me first, and only later love for the coming child.

That September dawn, listening to the rumble of Charles's voice through the walls, I left the sitting-room window and found myself restlessly dawdling into Maurice's nursery: his cot was empty and most of his toys had gone, for Helen had taken him for the next fortnight. There I was glancing at one of his picture-books when Charles March found me.

He was not shaved, his eyes were sharp with a doctor's interest, with his own fellow-feeling: he would drive her to the clinic, he said, and, with a sarcastic flick not unlike hers, added that it was better to err on the safe side.

It was only lately, when he had been married for years, that he had had a family himself. There had been a time during my separation from Margaret when he and I had sympathised with each other, knowing that we both wanted children and might be deprived of them. As I looked at him I remembered that we had spoken without reserve.

Nevertheless, if he had just been a doctor and not an intimate friend, I should have asked more questions. As it was, I went into the bedroom, where Margaret had nearly finished packing her dressing-case. She was wearing a coat over her nightgown: as I held her in my arms, she said:

"You might as well go to that dinner tonight."

Then she added:

"I'd rather be there than where I shall be. Yes, I'd even rather be at Lufkin's."

It might have been intended as a jibe, but as I held her, it told me more. I did not need even to think or reply:

this was the communication, deeper than emotion or sensuality, though there is sensuality in it, which two people close together cannot save each other from. I knew that her nerve for once had faltered: her imagination was showing her a lonely, hygienic room, the bedside light. Brave in so many ways, she had her phobias, she dreaded a lonely room: she even felt the sense of injustice that cropped up in her, in and out of place. Why did she have to go through with it, while others were enjoying themselves?

Enjoying themselves at Lufkin's—it was, however, not a reasonable description of peoples' behaviour there; it never had been, it still was not. I arrived ready to be elated, with the peculiar lightheadedness of an ordeal put off: for at breakfast time, a few hours after Margaret arrived at the clinic, they had told me that the child might be born within forty-eight hours, then at five o'clock had said that it was not likely for a week and that I could safely spend the night out.

Just as there used to be in Lufkin's suite, there was drink, there was noise: in my lightheadedness I could take the first and put up with the second, but as for elation, it did not bear up in many under Lufkin's inflexible gaze. The curious thing was that he believed it did. When the women left us, and Lufkin, as always indifferent to time, began a business talk that lasted an hour, he had a satisfied smile as though all his guests were feeling jolly.

Nearly all of them belonged to his own staff. He had not been forgiven by his fellow-tycoons for taking an honour from their enemies and socially they cold shouldered him. Not that he gave any sign of caring: he just went on inviting to dinner the younger bosses with whom by now he had filled the top places in his firm: men more educated, more articulate than the old ones, looking and speaking more like civil servants, and in his presence sounding less like a chorus of sycophantic cherubim. And yet, when he made a pronouncement which they believed to be nonsense and which everyone round the table knew they believed to be nonsense, none of them said so, though several of them had gone so far that Lufkin could do them neither harm nor good. His *mana* was as strong as ever.

I was glad to watch it all again. It gave me—I was relaxed, I should enjoy my sleep that night, the worry of the dawn, because it was put off, was washed away—the luxury of recalling a past less happy. Nights at that damped-down table before the war: other able men choosing their words: back to the Chelsea house. It seemed to me strange that I could have lived that life.

I had another reminder of it, before Lufkin let us go from the table. There had been talk of a legal case the firm was concerned with, and, among the names of the barristers, Herbert Getliffe's came up.

"You devilled for that chap once, Lewis, or am I wrong?" said Lufkin. On such points he was never wrong.

I asked whether he knew Getliffe. To nod to, said Lufkin.

I asked whether Getliffe would soon be going to the Bench.

Not on your life, said Lufkin.

He sounded positive, even for him.

"What's happened?" I enquired.

"Well, within these four walls, he's blotted his copy-book. He's been doing some jiggery pokery with his income tax, and they've had to be persuaded not to prosecute him." Lord Lufkin said it not so much with malice, as with the certainty and satisfaction of inside knowledge. "I've got no pity for the damned fool. It not only does him harm, which I can bear reasonably philosophically, but it does harm to the rest of us. Anyway, he won't be able to live this one down.

"That chap's finished," said Lufkin, declaring the conversation closed.

When, after midnight, the party broke up he drove me home himself, less off-handed with me than the others because I was no longer a member of his court. Sitting back as the car paced through the Mall, up St. James's, past the club windows, I felt a moment's disquiet, mysterious and heavy, the first that night; and then once more the sense of privilege and power which I still was subject to in his company. The car, as opulent as he was austere, moved up Piccadilly, past the Ritz, the Green Park. There was not enough men for the top jobs, Lufkin was saying: the number of top jobs was going up as society became more complex, and the number of competent men had not gone up at all. True, the rewards weren't much these days: perhaps we should have to deal out a few perks. If we didn't find enough good men to run the show, Lufkin said, the country was sunk.

For once his tone had lost its neutrality and become enthusiastic; but when the car drew up in front of my flat, he spoke as bleakly as though I were a stranger. What he said was: "Give my regards to your charming wife."

As I thanked him for the dinner, he went on:

"She'll have received some flowers from me this evening." He said it just as bleakly, as though his only gratification was that he had mastered the etiquette and had all the apparatus of politeness at his command.

Out of a deep sleep, into which I had fallen as soon as I left Lufkin and went straight to bed, I heard a distant burr, and my heart was thudding with dread before I was awake enough to be conscious that it was the telephone. As I stumbled across the room, across the hall, switched on and was dazzled by the light, my throat was sewn-up. The telephone burred loudly now, like all the bad news I had ever had to hear.

As I took up the receiver Charles March's voice came at

once, unusually loud even for him, so that I had to hold
the instrument inches away:

"Lewis? Is that you?"

"Yes?"

"You've got a son."

"Are they safe?"

"I think they're pretty well."

His voice came to me, still loud, but affectionate and
warm:

"You've had good luck for once and I envy you."

His own children were girls, he had wanted a son and had
apologised for it as a piece of Jewish atavism: but he knew
that I did too.

I could not see them until the morning, he said. He told
me the time her labour started, and the time of the birth;
he was full of happiness because he could give me some. "It's
not often we've had anything good to tell each other,
don't you agree?" His voice spoke out of our long friendship.
He said that I could do with some rest myself, and that I was
to get back to bed now.

I neither could nor wanted to. I dressed and went down
into the street, where the night air was thundery and close.
Just as, when expecting a joy and suddenly dashed with
disappointment, one has moments when the joy is still
expected—just so, the shadow of fear can survive the opposite
shock, the shock of happiness. I was still shaken, out of
comparison more so than I had been at Lufkin's table:
for an instant, it reached me that this was a happy night,
and then I reverted to feeling, with a hallucinatory sharpness,
that it had not yet occurred.

As I walked across the park the thundery cloud-cap was
so low that it was hard to make out the interlocking couples
on the grass; I passed close by, in the headaching and stale
air, the seat where Margaret and I had sat in the desolating
night when it seemed that we had worn each other out. Yet

that was unrealisable too, as unrealisable as Charles March's news.

Retracing without intention the way Lufkin had driven me, I came to the mouth of St. James's Street. It was empty now, and not one of the club windows was alight; all of a sudden I stopped repressing the disquiet that had seized me in Lufkin's car. For, looking into those windows from the car, I had not dared to think of another evening when I had dined out without my wife—when I had dined with Gilbert Cooke, and simultaneously Sheila was dying. Now I could let the past come back blank and harmless, so that, going slowly down the street, I did at last credit my reason for happiness.

It was not until I saw Margaret next morning, however, that I felt happy. Suddenly the sight of her in bed, her hair straight as a schoolgirl's, her collar-bone plain where the bedjacket and nightgown had fallen away, made the tear glands smart, and I cried out. I said that I had not seen her look like that; then when I let her go and gazed at her again, I had to ask:

"How are you?"

"What century do you think you're living in?"

She was tired, she spoke with the indulgence of not concentrating. She went on:

"I wish I could have another for you."

I interrupted her, and then she said, inspecting me:

"What do you think you've been doing?"

"Walking about."

"If you'd listened to me——" but she could not go on teasing me. When had I heard? What exactly had I been doing when I heard? Who told me? What did I say? She cried out:

"He's a dear little boy and I love him very much."

Sitting up, she turned her head on the bank of pillows and looked out of the window into the clinic garden. The cloud-cap was still dense, ominous over the trees. She said:

"The room where I first saw you—it must be somewhere in the wing over there."

It was part of the same establishment; until that morning I had not been near it again.

"It must have been about four in the afternoon, but it was earlier in the month, wasn't it?" she said, exact in her memory because she was happy.

She added:

"I liked you. But I don't believe I thought I should ever be your wife."

She said, in a tone relaxed and both diffident and proud: "At any rate, I've done something for you now."

Soon afterwards she rang and asked the nurse to bring the baby in. When she did so, I stood up and, without finding anything to say, stared at him for what seemed a long time. The nurse—she had a smooth and comely Italianate face—was saying that he was not a whopper, but a fine boy, 'all complete and perfect as they say': I scarcely listened, I was looking at the eyes unfocused, rolling and unstable, the hands waving slowly and aimlessly as anemones. I felt utterly alien from this being in her arms: and at the same time I was possessed by the insistence, in which there was nothing like tenderness, which was more savage and angry than tender, that he must live and that nothing bad should happen to him.

As the nurse gave him to Margaret his head inclined to her, and I saw his side-face, suddenly transfigured into a cartoon of an adult's, determined, apprehensive. Grasping him, Margaret looked at him with an expression that was no longer youthful, that held responsibility and care, as though the spontaneous joy with which she had spoken about him had been swallowed up in pity.

I stood and watched her holding the child. Partly I

felt I could not get used to it, it was too much for me, it had been too quick, this was only a scene of which I was a spectator. Partly I felt a tug at the fibres, as though I were being called on in a way I did not understand; as though what had entered into me could not yet translate itself into an emotion, into terms of anything I could recognise and feel.

CHAPTER XLIX

A CHILD LOOKING AT THE MOON

WHEN, fifteen months after the child's birth, I received a letter from Mrs. Knight saying that her husband had been very ill and wished to see me, I did not think twice before going. They were staying, so she told me in the letter, at Brown's Hotel—"so as to get him to the seaside by easy stages. Of course, he has such a sense of duty, he says he must get back to his parish work. But I trust you not to encourage him in this. He is not to think of returning to the Vicarage until the summer."

Apparently he was not to think of retiring either, it occurred to me, though by this time he was nearly seventy: they had never needed the stipend, it was negligible beside her income: but that did not prevent Mr. Knight from clinging on to it. As for his cure of souls, for years he had found that his ill-health got worse when confronted with most of his daily tasks, except those, such as preaching and giving advice, which he happened to enjoy.

When I first caught sight of him in the hotel that afternoon he looked neither specially old nor ill, although he was lying stretched out on his bed and only whispered a greeting. Mrs. Knight plunged straight into the drama of his illness. They were doing themselves well, I noticed: they had taken a suite, and I walked through a sitting-room lavish with flowers on the way to their bedroom. By Mr. Knight's bed stood grapes, books, medicine bottles and tubes of drugs: by Mrs. Knight's stood magazines, a box of chocolates, a bottle of whisky and a syphon of soda. It had an air of subfuse comfort, of indulgences no longer denied, that I had seen before in elderly couples travelling.

Mrs. Knight sat on her bed, describing her husband's symptoms: in a dressing-gown, his coat and collar off, Mr Knight lay on his, his eyes closed, his clever petulant mouth pulled down; he lay on his back, his legs relaxed, like a figure on a tomb or one in a not disagreeable state of hebephrenia.

According to Mrs. Knight's account, he had for a long time past been starting up in the middle of the night with his heart racing.

"I take his pulse, of course," she said energetically to me. "Ninety! A hundred! Sometimes more!

"I decided," she looked at me with her active innocent eyes, "that I ought to keep a diary of his health. I thought it would help the doctors."

She showed me a quarto day-book, two days to the page, and in it some of the entries in her large hand. . . .

'L. woke up as usual: pulse 104. Quietened down to 85 in twenty minutes . . .' 'Better day. I got his heart steady for twenty-four hours . . .'

It sounded to me like the physical condition of a highly strung and hyperæsthetic man, but it would not have been profitable to tell Mrs. Knight so. Apart from 'good afternoon', she had said nothing to me since I arrived that did not concern her husband's health.

"It was always the same, though," she cried. "We couldn't stop it! Him waking up in the middle of the night with his heart pounding away like this——"

Sitting on the bed she moved both her thick, muscular arms up and down, the palms of her hands facing the floor, at the rate of hundreds a minute. For the first time, the silent figure on the other bed joined in: Mr. Knight used one arm, not two, and without opening his eyes flapped a hand to indicate the rapid heart-beats, but not so quickly as his wife, not in time.

"And I couldn't get him to be examined properly," she

348

said. "He's always been frightened of his blood pressure, of course. He wouldn't let the doctors take it. Once I thought I had persuaded him to, but just as the doctor was putting the bandage round his arm he shouted 'Take it away! Take it away!'"

Mr. Knight lay absolutely still.

"Then one night three months ago, it was in September because he was just thinking about his harvest thanksgiving sermon, it was a nice warm night and he'd had a couple of glasses of wine with his dinner, I woke up and I didn't hear him at all, but I knew he was awake. As a rule, of course, he calls out to me, and I knew—it was just like second sight—I knew there was something wrong because he didn't call out. Then I heard him say, quite quietly, just as though he were asking me for a glass of water: 'Darling, I think I'm going'."

A sigh came from the other bed.

"I didn't say 'I think I'm *going*,'" came a whisper from Mr. Knight. "I said 'Darling, I think I'm *dying*'."

Still good-tempered, still urgent, Mrs. Knight accepted the correction: she told me of the visit of the doctor, of his opinions, encouragements and warnings, her own activity, Mr. Knight's behaviour. Oddly enough, despite her hero-worship of her husband, her narrative was strictly factual, and pictured him as comporting himself with stoicism perceptably less than average. After his one protest he did not object or open his eyes again, until at last he said, faintly but firmly:

"Darling, I should like to talk to Lewis just for a little while."

"As long as it doesn't tire you."

"I don't think it need tire me, if we're careful," said Mr. Knight—with a concern that equalled hers.

"Perhaps it won't be too much for you," she said. "Anyway I shan't be far away."

With injunctions to me, she removed herself to the sitting-room: but she did not go out of sight, she left the door open and watched as though she were a policeman invigilating an interview in gaol. Very painstakingly Mr. Knight hitched his head higher up on the pillow; his eyes were no longer shut, he appeared to be staring out of the window, but he gave me an oblique glance that was, just as I remembered it, shrewd, malicious, and sharp with concealed purpose.

"I don't receive much news nowadays, naturally, Lewis, but all I hear of you suggests that you're prospering."

He began again, just as I remembered, some distance from the point; I was ready for him to weave deviously until his opening came. "Should you say that, allowing for the uncertainties of life and not claiming too much, that that was true?"

"In many ways it is."

"I am glad for you, I am glad."

In part, I thought, he meant it; he had always had an affection for me. Then, probing again, he said:

"In *many* ways?"

"In more than I reckoned on."

"There is bound to be much that you and I find difficulty in asking each other, for reasons that would distress us both to think of, and yet I should like to think that you perhaps have known what it is to have the gift of a happy marriage?"

I was sure that this was not the point he was winding towards. He asked it quite gently, and in the same tone I said yes, I was coming to know it.

"It is the only good fortune I've been given, but I've been given it more completely than most men," said Mr. Knight. "And if you will let me tell you, Lewis, there is nothing to compare with it."

He was whispering, his wife could not hear: but again,

ngular as it might have seemed to a spectator, he meant
t. He went on:

"I seem to remember, forgive my meanderings if I am
vrong, that I caught sight of the announcement of a birth
1 the *Times*—or the *Telegraph*, was it? Or perhaps both?—
hat somehow I connected with your name. Could that
ossibly be so?"

I said yes.

"I seem to remember, though again you must forgive
ny mistakes I make, it was of the male sex?"

I said yes.

"It seems to come back to me that you announced his
ames as Charles George Austin. Somehow, not knowing
nything of your recent adventures, of course, I connected
he name George with that eccentric figure Passant, whom
 recalled as being an associate of yours in the days that I
irst heard about you."

Yes, I said, we had called him after George Passant.

"Not bad," Mr. Knight gave a satisfied smile, "for an
ld man in a country vicarage, long out of touch with
ll of you and the world."

But he was still skirmishing, right away from his point
f attack. He went on:

"I hope your boy gives you cause to be proud of him.
You may be one of those parents whose children bring them
appiness."

Then he changed direction again. He said, in a light,
eflective tone:

"Sometimes, when I've heard mention of an achievement
f yours, I go back to those days when you first came
nto my house, should you say that's because I've had
othing to occupy me? Does it occur to you that it was
 quarter of a century ago? And sometimes, with all respect
o your achievements and acknowledgment of the position
ou've secured for yourself, I find myself wondering, Lewis,

whether all that time ago you did not contemplate even mor
of the world's baubles than—well, than have actuall
accrued to you. Because at that age there was a formidabl
power within you. Of course I know we all have to com
pound with our destinies. But still, I sometimes felt ther
might have been hours when you have looked at yoursel
and thought, well, it could have gone worse, but never
theless it hasn't gone perfectly, there have been som
disappointments one didn't expect."

I was wondering: was this it? I replied:

"Yes. At that age I should have expected to cut mor
of a figure by now."

"Of course," Mr. Knight was reflecting, "you've carrie
a heavy private load so much of your life. And I suppose
if you'd been going to take a second wind and really go t
the top, you wouldn't at your present age have readjuste
yourself to a wife and child."

Was this it? Had he got me there simply to remind m
that my public career had not been wonderful?

If so, I could bear it, more easily than he imagined
But somehow I thought he was still fencing. It was jus
that at seventy, believing himself ill, taking such care of hi
life that he had no pleasure left, he nevertheless could no
resist, any more than in the past, tapping the baromete
of an acquaintance's worldly situation. And he was, also
as in the past, just as good at it as Rose or Lufkin. He ha
never been outside his parish, he had been too proud and
vain to compete, but at predicting careers he was as accurat
as those two masters of the power-ladder.

Curiously, when any of the three of them made mistakes
it was the same type of mistake. They all tended to writ
men off too quickly: they said, with a knell not disagreeabl
to themselves, he's finished, and so far as his climbing th
ladder in front of him went, they were nearly always right
But they forgot, or undervalued, how resilient human being

were. Herbert Getliffe would never be a judge: Gilbert Cooke would never be more than an assistant secretary: George Passant would stay as a managing clerk at eight or nine hundred a year until he retired: but each of them had reserves of libido left. They were capable of breaking out in a new place: it was not so certain as the prognosticians thought that we had heard the last of them.

"Should you say," Mr. Knight continued to delve, "we are likely to hear more of you in high affairs?"

"Less rather than more," I said.

His lids drooped down, his expression had saddened.

"Perhaps," he said, "if it hadn't been for my daughter, you would have got a better start."

"It would have made no difference in the end," I replied.

"I can't help thinking how you must have been held back."

"In the long run, I should have done much the same," I said.

Just for an instant he turned his head and looked at me with eyes wide open.

"I think of her and ask myself about her," he said. "And I've wondered if you do also."

At last. This was the point. Now he had led up to it, it turned out not to be a dig at me.

"I have done often," I said.

"I know you ask yourself what you did wrong, and how you ought to have helped her."

I nodded.

"But you're not to blame, I can't put the blame on you. Time after time I've gone over things she said to me, and how she looked when she was a girl. She had become strange before ever you met her or she brought you to my house."

He was speaking more directly than I had heard him speak.

"I keep asking myself, what I should have done for her. I suppose I pretended to myself that she was not so very strange. But I don't know to this day what I should have done. As a very little girl she was remote from either of us. When I told her she was pretty, she shrank away from me. I remember her doing that when she was six or seven. I was very proud of her, and I used to enjoy saying she was beautiful. I can see her eyes on me now, praying that I should stop. I don't know what I should have done. I ought to have found some way to reach her, but I never could."

He added:

"I ought to have helped her, but I never could. I believe now I did her more harm than good."

He asked:

"What could I have done?"

Just then Mrs. Knight came bustling out of the sitting-room, scolding him because he was tiring himself, indicating to me that it was time I left him to rest.

In an instant the veil of self-concern came over Mr. Knight. "Perhaps I have talked too much," he said. "Perhaps I have."

On my way home across the edge of the Park I was moved because I had seen Mr. Knight, the most hypochondriacal and selfish of men, bare a sorrow. How genuine was it? In the past his behaviour had baffled me often, and it had that afternoon. Yet I thought his sorrow lived with him enough so that he had to summon me to listen to it. I found myself sorry for him. It was the heaviest feeling I took away with me, although, when his invitation came and I knew that I should be reminded of Sheila, I had not been certain how much it would disturb me.

It seemed that I might feel the same pain as that which seized me the night I caught sight of R. S. Robinson at the party. But in fact I had felt it not at all, or very little.

Talking to her father, I had thought of Sheila with pity and love: but the aura which had surrounded her in my imagination, which had survived her death and lasted into the first years with Margaret, had gone altogether now. Once her flesh had seemed unlike any other's, as though it had the magic of someone different in kind. Now I thought of her physically with pity and love, as though her body was alive but had aged as ours had aged, as though I wished she were comfortable but found that even my curiosity about her had quite gone.

When I arrived, Margaret was in the nursery playing with the children. I did not talk to her about the Knights at once, although she detected at a glance that I was content. We did not speak intimately in front of Maurice because anxiously, almost obsessively, she planned to keep him from jealousy. Her nerves were often on the stretch for him; she not only loved him, but could not shut out warning thoughts about him.

That afternoon, we both paid him attention before I spoke to Charles. Maurice was sitting at a little table with a set of bricks and steel rods. He was now five and had lost none of the beauty he showed when I first saw him. By what seemed an irony, he had shown no perceptible jealousy of his half-brother. His temper, which had been violent in infancy, had grown neither better nor worse. Whenever he was placid a load lifted from Margaret's brow; that afternoon, he was building with a mechanic's interest, and in peace. We turned to Charles, lifted him from his pen and let him run between us.

Looking at him, I was suffused with pleasure, pleasure unqualified. In the days when Margaret and I first lay together watching the firelight on the ceiling, I thought that I had not known before the sweetness of life, and that here it was. Here it was also, as I looked at the little boy. He had learned to walk, but although he was laughing, he

355

would not move until we were both in place; he beamed
he was jolly, but he was also sharp-eyed and cautious
Rotating an arm, head back, he ran, trusting us at last.

He had none of Maurice's beauty. His face was shield
shaped, plain and bright: he had eyes of the hard strong
blue common in my family. A few minutes later, when
Maurice had gone into another room, Margaret touched
my arm and pointed—the child's eyes were concentrated
and had gone darker, he was staring out of the window where
the moon had come up among a lattice of winter trees
He kept reiterating a sound which meant 'light', he was
concentrated to the depths of his fibres.

It was then, in happiness, that I reported to Margaret
how Mr. Knight had pointed out the extent to which I had
failed to live up to my promise, and the number of dis
appointments I had known.

"He doesn't know much about you now," she cried.

"He knows something," I said.

"What did you say?"

"I said there was a good deal in it."

She read my expression and smiled, happy herself.

I added:

"I didn't tell him what I might have done—that I think
I could accept most miseries now, except—" I was watching
the child—"except anything going wrong with him."

She began to speak and stopped. Her face was swept clear
of happiness: she was regarding me protectively, but also
with something that looked like fright.

CHAPTER L

COMPARISON OF MARRIAGES

WHEN I was alone, I thought sometimes of the warning Margaret had not spoken. But neither of us so much as hinted at it, until a night over a year later, a night still unshadowed, when we had Gilbert and Betty Cooke to dinner.

To my surprise—I had expected the worst, and got it wrong—that marriage was lasting. They often came to see us since—also to my surprise—Betty and Margaret had become reconciled. Thus, by the most unexpected of backdoors, Gilbert's inquisitiveness at last found our house wide open. That inquisitiveness, however, had lost its edge. We had looked for every reason for his wanting to marry Betty except the simple one; but he was devoted to his wife, and humbly, energetically, gratefully, he was engrossed in making the marriage comfortable for her.

On the surface, it was a curious relation. They quarrelled and snacked. They had decided not to have children and spent much thought, disagreeing with each other, on food and drink and how to decorate their flat. With an income much less than ours, they had achieved twice the standard of luxury, and they went on adding to it, simultaneously attending to and criticising each other.

It was easy to imagine them at sixty, when Gilbert retired, knowing just the hotels to squeeze the last pound's worth out of his pension, badgering restaurant proprietors all over Europe, like the Knights without the hypochondria, a little cantankerous, a little scatty except about their comforts, carping at each other but, to any remark by any intruder, presenting a united front. It might have seemed a come-down, compared with Betty in her twenties, so kind and slap-dash, so malleable, anxious for a husband to give purpose to her existence: or compared with Gilbert at the same age who, enormities and all, was also a gallant and generous young man.

But they had done better than anyone saw. They were each of them unvain, almost morbidly so: the prickles and self-assertiveness which made them snack did not stop them depending on each other and coming close. They were already showing that special kind of mutual dependence which one occasionally sees in childless marriages, where neither the partners nor their relation ever seem to have quite grown up, but where, in compensation, they preserve for each other the interest, the absorption, the self-centredness, the cantankerous sweetness of young love.

Looking at them at our dinner table I saw Gilbert, in his middle forties, getting fatter and redder in the face; Betty, well over forty, her eyes still fine, but her nose dominating, more veins breaking through the skin, the flesh thickening on her shoulders. And yet Margaret, in years and looks so much the younger, was older in all else—so that, watching them, one had to keep two time-scales in one's head, one non-physiological: and on the latter, Betty, with her gestures as unsubdued as when she was young, allied with Gilbert in a conspiracy to secure life's minor treats, was standing delectably still.

That night they had come a little late, so as to avoid seeing the children; increasingly, like two self-indulgent bachelors, they were cutting out exercises which they found boring. But for politeness' sake Betty asked questions about the boys, in particular about mine: and Gilbert did his bit by examining and hectoring us about our plans for their education.

"There's nothing to hesitate about," he said, bullying

nd good-natured. "There's only one school you need
ink about," he went on, referring to his own. "You can
fford it, I can't conceive what you're hesitating for.

"That is," he said, his detective passion suddenly spurting
ut, gazing at Margaret with hot eyes, "if you're not going
o have a big family——"

"No, I can't have any more," Margaret told him
irectly.

"Well, that's all right then," cried Gilbert.

"No, it hangs over us a bit," she said.

"Come on, two's enough for you," he jollied her along.

"Only one is Lewis's," she replied, far less tight-lipped,
hough still far shyer, than I was. "It would be safer if he
ad more than one."

"Anyway, what about this school?" said Betty briskly,
little uneasily, as though shearing away from trouble she
id not wish to understand.

"It's perfectly obvious they can well afford it, there's
nly one school for them." Gilbert was talking across the
able to her, and across the table she replied.

"You're overdoing it," she said.

"What am I overdoing?"

"You think it's all too wonderful. That's the whole
rouble, none of you ever recover from the place."

"I still insist," Gilbert was drawing a curious triumph
ut of challenging her, he looked plethoric and defiant,
'that it's the best education in the country."

"Who's to say so?" she said.

"Everyone says so," he replied. "The world says so. And
ver these things the world is usually right," added Gilbert,
hat former rebel.

They went on arguing. Betty had reserved her scepticism
nore than he had; she recalled days when, among aristocrats
f her own kind, intellectuals like the Davidsons, it was
ommon form to dislike the class subtleties of English

education; she had known friends of ours who had assume
that, when they had families, they would break away fror
it. She said to Gilbert:

"You're just telling them to play the same game wit
their children as everyone round them."

"Why shouldn't they?"

Betty said:

"If anyone can afford not to play the same game, Lewi
and Margaret can."

Duty done, with relief they grumbled about their la
week-end. But I was absent-minded, as I had been sinc
Margaret spoke about the child. The talk went on, a dinner
party amiable, friendly, without strain, except that whic
gripped me.

"It would be safer——" She had meant something mor
difficult, I knew clearly, than that it would be a life-lon
risk, having an only son. That was obvious and hars
enough.

But it was not that alone of which Margaret was afraic
No, she was afraid of something which was not really
secret between us but which, for a curious reason, she woul
not tell me.

The reason was that she distrusted her motive. She kne
that she expected perfection more than I did. She ha
sacrificed more than I had; it was she who had, in breakin
her marriage, taken more responsibility and guilt; sh
watched herself lest in return she expected too much.

But in fact, though she distrusted herself, her fear wa
not that I should be compelled to lose myself in my son
but that, in a final sense, I should desire to. She knew m
very well. She had recognised, before I did, how muc
suffering a nature can bring upon itself just to keep in th
last resort untouched. She had seen that the deepes
experiences of my early life, unrequited love, the care
spent on an afflicted friend, my satisfaction in being

spectator, had this much in common, that whatever pain I went through I need answer to myself alone.

If it had not been for Margaret, I might not have understood. It had taken a disproportionate effort—because under the furrows of such a nature as mine there is hidden an inadmissible self-love—to think that it was not good enough.

Without her I should not have managed it. But the grooves were cut deep: how easy it would be, how it would fit part of my nature like a skin, to find my own level again in the final one-sided devotion, the devotion to my son.

When Betty and Gilbert, each half-drunk and voluble, had at last left us, at the moment when, after drawing back the curtains, I should have started gossiping about them, the habit of marriage as soothing as the breath of the night air, I said instead:

"Yes, it is a pity that we've only the one."

"You ought to have been a bit of a patriarch, oughtn't you?" she said.

She was giving me the chance to pass it off, but I said:

"It needn't matter to him, though, need it?"

"He'll be all right."

"I think I've learned enough not to get in his way."

I added:

"And if I haven't learned by now, I never shall."

She smiled, as though we were exchanging ironies: but she understood, the mistakes of the past were before us, she wished she could relieve me of them. And then I seemed to change the subject, for I said:

"Those two"—I waved the way Betty and Gilbert had gone "—they'll make a go of it now, of course."

On the instant, she knew what I was doing, getting ready to talk, through the code of a discussion of another marriage, about our own. It was stuffy in the room, and we went down into the street, our arms round each other, refreshed: the night was close, cars were probing along the pavement, we struck in towards one of the Bayswater squares and then walked round, near to each other as we spoke of Betty and Gilbert.

Yes, she repeated, it was a triumph in its way. She thought that what had drawn them together was not desire, though they had enough to get some fun, was nothing more exalted than their dread of being lonely. Betty was far too honourable to like Gilbert's manœuvres, but they were lonely and humble spirited, they would fly at each other but in the long run they would confide and she would want him there. If they had had children, or Betty had had a child by her first marriage, they might not have been so glued together, I said: I was trying to tell the truth, not to make things either too easy for myself or too hard: they were going to need each other more, at the price of being more selfish towards everyone else.

In the square, which had once been grand and had now become tenement flats, the last lights were going out. There was no breeze at all: we were holding hands, and talking of those two, we met each other, and spoke of our self-distrust.

CHAPTER LI

LISTENING TO THE NEXT ROOM

AS WE walked round the square that night, both children were well. A fortnight later we took them to visit their grandfather, and the only illness on our minds was his. In the past winter Davidson had had a coronary thrombosis: and, although he survived, it was saddening to be with him now. Not that he was not stoical: he was clear-sighted about what he could expect for the rest of his life: the trouble was, he did not like what his clear sight told him, his spirits had gone dark and he would have thought it unreasonable if they had not.

Up to the sixties he had lived the life of a young man. His pleasures had been a young man's, even his minor ones, his games and his marathon walks. He looked more delicate than most men, but there was a pagan innocence about him, he had not been compelled to adjust himself to getting old. Then it had happened at a blow.

He was out of comparison more stoical than Mr. Knight. Though Davidson believed that when he died he was going into oblivion, he feared death less than the old clergyman. He had found life physically delightful until he was sixty-five, while Mr. Knight had immobilised himself in hypochondria more than twenty years before. But of the two it was Davidson who had no consolation in the face of a sick old age.

What he did was concentrate fanatically on any of his pastimes still within his power. No one could strike another spark of interest out of him; that Saturday afternoon Margaret was screwing herself up to try.

As we entered his study with the children, he was playing the war game against Helen, the board spread out on a table so that he could be comfortable in an armchair. In the quiet both boys backed shyly to Margaret, and momentarily the only noise we heard was Davidson's breathing, a little shorter, a little more strenuous than a healthy man's, just audible on the close air.

The silence cracked as Maurice went straight to Helen, to whom he talked more fluently than any other adult, while the little boy advanced and stared from the board to Davidson. While Helen took Maurice away into the corner, Charles asked:

"What is Grandpa doing?"

"Nothing very dazzling, Carlo."

Although Davidson's voice had none of the spring and tone it used to have, although the words were mysterious to him, the child burbled with laughter: being called 'Carlo' made him laugh as though he were being tickled. He cried out that his grandfather called him Carlo, he wanted the joke repeated. Then Davidson coughed and the child looked at him, transparent indigo irises turned upon opaque sepia ones, the old man's face sculptured, the child's immediate and aware, so unlike that they seemed not to have a gene in common.

"Are you better?" the child asked.

"Not really. Thank you," Davidson replied.

"Not quite better?"

"No, not quite better."

"A little better?"

For once not replying with the exact truth, Davidson said:

"Perhaps a little better."

"Better soon," said the child, and added, irrelevantly and cheerfully: "Nanny is a little better." It was true that the nurse who came in half the week had been ill with influenza.

"I'm very glad to hear that, Carlo."

I wanted to distract the child from his grandfather. I could hear—beneath Davidson's tone, offhand rather than polite, which he used to the infant not yet three as to a Nobel Prize winner—I could hear a discomfort which by definition, as Davidson himself might say, was beyond help. So I asked the little boy to come and talk to me instead.

He replied that he would like to talk to his grandfather. I said that I would show him pictures. He smiled but said: "Grandpa called me Carlo."

He went round the board, nearer to Davidson, staring applaudingly into his face. Then Margaret spoke to Charles, explaining that he could come back later and that I had splendid new pictures for him.

"Go with daddy," she told him.

The child gazed at me, his eyes darkened almost to black.

As a rule he was amenable, but he was enjoying the clash of wills. He was searching for words, there was a glint in his eye which in an adult one would have suspected as merry, obstinate, perceptibly sadic.

"Go with daddy," Margaret said.

Clearly and thoughtfully he replied:

"I don't know who daddy is."

Everyone laughed, me included: for the instant I was as hurt as I had been at eighteen, asking a girl to dance and being turned down. Then I was thinking how implacable one's egotism is, thinking from mine just wounded to this child's.

Gazing at him beside his grandfather's chessboard, I felt unusual confidence, without any premonition, that, as he grew up, he would be good-natured: within the human limits, he would be amiable and think of others. But one had to learn one's affections: the amiability and gentleness one dressed up in, but the rapacious egotism had been there all the time beneath. It protruded again, naked as in infancy, as one got into old age. Looking from the smiling little boy to his grandfather, dispirited and indrawn, I thought that by a wretched irony we were seeing its re-emergence in that man, so stoical and high-principled, who only a year before had been scarcely middle-aged.

As we tried to persuade the child away from his grandfather's side, he was bad-tempered in a manner uncommon with him. He cried, he was fractious, he said he had a cough like grandpa, he practised it, while Margaret listened, not knowing how much was genuine, except that he had woken up with the faint signs of a cold that morning.

She put her hand to his forehead, and so did I. He seemed just warm with passion. Through anger, he kept telling us he would like to stay with grandpa: he repeated, as though it were a reason for staying, that he had a cough like grandpa, and produced it again.

"I think he's over-excited, I don't think it can be more than that," said Margaret to me in an undertone, hesitating whether to look after him or her father, her forehead lined. Then she made up her mind; she had come to speak to her father, she could not shirk it and leave him with his spirits dead. She called to Helen, telling her that Charles was upset, would she take care of him for half an hour? Helen nodded, and got up. It was curious to see her, trim yet maternally accomplished as Margaret would never be, since Helen's instinct was so sure that it left her no room for wondering whether she might not be taking the wrong course, saying the wrong thing. As effortlessly as a hypnotist, she led him and Maurice out of the room, other attractions wiped out of Charles's mind as though his memory were cut off.

Left with her father, Margaret's first act was to take Helen's side of the war game, at which she was the only person who could give Davidson a run. In silence, they finished the game. Davidson's expression had lightened a little: partly it was that Margaret was his favourite daughter, partly the anodyne of the game—but also, where many men would have drawn comfort from their grandchildren, to him the sight of them seemed a reminder of mortality.

He and Margaret were staring down at the board: his profile confronted hers, each of them firm and beautiful in their ectomorphic lines, their diagonals the mirror-image of each other. He had a winning position, but she contrived to make the end respectable.

"For neatness," said Davidson, his tone lively again, "I give that finish 65 out of a 100."

"Nothing like enough," said Margaret. "I want 75 at least."

"I'm prepared to compromise on 69."

He sounded revivified. He looked at the clock and said eagerly: "If we're quick, there's time for another one."

Reluctantly Margaret said no, they'd better leave it till next week, and his face went heavy, as though the skin were at last bagging out over the architecture of the bones. Afterwards, she had to ask him questions to keep him from sinking numb into his thoughts. His replies were uninterested and dull. Were there any pictures we ought to see? One exhibition, he said flatly, was possibly worth our time. When would he be able to go himself? Not yet. When? Margaret asked. They said—his reply was indifferent— that in a month or two he might be able to take a taxi and then walk through a couple of rooms. You must do that as soon as you can, she said. He hadn't the slightest inclination to, he said.

She understood that she was on the wrong tack. He had said all he had to say about pictures when he was well; he had written about them at the height of his powers; he could do so no more, and it was better to cut it out absolutely, not to taunt himself by seeing a picture again.

Casting about, she mentioned the general election of the past winter, and then the one she thought must soon follow.

"I should have thought," said Davidson, "that one had to be a morbidly good citizen to find the prospect beguiling."

"I don't think anyone does," said Margaret.

"I should have thought that it would lack picturesque features to a remarkable extent." He was making an effort to keep up the conversation now.

"No," he added, "there would be one mildly picturesque feature as far as I'm concerned. That is, if I had the strength to get as far as voting, which I must say seems improbable. But if I did manage to vote, I should be voting conservative for the first time in my life."

I was thinking how most of those I knew, certainly eight out of ten of my professional acquaintances, were moving to the right.

Margaret, taking advantage of the chance with Davidson, broke in.

"Going back to your voting," she said, "it would have seemed incredible thirty years ago, wouldn't it?"

"Quite incredible," he replied.

"You and your friends didn't have much idea of the way things would actually go, did you?"

"By and large," he said, "they've gone worse than we could possibly have imagined."

"Thirty years ago," he added, "it looked as though they would turn out sensibly."

"If you had your time again," she said, "how would you change what you were all thinking?"

"In my present form," he was not speaking dully now, she had stung him, "the thought of having one's time over again is fairly near the bone."

"I know it," she said: her tone was as sharp. "That's why you've got to tell us. That's why you've got to write it down."

368

"I don't trust the views of a man who's effectively done for."

"For some things," she said, throwing all gentleness away, "they're the only views one can trust."

She went on:

"You know very well, I've never much liked what your friends stand for. I think on all major issues you've been wrong. But don't you see how valuable it would be to see what you think——"

"Since the future doesn't interest me any more." They were each being stark; she was tired with the effort to reach him, she could not go much further, but his eyes were shining with interest, with a kind of fun.

"On most major issues," he caught her phrase, "we were pretty well right." He gazed at her. After a pause he said: "It might be worth thinking about."

Another pause, in which we could hear his breathing. His head was bent down, but in his familiar posture, not in dejection.

"It might give me something to think about," he said.

With a sigh, she said that now she must go and find the children.

"I'll think about it," said Davidson. "Mind you, I can't promise. It'd be a bit of a tax physically and I don't suppose I'm up to it."

He said goodbye to me, and then turned to Margaret. "I'm always very glad to see you," he said to her. It was a curious parting from his favourite daughter: it seemed possible that he was not thinking of her as his daughter, but as the only person who looked straight at him in his illness and was not frightened off.

We went into the drawing-room, where I had not been since the evening Margaret said she would come to me. In the summer afternoon, with Helen and the children playing

369

on the floor, it seemed much smaller, as diminished as one of childhood's rooms revisited.

In the contracted room, Helen was saying that Charles did seem a little out of sorts: perhaps we ought to take him home soon. The child, picking up most of the conversation, cried because he did not want to go; he cried again, in inexplicable bursts, in the taxi; in the nursery his cheeks were flushed, he laughed with an hysterical echo, but was asking, with a customary reasonableness, where Auntie Helen was and when he would see her again. Then he said, with a puzzled and complaining expression:

"My feet hurt."

There seemed nothing wrong with his feet, until Maurice said that he meant they were cold, and Margaret rubbed them between her hands.

"Clever boy," Margaret said to Maurice, already ambivalent about being praised.

"Shall we clap him?" said Charles, but his laughter again got out of control. He cried, became quiet, and then, with a return of the complaining expression, said: "My head hurts."

Under our eyes his cold was growing worse. His nose ran, he coughed, his temperature was a little up. Without speaking to each other, Margaret and I were thinking of his nurse's influenza. At once, no worry in her voice, Margaret was arranging for Maurice to sleep in the spare room: still not hurrying, as though she were ticking off her tasks, she had a word with me alone before she put Charles to bed.

"You are not to be too anxious," she said.

Her face, like many whose nerves are near the surface, was always difficult to read, far more so than the poker faces of Rose or Lufkin, because it changed so quickly. Now it was as calm as when she spoke to the children. Yet, though she was steady, and I was letting my anxiety go, I suddenly knew that for no reason—not because of any of his symptoms, nor anything she knew or noticed which I had not—her anxiety was deeper.

"If he's not better tomorrow, we'll have Charles March in straightaway," I said.

"Just to give you a decent night," she said, "perhaps we might as well have him now."

Charles March had arrived and was in the nursery before Margaret had finished putting the child to bed. Standing in the drawing-room I listened to their voices, insistent, incomprehensible, more ominous than if I could have picked out the words, just as their voices had been when I listened in this same room, the morning before he was born. It seemed longer than on that morning until they came to join me, but at once Charles gave me a kind, protective smile.

"I don't think it's anything very terrible," he said.

Just for an instant I felt total reassurance, like that of a jealous man who has had the moment's pretext for jealousy wiped away.

He sat down and, his eyes sharp and cautious, asked me about the nurse's ' flu '. What was it like? More catarrhal than usual? Had any of us had it? Yes, Margaret replied, she had, mildly: it had been going round the neighbourhood.

"Yes," said Charles, "several of my patients have had it."

He was thinking out what he could safely say. It caught my eye that his suit was old and shabby, fading at the lapels: he was seedier to look at than when I first knew him as a smart young man: but the seediness did not matter and he was wearing well: his hair was still thick and fair, his eyes bright. This life he had chosen, which had once seemed to me quixotic and *voulu*, was suiting him.

"Well, obviously," he said, "it would be slightly far-fetched to look for anything else in the boy's case. I am a bit of an old woman, and with very small children I can't help thinking of the rare things that might just possibly happen to them. But I can't see any justification for suspecting any of them here. No, we may as well call it 'flu', this brand of 'flu' that seems to be in the air."

As he spoke, he was setting out to reassure me. But, as well as being a man of strong feeling, he had made himself a good doctor. He knew that he started by being both over-cautious and over-ingenious. With any child—more than ever with the child of a close friend—his temptation had been to spend time over remote dangers. It had meant alarm, it was bad medicine, it was a private irritation. For Charles was a devoted man, but he had an appetite, personal as well as professional, for being right.

When Charles March had gone, the child had a bout of crying, and Margaret went to sit beside him. Afterwards she read to Maurice until his bed-time, making it up to him for having been so long away. It was not until eight o'clock, having spent herself on each in turn, that she came to me.

We were listening for a cry in the next room. She had gone dead tired; she talked, not of the child, but of her father: had she done him any good? When she spoke as she had had to speak to him, she did not like herself much. Ought she just to have left him to himself? She was tired out, she was asking nothing deep or new, just a guilty question from a daughter who had broken loose. I was listening to the next room, but that worry was a little lulled, and she wanted me to strengthen her. To her, who took so much responsibility, to whom much of love meant that, it was a final release of love to shed it.

Listening to the next room, I could lull that worry enough to attend to Margaret. And yet, for both of us, it was only just lulled, so that by a consent unspoken we did not allow ourselves any of the ordinary evening's pleasure, as though even a glass of wine with our meal, or standing outside on the roof garden and smelling the flowers in the humid air, were a provocation to fate.

CHAPTER LII

PHOTOPHOBIA

THE child woke three times during the night, but he had no more than a sleep-flush when we went in to him in the morning. He was lying on his back talking to himself, and when we looked down into the cot he smiled. I found myself asking him, as though he were an adult, how he was feeling: mechanically, imitating his nurse, he replied very well, thank you. I asked if his head were hurting: he looked surprised and then troubled, but at last said no.

When Margaret had taken his temperature, reading the thermometer by the window in the morning sunlight, she cried:

"It's gone down. It's only just over 99."

Her joy filled the room. Delighted with her because she told good news, I thought how absolute was her capacity for joy. Many thought of her as gentle and responsible: some, who knew her better, saw the fibre of her will: but perhaps one had to love her to feel her capacity for joy. I loved it in her.

I asked, didn't he seem easier? The catarrh was less, the look of strain had gone. After the night before, no adult would have looked as bright. Yes, we weren't imagining it, he was far brighter, she said.

As we talked about him over his head, the child had been listening: he knew that we were pleased with him. With something like vanity or gratification, he said: "Better now."

Then he told us that grandpa was a little better, nanny was a little better. Amiably he asked:

"Are we a little better? Are we quite better?"

He did not object, however, when Margaret told him that he was to stay in his cot. He was content to lie there while we read to him and showed him his toys: as it was Sunday morning Maurice was at home, and so I stayed alone in the nursery, reading Charles's favourite books time after time, watching for any change in his cough, his hand moving to his head or ear, with an intensity of observation that co-existed with boredom, with an emotion so strong that it seemed incredible I could at one and the same time be bored.

About midday Charles March called. The temperature was still down, and he was satisfied. He was so satisfied that he spoke to us sternly, as though we were careless or indifferent parents, and ordered us to ring him up at once if there were any deterioration. My tongue lightened, I said it was the most unnecessary advice that even he had ever given me: and as Margaret and I laughed he was taken off guard, his professional authority departed, he blushed and then guffawed.

We were standing in the hall, and from the nursery came the child's voice, shouting for his mother and father. As Margaret opened the door, he called out: "What were they laughing at?"

"Someone made a joke, that's all," she said.

"They laughed."

"Yes, we shouldn't have made such a noise," she said.

The child produced an artificial 'ha-ha-ha' which led to a genuine one, not hysterical, but somehow real mirth self-induced.

All that afternoon and evening, there was no change that either she or I could be sure of. I felt in myself, I knew it in her, that state of physical constraint in which one is aware of one's own footsteps, even knows that one's own breath is catching. I had seen it before, in a man who was waiting to be arrested. But in us it was a denial of the moment, the more we secretly thought that next day he might be well.

Most of the afternoon I played with Maurice, whilst she took her spell at the bedside. Among his birthday presents Maurice had been given a game similar to the halma I remembered in my own childhood: suddenly that sunny afternoon, refusing to walk with me to the Serpentine, he developed an obsession for it. When I won, he became ill-tempered and muttered to himself, but insisted on more; for a long time I sat there with him—the air brilliant over the Park, the sun streaming into the room, our corner shaded—not resenting the occupation, time dripping by that way as well as any other, letting him win. He mentioned the child only once, when without any explanation he referred to him by a pet name, and said:

"Will he have to stay in his cot tomorrow?"

"I expect so," I said.

"And the day after that?"

"Perhaps."

"And lots and lots of days?"

He did not seem to be speaking out of either malice or affection, but something more like scientific curiosity.

"Lewis," he asked, his handsome face lit up with interest, "has anyone had to stay in bed for a *thousand* days?"

"Yes," I said.

"Has anyone I know?"

He pursued his researches. Had I ever had to? Or Margaret? Or his father? Or his grandfather? Raptly, he asked:

"Has anyone ever had to stay in bed for a *million* days?"

"People don't live as long as that."

He thought again:

"If I had a space-ship, I could get to the moon in a thousand days."

"Yes, you could."

"No, I couldn't. You're wrong," he cried with superiority and triumph. "Of course, I could get further than the moon in a thousand days. I could get to Venus, you ought to know that anyone knows that."

Charles did not go to sleep at his usual time, and cried for his mother to stay with him: he was restless and cried again before nine o'clock; but neither her eyes nor mine could find any change. We stayed up for some time, but there was no sound, and at last we went to bed. Waking out of my first sleep, I was listening at once, but there was still no sound: all was quiet, I did not hear Margaret breathing in her sleep.

Trying to rouse myself, I said:

"Are you awake?"

"Yes," she replied.

"Haven't you been to sleep?"

"Not yet."

"Is anything the matter with him?"

"No, I've been in to see him once, he's sleeping." Her voice was clear, but also, now that I was awake myself, I could hear how wakeful it was, and tight with care.

"What are you thinking of?" I asked.

After a pause she replied:

"Yes, there is something."

"Tell me."

"I think he's on the mend, and we probably shan't need it. Perhaps we needn't say anything. But I've been thinking, if he should have a set-back, I don't want you to mind, I want you to let me have Geoffrey in to see him."

In the words, jagged with anxiety, I could hear the hours of her sleepless night: but now I was turned hard and angry.

"It seems strange," I replied.

"I don't care what it seems, he's a first-class children's doctor."

"There are other first-class children's doctors."

"He's the best I've seen."

"There are others as good and better."

My anger was sullen, hers on the flash-point. But it was she, more violent than I was, who controlled herself first.

"This is a good time to quarrel," she said in the darkness.

"We mustn't quarrel," I said.

"Let me try and come out with it."

But she could not make a clear explanation. She had been thinking, she said, just as I had been thinking, what it would be like if he got worse. And there was Maurice, she wanted to be sure that he was looked after. If Charles got worse, it would be too much to bear, unless she had complete confidence in a doctor. Her voice was shaking.

"Would it have to be Geoffrey?"

"I should know we'd done the best we could."

For each of us, the choice was dense with the past. I was jealous of him, yes: jealous as one can be of someone one has misused. Even the mention of him reminded me of the time I had lost her, my paralysis, the period in my life that, looking back, I liked the least. I had avoided seeing him since Margaret came to me. It was part of his bargain, in letting her keep Maurice, that he should visit him when he wanted. He made a regular visit each week, but on those days I had not once been there.

On her side, although she liked Charles March, she felt for him a fainter jealousy, the jealousy for parts of my youth that, except at second-hand, were for her unknown and irrecoverable.

There was something else. In a fashion that seemed right out of character, but one I had noticed in older women, she liked to hero-worship her doctor, make a cult of him; perhaps because of the past, she could not manage to do that with Charles March.

"All that matters," I said, "is that he is looked after. We can forget everything else."

"Yes."

"If you should need Geoffrey, then you'd better have him."

Very soon, not more than five minutes after, she was sleeping for the first time that night, but it was a long time before I got to sleep again.

In the morning, when we went in together to see the child, that anxiety in the darkness seemed remote. He looked as he had done the day before, he greeted us, his temperature was the same. As soon as Maurice had gone to school, the two of us sat beside the cot all the morning, watching him.

His cough had slackened, but his nose was still running. Otherwise he did not grumble, he lay there being read to, at times apathetic. At other times he became impatient with reading, stopping us when we were halfway through a book, demanding that we start again. It was a trick, I insisted to myself, that he often did.

Just after midday, looking down at him, I could not keep back the question—was he more flushed than ten minutes before?

For an instant I glanced at Margaret; our eyes met, fell away, turned back to the cot; neither dared to speak. Twice I took my eyes away from the child, to the floor, anywhere, while I counted the instants, in the hope that when I looked again I should see it had been an illusion.

Since my first alarm—not more than a few minutes past— I had not looked at Margaret. She was gazing at him. She too had seen. When our eyes met this time, each saw nothing but fear. When we looked back at the child, his expression was also strained with something like fear. His cheeks were flushed, and his pupils were dilating.

I said to Margaret:

"I'll ring up Charles March. If he's not already on the way, I'll tell him we want Geoffrey too."

She muttered thanks. As soon as I had returned, she would get on to Geoffrey.

Charles was on his rounds, so his wife told me. He would be calling at his house before coming to us, so I could leave a message. As I was re-entering the nursery, the child was crying resentfully:

"His head hurts."

"We know, dear," said Margaret, with the steadiness in which no nerve showed.

"It hurts."

"The doctors will help you. There will be two doctors soon."

Suddenly he was interested:

"Who are two doctors?"

Then he began crying, hands over his eyes, holding his head. As Margaret went to the telephone, she whispered to me that his temperature was right up; for a second she gripped my hand, then left me with him.

Crying with his head turned to the pillow, he asked where she was, as though he had not seen her for a long time. I told him that she had gone to fetch another doctor, but he did not seem to understand.

Some minutes passed, while I heard the trill of telephone bells as Margaret made calls, and the child's whimpering. Whatever I said to him, he did not make clear replies. Then, all of a sudden, he was saying something feverish, urgent, which seemed to have meaning, but which I could not understand. Blinking his eyes, his hand over them, he was pointing to the window, demanding something, asking something. He was in pain, he could not grasp why I would not help him, his cries were angry and lost.

Myself, I felt lost too, lost, helpless and abject.

Once more he asked, imploring me in a jumble of words. This time he added "Please, please", in anger and fever, utterly unlike a politeness; it was a reflex, produced because he had learned it made people do things for him.

I begged him to speak slowly. Somehow, half-lucid, he made an effort, his babble moderated. At last I had it.

"Light hurts." He was still pointing to the window. "Will you turn light off? Light hurts. Turn light off. Please. Please."

As I heard, I drew the curtains. Without speaking, he laid his face away from me. I waited beside him in the tawny dark.

CHAPTER LIII

ACT OF COURAGE

SOON after Margaret returned, the child vomited. As she cleaned him, I saw that his neck was stiff, strained like a senile man eating. The flush was crimson, his fingers pushed into his eye sockets, then his temples.

"Head hurts," he cried angrily.

He was crying with a violent rhythm that nothing she said to him interrupted. In the middle of it, a few minutes later, he broke into a new fierce complaint.

"My back hurts."

In the same tone, he cried:

"Stop it hurting. It is hurting me."

When either of us came close to him, he shouted in irritation and anger:

"What are they doing?"

The regular crying hooted up to us; neither she nor I could take our glance from him, his face fevered. We watched his hands pushing unavailingly to take away the pain. Without looking at Margaret I knew, as of something within one's field of vision, that her expression was smooth and young with anguish.

We were standing so, it was just on two o'clock, when Charles March came in. Impatiently he cut short what I was telling him; he glanced at the child, felt the stiff neck, then said to me, in a tone heavy, brotherly and harsh:

"It would be better if you weren't here, Lewis."

As I left them, I heard him beginning to question Margaret: was there any rash? How long had his neck been rigid?

I was dazzled by the afternoon light in the drawing-room; I lit a cigarette, the smoke rose blue through a gleam of sun. The child's crying ululated; I thought I noticed that since I first entered the gleam of sun had moved just perceptibly along the wall. All of a sudden, the ululation broke, and there came, pressing like a shock-wave, a hideous, wailing scream.

I could not bear to be away, I was just on my way back to the child, when Charles March met me at the drawing-room door.

"What was that?" I cried.

The scream had died down now.

"Oh, that's nothing," said Charles. "I gave him penicillin, that's all."

But there was nothing careless or even professional in his voice now, and his face was etched with sadness.

"If it could have waited I wouldn't have done it, I'd have left it for Hollis," he said.

He added that I did not need telling that his diagnosis had been wrong. He did not explain that it was a reasonable mistake; he could not get over what he felt he had brought upon me. He said in a flat tone:

"I've done the only thing for him that we can do on the spot. Now I shall be glad to see Hollis arrive."

"He's seriously ill, of course?"

"I'm afraid so."

"Will he get over it?"

"He ought to stand a good chance—but I can't tell you much——"

He looked at me.

"No," he said, "if we've got it in time he ought to be all right."

He said:

"I'm desperately sorry, Lewis. But what I'm feeling doesn't exist by the side of what you are."

He had been an intimate friend since we were very young men. At any other time I should have known that, both because of his tenderheartedness and his pride, he was ravaged. But I had no attention to spare for him; I was only interested in what he had done for the child, whether he had taken away any of the suffering, whether he was being any use to us.

In the same animal fashion, when at that moment I heard Geoffrey Hollis arrive, I felt nothing like embarrassment or remorse, but just a kind of dull hope, that here might be someone bringing help.

As we all four of us gathered in the hall, it was Geoffrey alone who seemed uncomfortable, the others were too far gone. As he nodded to me his manner was offhand, but not as certain as usual; his fair head looked as unchangingly youthful, but his poise was not as jaunty. It was with something like relief that he listened to Margaret's first words, which were:

"It's worse than I told you."

Once more I stood in the drawing-room, staring at the beam of sunlight along the wall. There was another scream, but this time it was minutes—I knew the exact time, it was five past three—before they joined me, Geoffrey speaking in an undertone to Charles March. The child's crying died down, the room was as quiet as when Charles had given us his opinion there less than forty-eight hours before. Through the open window came the smell of petrol, dust and summer lime.

"Shall I begin or will you?" said Geoffrey to Charles March, in a manner informal and friendly: there was no doubt of the answer. Geoffrey was speaking without pomposity, but also, even to Margaret, quite impersonally.

"The first thing is," he said, "that everything has been done and is being done that anyone possibly can. He'll have to be moved as soon as we have checked the diagnosis and my people have got ready for him in the isolation ward. You'll be able to drive round with the sample straightaway?" he said to Charles March.

Charles inclined his head. He was a man of natural authority and if they had met just as human beings he would have overweighted this younger man. But now Geoffrey had the authority of technique.

"I might as well say that the original diagnosis is one which we should all have made in the circumstances two days ago. The symptoms were masked to begin with and then they came on three or four hours ago, after that intermission yesterday, which is quite according to type, except that they came on with a rather unusual rush. If I had seen him on Saturday, I should never have thought this was a serious possibility myself."

Charles's face, drawn and pallid, did not move.

"And I shouldn't yesterday, and it's out of the question that anyone would. We ought to thank our lucky stars that Doctor March got the penicillin into him when he did. We may be glad of that extra half-hour."

It was, I remembered later, impersonally cordial, a little patronising, and scientifically true. But at the moment I actually heard it, I was distracted by this wind-up. I said:

"What has he got?"

"Oh, neither Dr. March or I think there is much doubt about that. Don't you agree?" He turned to Charles March, who nodded again without his expression changing.

"It's a meningitis," said Geoffrey Hollis. "A straightforward one, we think.

"Mind you," he said to me, not unkindly, with a curious antiseptic lightness, "it's quite bad enough. If this had happened twenty years ago I should have had to warn you that a large percentage of these cases didn't recover. But nowadays, with a bit of good fortune, we reckon to cope."

384

ACT OF COURAGE

It was after Charles March had left, and Geoffrey had rung up the hospital, telling them to expect him and the case, that he said:

"That's all we can do just now. I've got to see another patient. I'll be back to take the boy along in a couple of hours."

He spoke to Margaret.

"You must stop Maurice coming here until we've got things straight."

"I was going to ask you," she said.

He was businesslike, he said that he did not intend them to take even a negligible risk: Maurice had already been exposed to infection; she was to watch him for a vestige of a cold, take his temperature night and morning: at any sign, right or wrong, they would inject him.

As she listened, he could not have doubted that all he said would be carried out. He gave a smile of relief, and said that he must go.

I longed for him to stay. With him in the room, the edge of waiting was taken off. It did not matter that he was talking to her about their son. I said, hoping against hope that he would stay with us, that I had better go in and see the child.

"I'll do that myself on the way out," he said, again not unkindly, "but I don't see the point of it for you."

He added:

"I shouldn't if I were you. You'll only distress yourself, and you can't do any good. It's not pretty to watch. Mind you, we don't know what they feel in these conditions, possibly nature is more merciful than it looks."

In the hours when Margaret and I sat alone by the cot, the child did not cry so regularly: much of the time he lay on his side, moving little, muttering names of people, characters from his books, or bits of nursery verses. Frequently he complained that his head hurt, and three times that his back did. When either of us spoke to him his pupils, grossly dilated, confronted us as though he had not heard.

He seemed to be going deaf: I began to think that he no longer recognised us. Once he gave a drawn-out scream, so violent and rending that it seemed as though he were not only in agony, but horribly afraid. During the screams Margaret talked to him, tried piteously to reach him: so did I, my voice mounting until it was a shout. But he did not know us: when the scream was over, and he was babbling to himself again, his words were muddled, his mind had become confused.

When Geoffrey came back to us at a quarter to five, I felt an instant's dependence and overmastering relief. He glanced down at the child: his long, smooth, youthful face looked almost petulant, he clicked his teeth with something like disapproval.

"It's not working much yet," he said.

He had a nurse waiting outside, he told us: they would take him at once: he looked again at the child with an expression not specially compassionate or grave, more like that of someone whose will was being crossed. He said that he would give him his second shot of pencillin as soon as they got him into his ward; it would be early, but worth trying. He added casually:

"The diagnosis is as I thought, by the way."

"Yes," said Margaret. Then she asked:

"Can we come with him now?"

Geoffrey looked at her deliberately, without involvement, without memory, competent with his answer as if she had been nothing but the mother of a patient.

"No," he said. "You'd only be slightly in the way. In any case, when we've got him settled, I couldn't let you see him."

"You'll ring us up if there's any change," she said steadily, "for better or worse?"

For once his tone was personal. "Of course I shall."

He told us, once more antiseptic, that we could telephone the ward sister at any time, but there was no point in doing so before that night. If it was any relief to us, he himself would be glad to see us at the hospital the following morning.

After the ambulance drove away, my sense of time was deranged. Sitting in the early evening with Margaret and Maurice, I kept looking at my watch as though feeling my pulse in an illness; hoping for a quarter of an hour to have passed, I found it had only been minutes. Sometimes I was so much afraid that I wanted time to be static.

All the time I was watching Margaret look after her other boy. Before he came in, she was so sheet-pale that she had made up more than usual, not to alarm him. She had explained how Charles had been taken away with a bad cold, and how she would have to take his own temperature and fuss over him a bit. Then she sat with him, playing games, not showing him any anxiety, looking very pretty, the abnormal colour under her cheekbones becoming her; her voice was level, even full, and the only sign of suffering was the single furrow across her forehead.

She was thankful that Maurice's temperature was normal, that he seemed in the best of health.

Watching them, I resented it because she was so thankful. I took my turn playing with the boy: though I could not entertain him much, I could stick at the game and go through the motions: but I was resenting it also that he could sit there handsome and untouched, above all that he should be well. With a passion similar in kind to my mother's, who in an extreme moment of humiliation had once wanted a war to blot it out and destroy us all, so I wanted the danger to my son to hang over everyone round me: if he was not safe, then no one should be: if he should die, then so should the rest.

When she took Maurice to bed I sat in the drawing-room doing nothing, in that state of despondency and care combined, which tied one's limbs and made one as motionless as a catatonic, reduced to a single sense, with which I listened to the telephone. Without either of us speaking, Margaret came and sat down opposite to me, on the other side of the fireplace; she was listening with an attention as searing as mine, she was looking at me with another care.

The telephone rang. She regarded me with a question on her face, then answered it. The instant she heard the voice on the wire, her expression changed to disappointment and relief: it was a woman acquaintance asking her to dinner the next week. Margaret explained that the little boy was ill, we couldn't go out anywhere because of the risk of letting our host down: she was as gentle and controlled as when she played with Maurice. When she returned to her chair, she mentioned the woman's name, who was a private joke between us, hoping to get a smile from me. All I could do was shake my head.

The vigil lasted. Towards nine o'clock she said, after calling out my name:

"Don't forget we should have heard if he were any worse."

I had been telling myself so. But hearing it from her I believed her, I clutched at the comfort.

"I suppose so."

"I know we should. Geoffrey promised——" she had reminded me of this already, with the repetitiveness with which, in the either-or of anxiety, one repeats the signs in favour as though they were incantations. "He'd be utterly reliable about anything like this."

"I think he would." I had said it before: it heartened me to say it again.

"He would."

She went on:

"This means he's got nothing to tell us yet."

She said:

"Look, there can't be anything much to hear, but would you like to ring up the nurse and see what she says?"

I hesitated. I said:

"I daren't."

Her face was strained and set. She asked:

"Shall I?"

I hesitated for a long time. At last I nodded. At once she went towards the telephone, dialled the number, asked for the ward. Her courage was without a flaw: but I took in nothing, except what her expression and tone would in an instant mean.

She said she wanted to enquire about the child. There was a murmur in a woman's voice, which I could not catch.

For an instant Margaret's voice was hard.

"What does that mean?"

Another murmur.

"You can't tell me anything more?"

There was a longer reply.

"I see," said Margaret. "Yes, we'll ring up tomorrow morning."

Simultaneously with the sound of the receiver going down, she told me:

"They said that he was holding his own."

The phrase fell dank between us. She took a step towards me, wanting to comfort me: but I could not move, I was incapable of letting her.

CHAPTER LIV

"COME WITH ME"

IN the middle of the night, Margaret was at last asleep. We had both lain for a long time, not speaking; in the quiet I knew she was awake, just as I had listened and known years before, when Sheila was beside me in insomnia. But in those nights I had only her to look after, as soon as she was asleep my watch was over: that night, I lay wide awake, Margaret's breathing steady at last, in a claustrophobia of dread.

I dreaded any intimation of sound that might turn into the telephone ringing. I dreaded the morning coming.

I should have dreaded it less—the thoughts hemmed me in, as though I were in a fever or nightmare—if I had been alone.

It had been easier when I had just had to look after Sheila. Of the nights I had known in marriage, this was the most rending. Margaret had been listening too, lying awake, until she could be sure I was safe out of consciousness: it was only exhaustion that had taken her first: she wanted to look after me, she was thinking not only of the child but of me also.

She wanted to look after me but I could not let her. In this care and grief I had recessed, back to the time when I wanted to keep my inner self inviolate.

As a child I had not taken a sorrow to my mother, I had kept my sorrows from her, I had protected her from them. When I first loved I found, and it was not an accident, someone so self-bound that another's sorrows did not exist.

But with Margaret they existed, they were at the core of our marriage: if I kept them from her, if I did not need her, then we had failed.

In the darkness I could think of nothing but the child. The anxiety possessed me flesh and bone: I had no room for another feeling: it drove me from any other person, it drove me from her.

I thought of his death. In the claustrophobia of dread, it seemed that it would be an annihilation for me too. I should want to lose myself in sadness, have no one near me, I should not have the health to admit the claim of the living again. In sadness I should be alone: I should be finally and at last alone.

I thought of his death, as the light whitened round the curtains. The room pressed me in; I had a picture, sudden and sharp as an hallucination, it might have been a memory or a trick with time, of myself walking along a strip, not of sand but of pavement, by the sea. I did not know whether I was young or an old man: I was walking by myself on the road, with the sea, leaden but calm, on my right hand.

I slept a little, woke with an instant's light-heartedness, and then remembered. Margaret was already dressing. As she looked at me, and saw the realisation come into my face, hers went more grey. But she still had her courage: without asking me this time she said that she would ring the ward. Remaining in the bedroom I heard her voice speaking, the words indistinguishable, the cling of the bell as she rang off, the sound of her feet returning: they were not light, I dreaded to see her eyes. She told me:

"She said there's no change to speak of."

All I could make myself reply was a question about our visiting Geoffrey at the hospital: when would she be ready to leave? I heard my voice deaden, I could see her regarding me with pity, with injury and rejection, with her own pain.

Whilst she gave Maurice breakfast and got him off to school, I did not move from the bedroom. At last she returned to me there: I said that it was time we were setting out.

She looked at me with an expression I could not read. She said:

"I think perhaps it would be better if you went alone."

All of a sudden I knew that she understood. The night's dreads—she had divined them. She had endured her own suffering about the child, and mine also. What could she do now either for the child or me? She could not bear, any more than I could, not to be with him; yet she was trying to tend me. Her tone was tight, she was admitting as much as she could bear.

It was a moment in which I could not pretend. To refuse her offer just because she craved I should—that was not in me. To refuse out of duty, or the ordinary kind surface of love—that was not in me either. There was only one force out of which I could refuse, and that was not love, but need.

All of a sudden, I knew that the fugue of the night was over. That part of me, which she understood even if it cost her her last hope, was not overmastering now.

Somehow the moment held not only the strains of our past, but something like a prophecy. I thought of the child's death, as I had in the night. If I lost him, I knew —it was the certainty of the fibres, not of thought—I should not be much good to her, but I should need her.

"No," I said, "come with me."

CHAPTER LV

EFFECTS OF AN OBLIGATION

THROUGH the underground corridor of the hospital, which smelt of brick dust and disinfectant, Margaret and I were finding our way to Geoffrey's office. Along the passage, whose walls, as bare as those of a tube railway, carried uncovered water-pipes, went mothers with children. At a kind of junction or open space sat a group of women, their children in pushchairs, as though expecting nothing, waiting endlessly, just left there, children not specially ill, their fate not specially tragic, waiting with the resignation that made hospitals seem like forgotten railway stations littered with the poor and unlucky camping out for the weekly train. Nurses, their faces high-coloured and opaque, moved past them with strong, heavy-thighed steps as though they did not exist.

When at last we saw a notice, turned down a subsidiary passage and reached the office, which was still underground, Geoffrey's secretary told us that he was with the child, that he had been giving him his sixth injection. That if we liked, we could wait in the doctor's room until he returned. Like the nurses in the corridor, she was a strong young woman, her face comely and composed with minor power. When she spoke to us it was in a tone which was brisk and well ordered, but which held an undertone of blame, as though we were obscurely responsible for our ill fortune. It was the tone which is not far distant from most of us, when we have to witness suffering and address it, as though when the veils of good nature were off we believed that the suffering were merely culpable, and suffering a sin.

In the office so small that the walls pressed round us, the light was switched on although through a window one could look up to the sky. The room glistened under the light, both naked and untidy—a glass-fronted bookcase full of text-books and sets of journals, a couple of tubular chairs, a medical couch. We sat down, she put her hand on mine: there we stayed like those others in the corridor, waiting as they were, not expecting to be picked up, too abject to draw attention to ourselves.

I was aware of her palm touching the back of my hand: of my own breathing: of the sheets of typescript on the desk, which looked like a draft of a scientific paper, and the photograph of a woman, handsome, dashing, luxurious.

The telephone rang, the secretary swept in and answered it. It was the mother of a patient: there was a misunderstanding about an address and the secretary was confused. As it happened, I knew the answer: I could not get the words out. It was not malice, I wanted to help, I even wanted to propitiate her, but I was dumb.

When she went out, having at length solved the problem, I muttered to Margaret that I had known all along, but she did not understand. At last she had become no braver than I was, all she could do was press my hand. We had each got to the point of apprehensiveness which was as though we were not thinking any more, as though we were no longer waiting for release. This was all we knew, sitting there together; we were incapable of looking for an end to it.

There was a noise outside, and Geoffrey banged the door open. As soon as I saw his face, I realised. He was shining with a smile of triumph and elation, with a kind of repleteness such as one might see in a man who has just won a tennis match.

Margaret's fingers touched me. Suddenly our hands were slippery with sweat. Without a word said, we were certain.

In the same instant, Geoffrey cried:

"He'll be all right. He'll do."

Margaret exclaimed, the tears spilled down her cheeks, but Geoffrey was oblivious of them.

"It's interesting," he said, "I've noticed it before, how the very instant the objective signs are beginning to go right, then the child seems to know it himself, one's only got to look at his face. It's interesting, one might have thought there'd be a time lag. But the minute that the count in the lumbar fluid showed we had really got this one under control, then the boy was able to hear again and his mind began to clear."

Suddenly he said, still wrapped up in his triumph:

"By the way, you needn't worry, there oughtn't to be any after-effects. He's a fine boy."

It was not a compliment, it was just his statement of biological fact. He was brimming with his own triumph at seeing the child recover: but also, uninterested in so many things which preoccupied the rest of us, not reading the news, contemptuous of politics, laughing off art as a plaything, he nevertheless was on the side of the species. He drew his most unselfcentred happiness, with a kind of biological team spirit, from the prospect of a strong and clever child.

I was giddy with Margaret's joy, which resonated with mine, so that I could not have distinguished which was which. I wanted to abandon myself to praise of Geoffrey: I was in the sublime state in which all my extravagance, so long pent in, was pelting against the wall of tact, or even of ordinary human consideration. I wanted to patronise him and be humble; I wanted to ask him outright whether he intended to marry the woman in the photograph. I should have liked to ask him if I could be of any use to him.

But I was moved by a compulsion which came from something deeper among the three of us.

"He's a fine boy," Geoffrey repeated. I was compelled to say:

"So is yours."

For an instant he was surprised—

"Yes, I suppose he is."

He added, with his head tossed back, with his student vanity: "But then, I should have expected him to be."

He was staring at Margaret. Her tears were not dry, her expression was brilliant with rapture and pain. She said:

"I'm watching for the first sign of anything wrong with him."

"Yes," said Geoffrey. "If nothing happens within a fortnight from now, then he's clear."

"I shall do anything you tell me," she said.

He nodded.

"I'd better see him two or three times a week until the period of incubation is over."

She cried:

"We must save him from anything we can!"

She had known, when she came to me, the loads that she was taking: some could shrug them off, not she: even now, in the midst of rapture, they lay on her, lay on her more heavily, perhaps, because she was uplifted. Somehow the boy's chance of infection stood before her like an emblem. When she spoke of it, when she said we must save him from anything in our power, she was speaking, not only of the disease, but of the future.

I said:

"Yes, we must save him from everything we can."

It was a signal of understanding between us. But Geoffrey, who had also heard her affirmation, appeared to have missed it. He replied, as though illness was the only point:

"Well, even if he does show any signs, which incidentally is much less likely than not, you needn't take it too tragically. We should be pretty incompetent if we didn't get it in time.

And children are very tough animals, you ought to remember that."

He said it with detached satisfaction. Then, in a totally different tone, he said:

"I'm glad I was able to do something for your child."

In the constricted office, he was sitting on the desk, above us, and as he spoke he looked down first at her, then at me. In the same tone, which was sharp, insistent, not so much benevolent as condescending, he said:

"I'm glad I was able to do something for you."

He was free with us now. Before, he had been constrained, because he was a man, light-natured but upright, who did not find forgiveness easy, who indeed felt not revengeful but inferior and ineffective in the presence of those whom he could not forgive. Now he had us under an obligation. His was the moral initiative. He was ready to be fond of her again: he was even ready to like me. He felt happy, released, and good.

So, it might have seemed incongruous, did we. She, and I also, had previously felt for him that resentment which one bears towards someone to whom one has done wrong and harm—a resentment in which there lurks a kind of despising mockery, a dislike in which one makes him smaller than he is. Now he had been powerful when we were abject. We had been in his hands; and, for both of us, for her more violently, but for me also, the feeling swept hidden shame away.

He sat there, above us, his head near the light bulb. Margaret and I looked up at him; her face was blanched with sleeplessness and anxiety, her irises were blood-streaked; so must mine have been. He showed no sign of a broken night: as usual, vain about his appearance, he had his hair elegantly brushed and parted, he smelt of shaving powder.

He was happy: we were sleepy with joy.

397

CHAPTER LVI

THE SHORT WALK HOME

JUST over a fortnight later, on a humid July afternoon, the clouds so dense that some windows were already lit at six o'clock, Margaret called at my office to take me home. She was wearing a summer frock, and in the heat she was relaxed with pleasure, with delectable fatigue, coming from the hospital, where she had been arranging for the child to return to us next day.

He was well and cheerful, she said. So was Maurice, who had escaped the infection altogether: there was no one in her charge to worry her now, she was lazy with pleasure, just as she had been when Gilbert first brought her into my sick room.

Just then there sounded Rose's punctilious tap at the door. As soon as he saw Margaret, whom as it happened he had not met, he broke into apologies so complex and profuse that even I began to feel embarrassed. He was so extremely sorry: he had looked forward all these years to the pleasure of meeting Mrs. Eliot: and now he had just butted in, he was making a nuisance of himself, he only wanted to distract her husband for a moment, but even that was an infliction. They had neither of them got better at casual introductions: Rose, inflexibly, wearing his black coat and striped trousers in the steaming heat, went on talking according to his idea of gallantry, his eyes strained; Margaret faced him as she might as a girl at one of her father's exhibitions, hating the social forms, doing her best to be easy with an awkward and aspiring clerk.

I saw that they mildly liked each other, but only as partners in distress. When Rose had finished his piece of business with me, which with his usual economy took five minutes, he made his protracted and obsequious goodbyes. After he had at last departed, I told her that he was one of the most formidable men I had known, in some ways the most formidable: she had heard it before, but now in the flesh she could not credit it. But she was too tired, too happy to argue; she did not want to disagree, even on the surface: she said, let us go home.

As soon as we had left the well-like corridors of the old building and went into the street, we pushed against the greenhouse air: sweat pricked at the temples: it was in such weather, I remembered, holding Margaret's arm, as when I first walked from Lufkin's office to the Chelsea house, getting on for twenty years before.

Now, in the same weather, we turned the other way, sauntered up Whitehall towards Trafalgar Square, and there got a bus. I told her how I had once sat on a bus close by with old Bevill, and he had mentioned her father's name, which gave me a card of re-entry into her life. As the bus spurted and braked up Regent Street, we talked about the child as we might have done in bed between waking and sleeping, the diary of his days, the conspiracy of hope which, during his illness, we had put away as though we had never played with it.

We talked of the children and then put them aside: along Oxford Street we were talking of ourselves. We talked at random, of the first nights we spent together, of what we had feared for each other in the last month, of thoughts of each other during the years we were separated.

As we got off at Marble Arch and walked along the pavement rustling with litter, under the trees, Margaret gave a smile of pretended sarcasm, and said:

"Yes, I suppose there are some who'd say we had come through."

I put my arm round her and held her to me as we walked slowly, as slowly as though we planned to spin the evening's happiness out. The vestigial headache, seeping in with the saturated air, seemed like a sensual ache. There was a smell of hot grass and fumes, and, although the lime was almost over, just once I fancied that I caught the last of it.

Her smile sharp, she said:

"I suppose some would really say that we'd come through."

She had more courage than I had. She was not anything like so given to insuring herself: her spirit was so strong that when she rejoiced, she rejoiced without qualification. To her, victories were absolute; at that moment, as we walked together, she had all of them she wanted: she wanted no more than this. And yet, by a perversity which she would not lose, she, whose fibres spoke of complete happiness, could not use the words.

That evening she had to dissimulate her faith, put on a smile that tried to be ironic, and deny the moment in which we stood. Just as I had done so often: but now it was I, out of comparison more suspicious of fate than she was, who spoke without troubling to placate it.

We were in sight of home. A light was shining in one room: the others stood black, eyeless, in the leaden light. It was a homecoming such as, for years, I thought I was not to know. Often in my childhood, I had felt dread as I came near home. It had been worse when I went, as a young man, towards the Chelsea house. Now, walking with Margaret, that dread had gone. In sight of home my steps began to quicken, I should soon be there with her.

It was a homecoming such as I had imagined when I was lonely, but as one happening to others, not to me.

PRINTED BY PURNELL AND SONS, LTD.
PAULTON (SOMERSET) AND LONDON